The Stranger Times

www.penguin.co.uk

The Stranger Times

C. K. McDonnell

BANTAM PRESS

TRANSWORLD PUBLISHERS
Penguin Random House, One Embassy Gardens,
8 Viaduct Gardens, London SW11 7BW
www.penguin.co.uk

Transworld is part of the Penguin Random House group of companies
whose addresses can be found at global.penguinrandomhouse.com

First published in Great Britain in 2021 by Bantam Press
an imprint of Transworld Publishers

A CIP catalogue record for this book
is available from the British Library.

ISBNs 9781787633353 (hb)
9781787633360 (tpb)

Typeset in 12/18 pt Van Dijck MT Pro by Jouve (UK), Milton Keynes.
Printed and bound in Great Britain by Clays Ltd, Elcograf S.p.A.

The authorized representative in the EEA is Penguin Random House Ireland,
Morrison Chambers, 32 Nassau Street, Dublin D02 YH68

Penguin Random House is committed to a sustainable
future for our business, our readers and our planet. This book
is made from Forest Stewardship Council® certified paper.

To Manchester – for the magic and the mayhem

PROLOGUE

The two men stood on the rooftop, watching the city toss and turn in its sleep. The shorter of them looked at his watch – it was 4 a.m. In his experience, no city that was worthy of the name actually slept. Even now, there were signs of activity: the occasional lonesome wanderer and the odd taxi light, trying to find each other in the night. Still, this was the moment when it got as close to truly quiet as it ever would. The sliver of time before the day shift took over from the night.

'And there's definitely no other way?'

The shorter man sighed. 'No.' He pulled his coat tight around him. The internet had told him the climate of Manchester was 'mild', which it turned out was a euphemism for 'permanently miserable'.

'Only . . .' started the taller man.

'Only what? We're not here to negotiate.'

The taller man glared down at his companion. 'This isn't easy, y'know?'

'Believe me, my part is considerably harder than yours.'

'It's forty-two bloody floors!'

'Yeah, but you only really have to worry about the last one.'

Anger flashed in the taller man's eyes. 'Is that supposed to be funny?'

'No, none of this is funny. You have no idea how much giving you this chance has cost me, and now we get up here and it turns out you're a pussy. Believe me, I am not amused.'

'I'm . . . Could I not take something to take the edge off?'

The shorter man turned and walked a few steps. He looked up at the full moon hanging low in the sky. Irony of ironies, he needed to stay calm. He couldn't say what he wanted to: that he'd let the last guy pop some pills to 'take the edge off' and it had resulted in a very nasty crater in the ground. This time it had to work, which meant that this guy needed to be a lot of things, not least of which was entirely unaware of the last guy. It had taken every ounce of the shorter man's ingenuity to find another suitable candidate in just a week, but still, time was running out. He turned back, spread out his arms and smiled. It all came down to how you sold it.

'Look, it's very simple. You have to do this of your own free will, and for it to work, your adrenalin levels have to reach a certain critical level in order to react with the mixture I gave you – or the transformation won't happen.' He avoided using the word 'potion' – it set the wrong tone. This was the age of science – because they'd done such a good job persuading the masses that magic did not exist. He moved forward until they were standing side by side again and lowered his voice. 'You've seen what I can do and you know I want to help. You just need to do your part.'

The taller man returned to his moody silence.

That was it. No more Mr Nice Guy. It was time to move this along.

'OK. I'm calling it a night. I know when people say "I'll do any-thing", they don't really mean it. It's an expression. I thought you were different. I thought wrong. There's a flight back to New York in three hours. See ya—'

The shorter man turned to leave but the other man grabbed his arm. His grip was vice-like.

'Just . . .'

The shorter man looked down at the hand that was currently gripping his bicep. 'Believe me when I say you do not want to do that.'

After a moment's hesitation, his arm was released. He looked up into the taller man's teary eyes. Anger, fear and a large dollop of hate swirled around in there. It was nothing he didn't expect. 'You told me you wanted to do this. You begged me, in fact. To use an expression from home, it's shit-or-get-off-the-pot time.'

The taller man reached into the pocket of his jeans and pulled out a photograph. He looked at it for a long moment, then tossed it away and started running as fast as he could.

The wind caught the picture and it hung in the air for a moment: a smiling blonde woman, her arms wrapped around a dimple-cheeked young girl with the same sparkling blue eyes, who beamed a gap-toothed grin up at the camera. Then it was gone, swept away into the night.

The taller man didn't slow as he disappeared over the edge of the building. Surprisingly, there was no scream on the way down; or if there was, it was carried away by the wind.

The shorter man ambled forward and looked over the side. Forty-two storeys beneath him lay pavement – gloriously craterless pavement. The tall man was not dead, merely transformed. Now, he was something else. Something useful.

'Looks like we got ourselves a ball game.'

The shorter man turned and walked away, whistling a happy tune to himself.

Somewhere near by, what sounded like a very big dog howled.

CHAPTER 1

Hannah glanced around as quickly and discreetly as possible, and then threw up in the bin. It had not been a good day. In fact, even though it wasn't yet lunchtime, today stood out as one of the worst days of her life – or it would have, if it wasn't for the fact there had been so many of them recently. Life had become one long stress dream she didn't seem capable of waking up from.

In her bag sat *Only One Direction*, the self-help book by Dr Arno Van Zil, the South African life coach. 'The past is unwanted luggage we don't need to carry.' She had been clinging to the book like a life raft. The author's warm smile on the front cover had started to feel slightly mocking now. 'All that matters is the next step.' She couldn't look back; she had to keep moving forward.

Having said that, she did need to sit down for a second so she could scour her bag for the mint that, please God, would be in there. She perched on a bench beside the bin. She was in a park not far from the centre of Manchester. The sound of kids whooping and hollering in the nearby play area mixed with the wash of ever-present traffic in the background. She shoved her phone into her coat pocket. She was starting to really hate the bloody thing.

When she had made the decision to walk away from her old life and not take anything with her, the phone had been one of the few exceptions. She might not want the money or the houses, but she still needed to communicate with the world.

Unfortunately, the phone contained social media, and Hannah was unable to stop herself from looking at it. A window back into a world of summers spent in London and the rest of the year in Dubai. Of wealth. Of conspicuous consumption. The feature that showed you pictures of what you'd been doing at the same time the previous year was particularly brutal. On the one hand it reminded her of the empty and soulless vacuum her life had been, but on the other . . . God, it had been easy. Comfortable.

Last week she'd heard the Pulp song 'Common People' in a shop and had felt like bursting into tears. There she had been, staring at tins of suspiciously cheap peas in a budget supermarket, wondering how long she could live on them for, when Jarvis Cocker of all people decided to put the boot in.

She had just come from an interview for her dream job. It had not gone well. She'd bet good money that it would still appear in her dreams, albeit in a nightmare that she would be reliving over and over again.

Storn was a range of upmarket Norwegian furniture. Exquisitely handcrafted and elegantly minimalist, it had quickly become a must-have for those who could afford it. Hannah loved it. Hannah had furnished two houses with it. Hannah could very probably never look at another piece of Storn furniture again without being violently ill.

When she'd seen the job advertised, it had felt like a sign from

God that she was going to get through this. That, despite what everyone had told her, she was making the right decision.

She had plucked up the courage to ring Joyce Carlson. Amongst the numerous 'friends' from her 'old life', Joyce was one of the few who had felt like a real friend. Once she'd known her for a while, Hannah had come to realize that, while being part of that life, Joyce had a healthy sense of realism that allowed her to simultaneously recognize the ridiculousness of it all. She was also one of the few women in that crowd who had got herself a job. An actual job. Joyce had met the CEO of Storn through her husband and been hired in a 'marketing' role when the company had launched the shop in London. Joyce knew the right people and had thrown the right parties, giving the brand exactly the kind of splashy landing they'd been hoping for. So much so, they'd now opened a second store in Manchester, catering to the Cheshire set, and they were looking for staff.

So Hannah had swallowed what little pride she had left and contacted Joyce.

The small talk had been as awkward as she had expected it to be. Joyce had expressed solidarity with Hannah while being classy enough not to ask any questions. In any case, Hannah was sure Joyce already knew much of what had happened. The most salacious details had, after all, made the newspapers. Undoubtedly, for the previous three weeks, Hannah's fall from grace would have dominated the gossipy conversations over lunch among the old set. She had been very aware when making the call that she was handing Joyce a tasty morsel to share if she so chose: *Oh yes, she rang me – she's looking for a job now!*

Still, she had needed the help. Once Hannah had raised the

subject of the job, Joyce had seen where she was heading immediately and had seemed extremely sincere in her assurances that she would do all she could to assist her. After all, Hannah had been one of her first and most loyal disciples in the cult of Storn. By the end of the call, Hannah had been all but assured that the job would be hers. She had put down the phone, light-headed with the thought that not only would she soon be able to support herself, but also that she had at least one real friend. The last eleven years might not have been a complete waste.

She had gone into the interview with real confidence.

'I'm really sorry, Ms Willis, I think my assistant must have made a mistake when printing your CV out.'

'Oh?'

'Yes. I've got you down as having read English at Durham University.'

'Right.'

'But you didn't graduate?'

'Ehm. Well, yes, about that—'

'Then there's nothing else on there apart from your hobbies and some charity work. If you give me a moment, I'll just ring her and tell her to print out the full thing. I do apologize. Are you OK for tea, coffee, espresso, cucumber water?'

'Yes, ehm – yes. Actually, that is all of my CV.'

'Ah, I see . . .'

That had been bad, but nothing compared to when the other interviewer had recognized Hannah's name. As she'd fled the Storn premises, Hannah had checked her watch. Her first proper interview had lasted seventeen excruciating minutes.

Sitting on the park bench, she found what she was fairly sure was a Tic Tac at the bottom of her bag. Beggars can't be choosers. She popped it in her mouth.

As well as the Storn interview, Hannah had another one lined up for today – mainly because she had forgotten to cancel it. The advert on the website had been, well, different: 'Publication seeks desperate human being with capability to form sentences using the English language. No imbeciles, optimists or Simons need apply.'

She hadn't been sure it was even a genuine advert, but still, she had sent in her CV regardless. A nice lady called Grace with an accent somewhere between Mancunian and West African had called up and offered her an interview. She'd accepted it, but then the Storn thing happened and, well, this one had completely dropped out of her consciousness. On her way into Storn this morning, she had even debated whether to ring Grace and tell her that she couldn't make it, but had decided against it – it was good to have a back-up plan. If the last couple of months of Hannah's life had proven anything, it was the importance of having a back-up plan.

So here she was, sitting in a park in an unfamiliar city, sucking on what she was increasingly less sure was a Tic Tac, heading for an interview for a job she knew absolutely nothing about and now desperately needed. She glanced at her watch. Christ, she was late now too. She pulled her phone back out of her coat pocket. The map showed the blue dot of the location as being behind an old church on the far side of the park.

She stood and brushed herself down. As she did so, a homeless guy with an eyepatch and a long brown beard that stretched down to his chest wandered up to the bin and looked in it. He wrinkled his nose in disgust and shook his head.

'I tell ya, love, there's some bloody monsters around here.'

CHAPTER 2

Hannah rushed around the corner and looked up and down the street. The park lay behind her, there was an all-weather football pitch to her right and a church to her left. The rest of the street was a stretch of wasteland, with some terraced houses at the far end. At the edge of the empty plot of land was a sign indicating that the site was going to be developed into luxury apartments, but the board was so battered and covered in graffiti that it now looked like someone's big idea whose time had passed.

Hannah started digging around in her bag for the scrap of paper she had written the address on. Maybe she had typed it into her phone wrong?

'Excuse me, sweetie, would you mind moving?'

Hannah immediately started to apologize – although, as she looked around, she couldn't find the source of the voice. She was entirely alone on the street.

'Up, dear. Always look up.'

Hannah took a step out into the road and did as she was told. The church was red brick, with bars on many of the windows. It possessed a sort of shabby, unloved beauty. The pockmarked brickwork climbed to a black slate roof. As Hannah looked further up, she saw a round, unbarred window of multicoloured stained glass. To her untrained eye, it would have been the building's most notable feature – had it not been for the portly man in a tartan three-piece suit who was standing on the roof above it.

'Oh my God,' said Hannah.

'No, sweetie, I'm definitely not him.' The man spoke with a plummy accent, like that of a camp Shakespearean actor. 'Could you be a dear and scooch over a smidge?'

Hannah realized she was directly below the man and scampered out of his projected flight path.

'Are you . . . Are you OK?'

'Sweet of you to ask, although it does demonstrate a frightful inability to assess a situation. Still though, no need to concern yourself. Off you pop.'

He cleared his throat and raised his voice to address the world at large. 'Fare thee well, cruel world. You shall have Reginald Fairfax the Third as your plaything no more!'

Hannah looked up at the man, desperately trying to think of something to say. However, she was beaten to it.

'Oh no, please don't do it, Reggie,' came a voice with the over-enunciated vowels she was already learning were a signature feature of the Mancunian accent.

Hannah took a few steps further back and found its source: an East Asian man with an unkempt beard who was leaning out one of the side windows of the church, looking up at the other man.

'You have so much to live for,' he continued.

What struck Hannah as odd was the relaxed tone of the second man, as if he were engaged in a half-hearted read-through of a script for which he had little enthusiasm. He seemed considerably more enthusiastic about the large bag of Kettle chips he had on the go.

'No, Ox, my dearest friend. I shall cast off these mortal chains and free myself from this sullied flesh. I leave you all of my earthly possessions.'

'Oh great,' said Ox, as much to himself as anyone else. 'A collection of waistcoats and a sink full of washing-up you said would be done first thing.'

'What was that?'

He raised his voice. 'Nothing.'

Reggie looked thoroughly put out. 'And you can talk! Leaving the house permanently stinking of Chinese food.'

'In my family we just call it food,' responded Ox.

'Oh, how lovely – my final moments and you mock me. Bloody typical.'

'Would you calm down? You don't have to make everything into a . . .'

Ox stopped as he looked down and noticed Hannah for the first time. 'Do you mind, love? This is a private conversation.'

Hannah looked between the two men before pointing at Reggie, up on the roof. 'He . . . He's going to kill himself.'

Ox nodded with a mouth full of crisps. 'Yeah, but almost all of the world's major religions believe that death is not the end, so, y'know . . .'

'But . . .'

Reggie spoke again. 'Please, sweet lady, spare yourself this scene. I could not forgive myself if my passing scarred you for life.'

'Yeah,' agreed Ox. 'You're still very much in the splatter zone there, sweetheart.'

'You are such an uncouth beast.'

'I'm just saying. She's got a nice suit on. She might be off to something important. She doesn't want your blood and guts all over her best rags.'

Reggie shook his head in disgust. 'Ignore him, but please do be on your way.'

Hannah looked at him and then at her phone. Even as she spoke, the words coming out of her mouth – said to a man standing on a rooftop – seemed so surreal. She felt as if she were watching herself from the outside.

'Well, ehm . . . You don't know where *The Stranger Times* is, do you?'

Ox laughed. 'Job interview, is it?' He shouted over his shoulder, 'Grace, have you got someone coming in to be the new Tina?'

Hannah could hear another voice yelling back but couldn't make out what was said.

'Yeah,' replied Ox. 'She's currently in Reggie's flight path.'

Something else was shouted, in a noticeably more forceful tone.

'All right, all right. How is this my fault?'

The voice inside snapped for a third time.

'OK, relax.' Ox looked down at Hannah again. Oddly, he only now seemed worried. 'You're in the right place, love. Front door is around the corner.' He jerked his head in Reggie's direction. 'Lucky you – we're about to have an opening.'

'You are an utter, utter bastard, Ox,' howled Reggie.

'Ah, what? Am I not allowed to grieve in my own way? You're always telling me what to think.'

'I wasn't. I was merely pointing out that—'

Hannah looked at the phone in her hand and then blurted out, 'Should I call somebody?'

'For what?' asked Ox.

Hannah gave an upwards nod in the suicidal man's direction.

'Ah, don't worry. This situation is under control.'

Reggie scoffed. 'That's what you think!' He then turned to Hannah. 'Off you pop, dear. Best of luck in your interview. Believe you me, you are going to need it.'

Hannah shifted her gaze between the two men. They both looked down at her with impatient expressions.

'Right.'

She shoved her phone into her pocket and hurried down the pavement, glancing back a couple of times as she did so – if anything, to double-check she hadn't imagined what had just happened.

She rounded the corner to find what must have been the church's original entrance. Patterned into the brickwork of the porch were the words 'Church of Old Souls'. Dangling beneath, at a precarious angle, was a sign that read 'The Stranger Times'. Scrawled below that were the words 'This is no longer a church. Please go bother God somewhere else.'

Sitting on a camping chair beside the door was a young man of about eighteen, with an expensive-looking camera dangling from around his neck. He was tall and skinny, his gangly frame emphasized further as he was wearing only a T-shirt and jeans. On a day that called for at least three layers, he was two layers too few.

'Hello!'

He leaped to his feet so quickly that his thick glasses fell to the ground.

'Oops,' he said in a cheerful voice. 'Don't worry. I got 'em, I got 'em.'

He scrabbled about on the ground, knocking over a Thermos and a pile of books in the process.

Hannah stepped forward and picked up the glasses before the man could crush them. She held them out. 'Here you go.'

The young man's hand wafted around in the air until it found Hannah's. Clearly he was near blind without them.

'Thank you very much.' He sprang to his feet, his fingers holding his glasses in place this time. 'Hello, again!'

Hannah winced as he snatched the camera from around his neck and took her picture.

'Hi,' said Hannah. 'There's a man around the corner there, threatening to jump off the building.'

The young man smiled and nodded. 'Yes, there is. I noticed that too. Keeping your eyes open is an important part of being a journalist. Speaking of which . . .' He snatched up a notepad from the table beside his chair and started scribbling. 'What is your name and age?'

'I'm Hannah, Hannah Drinkwater. Crap, I mean Willis. Hannah Willis.'

'Right,' he said, furiously scribbling away on his pad. 'And your age?'

'Well . . .' She tried hard to make the rest of the sentence sound playful in tone. 'That's a bit rude, isn't it?'

'Is it? Oh God, it probably is, isn't it?' He drew himself up to his full height, smiled and extended his hand. 'Hello, my name is Simon Brush. Delighted to make your acquaintance.'

Hannah shook his hand. Up close, she could see that his skin was an unhappy testament to the cruelty of teenage years. He looked old enough to have got over the worst of it, but nobody had told his face.

'Likewise.'

'Now,' he said, withdrawing his hand, 'what was your age?'

Hannah stepped back and eyed his T-shirt. The slogan on it read 'I work for *The Stranger Times*'.

'Oh, you work here?'

Simon shook his head. 'No, not yet. I am engaging in positive re-inforcement. Dress for the job you want, so they say. So, y'know . . .'

'Oh, right. I see. I'm here for an interview too.'

'I'm not here for an interview,' said Simon. 'I'm not currently allowed to enter the building. To quote Mr Banecroft' – he snatched up another of his notebooks and flicked through it to find what he wanted – ' "under no circumstances is that forlorn four-eyed freak to be allowed in this building". He has quite the flair for alliteration, doesn't he?'

'Well, yes, but that does seem rather mean.'

'Oh no – y'see, this is like that scene in *Doctor Strange* when he wants to study at the temple but they won't let him in, so he sits outside. That's what I'm doing. I think Mr Banecroft is testing my resolve. I'm showing him my stick-to-it-ed-ness. My determin-ation. This is my one goal in life, and I'm not going to stop until I achieve it. That's why I'm practising my shorthand.'

'Ah, OK. I see.' Belatedly, the wording of the ad came back to her. *No imbeciles, optimists or Simons need apply.* Oh dear.

'I'm doing everything I can to be ready when opportunity strikes.' Simon pulled down on the hem of his T-shirt to show more clearly the message emblazoned on it. 'See the goal. Be the goal!'

Hannah reread it and then paused, unsure of what to say next.

'What?' asked Simon.

'Nothing. Only it's, well . . .'

Hannah realized that, on first scan, her eyes had tricked her into seeing what she expected to be there, rather than what was actually there.

'What?' repeated Simon.

'It's just, your T-shirt – it's missing an "e"?'

'No, it's . . .' Simon looked down and read the wording upside down.

Hannah smiled awkwardly as he did so, already regretting pointing out the mistake.

'I work for *The Stranger Tims*.' Simon looked crestfallen. 'Tims? What the . . . ? Bloody dyslexia. I've been wearing this for weeks! Why didn't anyone tell me?'

'You've been here for weeks?' asked Hannah.

'Yeah. At least it's stopped snowing – that was a rough couple of days.'

'Right. Sorry. I shouldn't have mentioned it.'

'It's not your fault.' Simon slapped on a smile even bigger than the one he had worn previously. 'Every failure is just an opportunity to succeed the next time.'

'That has not been my experience,' replied Hannah.

'What?'

'Never mind. I should get going.'

'Best of luck with your interview.'

Hannah smiled at Simon as she moved past him towards the front door. He stood there giving her two thumbs up, like a shivering monument to misplaced optimism.

The big wooden doors that opened on to what Hannah assumed was the nave of the church were firmly locked, but a rickety stairway beside them led to an upper level. The walls were damp, the paintwork flaking and faded. The fourth step from the top was broken and Hannah had to hop over it.

She stepped through a doorway into the reception area of *The Stranger Times* – a long, narrow room. At the far end a short, plump black woman sat behind the reception desk, typing furiously at a PC that still had one of the old, full-bodied monitors. Hannah hadn't seen one of those in a decade. Foldaway metal chairs sat stacked in one corner, and a battered leather sofa that'd seen better millennia was pushed up against the wall.

The woman looked up and beamed a warm smile. 'Hello, are you here for the interview?'

'Yes, ehm, I'm Hannah Drinkwater – I mean Willis.' Hannah glanced at her watch: twelve fifteen. 'Sorry I'm late.'

The woman waved a hand in her direction. 'Oh, don't worry about that. He hasn't stirred yet. I'm Grace, the office manager.'

She extended her hand. Hannah moved across to shake it. She noticed a couple of framed pictures on the desk: one of Jesus and the other of Phillip Schofield. Grace had long painted nails, and jangly bracelets around each wrist, which gave every movement a musical accompaniment. She had a very warm, re-assuring smile.

'Take a seat. *STELLA!*'

The last word was screeched with such ferocity that Hannah jumped back involuntarily.

'Sorry,' said Grace. 'Please take a seat – we'll be right with you.'

Grace went back to clacking away at her keyboard. Hannah nodded and sat down on the sofa. It was one of those couches you sank into whether you liked it or not, which made it damn near impossible to find a comfortable way of sitting. She moved around, trying to find a dignified compromise, while the leather made embarrassing little parpy noises and her skirt rode up. Tufts of stuffing poked out of one of the holes in the upholstery.

'Did you have any trouble finding the place?' asked Grace cheerfully.

'Oh no, I . . . Well, a bit . . . Actually, ehm, are you aware there's a man trying to jump off your building?'

Grace didn't even look up. 'Well, it is Monday.'

'Right.'

On her way to the interview at Storn that morning, Hannah had been so nervous she'd walked out in front of a car and been greeted by a screeching of tyres and some furious honking. She was beginning to consider the possibility that she'd died at that moment and everything that had happened since was, in fact, hell. It would explain a lot.

On the wall behind the sofa, some front pages of *The Stranger Times* were displayed in grotty frames. 'Nessie Is the Father of My Child' hung beside 'Virgin Mary Halts Terrorist Attack' and

'Switzerland Doesn't Exist'. Reading these made Hannah realize that she was criminally underprepared for the interview – she knew absolutely nothing about the job she was going for. *The Stranger Times* appeared to be a newspaper, although the word 'news' was something of a stretch.

Hannah jumped as Grace hollered 'Stella!' again.

There came a thump from behind the double doors opposite the sofa, followed by the sound of stomping feet on wooden floorboards. The face of a pretty girl, wearing a sour expression and topped with a head of badly dyed green hair, popped through the doorway.

'What are you shouting at me for?'

Grace didn't even move her head. 'Because I need you for something.'

'There's no need to shout.'

'If I do not shout, you do not come.'

The girl sucked her teeth. 'Treating me like I'm some dogsbody, innit.'

'That is exactly what you are, and don't you suck your teeth at me, young lady.'

'What? I can't express myself no more? You want a robot?'

'If it'd clean up its room, then yes. This lady is Ms Drinkwater—'

'Willis,' interjected Hannah.

'Right.'

The young girl, who Hannah assumed was the hollered-for Stella, gave her an appraising look. 'She tryna be the new Tina?'

'Speak properly. And yes, she is. She's got an interview with Vincent.'

Stella shook her head. 'I give her two minutes.'

Grace stopped typing and glowered at Stella. 'I did not ask for your opinion. I want you to show her through.'

'I'm just keeping it real.'

'How about you keep it zipped and do what you are asked?'

Stella rolled her eyes.

Grace rolled her eyes.

Hannah smiled nervously at them both, now feeling a whole different kind of uncomfortable.

Stella opened the door and stepped back. 'Well, come on, then.'

Hannah stood, quickly brushed down her skirt, and followed Stella through the door.

'Good luck,' said Grace.

'Thank you.'

What Grace said next was lost under the sound of Stella closing the door behind her with more force than was strictly necessary, but she could've sworn she heard the words 'You'll need it.'

Hannah found herself in a long hallway, with stained-glass windows down the right-hand side that threw explosions of colour across cardboard boxes piled haphazardly against the opposite wall.

She smiled nervously at Stella. 'My mum and I always argued too.'

'Yeah, cos all black people are related. Grace is my mum, Oprah is my auntie and Barack Obama is my cousin, yeah?'

'Oh God, I'm sorry. I didn't mean to . . .'

'Whatever.' Stella stomped down the hallway a few feet, and

then stopped and turned around. 'You don't want to keep the boss waiting.'

'Right.'

Hannah fell into step behind Stella as she carried on.

'He's a white dude, so he's probably your brother or something.'

'Honestly, I'm . . . It was just . . .'

'Whatever, Maybe-new-Tina.'

Hannah guessed the girl couldn't be much older than fifteen. She wore ripped jeans, Doc Martens, and the kind of pissed-off body language that could be read from space.

Hannah stumbled over a box of browning newspapers, which spilled out across the floor.

'Careful, I is filing those.'

'Sorry. So, ehm . . . when did Tina leave?'

'I dunno, never met her. I've only met the seven or eight people who've tried to be the new Tina.'

'But . . .'

'Nobody has lasted long enough for anyone to remember their name.'

'You mean . . .'

Stella held up her hand for silence; they had reached the end of the corridor. She stepped to the side and then leaned forward to knock loudly on the door three times.

A soft groan issued from inside.

'Boss. We got someone wants to be the new Tina.'

No response.

'Maybe now isn't a good time,' said Hannah.

'It never is,' said Stella. 'Count of three, I'm gonna open the door, you run in. My advice – stay low, move fast.'

'What do you—'

'One-two-three.' Stella said it as if it were a single word before reaching across, grabbing the handle and throwing open the door in one swift motion. She leaned back quickly, as if she were expecting a torrent of water to come rushing out.

'Should I—'

'Go, go, go!'

Hannah moved inside and the door slammed shut behind her.

Dawkins IS God

A church has been formed in Lancaster based on the premise that well-known atheist Richard Dawkins is really the son of God. High priestess and part-time mobile hairstylist Veronica Clift, 41, says it makes perfect sense. 'Revelations clearly states that only 144,000 people can fit into heaven, and the divine Richard is doing everything in his power to get the numbers of true believers down to prevent overcrowding.'

CHAPTER 3

Hannah found herself standing in what was technically a rather large office. The reason it was 'technically large' as opposed to 'actually large' was the number of box files and piles of newspaper that occupied almost every available space. The only light in the room came through the stained-glass windows, the sunbeams capturing the dusty air and giving the place a sense of dilapidated charm. While it might have been a delight for the eyes, it fared less well with the other senses – particularly smell. The stench was that of a compost heap that smoked sixty a day.

'Hello?'

No response. Hannah stood still and listened. There seemed to be a soft snoring sound coming from the desk in the corner, but she couldn't see its occupant thanks to the piles of books, files and general detritus that littered it. She tentatively took a step forward, careful to avoid the silver foil container, the contents of which might once have been from an Indian takeaway, but now appeared close to an exciting breakthrough in the field of biological warfare.

As she moved nearer and was able to see past the largest pile of files, a mop of hair came into view. It was lying on the desk, snoring loudly.

Hannah cleared her throat to no noticeable effect.

'Hello?'

Nothing.

She tried clearing her throat again, at maximum volume. Still nothing.

She looked around, then picked up a large book from atop one of the piles, surprised to discover it was a copy of *Quirk's Peerage*. She dropped it to the ground with a loud *thunk*.

'Gah!'

The man sat bolt upright, a sheet of paper stuck to his face with his own drool. 'Ahhh! I'm blind, I'm blind!'

His arms flailed around his head, as if trying to fend off an attack of invisible wasps. The piece of paper fell to the floor just as his elbow encountered a half-full bottle of whiskey sitting on the desk, sending it toppling off the edge. With unexpectedly sharp reflexes, the man shot out his right hand and caught the bottle before it reached the floor.

'Thank Christ!'

An unseen intercom sprang into life somewhere, delivering Grace's voice into the room. 'That's one.'

The man looked around. 'How is that one? That can't be one. If I say it when there's only me in the room, then it's basically thinking out loud. You cannot deny a man his right to think!'

'You're not alone in the room.'

'Yes, I . . .'

The man looked up, only now seeing Hannah.

'Who is that?'

'Hello, I'm—'

The man held his hand up to silence Hannah.

Grace's voice continued. 'Her name is Hannah Drinkwater—'

'Willis,' interjected Hannah.

'Willis,' continued Grace, 'and she's here for an interview.'

'What? Why? Who put this in?'

'You did. We need a new Tina.'

'But we've already got a new Tina.'

'He resigned, remember? He threw a stapler at your head.'

'Right,' said the man, holding his head in his hands. 'That explains the splitting headache I've got.'

'It was two weeks ago, and he missed.'

'Ah yes, it hit whatshisname instead. That was enjoyable.'

'Ox. And it wasn't enjoyable for him. The reason you've got a splitting headache is the usual.'

'Yes, all right.' The man pulled a face.

'Vincent Banecroft, don't you pull a face at me!'

Banecroft looked around the room. 'How could you possibly know that I—'

'I know.'

'Oh, for—'

'That's two.'

He held out his hands in outrage. 'But I didn't say anything.'

'It was implied.'

'This is ridiculous.'

'Rules are rules.'

'And these rules are ridiculous.'

'Would you like me to show you the agreement you signed, Vincent? Again?'

'No, I would not. Legally, I'm not even sure it would hold up. I was drunk when I signed it.'

'If I had to wait for you to be sober—'

'Yes, yes, yes,' interrupted Banecroft. 'Thank you, Grace. I do not need you to embarrass me in front of our interviewee.'

He looked properly at Hannah for the first time, blinking as he did so, as if trying to focus.

'Ha,' said Grace. 'Like you were particularly impressive up until this point.'

'Right, that's it. As soon as this is done, I'm going to find wherever the hell the intercom is and I'm pulling it out.'

'Best of luck finding anything in that pigsty.'

'Enough. Turn it off immediately, Grace. I am about to conduct a private interview with Ms . . .'

'Drinkwater,' supplied Grace.

'Willis, actually,' corrected Hannah once more.

'Yes,' said Banecroft, 'with all of the above. Turn it off.'

'With pleasure.'

There was a loud beeping noise.

Banecroft shook his head in frustration, resulting in a cigarette dropping out of his hair and on to the table in front of him.

'Ah, excellent.' He snatched it up and started rummaging around on the desk. 'Well, come on, then . . .' He shot an irritated look at Hannah and nodded towards the chair opposite him. 'I haven't got all day – I'm a busy man. Where's my bloody lighter?'

He looked at her as if expecting an answer. Hannah shrugged.

'Well, you've failed the first test. Observation is a key skill. Grace?'

Grace's shout carried down the hallway. 'I can't hear you. You told me to turn off the intercom.'

'So how did she . . . ? Never mind.' Banecroft cupped his hands around his mouth and shouted back. 'WHERE'S MY LIGHTER?'

'I DON'T KNOW.'

Hannah pulled out the chair she had been directed towards.

'I bet she's nicked it. She's always throwing out stuff she doesn't like. That's probably why she's had three husbands. Do you have a lighter?'

Hannah didn't respond.

Banecroft clicked his fingers irritably. 'Hello, Earth to blondie. Come in, blondie.'

'Sorry, I wasn't listening. There are things on this chair.'

'Well, move them off and sit down. C'mon, c'mon, c'mon. I've not got all day.'

Hannah wrinkled her nose in disgust. 'There's a slice of pizza here.'

'Ah, excellent.' Banecroft reached across the desk and plucked the pizza from its perch on the pile of books, revealing a Zippo lighter underneath it. 'Ohhh, double bubble. Today is starting to look up.' He snatched up the lighter in his other hand and sat back down.

Hannah carefully removed the pile of books and placed them on the floor. She did so slowly, to avoid having to look at Banecroft and confirm her strong suspicion that he was eating the slice of pizza.

The chair cleared, Hannah sat down on it, trying not to focus on how the stains on its worn upholstery might now be transferring themselves on to her best suit.

Once in position, she got her first proper look at Vincent Banecroft. Under the destroyed bird's nest of hair sat grey-green bloodshot eyes in a face of pale, unshaven skin. He wore a suit that a charity shop would politely thank you for donating and then burn as soon as you'd walked out the door. He was probably somewhere in his forties, but the generally unhealthy air of the man threw off Hannah's readings. He somehow managed to look both fat and skinny. His face had a hangdog air to it, although that might be explained in part by the chewy piece of prehistoric pizza he was grimly masticating. In short, he looked like his own corpse waiting to happen.

With difficulty, Banecroft swallowed, belched loudly and then leaned back in his chair before placing his feet on the desk. He retrieved the cigarette he had discovered earlier and positioned it in his mouth.

'Is smoking allowed in this building?' asked Hannah.

'Well now, that depends. *You* are not allowed to smoke. I, however, am positively encouraged to do so. It is one of the few comforts I have for being shipwrecked among this confederacy of dunces.' He spoke with an Irish accent, more on the growling than the lilting end of the scale.

'I have asthma.'

Banecroft shrugged. 'We all have our crosses to bear. I myself have crippling athlete's foot.' He lit the cigarette. 'So, let's do this, shall we? Where do you see yourself in five years' time?'

'Well, I . . .' Hannah was thrown. She tried to remember what she had read in *Dynamite Answers to Interview Questions*, which she had pored over the night before. 'I look forward to developing my skill set and building on my—'

'Trick question. Nobody comes here if they have any future. This is where futures come to die. Take it from one who knows.'

Banecroft leaned forward and pulled two sheets of stapled A4 paper from a pile of other papers on his desk, causing several of them to tumble on to the larger pile on the ground below. 'Let's take a gander at the old curriculum vitae, then, shall we?'

Hannah recognized her CV, although when she had sent it in there hadn't been quite so many food and drink stains on it.

'Page one – you've been to school. Well done on fulfilling a basic legal requirement.'

'Well, yes, I—'

He flipped the page. 'Page two – you went to Durham University to study English.'

'Yes, I have always been—'

'Which you did not finish. And then . . . you disappeared.'

'I was—'

'No, wait – tell a lie – you organized a couple of charity fun runs and a ball. Well, well. "Fun run". That surely ranks up there with "friendly fire" and "vegetarian meal" in the list of oxymorons.'

Hannah said nothing.

Banecroft looked up from the CV. 'Nothing you'd like to add?'

'Do I get to speak now? I was getting the impression you just wanted to monologue.'

'Ohhh, the kitty has claws. Good to know. So, who was it? Nanny? Personal trainer?'

'Excuse me?'

Banecroft took his feet off the table and picked up the bottle of whiskey. 'Who was he screwing?'

Hannah shifted in her seat. 'I don't know what you mean.'

Banecroft fished a grimy glass from his desk drawer and filled it with a generous-verging-on-suicidal measure of whiskey. 'Sure you do.' He placed the whiskey bottle in the bottom drawer and looked across at Hannah. 'You left university mid-degree and disappeared. Can't have been to prison as, unless the rules have been even further relaxed, you can't organize a charity ball from Wormwood Scrubs. That means the other kind of incarceration: marriage. Seeing as you didn't have to work, I'm guessing he had a good job. City-boy type? He's not dead, otherwise you'd be wearing the ring still, and you'd not be here, because being here is desperate and most big jobs have nice parachutes if your spouse pops his Gucci loafers. You were married, you're at least separated, and the suit you're wearing shows you had money, even if you don't any more. Probably turned your back on all his ill-gotten gains to start a new life without the bastard. You're a strong, independent woman who doesn't need him – but you still kept a few of the outfits. So, who was he screwing? Nanny? Personal trainer? Do people still screw their secretaries? That seems like a bit of a cliché.'

Banecroft and Hannah locked eyes for a long moment.

'We just grew apart as people.'

'Poppycock.'

'Poppycock?'

It was Banecroft's turn to look put out. 'I have an agreement with my receptionist.'

'Office manager,' interjected Grace's voice, from the unseen intercom.

'So help me, Grace, get off that accursed thing this instant!'

There was another loud beep.

Banecroft took a swig of whiskey from his glass. 'I have signed an agreement with my . . . office manager, which states that I am not allowed to swear or take the Lord's name in vain more than three times a day.'

'What happens if you do?'

'She leaves. It turns out the place cannot function without her. In this receptacle of ineptitude, broken dreams and hard-luck stories, she is that most dangerous of things – a bona fide useful employee. Speaking of leaving . . .' Banecroft interrupted himself by coughing violently, requiring Hannah to duck as the lit cigarette flew out of his mouth and spiralled towards her head.

'Damn it. Excellent reflexes, though – well done. You've passed the physical.'

Hannah glanced over her shoulder, but the cigarette was nowhere to be seen amidst the piles of newspapers. She looked back at Banecroft, who was in the process of lighting another one.

'Shouldn't you get that?'

'It'll probably be fine. The whole building is riddled with damp. Terrible kindling. What were we discussing?'

Banecroft leaned back once more and placed his feet on the desk again.

'You were telling me what this job entails.'

'No, that doesn't sound like something I'd do.'

'You were explaining how you've been emasculated by your own office manager.'

'Before that.'

Hannah wasn't looking at him at all.

'I'm sorry, do I not have your full attention?'

'Apologies, I was slightly distracted by your office now being on fire.'

Hannah leaned to one side to give Banecroft a clear view of the smoke coming from one of the newspaper stacks.

'Oh, for— No need to be so dramatic – it's not a big fire. GRACE! Can you . . . ? We need a whatchamacallit . . .'

The door to the office flung open and Stella stomped in carrying a fire extinguisher.

'Yes, one of them. Excellent.'

Stella sprayed foam on the smouldering papers while simultaneously glowering at Banecroft. When she eventually stopped, she kicked the papers with a well-placed Doc Marten to ensure no flames had survived.

'Excellent. Have you met my protégée?'

Hannah looked between them and nodded. 'Stella. Yes, I have.'

'She's just a bundle of joy, aren't you, Stella? Big fan of old buildings such as this one. I first met her when she was clambering in our window for a midnight tour.'

'Oh man, not this shit again?'

'GRACE?'

'She didn't sign the deal – you did,' came Grace's voice.

'How is that fair?' Banecroft turned back to Hannah. 'Anyway, she happened to catch me polishing my prized possession.'

'Ain't that the truth.'

Banecroft reached down and picked up an object that Hannah

could best describe as a gun, although she had never seen one quite like it before. It started out like a normal rifle at its butt, but its muzzle resembled nothing so much as a trumpet. Banecroft held it aloft.

'A one-of-a-kind Balander Blunderbuss. Passed down from Lord Balander to Lord Balander for generations, until the last of the line lost it to me in the mistaken belief that a full house beats a straight flush.'

'It's, umm, very nice.'

'Yes. Angsty the Teenager didn't think so when she first met it, but then some people don't take a shine to me right off the bat. My young apprentice was given a choice – prison or an exciting career in the newspaper business.'

'Yeah,' said Stella. 'If I knew what it was gonna be like, I'd have asked him to shoot me.'

'Oh, she doesn't mean that.'

With a two-fingered salute and a slam of the door, Stella left the room.

Banecroft sat back in his chair again. 'I like that kid. She's got a wonderful angry energy. Like she's decided life is crap and we're all just killing time until we meet a slow and painful death. She is well ahead of the game on that front. At her age, I still held out hope for something. Anyway, where were we?'

'You were insulting me and then you set fire to your office.'

'Now that does sound like me. Wait a second . . . Speaking of fire, Drinkwater!'

Hannah's heart sank. 'So, the role – exactly what does it—'

Banecroft drummed excitedly on the desk. 'I remember now.

You made the papers: the woman who burned down her cheating husband's house. I can see why you're so big into fire safety now.'

Hannah felt her anger rise. 'I didn't burn down a house. I was burning his clothes in the back garden and the wind changed.'

It had taken quite a lot of wrangling to avoid an arson charge.

'I see,' said Banecroft. 'And was this before or after you, what was it, "just grew apart as people"?'

Hannah folded her arms. 'Did you bring me here just to humiliate me?'

'No, but it's a fun bonus. So, to go back to my original question: nanny or personal trainer?'

Hannah felt something snap inside her. She was on her feet before she realized. 'Oh, to hell with you. Who are you to pass judgement on anyone? Sitting here in your own filth. What kind of a place is this anyway? Listen to yourself, you disgusting man. "Nanny or personal trainer? Nanny or personal trainer?" If you must know, marriage guidance counsellor. That's right, I caught him banging the woman who was supposed to be saving our marriage after he'd already screwed his personal trainer, the neighbour's nanny, a couple of my supposed friends and yes, a secretary. That is still a thing – at least in my crappy life. This is how bad things have got. My last chance of a job is begging some drunken sop whose own staff hate him so much that they have to blackmail him into signing agreements to behave with basic common decency, and even then one of them is outside right now, threatening to throw himself off the roof.'

Banecroft paused, the glass of whiskey halfway to his lips. 'He's what?'

Hannah took a deep breath, trying to regain some composure. 'Yes. And to think, I was daft enough to try to talk him out of it.'

'Bloody Mondays. Excuse me a moment.'

Blunderbuss still in hand, Banecroft turned, opened the stained-glass window behind him and leaned out.

'Right!' he hollered. 'This is it!'

'You stay away from me, you monster!'

The voice was that of Reggie, the man in the tartan three-piece suit whom Hannah had met earlier – although 'met' didn't seem like the right word, given the circumstances.

'Every bloody Monday,' shouted Banecroft. 'Enough is enough. I'm going to shoot you.'

Hannah watched as Banecroft dangled precariously out of the window, aiming the blunderbuss up at the roof.

'You're too late, I'm jumping.'

'Good, I like a moving target. It's been a while since I killed a man, but I guess it's like riding a bike. You never forget.'

Banecroft cocked the hammer on the blunderbuss and placed the butt against his shoulder.

'Leave me alone, you beast. That gun probably isn't even loaded.'

'Really? I'm an alcoholic with nothing to live for. You seriously think I'd have a gun and not keep it loaded?'

'Well . . .'

'And rest assured, I'll definitely do it. Do you know why? Because I can't stand the idea of you killing yourself, because then you'll actually have achieved something. I can't live in a world where someone of your ineptitude has even the briefest moment of accomplishment. Now get back inside and give me twelve hundred words on the banshee of wherever.'

'Never.'

'OK, then jump. I've had a better idea. I'm not going to shoot you. Instead, I'll let you jump and then I'll continue to publish your articles.'

'What articles?'

'You know, the ones where you admit that all this ghost stuff is nonsense.'

Hannah heard a gasp.

'You wouldn't dare.'

'Sure I would. Then I'll publish one about how all the UFO stuff is a load of guff too.'

Hannah heard the voice of the man she'd seen leaning out of the window earlier – Ox. 'Hey, what did I do?'

'Well, when your soulmate here takes the jump, I assume you'll follow in a grand romantic gesture.'

'For the last time, we're just flatmates!'

'All right, that's enough.' Grace's voice boomed over the others'. 'All of you, back inside, right this minute. Nobody is jumping off anything or shooting anyone. There is a young, impressionable girl in the building – have you all forgotten that?'

'I don't care,' came the aforementioned impressionable girl's voice from somewhere else.

'Shut up, Stella! I will not tell all of you again. Now – I am doing the lunch orders. Ox?'

'Quarter pounder with cheese, chips and gravy.'

'Reginald?'

'I'm . . .'

'Reginald?' Grace repeated.

'Halloumi salad, please.'

'Certainly.'

'I'll have the all-day breakfast,' shouted Banecroft.

'I told you that you would not get lunch if you threatened to shoot anybody again.'

'It's not even loaded.'

'All right, fine.'

Banecroft leaned back in the window and looked at Hannah. 'What do you want?'

'Excuse me?'

'Lunch. Don't tell me you don't know what that is? You've done bugger all except eat it for a decade.'

Hannah opened her mouth and then closed it again. 'Wait, you're hiring me?'

Banecroft sighed. 'Yes. Your CV may contain absolutely nothing, but out of thirty-eight applicants, it was one of only two that contained fewer than three spelling mistakes. This newspaper may be a pile of excrement, but as long as I'm here, it'll be correctly spelled excrement.'

'But . . .'

'Incidentally, the other applicant with fewer than three mistakes had written the CV in his own blood.'

'I'm surprised you didn't give the job to him.'

'I tried. He turned us down. He got a job at Subway, apparently. So, what'll it be?'

Hannah looked about the room and took a deep breath. 'Yes, OK, I'll take it.'

'What?' said Banecroft. 'The job? Of course you'll take it. You wouldn't be here if you had a choice. For the last time, what in the name of all that is good and holy do you want for lunch?'

'A chicken sandwich?'

Banecroft stuck his head out the window again. 'The new Tina will have a chicken sandwich.'

He leaned back inside and closed the window. 'Now, if that will be all, it's nearly lunchtime and I have yet to drink my breakfast. I can't face the afternoon editorial meeting sober.'

He sat back in his chair heavily and tossed the blunderbuss into the corner, where it promptly fell over and shot him.

CHAPTER 4

Jace needed to keep the excitement from his voice, or at least try to pretend it was something else. He turned and smiled at the client, who beamed back at him. Luckily, this idiot was American. The Yanks were so gosh-darned optimistic and positive about everything that he probably saw fevered excitement as a default setting. One look at this short-arse's great big gullible face and Jace's heart had leaped for joy.

The guy had walked into the agency's offices eating a kebab, for God's sake – who does that? It had taken every ounce of Jace's self-restraint not to say anything when the slob wiped his hands on the upholstery of Jace's BMW on their way to the viewing. He hadn't got himself in serious debt so some gluttonous pig could mess up his perfect ride. Still, seeing as there was a thousand-pound bonus for anyone who could shift this dump, there was a chance he was about to get a bit of breathing room on that front. Fiona had stopped him from using the agency cars when he'd been caught – well, no time to think about that now.

Normally, Mondays were pretty dead in the office. Most staff at the estate agency had the day off, given the vast majority of viewings took place on a Saturday. Jace was only working it as a punishment. Fiona was penalizing him because, well – all right, he had messed up. He'd been showing that apartment in Macintosh Mill only for the client to come home and find Jace in bed with the woman he'd been showing it to. Fiona had said it was unprofessional, which Jace had to admit it was, but that wasn't the main source of her annoyance and they both knew it.

Jace should never have gone back to her room after the Christmas party. It had been a mix of pity, convenience and free alcohol. Fiona had threatened to fire him after the Mac Mill incident and he had threatened to tell her husband if she did. The atmosphere between them had been toxic ever since. He felt like the whole thing was very unfair. He'd initially thought giving a taste to grateful older women was his secret weapon; it had sold that penthouse over in Ancoats after all, but now it had backfired spectacularly. Not only had the Mac Mill woman walked away from the sale, but she had left him with a nasty itch down there. He was going to have to go and see somebody about that. He also needed a holiday, but there was zero chance of that if Fiona carried on keeping him away from all the juicy commissions.

Mostly, the agency dealt in residential sales and lettings. The money was in sales, but that's why Fiona used them as an incentive, dangling them in front of her acolytes like carrots. They also had a few commercial properties, mainly because Fiona was greedy and incredibly good at convincing people she could sell anything. Still, in over a year, nobody had been able to lease this place. The one prospective client they'd had in the last six months had walked out on the viewing, offended that they had even dared show it to her.

It was an old warehouse. If the owner had any sense he would have gone to the right pub, dropped an envelope containing a couple of grand on the right table, then waited for the police to call and regretfully inform him that it'd been gutted in a suspected arson attack. Bloody kids.

As the metal shutters juddered up slowly, Jace realized he needed to cover the pained squeal with some small talk. What did you say to men? They'd never been his target demographic.

'So, have you been in Manchester long?'

'Couple of weeks.'

'And where were you before that?'

A particularly loud screech meant Jace didn't catch the answer. He could have sworn the guy said prison, but he must have heard wrong. The bloke was five foot nothing and looked way too soft to have done time. Not that Jace knew a lot about such things. He smiled and nodded, and the Yank smiled and nodded back.

The location was bad. The condition of the property was worse. Still, neither of those things was the warehouse's really big problem. Or rather, one of its four really big problems. In reverse order, the place was filled with mouldy old furniture that looked terrible and smelled horrendous. Human beings hated it but apparently rats didn't, hence problem number three. Jace was just hoping the little shits wouldn't pop out during the viewing. Problem two was the lack of plumbing, which seemed doubly ironic given problem one: the foulest of foul stenches from a blocked-up sewer under the property which, despite some less than subtle hints, the vendor had no inclination to get sorted.

As the shutter door ground its way upwards, the smell hit Jace so hard he had to take a step back.

'Sorry about the pong. The place hasn't been open for a couple of weeks.'

'Oh, is it bad? I don't have much of a sense of smell.'

Jace's heart leaped but he didn't miss a beat. 'No, not really. Just a little musty. It'll be fine with a bit of air going through it.' He reached over and flipped on the lights, which slowly blinked into life. 'So, no sense of smell?'

'Yeah,' said the Yank. 'It's one of the weird side effects of the particularly brutal torture I was subjected to.'

'Right,' said Jace.

Was that a joke? It could be one of those peculiar-sense-of-humour things. People were weird. Only last week Jace had visited a flat in the Northern Quarter on the landlord's request to discover the tenant was living with fourteen rabbits roaming free in the property. An argument had ensued as the guy disputed whether they were considered pets.

Jace needed to press on. 'As you can see, plenty of space.'

The place was filled with random piles of broken furniture that stretched back into the darkness. Apparently, at some time or another, someone had had the brainwave that loads of furniture nobody wanted in the first place could be upcycled and resold. It had proven to be as bad a business idea as it sounded.

'The owner wouldn't mind if you wanted to get rid of all the furniture, and just look at all this space. I mean, you will never find this amount of space anywhere else in this price range.'

'It's off the beaten track, isn't it?'

'Well, yes and no,' said Jace. The whole area was a sinkhole. Storage units and dodgy garages were interspersed with abandoned-looking premises. The only reason they were still standing was that nobody had been inclined to bulldoze them and put up something useful in their place. 'It has access to lots of local amenities and again, you will not find this kind of space so close to the city centre. It's a rough diamond.'

'You say the word "space" a lot.'

Jace forced a laugh. 'Ha, sorry. Well, it's just that there's so much of it.'

'And the smell?'

'It really isn't that big a deal.'

Jace used every ounce of his self-control to resist the urge to retch. It really was that bad. He needed to get this idiot to sign the forms today before he brought somebody with him who had a functioning sense of smell. Jace felt peculiar. Like there was a buzzing in his head. He wasn't sure if he'd asked the man already, but for the life of him he couldn't remember either the client's name or what he actually wanted the space for. He looked down at the clipboard in his hands, where those areas on the paperwork were blank.

'Actually, I . . . Sorry . . . Could you give me your name again?'

The Yank smiled. 'I didn't give it to you the first time. It's Moretti.' He was digging around in his leather satchel as he spoke.

'Right. And what is it you'll be using the property for?'

'Oh, I'm going to be saving a sick child's life.'

'Wow,' said Jace. 'So, like, medical research?'

Moretti smiled. 'No, no. It'll be blood magic. Highly illegal.'

Jace stood there with his pen poised over the clipboard and looked at Moretti.

'I see.' This guy was clearly completely mental. He decided to choose his next words carefully. 'I don't know what you mean by that. Obviously, I can't rent it to you if you tell me you'll be using it for an illegal purpose.'

Moretti laughed. 'My kind aren't governed by your laws.'

'When you say "my kind" . . . I appreciate you're American, but obviously in Britain – British laws apply.'

Moretti pulled a couple of what looked like steel ball bearings out of his bag.

'Here they are. And no, I don't mean countries. You see, I am a member of the cabal of immortals that secretly runs your sad little world. I view you as you view those rats you're trying to pretend aren't running around over there.'

The buzzing noise in Jace's mind was growing louder. This man was clearly insane. He was still wearing the same grin as when they'd first met, but somehow it now looked demented rather than clueless. Jace needed to get out of there. Some part of his brain, still focusing on the sale, spoke next.

'Rodents are always a problem in any warehouse-type space. I'm sure some traps will fix that.'

'What a good idea.' There was now an air of malevolence to Moretti's smile. 'I've actually got myself a little trap right here.'

He casually tossed one of the ball bearings up into the air, where it stopped dead, floating about ten feet off the ground.

'How . . . how are you doing that?' asked Jace.

'That's not the question you should be asking.'

'No?' said Jace, shuffling his feet, angling himself towards the door.

'No,' said Moretti. 'The question you should be asking is: why am I not running?'

Jace sprinted for the open door, not looking back. He heard Moretti whistle. With a flash of silver, the ball bearing zipped through the air, coming to a stop in front of him. It expanded before his eyes. Where there had been one tiny ball of steel, there was now a rectangular plate of metal. Three. Five. Seven rectangular plates of metal.

Jace turned around to run the other way but Moretti was standing with his arms folded, smiling at him. He began to feel the metal grasping around his wrists, ankles, neck. He wanted to shout for help as a force lifted him off the ground, but no noise would come. He felt himself somersault through the air and then slam into the corrugated steel wall. He drew in a breath to scream but metal wrapped itself around his mouth, sealing it closed.

Eyes wide, he looked about him, his heart pounding. He was pinned to the wall ten or so feet off the ground. Metal bound his ankles, wrists, neck and stomach, holding him very firmly in place. Below him, Moretti took a handkerchief out of his pocket and blew his nose messily. He then looked up at Jace, a wide grin beneath his wild eyes. He nodded his head in satisfaction.

'Good, good. They work. Needed to check that.' Moretti ran a hand over his bald pate, smoothing down the hair he still had left around his ears. 'So, whatever your name is, couple of things you need to know about me. One – my sense of smell is perfectly fine, and two – I really dislike being lied to.'

Jace tried to speak but it was impossible.

'Oh, and three – I'm, y'know . . .' Moretti wiggled his fingers in the air. 'Magical. I'm also a little bit . . .' He twirled a finger at his own temple. '. . . crazy, but torture really does have that effect on you. Do you have any idea what kind of torture a bunch of immortals can come up with when they want to punish you but they aren't allowed to kill you? You see, when I say we're immortal . . .' Moretti stopped himself and waved his hand. 'Oh, never mind. Look at me, gabbling on. I must not forget my purpose – I'm here to save a child's life.' He clasped his hands to his chest. 'You see, I'm not all bad. I like to help the needy. I want you to know that this inconvenience to you does serve a higher purpose.'

Moretti looked at his watch. 'Speaking of which, we must move this along. So, you've got ten seconds to see if you can escape those bonds and if you can't, I'm going to kill you.' He looked up into Jace's eyes. 'Don't look so scared, we all have to go sometime. I mean, not me – but you do.'

Jace tried to move his arms as panic surged through him.

'Come on,' hollered Moretti cheerfully. 'It feels like you're not really trying. Perhaps you work better with an audience?'

Moretti made a motion with his hand and Jace heard a squeal from within the jungle of furniture. A shape rose up and flew towards him. As it grew larger in his vision, he clenched his eyes shut, bracing himself for the impact that didn't come. After a second he opened his eyes. Floating in the air, inches from his face, close enough that he needed to close one eye to focus on it, was a large rat. He could make out the wild terror in its eyes as it attempted to squirm away from the invisible hand that was holding it. Jace could sympathize.

He couldn't see Moretti any more but his voice rang out. 'So . . . ten . . .'

Jace tried with every fibre of his being to twist and turn any of his limbs, to gain any sort of wiggle room, but nothing gave. It felt as if the metal were moving to counter him, resisting his attempts. All the time he did so, the calm, almost bored-sounding voice continued to count down.

'. . . three . . . two . . . one . . . zero, and – you're dead!'

Jace watched numbly as the rat soared away from him and, with a sickening squeal, collided with the back wall of the warehouse.

He heard Moretti whistle, and before he knew what was happening the metal that had bound him so tightly wasn't there any more. Jace tumbled messily to the ground. He looked up to see Moretti holding out his hand, palm up, as the plates of metal reformed above it into an impossibly small ball bearing.

Jace started to get to his feet.

'Relax,' said Moretti, moving towards him. 'I just needed to test these bonds worked as advertised. Don't worry – I'm not really going to kill you. You're not important enough for me to kill. Oh, and hey – little bit of good news.'

Moretti mouthed a word, wafted his hand and the air was filled with the pleasing scent of lilacs.

Jace felt numb, as if his mind could no longer process anything that was happening to him. He watched as Moretti took something from the inside pocket of his jacket. A gold coin on a chain now dangled before Jace's eyes.

'Relax, buddy, it's almost over. Just watch the shiny coin . . .'

With a flick of Moretti's wrist, the coin started spinning impossibly fast.

'That's right. Now, you're going to forget everything that happened over the last couple of hours, and when you go back to the office you're going to remove this property from your files. If anyone asks, it's not available. Give me the keys.'

Jace handed them over compliantly.

'Good boy,' said Moretti. 'Oh, and one last thing. For the next two weeks, every time you say the word "space", you're going to excuse yourself from the room, find a quiet spot and punch yourself in the nuts. Hard. Got it?'

Jace smiled and nodded. 'Got it.'

Moretti patted him on the head. He stopped the coin spinning and placed it back in his jacket pocket. 'Now run along. I've got shit I need to do.'

Jace stood and walked out into the sunlight, throwing a happy wave over his shoulder as he did so.

Moretti looked around him and then jingled the set of keys he held in his hand. He drew in a deep, satisfied breath.

'And to think, people say the Brits aren't friendly.'

CHAPTER 5

It was, in many ways, the most British response imaginable to a situation. Their boss had shot himself in the foot in an extremely non-metaphorical way. There had been quite a lot of blood. Enough for Ox to have promptly fainted when he ran into the room. Grace had come in and taken control of the situation – calling an ambulance, raising the foot and wrapping it in most of the contents of the first aid kit. Banecroft had spent the entire time screaming and hollering while, remarkably, managing not to swear or take the Lord's name in vain.

Hannah had stood to the side, too dazed to feel she could be of any use to anyone. This was only her second ever job interview, but she strongly suspected that they didn't normally end in this much gunplay and bloodshed. Through it all, a little voice in the back of her mind kept saying, 'Ohhh, you got a job, though. That's pretty good, isn't it?' It was. A second voice kept trying to butt in with, 'Yeah, but look where it is. I mean, you're working for an appalling human being who screams abuse at everyone and just shot himself in the foot.' To counter this, the first voice began singing 'Things Can Only Get Better' by D:Ream.

The ambulance crew had examined Banecroft and determined

that most of the damage was 'superficial'. The blunderbuss had been loaded with sand and what could best be termed detritus. It was less a gunshot and more a directed explosion of random crap. Still, when the police had turned up a couple of minutes after the ambulance, they'd quickly decided that they should impound the weapon.

Banecroft had been less than pleased about the situation. He had waited until the ambulance crew had moved him on to the stretcher, down the stairs and outside into the brisk March air before giving the police both barrels of his impressive swearing capabilities. His agreement with Grace clearly only covered profanities uttered inside the building. The police looked as if they were considering charging him, but that would've meant spending more time in his company, and from their slumped shoulders and glassy-eyed stares, Hannah guessed they were near the end of a long shift.

Hannah, Stella, Ox and Reggie watched as the ambulance pulled away. Grace had elected to go with Banecroft to the hospital, reasoning that the paramedics, who weren't paid anywhere near enough to put up with such a patient, might otherwise find themselves tempted to open the vehicle's rear doors at the first steep hill they reached and let gravity take its course. Banecroft had the ability to make a first impression that ranked just below that of a landmine.

Simon, despite Ox trying to talk him out of it, hopped on his bike and followed the ambulance, keen to 'report the story'.

'So,' the now-recovered Ox said. 'Pub?'

★

The Admiral's Arms had three things going for it: location, location, location. It was close by.

The building beside it looked a lot nicer and it was in the process of being knocked down. Conversation was limited as the group of four walked past the demolition site – the hypnotic spectacle of a wrecking ball ploughing into a wall took up all of their attention. Lots of men in hard hats were standing around, each no doubt secretly jealous that they weren't the guy in the cab of the crane, swinging the ball.

Once inside the pub, Hannah realized that beneath its gruff exterior, the Admiral's Arms' interior was even gruffer. It wasn't a 1970s-themed pub; it was a pub that had been built in the 1970s and had remained exactly the same, only somehow it had also grown worse. The carpets were threadbare, the wallpaper was peeling, and the leather of the booths was the texture of Keith Richards' face.

'Afternoon, Dennis,' said Ox cheerfully as they entered. The man behind the bar looked up briefly from his newspaper and mumbled something unintelligible. He was in his sixties, and had no hair on his head but a remarkable amount coming out of every other orifice.

The group moved to occupy a booth near the door. As Hannah sat down, she noticed a sign on the wall: 'Due to ridiculous health and safety regulations, this establishment will no longer be serving food. Tough!'

'Are we sure Mr Banecroft will be OK?' she asked.

'Honestly, dear,' said Reggie, 'do not give it a moment's thought. He will be absolutely fine.'

'Yeah,' agreed Ox. 'After the inevitable nuclear holocaust, the only things left will be cockroaches and Vincent Banecroft. Personally, I feel sorry for the cockroaches.'

Stella – who, upon taking her seat, had instantly pulled out a book from her satchel – didn't look up. 'Cockroaches can hold their breath underwater for, like, forty minutes and can run up to three miles in an hour. Innit.'

Hannah looked at her. 'Wow. Is that right?'

'Yep,' she said, turning a page. 'For reals.'

Now that she wasn't freaking out about an impending job interview, Hannah noticed that Stella's attempts to be street were just that: attempts. Hannah was no expert, but it all sounded a tad forced.

'Our girl here is a fount of trivia,' said Ox. 'She's the reason Dennis got rid of the quiz machine.'

'Yeah,' said Stella, 'and it was the only thing in this dive that was any fun.'

'Shush,' said Reggie. 'You know how sensitive Dennis gets. This place is his pride and joy.'

All four of them looked around the room.

'Well,' said Reggie, 'that may be overstating the case slightly. Would you believe that the toilet facilities are kept in pristine condition?'

'Really?' asked Hannah.

Reggie gave her a tight smile. 'Sadly no, but needs must.'

And with that, he headed off in the direction of the gents. Hannah watched him go.

'Are you sure this is a good idea?'

'What?' asked Ox.

'Bringing a suicidal man to the pub?'

Ox looked genuinely shocked. 'Suicidal? Who's suicidal?'

Hannah looked pointedly at the door of the gents' toilet.

Ox waved a hand dismissively. 'Reggie? Don't be daft. He's not suicidal.'

'But he threatened to jump off a building!'

'A pretty small building,' interjected Stella.

'Yeah,' agreed Ox. 'And he's been doing the same thing every Monday morning for months now. Like clockwork.'

'But . . .' started Hannah, but she couldn't think what else to ask.

'Look,' said Ox. 'Every Monday we've got the editorial meeting with Banecroft and, well, you've met him.'

Hannah nodded.

'Some people get themselves psyched up for something like that by, I dunno, mainlining coffee or going for a jog or summat. Reggie does it by having one of them historic fits.'

'What?'

'He means histrionic,' said Stella, who now held her book in one hand and her phone in the other.

'That's what I said. Reggie is a very calm bloke most of the time.'

'Really?'

Both Ox and Stella nodded.

'Although,' continued Stella, 'he did lose it with one of them other new Tinas when they had a discussion about the Oxford comma.'

'Yeah,' agreed Ox. 'Apart from that.'

'Right,' said Hannah.

They lapsed into silence as Ox checked his phone and Stella read her book. Hannah used the time to take a proper look at the Admiral's Arms' other patrons. An old man sat at the bar, staring at his half-drunk pint as if he were expecting it to give him bad news any minute. At his feet sat an incongruously happy-looking dog, panting away cheerily. In the corner, a couple of women sat knitting. Oddly, they were knitting the same garment from either end. It seemed to have more sleeves than could possibly be needed. The final customer was a tall man in his twenties who wore a peaked cap and had a nervous, jerky energy to him. It meant that even as he sat on a stool at the bar, texting, he was neither sitting down nor standing up, but in a permanent state of flux between the two.

Reggie returned from the gents, careful to dust down his seat before taking his place at the table.

'Right,' said Ox. 'Time for a round, I think.'

He looked at Hannah expectantly.

She smiled. 'I'll have a white wine, please.'

'Guess again,' said Ox.

Reggie sighed. 'What Ox is trying to say, in his own inimitably abrupt style, is that it is traditional on these occasions for "the new Tina" to get the first round in.'

The rest of the table nodded.

'Oh. Right. Of course. Sorry.'

'I'll have a pint of mild, please,' said Ox.

'A gin and tonic,' said Reggie.

'Same,' said Stella.

'She'll have a Coke,' said Reggie.

Stella lifted her gaze and, from between strands of green hair, shot Reggie the dirtiest of looks.

'Come now, Stella, dear. What would Grace say?'

'She's not my mum.'

'She's everybody's mum,' said Ox.

Stella tutted and went back to her book. 'Fine. Whatever. Coke.'

'Ooh,' said Ox, 'can we get some nuts too? I'm starving – since we didn't get a lunch because of you-know-who doing you-know-what.'

Hannah went to the bar and ordered the drinks and nuts. From the look Dennis the barman gave her, it appeared that her doing so had entirely ruined his day. She tried to engage him in conversation, but he regarded her with undisguised suspicion. When he'd finished pouring the drinks, Hannah's polite request for a tray was met with, 'We used to have one but somebody borrowed it for Princess Diana's wedding and never brought it back.'

As she stood at the bar, Hannah had her first moment alone with her thoughts since she had entered the doors of *The Stranger Times* a couple of hours ago. She had a job! She had co-workers! Admittedly, they were a tad eccentric, but it was a refreshing change from the stultifying life she'd known previously, where anything that didn't fit into rigorous parameters was mocked and derided, although never openly. That old crowd had too much class to practise honesty. If you wanted to hear what they really thought of you, you'd need to somehow be in the room you'd just walked out of. It left you in a permanent state of unease, thinking that at any given time people were talking about you.

After her break-up with Karl, that unease disappeared. Hannah was now certain they were talking about her. This job was a fresh start. Reggie seemed nice. The accent was luvvie in the extreme, but he appeared to be a gentle soul. Ox was quite abrupt, but he was lively. She bet he'd be good fun when she got to know him. Stella was clearly very smart. Hannah hoped she could get on her good side – assuming she had one. Simon had seemed like an enthusiastic, if odd, kid. After the life she had led to this point, being around unvarnished, unapologetic enthusiasm for anything was a refreshing change. Grace, too, had seemed nice. Yes, she decided, while Banecroft was an 'issue', overall, things were definitely looking up.

Hannah ferried the drinks to the booth in two trips and then retook her seat.

'So,' said Reggie, 'how is our new assistant editor settling in?'

'Excuse me?'

Reggie sipped at his gin. 'Oh, my dear, did you not know? You're our assistant editor.'

'I am? That was never mentioned in the . . . Gosh!'

'Wow,' said Stella, not looking up from her book. 'The new Tina literally just said "gosh". She'll be asking for lashings of ginger beer next.'

Hannah elected to ignore her. 'So, I . . . What does the job entail exactly?'

'Well,' said Reggie. 'Quite a lot really. You're in charge of subediting the paper, so cutting things down as needed, corrections, that sort of stuff. And you're also the conduit between the editor and the journalistic staff.' Reggie wafted his hand in front of himself and Ox.

'Are you all of the writers?'

'Oh no,' said Ox. 'We're just the only two full-timers. We've got a load of others who send stuff in. There's a bloke in Brazil who sends us stories from South America . . .'

Reggie nodded. 'Lots of rather bizarre occurrences happen down there. Just last week they had a rain of frogs in Peru, a mummy attacked someone out hiking in Venezuela, and a woman became pregnant in Argentina when she got caught in a tornado and accidentally fell on to a gentleman's . . . Well, y'know.'

'Right,' said Hannah, wondering how long it had taken for someone to come up with that excuse.

'Yes,' continued Reggie. 'I am *The Stranger Times*'s paranormal consultant and Ox here is our ufologist and general paranoid.'

'It's not paranoia if people are really out to get you.'

'Yes, well—'

'Sorry,' interrupted Hannah, a new urgency in her voice. 'I'm the assistant editor? I'm, like, the second in command?'

Reggie nodded. 'That is one way of looking at it.'

'Technically,' conceded Ox. 'In reality, you're the thing standing between us and Banecroft. If it helps, think of yourself as, like, one of them rodeo clowns.'

'Yes,' agreed Reggie. 'I'm afraid so. The best explanation for Vincent Banecroft is that he is Ireland's gift to the English to thank us for all the nice things we've done to them over the years.'

'I mean,' said Hannah, 'since our editor is currently out of commission, should we all be in the pub? Shouldn't we be, I don't know, working on something or . . .'

'Relax,' said Ox, 'there's no need to panic.'

'OK, but—'

Hannah stopped talking as Ox, in one fluid motion, slid under the table.

'Ehm, Ox, what are you doing?'

'Nothing. Everything is absolutely fine.'

For a man in the duck-and-cover position he sounded remarkably cheerful.

'Oh, good God,' said Reggie.

Hannah followed his gaze across the room. Two men had just walked in. One was tall and shaven-headed, the other short with long hair and a beard.

Reggie spoke in an urgent whisper while pointedly not looking under the table. 'Would it be safe to assume that you borrowed money from the Fenton brothers?'

'No, actually. Smart-arse. I placed a bet with them.'

'I'm going to guess that you did not win.'

'Now is not the time, Reggie. I need a distraction. Stella, be a good girl and go outside and set something on fire.'

'Do no such thing,' snapped Reggie before Stella could reply.

'Fine,' said Ox. 'Everyone just carry on like I'm not here.'

'That's easy for you to say,' said Hannah. 'You're not wearing a skirt.'

'He's gay,' said Stella, without looking up.

'Oh,' said Hannah. 'Well . . . that's all right, then.'

'Thank you for your approval of my life choices,' came the voice from under the table. 'What are they doing?'

'Well,' said Reggie. 'They're at the far end of the bar, talking to

Dennis. Oh, the big one just clocked us. He's pointing us out to the little one.'

'Oh no, oh no, oh no.'

Stella reached into her satchel, which was festooned with stickers, and took out a lunch box containing half of a home-made ham sandwich.

'You owe me big time for this,' she said, to nobody in particular.

She pulled out a sliver of ham and, with a surreptitious underarm toss, sent it flying across the room towards the main doors. Nobody noticed – or at least no person noticed. One canine certainly did. The dog, which had been sitting so obediently at its owner's feet, flew to the doors in pursuit of a treat, its lead still wrapped around the leg of the tall stool. The owner fell forward, throwing a large part of his pint into his own face.

The scene drew the attention of everyone in the room.

'Go,' hissed Stella.

Hannah tried to keep a demure expression on her face as a grown man quickly crawled under her legs and out towards the back door. While the dog owner gave his wayward pooch a severe talking-to, the door opened and Ox made his escape.

'Right,' said Reggie. 'Well, that was all very dignified.'

Hannah glanced at the two men at the bar. 'Ehm, I don't know if anyone else has noticed, but those two guys are looking over here again, and they don't seem happy.'

'Yes. We should probably depart before it dawns on them that they might have been bamboozled.'

Hannah, Reggie and Stella got to their feet. Maintaining a determined focus in the opposite direction to the Fenton brothers, they made for the back door. If they'd looked in the direction of the two men, however, they would have noticed one of them nudging the other before they both headed out the main doors.

'Afternoon,' said the tall one.

The two Fenton brothers were taking up the whole pavement.

'Hello,' said Hannah with a nod as she tried to move past them.

The short one moved to block her. 'We're looking for your friend.'

'I don't know who you mean.'

'Yeah, but *he* does.' The big one shoved a finger in Reggie's face. 'Where's the little Chinky fella?'

'Well, now,' said Reggie, 'that is highly inappropriate language to describe Ox's proud Chinese ancestry.'

'Is that right?' The big one replaced his finger with his whole face, now inches from Reggie's. 'Seeing as the little Chinky fucker owes us three grand, I'll call him what I like.'

'OK, look,' said Hannah, 'this is nothing to do with us.'

'Yeah?' said the shorter one. 'Well, I'm afraid we're making it your problem. If Ox wants to play hide-and-seek, then we've got to send him a message. Ain't we?'

'OK,' said Hannah. 'What is the message?'

Stella tutted from behind her. 'I don't think it's a *message* message, New Tina.'

Hannah's face reddened briefly, but the colour drained quickly when she realized embarrassment was the least of her problems. 'All right, look—'

The tall Fenton ignored her and turned to his brother. 'What d'ye reckon? The kid, the MILF or the poof?'

Reggie stepped forward. 'Gentlemen, there is no need for violence. I'm sure Ox will sort out his business with you promptly. We shall inform him of your displeasure.'

'Oh, la-di-da,' said the short one. 'This one, Terry,' he said, with a jut of his head towards Reggie. 'Let me do this one. Understand, like, it's not cos he's a poof – I just always really hated Rupert the fucking Bear.'

He leaned forward and patted Reggie's waistcoated paunch. 'Our nan had a settee that looked just like you. I never liked it – or her.'

Reggie sighed. 'Gentlemen, a couple of points of note. Firstly, you have made the common, if lazy, mistake of confusing decorum and a sense of individuality with homosexuality – even in this more enlightened age, a tediously frequent occurrence. As it happens, I am rampantly heterosexual. And secondly . . .'

It was fast. So fast that there didn't seem to be a moment where it was happening. It went from being an impossibility to being something that had already happened. One second the Fentons were snarling at them, and the next, each of them had one of Reggie's hands at their throat, hands that were holding knives, pressed up against their skin.

'Either of youse muppets threaten me or my friends again and it'll get tasty. Are we clear?'

Reggie's voice had dropped an octave and fallen into an entirely different accent. To be polite, Hannah would have called it Liverpudlian, but most would simply label it Scouse.

The big Fenton went to speak, but stopped when the blade was pressed slightly harder against his throat.

'Don't speak, la', just nod – real slow, like.'

They both nodded.

And just like that, as soon as it had happened, it had unhappened. Reggie withdrew his hands, the knives disappeared back to wherever they had appeared from, and Reggie's plummy diction returned.

'Excellent. Lovely to chat, but we must dash. Ladies, if you please.'

The Fenton brothers stood statue-still as the group hurried up the pavement past them.

'Whoa,' said Stella when they were out of earshot. 'What in the . . . what?! That was stone-cold badass, Reggie.'

Reggie didn't look back, but hurried on. 'Now, now. It was an unfortunate necessity. Let's not bang on about it. In fact, I'd be very grateful if nobody mentioned it again. You should head home, Stella. I don't want Grace getting upset.'

He threw them a wave and was off across the road, looking like a flustered librarian on his way to a cello recital.

Stella and Hannah shared a blank look as they watched him go – a portly, middle-aged man who freaked out at the prospect of an editorial meeting but who could have blades at the throats of two thugs in the blink of an eye.

CHAPTER 6

Jimmy woke with a start.

This was a good spot, normally. Under the railway arches in Castlefield. Central, but far enough out of the way that you wouldn't have some drunken student tripping over you on the way back to his digs. It was dry, unless it really wasn't – like in the summer when the rain was heavy and the guttering above had flooded – but tonight there was only a light drizzle. If you huddled in the corner between the red-brick walls, it was generally all right, although when the wind changed and blew in at just the right angle, it'd cut right through you.

Was that what'd happened? Jimmy felt cold, but no more than you'd expect for Manchester in March. It was supposed to be bloody spring, but there'd been snow last week. Most of the country had come to a standstill, but Manchester never got that much. Jimmy was from Glasgow and took pride in telling people how they had real cold up there; this was nothing. Sleeping rough up that way was hardcore.

Leaky and Jen used to hang here at night, but then Leaky'd got done for thieving and she'd cleared off. People were always moving on like that – disappearing only to reappear months or even years later, but sometimes never again. Jimmy had liked Jen; she'd had a kind heart. He'd had suspicions that she was one of the Folk, but she'd played dumb when he'd dropped hints. He supposed he couldn't blame her. Folk who'd run had always done it for good reasons, and they always wanted to stay lost. He knew he did.

He liked Castlefield. It had the feel of the old. There was a sign up for the tourists, telling them it'd been the town from which the whole city had grown, having appeared on the side of the Roman fort of Mamucium and supplying it with 'necessary services'. Jimmy's brother had been a squaddie, and he knew exactly what 'necessary services' soldiers went looking for. He had once made the mistake of joking that the whole city had grown out of a knocking shop, and Carol Newell had belted him round the ear-hole something rotten. Weird burst of civic pride from a girl who'd seen her fair share of passenger seats until she'd got sick.

You could still see some of the skeleton of the original fort. There were old bits of wall knocking about, in between the yuppie flats and that. The normals needed plaques to tell 'em it existed, but Jimmy could feel the history. It seeped into the soil. History was a different thing to his kind. It wasn't to be found in books.

He pulled his sleeping bag tighter around himself and rolled over. He needed to get a bit of kip before the trains started rolling overhead and the ordinary world burst into irritating life around him. What he wouldn't give for just one solid block of eight hours. He could change a lot of things with a decent night's sleep.

He sat up when he heard the sound. It wasn't much, but maybe that was the point. Maybe it was the kind of sound somebody would make when they were trying not to make one. His heart was pounding.

Tanner was going to come looking for him. Jimmy had been hurting and he'd nicked some of his stash. Tanner knew. He and Jimmy had been tight, but he wasn't the forgiving sort. Jimmy knew he had a beating coming. All of his life, it'd felt as if he had a beating coming – like he'd popped out of his ma down on his luck and had never got back to even. Like all the Folk, he had to pay the cost. You couldn't avoid it even if you ran. They always found you.

There it was again. The noise. Above him. On the arches. How was it up there? There were no trains at this time of night. Maybe there were workmen checking the line? He'd seen them before.

Still, something down around his nutsack was telling him to run, baby, run.

He slipped out of his sleeping bag as quietly as he could. Most of what he had he was wearing. The rest was in his rucksack beside him. It was as he leaned down slowly to pick it up that he saw them: the eyes. They glowed. Once you'd seen them, the mind could feel out the rest of the creature's form. It hung upside down from the railings. Only it couldn't be . . . It was impossible. There were rules now. He'd never seen one, but there had been bedtime stories – the kind that kept you up at night. The thing . . . yawned? It yawned. Above those eyes, he could see its white fangs in the dim light as its powerful jaws stretched open. It wanted him to run. It was going to get its wish.

His feet were already moving before the thought had formed.

Jimmy bounced off the wall beneath the arch and found himself in the wide-open area between the bridge and the canal, his feet barely touching the cobbled ground. He heard something land softly behind him and then came the skitter of claws on stone.

Jimmy headed for the footbridge, his heart thumping so hard in his chest that he thought it might explode.

He heard the rush of air a millisecond before it hit. Something big and heavy crashed into his back, knocking him so hard that he couldn't put out his hands in time and his face met the pavement. His nose shattered and that row of replacement teeth, which the nice dentist lady had done for him after he'd caught a beating last year, smashed messily. He rolled on to his back and spat out the broken dentures. He could taste the blood as it washed down his face from his shattered nose.

Then it was on top of him. The red eyes inches from his. Claws dug into his shoulders. The jaws were open, drool spilling from them in long ribbons, as the creature panted.

'No, no. S'not possible. You're a . . . You dinnae exist. Not any . . .'

It leaned forward and licked at the blood on Jimmy's face.

He whimpered and clenched his eyes shut, wishing this to be a nightmare he could wake up from, even though he knew for certain it was no such thing.

'What in the—?'

Jimmy opened his eyes at the sound of a voice he recognized. Long John was as Manc as they came. When someone did an impression of a Manc accent, whether they'd met him or not, it was Long John they were doing. He must've just wandered around the corner, looking for a place to crash. He stood there, a bottle of something in his hand, looking down at them, his mouth wide in an O of disbelief.

He turned, but his chances were as hopeless as Jimmy's had been. The creature reached out a long arm and snagged the back of Long John's coat. The bottle smashed to the ground beside Jimmy's head, the liquid splashing on to his lips. Vodka. Long John must've come into some dosh. The beast wrapped its massive claws around Long John's throat.

The last thing Jimmy saw was the surprised expression on Long John's face as he flew through the air and over the canal before hitting the wall on the far side and sliding down it.

Then, mercifully, Jimmy passed out.

Homework Eats Dog

A woman in Norway has claimed that her child's art homework consumed the family pet. Elana Niddlestrom, 37, says that her son, Eric, drew a particularly unsettling picture of a troll that appeared to him in a dream. It was left alone with their pet terrier, known as Donkey, when the family went to the cinema, only for the dog to have disappeared without trace when they returned. An extensive search produced no sign of Donkey, but Elana noticed that the troll's facial expression had changed and it was now smiling in 'a disturbing way'. Mrs Niddlestrom would not give her permission for the picture to be reproduced in the press as she expressed her concern that it may 'add to its power'.

CHAPTER 7

Grace looked at the clock on the wall and sighed. Eight fifty-nine a.m.

The new girl had seemed quite pleasant, and it would've been nice to have another woman around the place. It would've been nice to have anyone else around the place, come to that. Oh well, she'd put the ad up again after the meeting.

She looked up to see Ox, whose expression was akin to that of a child waiting for Christmas.

He spoke in a low, excited whisper. 'She's not here.'

'I can see that, Ox.'

'I had her lasting less than a day in the office pool.'

'Technically, if she doesn't turn up, she never started, so . . .'

Ox's expression changed to one of outrage. 'What? No way, man. That is f—'

'Ox,' interrupted Grace, whose feelings on foul language were well known.

'That's not right,' finished Ox. 'I won the bet, fair and square.'

'It'd be the first time in a while.'

Grace disapproved of gambling, bar the occasional office pool and five pounds every year on the horse in the Grand National with the most God-fearing name. To be fair to Ox, you couldn't call what he did 'gambling' – he had a system, which, as far as Grace could tell, could guarantee a loss with unerring accuracy.

'Where's Simon?' asked Ox, looking to change the subject. 'He's not outside.'

'Isn't he? Poor child, maybe he finally had enough of standing around in the cold. That boy has a proper education, should be making something of himself. Maybe seeing someone else getting taken on made him realize it was time to give up the ghost.'

Reggie looked up at the mention of ghosts. 'What?'

'Nothing, dear.'

Reggie nodded and went back to staring at the floor. They were all more than aware of how much he dreaded these meetings. Grace had made sure to position herself between him and the most direct route to the roof, as she didn't want a repeat of yesterday. Banecroft may no longer have his gun, but the man had something far worse: an imagination. Reggie looked pale and kept closing his eyes and taking deep breaths, but so far, he hadn't given any indication that he was considering bolting.

Reggie and Ox sat opposite Grace, with Stella in the corner beside the laptop, playing on her phone while reading a book. Grace had given up trying to figure out how that worked. She returned to watching the clock on the wall as the second hand clicked around towards 9 a.m. The quartet sat in silence. It was the kind of silence you probably encountered right before a parachute jump into enemy territory. Grace made an effort to smile reassuringly in Reggie's direction, just in case he opened his eyes at any point.

Normally, the editorial meeting happened on a Monday

afternoon. But, normally, the editor had not shot himself in the foot immediately beforehand. As the paramedics had taken Banecroft away, the last thing he had hollered was that the editorial meeting would be at 9 a.m. the following day. So here they were – she, Ox, Reggie and Stella – sitting in the bullpen, waiting for the arrival of the bull. And the new girl hadn't turned up.

The 'bullpen' had been called that for longer than Grace could remember, and she'd been there a while now. It was a grand title for an office space that held enough desks for about a dozen people – not that they needed that many. It was only the four of them, plus Banecroft and whoever the next new Tina would be – on this floor, at least. There had been more employees when Grace had started, about a decade ago, but the numbers had been slowly going down. Banecroft's arrival six months previously had prompted a scramble for the lifeboats. Life under Barry, the previous editor of *The Stranger Times*, had been like snuggling up beside a fire with a warm cup of cocoa. With Banecroft it was like being in the fire.

The furniture was mismatched and wobbly. The wooden floorboards were so wonky there was now a dip in the centre of the room – which was a worry, given how high up they were. The floor they were on must have been put in when the Church of Old Souls was converted. Not for the first time, Grace looked beneath her feet and wondered what kind of building regulations were in existence at whatever deep and distant point in the past the conversion had happened. *The Stranger Times* had been here longer than anyone could remember.

The clock ticked over to 9 a.m. and the door linking the bullpen to Banecroft's office flew open. His office had one door that led into reception via the corridor but a second one opened directly into the bullpen. It meant that at any given time the staff could never be entirely sure where he was. A fact he used to his full advantage.

Reggie flinched as Vincent Banecroft emerged, but thankfully he remained seated. The editor limped in, crutch in his right hand, looking even less in love with life than usual, if such a thing were possible. He was wearing his grey pinstriped suit. As far as Grace was aware, he owned three suits, all of which looked as if they might stand up and walk out of the office of their own accord. He'd be down to two now, the trousers of the black one having been shredded by yesterday's incident. Sartorial elegance was one of the first casualties of war.

Grace found herself wondering how he'd got back here last night and, come to that, what he'd been wearing when he had done so. Somewhere, a taxi driver had a tale to tell.

Banecroft limped towards them. 'Where in the hell is the new Tina?'

Grace answered. 'She hasn't shown up.'

Banecroft threw himself into the office chair that Grace had left out for him. 'I knew it. First sniff of the real world and she's run home to hubby. She'll be back in his cheating arms as we speak. I have a sixth sense for these things.'

'Yes,' said Grace. 'You are quite the people person.'

Banecroft stopped, a cigarette halfway to his mouth. 'Are you mocking my finely honed intuition, Grace?'

'No.' She had found that the trick with Banecroft was not to push him too far, otherwise he'd take his bad mood out on one of the others.

'Right,' said Banecroft, lighting his cigarette. 'Due to yesterday's workplace accident, caused by that one' – he jabbed his lighter in Reggie's direction – 'we're already behind schedule.'

Reggie looked suitably outraged. 'How on earth was that debacle my fault?'

'Because,' said Banecroft, inhaling half a cigarette in one breath and expelling the smoke from his nostrils, 'I'd have never touched the damn gun if you'd not been on the roof having yet another melodramatic Monday meltdown.'

'Most people don't try to deal with such a situation by threatening to shoot the person involved.'

'Well,' said Banecroft, 'you were too far away to stab. Come to that, I distinctly told somebody after last week's episode to block off access to the roof.'

Stella raised a hand without looking up from her book. 'Yeah, that was me. Didn't do it.'

'And why not?'

'Cos we got one set of stairs out of here and I ain't dying in no fire, you get me?'

'What are the odds of that happening?'

'You started a fire yesterday.'

Ox nodded. 'She's got a point there.'

'Does she?' Banecroft glowered at Ox, who shifted in his chair.

'How am I in trouble?' he asked.

'It'll come to me in a minute.'

Grace heard a thump outside in the reception area. 'Oh, for the love of the Lord, I put a sign up saying not to come in.'

'Did you use diagrams?' asked Banecroft. 'I get the definite impression that most of the loons who buy this rag do so mostly for the pretty pictures.'

'Hello?'

Grace smiled. It was Hannah.

'So much for your finely honed intuition.' She raised her voice. 'In here, darling.'

Banecroft matched her volume. 'Get out. You're fired.'

Hannah limped through the door. 'What?'

Her outfit had no doubt started the day in fine fettle; however, the left sleeve of the jacket was now torn, the blouse was missing a couple of buttons, and there was some blood on it, presumably from the nosebleed she was trying to stem with a tissue.

'Sorry. I had a bit of an issue getting here.'

'Better luck getting home. You're fired.'

'No,' said Grace, 'you are not.'

Grace and Banecroft locked eyes. 'I can't have people rolling in whenever they like – it sets a dangerous precedent.'

'Look at the girl. She's bleeding, panting, clothes all messed up – I'm guessing she didn't just forget to set her alarm clock.'

'It's the principle of the thing.'

'You're a man of principle now, are you?'

They continued to stare at each other.

'Five,' said Banecroft. 'I want five swears.'

'No way. We need more staff and you know it. Where are we going to get a new Tina from at this rate?'

Banecroft shrugged. 'I could ring the old Tina, see if she'll come back.'

'She . . .' Grace turned to the others. 'What's the word for it?'

'Headbutted,' said Ox.

'Thank you,' said Grace, before turning back to Banecroft. 'She headbutted you.'

'Yes, but not that hard.'

'Four.'

'And I want my gun back.'

'I do not have your gun.'

'No,' said Banecroft. 'But you can ring up and get it back by asking nicely. People like you. You are likeable.' He managed to say this as if it were a serious character flaw on Grace's part.

Grace looked up at the ceiling, quite possibly making a silent prayer. 'OK. Fine. I shall try.'

'Excellent.'

'But no guarantees. As far as I understand it, the police are in the business of taking guns away from people, not giving them back.'

'I know. It's political correctness gone mad.' Banecroft looked up at Hannah. 'All right, Real Housewife of Wherever, you're not fired. You're on a final warning.'

Hannah nodded nervously. 'OK.'

'So what happened?'

'I'd rather not talk about it.'

'I'd rather not be here,' said Banecroft, 'but I am. Go.'

They all looked at Hannah, who puffed out her cheeks.

'If you must know, I'm living with a friend of mine and her husband, and—'

'You got into a fight with them?'

'No!'

Banecroft twirled his finger in the air. 'Then skip forward.'

'I got on the wrong bus.'

'And then you tried to hijack it?'

'No.'

'Then skip forward.'

Banecroft added rhythmic stomping of his good foot to the finger twirling.

'All right. But—'

'Forward, forward, forward.'

'All right! I was late, running through the park, and this woman was walking her six dogs. I mean, who has six dogs?'

'Forward, for—'

Hannah stamped her foot. 'This is the last bit!'

'And?'

'I . . . tried to run around her, got tangled up in one of the leads and sort of ended up in a fight with this bloody woman and her six dogs. She was . . . They were . . .'

'Bloody hell,' said Banecroft, 'we've hired Inspector Clouseau.'

Grace cleared her throat. 'Need I remind you, you shot yourself in the foot.'

'Yes, but that was yesterday. Let's all just move on, shall we? We have a piss-poor paper to produce.'

'That's one.'

'Damn it.'

Grace patted the chair beside her. Hannah limped over and sat down.

'Right,' said Banecroft, 'let's kick off this parade of inadequacy, then, shall we?'

Grace opened her notepad to take what could loosely be referred to as the minutes.

Banecroft pointed his crutch in Ox's direction. 'Let's start with the Chinese one and then we'll do the fat one.'

'Sorry,' said Hannah, 'but that is totally inappropriate.'

Banecroft flicked some cigarette ash on to the floor. 'Oh, the late one has something to say.'

'Yes,' said Hannah. 'Yes, I do. I know you've got your whole being-horrible-to-everyone thing going on here, but you cannot refer to somebody as "the Chinese one". It is racist.'

'No, it is not.' Banecroft turned to Ox. 'Are you Chinese?'

Ox looked at Hannah and then nodded. 'I am. I'm proper Chinese, me.'

'See? So thank you for your input, Ms Moral Outrage, but we have a very good system here.'

'You could just use people's names?'

'I could do, yes. But then I'd worry that the unwarranted rush of self-esteem it would result in might give the staff the incorrect impression that they're good at their jobs. As soon as someone actually does something competently, I'll let them know. It hasn't happened yet, but rest assured, I am on constant alert for even the slightest indication that it might. Now, if Malcolm X of suburbia is done trying to empower the oppressed workers, we've got a paper due out Friday, and so far it contains nothing but some of the most depressing lonely hearts ads you'll ever see, three letters of complaint, and a picture of a Japanese goat that looks like Kylie Minogue. In other words, editorial meeting is in session!'

CHAPTER 8

Two hours into the editorial meeting and Hannah had an aching wrist, a sore head and a desperate need to use the bathroom. There didn't seem to be a good moment to excuse herself, mainly because of the meeting's relentless pace. Most of the time, Banecroft sat slouched in his chair, his face covered with an open copy of *The Catcher in the Rye* and his bandaged foot up on the desk. His hands gesticulated as he issued occasional instructions amidst a torrent of reprimands, admonishments and swear-free insults.

Hannah was too busy trying to keep up to ask any questions, attempting to interpret Banecroft's barked commands with nothing but whatever clues Grace could slip in to assist her. While she tried furiously to scribble notes – which she assumed she was supposed to do, as Grace had handed her a notepad – Stella sat in the corner, tapping away on a computer.

There seemed to be a rough structure to the whole process, with the emphasis on 'rough'. Proceedings opened with Grace running through articles that had been submitted by what Hannah supposed could be called freelancers, although Banecroft preferred 'the idiots I don't have to see every day'.

Ox and Reggie, the ones she very definitely wasn't referring to as 'the Chinese one' and 'the fat one', apparently made up the paper's features department. This seemed a rather grandiose title, but Hannah was trying to keep an open mind. Of the two, Ox seemed to have a better feel for managing Banecroft, at least in the sense that he got shouted at marginally less frequently. His collection of UFO sightings, wild conspiracy theories and weird robots invented by Japanese people seemed to fit mostly what Banecroft was looking for.

In contrast, Reggie kept pitching stories that he assured everyone were 'of interest to the serious paranormalist'. Banecroft, one eye on Grace and her swear count, eventually resorted to making rude noises to express his displeasure. It would be unfair to say he was acting like a spoiled child – Hannah had never seen a child who could be so consistently and creatively rude. By the end of Reggie's pitching session, Banecroft was red in the face and surely running out of saliva, such was the raspberry count. While Hannah didn't know much about any of this stuff, it appeared Reggie was trying to move the paper in a more 'serious' direction. Best of luck with that.

Yesterday, Hannah had taken home a copy of the most recent edition of *The Stranger Times*. Its stated task was to report the weird and wonderful from around the world 'and beyond'. Hannah could hear the voice of her father roaring 'Nonsense!' as she read articles about sightings of mythical creatures, discussions of outlandish conspiracy theories, and stories of people doing all manner of disturbed and disturbing things, an alarming number of whom had been naked while doing them.

Hannah didn't consider herself a prude, but the euphemistically titled 'Coming Togethers' column, seemingly a regular piece, had been rather shocking. It contained a list of things women had 'married' and men had tried to have sex with. Her soon-to-be-ex-husband had been some kind of sex addict, but at least he'd never been caught attempting to have his end away with the statues of a terracotta army. Mind you, if Hannah had followed the path of a woman from Wyoming and married a combine harvester, think how differently her life could have turned out . . .

Hannah had closed the paper and given herself a long, hard talking-to. For the first time in her life, she had a job. And if that job consisted of publishing nonsense, then she was going to be the best damn publisher of nonsense she could be. There were undoubtedly worse jobs in the world, although Banecroft was quite possibly a top-five worst boss.

He had an unusual system of editorial decision-making, which revolved around marine life. Someone would mention a story and then he would either ask further questions or shout out the name of an aquatic lifeform along with a number, then they'd move on. After being confused initially, Hannah eventually caught on that it was a way of determining how big a story should be, along with a page number.

'Plankton' were tiny – a couple of lines; 'prawns' were a single paragraph; 'trout' a couple; 'salmon' three; 'dolphins' a page; and 'sharks' were a two-page spread. When he asked 'Fried?' it apparently meant 'Does the story have any pictures with it?', and 'bubbles' were quotes – both of which were good things. If he didn't like a story, it was 'thrown back' or else there was the 'ice-box', which Hannah guessed meant that it was to be kept for a later date. A 'whale' – well, a whale was something they hadn't found yet, which was why the atmosphere in the room was becoming increasingly tense. That and the fact that Banecroft had taken off the shoe on his good foot, although the stench that ensued meant that 'good' was a relative word.

'Right,' said Banecroft, whom Hannah had suspected of being asleep, so long had been the pause since he'd said anything from under his book. 'Let's go round again.'

This declaration was met with a widespread groan. Banecroft sat up and looked around.

'Oh, I'm sorry – are we not feeling it? You should have said. I do apologize. Let's all take a break, maybe get some fresh air and just, y'know, chillax.'

Even as Hannah stood up, a voice in her brain was screaming at her to sit back down. The others looked at her as if she were the herd member who had just started limping on a really dodgy area of the African plain.

'Yes,' continued Banecroft, 'let's all follow the new Tina's example and toddle off to have a nice long lunch – maybe some light shopping – as we have, after all, not a care in the world. I mean, who really cares that we'll be publishing a newspaper on Friday with a wide, gaping monumental *nothing* on the front page, because we have found absolutely nothing worthy of it?'

'Oh,' said Hannah. She sat back down, having just grasped what a 'whale' was in the Banecroft nomenclature.

'All right, Vincent,' said Grace. 'You have made your point.'

'Have I? Have I? It doesn't feel like I have, as we are currently sitting here with our collective thumbs up our . . .'

Grace shot him a warning look.

'Our you-know-wheres . . . and nobody – but nobody – has come up with what we need.'

'Could we not just . . .'

Hannah was shocked to realize the voice that was talking was hers.

Banecroft's eyes narrowed as he turned in her direction. 'What?'

'Make something up?'

When at home for Christmas a few years ago, Hannah had made the mistake of allowing Karl to drive in the snow. He'd said something about how most drivers were wimps and that modern tyres were designed to cope with all-weather conditions. He'd then taken a corner too fast and the car – along with its modern tyres, designed to cope with all-weather conditions – had gone into a long skid. A very long skid. It had been the weirdest of experiences. As the car had spun and spun, Hannah had had enough time to tut at Karl's idiocy and he'd had enough time to explain how this wasn't his fault, and only then had they hit the side of the tractor. The farmer had been very good about it, even when Karl had – against all available evidence and notions of decency – tried to claim it was somehow the farmer's fault.

The memory of that incident came back to Hannah now. She could see the inevitable collision careering towards her and there was nothing she could do to save herself. She hadn't said the wrong thing. She had said *the* wrong thing. Banecroft's eyes were small pinpricks of red, like a forest fire in the distance that was coming to burn down all the little piggies' houses.

'Make something up?'

His voice chilled her to the bone. Hannah had never heard him speak softly before.

Grace opened her mouth to say something, but a look from Banecroft silenced her.

'Make something up?' he repeated.

'I mean,' offered Hannah, 'it's just that . . . seeing as . . .'

'As what? As everything we report is nonsense, we could just save ourselves the effort and make it up?'

He stood and stared at her for an uncomfortably long time. When it became apparent that things weren't going to proceed until she had given some kind of answer, she nodded.

He pointed towards the window. 'What does the sign above the door outside say?'

His tone of voice was almost casual, in the way that a log could look casual, drifting down a river, if you ignored the large reptilian eyes blinking at you as it approached.

'It says *The Stranger Times*,' said Hannah.

'It does,' confirmed Banecroft. 'And what does it say under that?'

'Ehm . . . It says this is no longer a church, please go bother God somewhere else.'

'That's right, it— Wait, what? It doesn't say that. It says "newspaper".'

'Actually,' said Grace, 'it doesn't say "newspaper". You changed it after that nice God-fearing man came round and knocked on the door and . . .' She noticed the look on Banecroft's face. 'Well, I was just saying.'

Banecroft turned back to Hannah. 'What it should say is "newspaper". We are a newspaper. We do not make up the news, because if we did then it would no longer be news. It would be lies.'

'But . . .'

'But nothing.' Banecroft almost stumbled as he leaned over to one of the desks and picked up a newspaper. It was the same edition that Hannah had taken home yesterday. He read out the headline: ' "Wolverhampton Invaded by UFOs". This is made-up nonsense, is it?'

Hannah said nothing, having realized belatedly that it was not her role to participate in this conversation.

'It's complete hokum, isn't it? Balderdash. Claptrap. Drivel. Twaddle. Tripe. Hogwash. Who could possibly believe it? Well, I'll tell you . . .'

Banecroft jabbed his finger at the first paragraph. 'Mrs Stade, forty-two, from Blakenhall. That's who. You see, *we're* not saying it's true. What we're saying is look, this mad woman believes this and here's why she does. Here's some other people who think something similar on pages five, six and seven, and we have an artist's rendering of the series of crafts she claims to have seen. We have an interview with her husband, who claims to have been taken up by said crafts, had his genitalia examined thoroughly and then been dumped outside a bookies with, I kid you not, a hot tip for that day's racing at Kempton.'

Banecroft tossed the newspaper back on the desk.

'We are a newspaper that reports the weird and wonderful from around the world. What would you call it when a couple from Wolverhampton believes that alien beings – as in highly sophisticated creatures capable of intergalactic space travel – are inexplicably interested in not just Wolverhampton, but the meat and two veg of a bloke called Clive from Wolverhampton? Do you know what I'd call it? I'd call it weird. The belief is weird and it is news. We aren't reporting the story as fact; we're reporting the existence of the story as fact. That might not mean much to you, but that is a little thing I call journalism.'

Hannah didn't know where to look. She nodded. She blinked, hoping the tears she could feel rising would not come.

'If you don't have any respect for that, then maybe this is not the job for you.'

'All right,' said Grace, in a vain effort to halt the landslide.

'Maybe you should run off back to hubby and make up your own happy ending. Where his wandering wang is actually not doing so.'

'Vincent!'

'Where you've not wasted your life on—'

'Falkirk!'

Everyone turned to look at Reggie, who was now standing up, having loudly proclaimed the name of a large town in central Scotland.

Banecroft continued to glare at Hannah, but he spoke to Reggie. 'What about it?'

'It has a toilet.'

'I'd imagine it has several.'

'Yes,' said Reggie with a sigh, 'but only one that the locals claim is possessed by the devil.'

Banecroft's eyebrows rose slightly. 'Go on?'

'It's in a pub. People claim that it speaks – issuing death threats, ominous predictions and . . .'

'And?'

'Shortbread recipes.'

Banecroft stopped and looked at the ceiling. He remained motionless for long enough that Hannah looked at Grace, who gave her an attempt at a reassuring smile.

'I . . . smell a whale.'

The rest of the room looked relieved, but Reggie's shoulders sagged. 'Yes, I rather feared you might.'

Banecroft turned. 'You're going up there – right now.'

'What? But, no . . . I have plans for the evening.'

Banecroft nodded as if agreeing. 'Yes. Yes, you probably did. Now you have them in Scotland.'

'But I can't drive.'

'I thought you were the one who could drive?'

'No,' said Reggie, pointing at Ox. 'That's him.'

Ox looked as if he'd just received the package in a game of pass the parcel and it was ticking.

'What? No, I . . . I can't . . . He's the expert in, y'know, this stuff.'

'That's why you're both going. And you can drop by and do a story on that spate of UFO sightings outside of Glasgow. That woman is still writing to us, isn't she?'

He looked at Grace, who nodded. 'Every week.'

'Excellent.'

'But I have articles to write up,' pleaded Reggie.

'You can do that while he's driving,' said Banecroft.

'But I get carsick.'

Banecroft clapped his hands together. 'Tremendous. Let's consider that a happy bonus.'

'Hang on,' interjected Ox. 'When am I supposed to get *my* articles written up?'

'You can do it while he's throwing up! This has all worked out perfectly.' Banecroft picked up his crutch and hobbled towards his office door. 'Good meeting. Now, whose leg do I have to hump around here to get a cup of tea?'

CHAPTER 9

DI Sam Clarke and DS Andrea Wilkerson leaned against the low wall and watched the SOCOs work as a train rumbled by overhead.

'Are you sure he'll want it?' asked Wilkerson.

'Yes,' responded Clarke. 'The yappy little sod can't resist trying to show how much cleverer he is than everyone else.'

'Right.'

A silence descended between the two of them, save for the sound of Wilkerson slurping at her tea and Clarke passing wind unapologetically. They were standing about thirty feet away from the area between the canal and the red-brick side of the building as the SOCOs needed space, and this particular crime scene was only about six feet wide. On the far side of the canal, a crowd of onlookers gawped. People never got tired of watching the police work, especially when there was a dead body in the offing.

There wasn't enough room to erect screens, so they'd covered the body and Clarke had dispatched a PC to tell people there was nothing to see, when there clearly was. They'd already had to ask an office worker from the building to stick his head back inside the window. Couldn't have some moron's DNA appearing on the body because he'd dribbled on to it from a height in his excitement to see a real-life tragedy.

The corpse, one John 'Long John' Maguire, was a homeless guy known to the Greater Manchester Police. He had a history of alcohol abuse and a long list of convictions for petty, non-violent crimes. It was a cruel irony: people who had quickened their pace to speed by and ignore him in life were now fascinated by him in death. DI Clarke was not one of those people.

'Still, guv,' said Wilkerson, 'shouldn't I talk to the SOCOs and maybe get the canvass started?'

Clarke waved his hand about. 'Look around you, Wilkerson. We're in the middle of Castlefield. Where are you going to start? The apartments? Anyone who can afford to live here is at work right now, and besides, they didn't see anything that happened at four in the morning because they were tucked up in beddy-byes. The vic was homeless – do you want to start canvassing that lot? Getting incoherent dribblings from a bunch of drunks and junkies who see spiders crawling across their skin half the time? Or would you like to go through the nearby CCTV and try to chase down the hundred pissed idiots it'll give you who were seen "acting strangely" in the area? Pissheads act strangely – it's what they do. I'm telling you, this is an unsolved waiting to happen and we don't want it on our board.'

'And Sturgess will?'

Clarke nodded. 'Sturgess will.'

'But—'

DI Clarke cut her off. 'Because he's a smart-arsed little scrote who thinks he's better than the rest of us.'

DS Wilkerson jumped as DI Tom Sturgess appeared behind them. 'Can't imagine where I got that idea from.'

Sturgess was standing on the other side of the low wall, a bottle of Diet Coke in his hand. The bloke didn't drink tea or coffee, which was weird for a copper. He also didn't drink alcohol, which was damn near unprecedented. Slight of build, with long black hair and a full, trimmed beard, Sturgess had piercing blue eyes that'd set more than a few female hearts aflutter down at the station. There were rumours he was gay, but as far as Wilkerson could tell, those rumours came from a couple of people who always assumed as much when a man showed zero interest in them. Wilkerson hated beards personally and didn't like men who took everything, including themselves, as seriously as Sturgess did. Still, if she were the corpse, she knew who she'd want working the case.

'Sturgess, didn't see you there,' said Clarke.

'Well, observation has never really been your thing.'

'Do you work at being this unpopular or does it just come naturally?'

'There's an extra course we can take. I'm surprised a go-getter like you didn't know that.' He nodded towards where the SOCOs were working. 'So, what are you trying to dump on me this time?'

'One of these days,' said Clarke, throwing the remnants of his cup of tea into the canal, 'that mouth of yours is going to earn you a slap.'

Sturgess raised an eyebrow. 'Is that right? And who will you be getting to do that?'

As Clarke turned and squared up to Sturgess, for one brief

moment Wilkerson wondered if something was going to happen. Instead, Clarke grinned a humourless grin and nodded towards the corpse. 'John "Long John" Maguire, late of this parish. Reported by a jogger who noticed him from the far side of the canal, and then found by PC Marcus Raven this morning at seven thirty-five. Took SOCO a while to get here because of that thing up in Moss Side – a dead homeless guy being, well, y'know.'

'And?' said Sturgess.

'And,' continued Clarke, 'on examination by the paramedics, injuries were found to the chest and the back of the head, which had been smashed in. Nasty way to go. Initially they thought he'd somehow got on to the roof and fallen, but, well . . . Take a look.'

Sturgess turned to where Clarke was pointing – the wall of the building above the body. Fifteen feet up was an indent in the brick-work. It looked as if something had hit it hard – really hard. Sturgess scanned the surrounding area. Wilkerson could see him making the calculations – the train tracks were too far away, as were the nearby buildings. There was nothing that could explain how a body could possibly have made contact with that section of the wall.

'The building manager assures us there was no damage there prior to this. They had someone in last week about something else – swears he would've noticed. Anyway—'

Sturgess spoke, his eyes fixed on the indent in the wall. 'I'll take it.'

'Maybe I don't want to give it to you.'

'Yes, you do. I'm here because you're trying to dump it, just like that thing last year up at the Mill, because you like easy tap-ins. I said I'll take it, now get your lazy arse out of my crime scene.'

With that, Sturgess strode off towards the SOCOs.

'Obnoxious little . . . Who is he calling lazy?'

DS Wilkerson said nothing.

Sturgess stopped and turned around. 'Oh, and DS Hadoke is off with an impacted wisdom tooth, so I need a DS if I'm to take this.' He looked pointedly at Wilkerson.

'No,' said Clarke. 'She's working with me.'

'I don't mind,' said Wilkerson, which earned her a glare from Clarke. 'I mean, if Hadoke isn't available . . .'

'Fine,' said Clarke, looking at her as if she were something he'd just scraped off his shoe, before turning and striding in the direction of his car.

Wilkerson turned to look at Sturgess, but he had already spun back around and was staring at the inexplicably damaged brickwork fifteen feet above the body of Long John Maguire.

CHAPTER 10

Paulo nodded.

'I mean,' continued Leeohnel, 'this salt lamp just has a wonderful energy to it and I think the negative ions it releases are just vital. People don't understand the word "negative" in this context is actually a positive thing. A lot of technology produces "positive ions"' – he formed the bunny rabbit ears in the air with his fingers – 'which are actually really negative. They can lead to insomnia, mental illness, cancer . . .'

Paulo nodded again. He really hated hippies, which was ironic, as his shop's primary purpose was to cater to them. Supposedly. People hold a lot of false assumptions about hippies. For a start, they're not the relaxed individuals people imagine them to be. If you were to leave two of them in a room for long enough, you could guarantee a heated and bitter argument. They all have remarkably entrenched ideas about how the world, the human body, and damn near everything else works. The only thing a lot of them have in common is a fevered certainty that the world would be a better place if everyone just listened to them. Only two weeks ago, he'd had to separate two middle-aged women who had come to blows over the Dalai Lama.

While the exchange Paulo was currently involved in was nominally about the £140 Himalayan salt lamp, it was really about something else. Leeohnel, with his long hair, ridiculously sculpted beard and an earring that looked like a fishing lure, was paying a tenner for a lump of pink salt rock with a dodgy bulb in it. The other £130 was the unspoken price for having to listen to him bang on.

Leeohnel was a regular customer. Paulo knew from taking credit-card payments that the guy was really called Lionel and had contrived the whole Leeohnel persona. Paulo had seen him a couple of times up on Deansgate in a suit, heading into his job at an insurance company.

He'd been running Paulo's Emporium for nearly ten years now, and he wasn't sure how much more of this crap he could take. Day after day of people droning on at him. He kept having a recurring dream where he beat a customer to death with an aboriginal spirit carving. He had dozens of the things; a bloke in Bolton cranked them out dirt cheap. He'd opened the store as a cover for his other activities, but it actually turned a very healthy profit.

Paulo was surrounded by dreamcatchers, wind chimes, all manner of crystals, indigenous carvings, and so on and so on. Every time he brought in a new line, a small part of him hoped that this would finally be the useless bit of crap that would make his dedicated – if demented – customer base finally realize it was all nonsense, but they just ate up every fad. Trying to fill whatever hole life had left them with.

Leeohnel pushed his curtain of hair back behind his ear and Paulo noticed the spider crawling in it. Experience had taught him not to mention such things. Leeohnel was probably letting it live there in the hope that somebody would ask him about it. Paulo wasn't paying any attention to the man's monologue – he didn't need to in order to nod in the right places. It was a conversation in name only. He'd give him another two minutes and then hit the button under the counter that made a fake phone ring in the back office. It was comfortably Paulo's best ever purchase, and was unique amongst the things in the outer shop in that it actually worked.

Paulo's eye was drawn to the shop's door as the bell above it rang. A bald, portly man had just entered. He was looking around with a smirk on his face.

Paulo forced himself to tune back in to Leeohnel's rambling stream of consciousness for a moment.

'. . . balance really is the key. So much of modern life is out of balance with the natural world.'

'Absolutely,' interrupted Paulo. 'Well, I hope you enjoy the lamp, Leeohnel. It does have a wonderful energy to it. Now, if you'll excuse me, I love our chats but I need to assist this customer.'

Leeohnel glanced over his shoulder at the other man and, with an undisguised look of disappointment on his face, said, 'Right, of course.' He picked up his linen bag containing the lamp, brought his hands together and bowed. 'Namaste.'

'Namaste,' said Paulo, mirroring his actions.

Leeohnel moved off towards the wind chimes and incense, and Paulo smiled at the new customer.

'Good afternoon, sir, and how can I help you today?'

The man stepped up to the counter and returned Paulo's smile. 'Well now, that depends . . .'

He spoke with an American accent, which was unexpected, but not as unexpected as what he did next. He placed his left hand on the counter and, with his index finger and thumb tucked into his palm, tapped the tips of his other three fingers on the counter three times. Paulo raised his eyebrows in surprise before giving the man a subtle nod.

'I'm sure we can help you, sir.' Paulo looked meaningfully to where Leeohnel was still perusing the incense. 'Take a look around and we can talk later.'

'I'm in kind of a hurry.'

Paulo looked in Leeohnel's direction more pointedly. 'I appreciate that.'

Paulo didn't care what kind of a hurry this guy was in, protocols were there to be followed for a damn good reason.

The man sighed. 'Fine.' He walked directly over to Leeohnel and engaged him in conversation.

Paulo couldn't hear what was said but Leeohnel went an even paler shade of white, turned on his heel and fled from the shop. Paulo watched him scurry up the lane, his shopping bag clutched to his chest. He dropped the deliberately spaced-out tone he typically adopted in the shop and threw up his hands. 'Ah, for fuck's sake, don't run off the civilians.'

The American shrugged. 'I didn't do anything except tell the man some home truths.'

'No, no,' said Paulo. 'I don't know how they do it where you come from, but this is not how this shop does business. Get out.'

The man took something out of his pocket and tossed it on the counter. Paulo managed to resist the urge to gasp as the gold coin rolled around on the table top. When he spoke again, his tone was guarded but a lot more friendly. 'I, ehm . . . Is that real?'

'It's real,' said the man. 'Test it if you don't believe me.'

Carefully, Paulo picked it up. He had held something like this only once before in his forty-eight years, but it had the feel of real Grandon Gold. It was cold to the touch and had the tell-tale subtle vibration to it. The value of the coin lay not in the gold, but in the energy the gold contained.

'I, ehm . . . I might have a bit of difficulty breaking this.'

'I'm looking to spend it all.'

Paulo nodded and licked his lips. 'Right, well, we've got a lot of potion ingredients, thaumaturgical objects. Either we'll have what you need or I can get it in if you give me a little time.'

The man laughed. 'Yeah, I'm trading that for some herbs and knick-knacks. Maybe throw in a wind chime while you're at it.'

'OK,' conceded Paulo. 'Well, what do you want?'

The man placed his hands on the counter. 'I need a Knife of Carathan.'

Paulo felt his stomach lurch. 'We wouldn't have anything like that.'

The man smiled. 'Sure you do.'

Paulo shook his head vigorously. 'Absolutely not. Under the Accord, blood magic is illegal and punishable by—'

'Believe me,' said the man, the smile falling from his lips, 'I know how it is punished. I also know you've got the knife, so let's make a deal.'

'Vinny,' called Paulo.

From the back office, the sound of furniture straining under an immense weight reached them, and Vinny lumbered through the beaded curtain. Paulo kept him out of the way because he had a tendency to scare the civilian customers. He also kept him close at hand for when it came to dealing with the more awkward elements of the Folk. Most just wanted ingredients and powered objects, but to run a shop such as Paulo's really was, you had to have protection.

'Problem?' said Vinny in a sonorous growl.

He stood at six foot ten and was the size of a small van. His hands were like baseball mitts on a normal human. The food bill alone to employ him was enormous, not to mention the cost of the breakages he was responsible for before Paulo had banned him from going beyond the counter. He worked a nightclub door some nights too – looking human enough that the normals wouldn't question it.

'Got yourself a troll,' said the Yank in a disconcertingly cheerful tone. 'Very sensible to have some protection in your line of business.'

Paulo nodded. 'He's just one of the many layers of protection this shop enjoys, so don't get any stupid ideas.'

'Hey,' said the man, holding up his hands. 'I come in peace, buddy. Just trying to do a little business.'

'I recognize him,' said Vinny, his lightning-sharp mind not being the reason for which he was employed.

'What?' said Paulo.

'He was at my boxing gym. Last night.'

Paulo had a sinking feeling in his stomach. 'Oh Gods, you didn't . . .'

The American put his hand in the pocket of his overcoat and pulled out something. Paulo caught the briefest flash of a small brown figurine before Vinny's massive hand clamped around his boss's throat. He looked sideways to see Vinny's mouth drop open, his face a picture of confusion.

Paulo's voice came out as a croak. 'Vinny, you moron!'

'What's happening?' asked Vinny, a note of terror in his voice.

'Well, Vinny,' said the Yank, holding out his hand, palm up, where the small figurine, all of three inches tall, now stood. 'I'd imagine your boss would tell you – if he were more free to speak – that if you engage in pugilism and end up bleeding, it really is very important to dispose of the blood properly. You see, if a powerful practitioner' – he pointed to his own grinning face – 'were to get hold of it . . . Well, let me put it this way: punch yourself in the face.'

Vinny punched himself in the face with his free hand. His mouth remained open as his head swivelled from his boss to the Yank and back again. 'Sorry, Paulo.'

'Moron.'

'Now, now,' said the Yank. 'Let's not be harsh. We can all get what we want out of this situation. You know what I want.' He pointed to the gold coin on the counter. 'And I'm willing to pay top dollar for it.'

'If I—' started Paulo, but he stopped. He looked at the Yank, who rolled his eyes and nodded. He could feel Vinny's grip on his throat loosen slightly. He drew in a breath before continuing.

'Selling a Knife of Carathan – if the Council finds out, that's an automatic death sentence.'

The Yank looked from Paulo to Vinny and back again. 'Let's not underestimate the chances of Death in the next thirty seconds. I just have to think it and this moron will pop your head clean off.'

'Fuck you,' said Vinny. The Yank blinked and Vinny punched himself in the face again.

'This place has cameras,' said Paulo.

'Good point,' replied the Yank. He put his hand back into the pocket of his overcoat and withdrew a second item. Paulo saw only a flash of blue light as whatever it was zipped around the room. Then came a sizzling noise and the smell of burning circuitry.

'Ahhh, those were nearly new.'

'I hope you filled out the guarantee.'

Paulo gulped. His mouth was getting dry. 'What are you going to use it for?'

'That's none of your concern.'

'It is if—'

Paulo winced as the Yank slammed his fist on the counter, the mask of joviality having fallen from his face. 'I'm done pretending this is a negotiation. My preference is to do this the easy way, but if I have to leave bodies and waste hours breaking through whatever security you have, I will. Now, there's one for the knife and' – he tossed another gold coin on the counter, where it rolled to a stop beside the first – 'another for you to forget I was ever here. Now, are we done pussy-footing around?'

The small part of Paulo's mind that was not filled with terror at the prospect of his imminent death looked down at the two coins and whooped for joy. It was more than he had ever seen.

'OK,' said Paulo, 'but I'm going to need some assurances.'

The Yank clicked his fingers and the shop's entire stock of baubles, crystals and other pseudo-mystical nonsense simultaneously rose a foot off the shelves it had been sitting on. Every last item was now floating in the air.

'The only assurance you're getting is that this is happening. You can choose the hard way or the easy way.'

'All right,' said Paulo. 'OK, don't . . . There's no need to.' He looked down the length of Vinny's massive arm where his soon-to-be-former bodyguard watched on in confused silence. 'And you'll leave the doll.'

The Yank snorted. 'Like I have a use for this idiot after today.'

Paulo took a final moment to consider his options, not that there was any real choice to be made. 'OK, fine.'

He performed a series of gestures with his hand, under the counter and out of sight. There followed a soft ripping noise.

'Ah,' said the customer. 'A Negari pocket. That takes me back.'

Paulo looked at the seam that had appeared in the air to his left and dipped in his hand. He had only ever rented the knife out to customers he knew really well, and for specifically agreed uses. There were many things it could be used for that nobody minded. The Council turned a blind eye on certain matters. The problem was that there were a few things it could be used for which a lot of people minded an awful lot. That was why objects such as the knife were banned. Paulo agreed with the ban, even if he didn't actually respect it.

He reached into the pocket, arm in up to the elbow, felt around for a few moments, and then pulled out a foot-long mahogany box. He placed it on the counter and carefully snatched up the two coins.

The Yank opened the case and his face lit up. 'Oh yes, this will do nicely.' He snapped it shut and beamed a smile at Paulo. 'A pleasure doing business with you.'

'Yeah,' said Paulo, resisting the urge to say anything that might antagonize his customer.

'Don't forget our deal.'

The Yank smiled as he tucked the box inside his overcoat and began to move towards the door. 'I was going to say the same thing. I was never here.' He tossed the small brown doll on to the counter, just out of Paulo's reach.

With a final wave, the American backed out of the shop's door, the bell above it tinkling as he did so.

For what seemed like a very long moment, Paulo and Vinny stood there, Vinny's hand still wrapped around his boss's throat. Then, the silence was broken by a cracking, smashing, shattering cacophony as the shop's stock came in to land.

Vinny's hand dropped from Paulo's throat. He leaned over to look at the mass of debris on the floor.

'Oh, shit.'

Paulo snapped up the small brown figurine from the counter and closed his eyes.

'What are you—'

The troll was interrupted by his own fist slamming into his face really hard.

CHAPTER 11

Grace looked down at the shelf and pursed her lips. 'I do not know, I just do not know.'

Hannah stood behind her with the shopping trolley, trying to be patient.

Grace sucked her teeth. 'It is tricky, very tricky.'

'Could you maybe just get a selection?'

Grace looked back at her. 'If only it was that simple.'

'They're just biscuits.'

'Biscuits are never just biscuits. They send a message. Offering someone a rich tea is a slap in the face; a chocolate Hobnob is downright solicitous. You have got to strike the right balance.'

'OK, so what message are we trying to send? I mean, who are these people? What is Loom Day?'

'Loom Day? Loom Day is not a thing. Today is Loon Day – when the paper opens its doors to allow the public to bring us their stories of the weird and whatnot. Tradition. First Tuesday afternoon every month, come rain, come shine, is Loon Day.'

'Oh. Right.'

'I don't like the name, personally, but that's what everybody else calls it so I have no choice. It's not exactly inappropriate – we get some . . . unusual people, no doubt.'

'And we give them tea and biscuits?'

'Yes. It is tradition. The first month Vincent was here, he tried to stop it. There was nearly a riot. One gentleman tried to set himself on fire.'

'Oh my!'

Grace waved her hand dismissively. 'He did not have petrol or anything; he just tried to set his anorak alight with a box of matches. He didn't even manage to set off the smoke alarm. Still though, we have to get biscuits.'

'OK. Well, I vote for chocolate Bourbons, then.'

'Are you insane!'

'What? They're nice.'

'Exactly. Too nice. We cannot have people enjoying the biscuits too much – then the timewasters will keep coming back every month. We will be overrun!'

'Digestives, then?'

'We are not trying to insult people either. Damn it, there will be complaints, but I am going to get ginger nuts again. It is a good, God-fearing biscuit, but nobody is crossing a road to get one.'

Twenty minutes and a discussion about instant coffee – into which two members of supermarket staff had to be brought as arbiters – later, Grace and Hannah were walking back from the shops, weighed down with inoffensive snacks, toilet rolls and antiseptic wipes. The Tuesday-morning traffic rolled by on Chester Road

and clouds hung overhead, not threatening rain but at least insinu-
ating the ever-present possibility.

'So,' said Hannah, searching for a conversational gambit, 'how
long have you worked at the paper?'

'Oh, me? About ten years now.'

'And is it always like this?'

'Like what?'

'With Banecroft being such a . . .' Hannah paused, keenly aware
of Grace's stance on bad language. 'I'm struggling to come up with
the right word.'

'Yes. He is quite something. The man needs his mouth washed
out with soap and water.'

'And the rest of him too.'

Grace nodded. 'It is not right, a grown man living in his office
like that.'

'Wait – he lives there?'

'Oh, yes. He has done since he took the job about six months
ago.'

'I take it he hasn't got a wife or, well, anything. I can't say I'm
surprised.'

'He used to.'

'Really? And I thought *I* needed a divorce.'

'She died, heaven rest her.'

'Oh.' Hannah winced. 'Sorry. When . . .'

Grace waved away her discomfort. 'Before he worked here – a
few years ago now. I take it you didn't google him?'

Hannah shook her head. The idea had never even occurred
to her.

'You should. It would be most educational. The man was a big deal on Fleet Street – editor of tabloid newspapers. Real high-flyer. Look . . .'

Grace shifted her shopping bags into one hand, fished out her phone and started to thumb something in nimbly. Having found what she wanted after a couple of clicks, she held out the phone to Hannah.

Hannah looked at the photo. 'Wow.'

Before her was a picture of a couple, one half of which was Banecroft. It took a few moments for that to sink in, as the difference from the foul-smelling, foul-mouthed and foul-tempered individual she knew was vast. He beamed a smile out of the screen, and was immaculate in a sharply tailored suit. The reason for his demeanour and appearance was, quite possibly, the other person in the picture: a stunning blonde woman in dazzling eveningwear. They were every inch the power couple.

'Wow,' Hannah said again, handing back the phone.

'Yes. Such a sad thing. She died and he – well, you have met him. Apparently he lost his mind after she passed, gave up on any and every thing, obsessed with trying to contact her. Getting taken in by every quack and charlatan in the book. There used to be an article about it online, but it got taken down. Maybe some of his old friends from back in the day did not like it. Who knows?'

'And he went from Fleet Street to here?'

Grace nodded as they turned the corner. 'Yes, via the gutter. We needed an editor after poor Barry died. He was the previous editor – a nice man. He died when . . .' Grace looked away.

'What?'

'Well, he was engaged in . . . unchristian behaviour.'

'Such as . . . ?'

'Let us just say he was doing something inappropriate with himself of a sexual nature and it did not go well. May he rest in peace, the poor little pervert.' Grace blessed herself.

'Ah . . .'

'Even before that, we were in trouble. Barry was nice, but he was not exactly the world's greatest newspaperman. The paper was tremendously dull – not to speak ill of the dead.' Grace blessed herself again as her bracelets jangled out a brief rhythm break. 'Say what you want about Banecroft, and I could say plenty, but it has not been dull since Mrs Harnforth dumped him on our doorstep.'

'Who is she?'

'She is the lady who owns the paper. A very fine woman. She is a bit of an oddball, but very "proper English". Refined. She drops in occasionally. You will see what I mean. I do not know where she found Vincent, but she plonked him down in that office, drunk as a skunk and smelling as bad. She said he was in charge, and then she was gone.'

'That doesn't seem like any way to run a paper – putting a drunken lunatic in charge.'

'It has worked, though. He has increased our circulation three hundred per cent.'

'Really?'

'Yes. The man has a nose for what people want and he is very good at giving it to them. Ox and Reginald moan about him, but we all thought we were going to lose our jobs under Barry,

God rest his soul. The last edition he produced had the headline "Inside: Eight-page Pull-out on Ancient Rituals of the Druids". Banecroft's first was "Three-headed Chicken Predicts End of Days". It might not be very God-fearing, but it does get people's attention.'

'And do you . . .' Hannah was unsure how to ask what she wanted to ask.

'What?'

'Do you believe in all this stuff?'

'Oh, no. I abide in the Lord. It is not about that, though. You heard Banecroft: we are not saying any of it is true, we are cataloguing all the crazy nonsense happening in the world. There is nothing wrong with it. Have you seen a normal newspaper recently? It is nothing but war and hate and people being awful to people. A rain of frogs in Cambodia, a man who thinks a ghost stole his car, and all kinds of people thinking aliens are sending them signals? I'd much rather that kind of crazy than the other kind, thank you very much.'

'I suppose.'

'It does not matter if you believe it or not. Reginald believes in ghosts but thinks UFOs are nonsense; Ox believes the exact opposite. Vincent does not believe in anything. At least not now.'

'But you said he—'

'Oh, he wanted to believe, back when he was going to all those mediums and whatnot, but we ran an article on them a few weeks ago. I did not say anything, but let us just say he has clearly decided there is nothing to it. I had never met a man who believes in nothing until I met him. May God bless his soul.'

'Maybe he doesn't have one!' Hannah meant it as a joke, but the look on Grace's face was one of outrage.

'Everybody has a soul.' She almost whispered it.

'Right.'

As they turned on to Willoughby Street, Hannah was painfully aware she had killed the conversation stone-dead. The silence hung between them for an uncomfortably long time, until Grace decided to break it. 'Can I ask a question?'

'Sure,' said Hannah, trying to sound bright and cheerful, although she had a strong idea of where this was heading.

'What are you doing here?'

'You asked me to come help with the—'

'No, no,' said Grace, 'but thank you very much for that. I mean, you are a rich lady, what are you doing coming to work with us?'

And there it was. 'I'm not rich.'

'But . . . ?'

'I was rich. Or at least I was married to a rich guy, but we're getting divorced.'

'Right, but you can get a lawyer and . . .'

Hannah took a deep breath. 'I decided I didn't want any of his money. I want an entirely fresh start – on my own. I want nothing from him.'

Grace's eyes widened in disbelief. 'Why would you do that?'

Hannah was taken aback. 'What do you mean? I'm standing on my own two feet.'

'But you could have done that while also kicking him right in the . . . you-know-wheres. In financial terms, I mean.'

Hannah shook her head. 'I'd rather do it in real terms. Besides, I don't care about the money.'

Grace tutted. 'Forgive me, but the only people who say they don't care about money are those who have always had it.'

'Well, that was the decision I made.'

'It was a terrible decision.' Grace held her hand up in apology. 'Sorry. The good Lord has blessed me with a very truthful nature.'

'Yes, he certainly has.'

Grace stopped walking and placed her hand on Hannah's arm. 'I am sorry. I did not mean to be disrespectful to you.'

Hannah shrugged. 'Don't worry about it. It's not like you're the only one. My own mother thinks I've lost my mind. She keeps ringing to ask if he's taken me back yet.'

'Oh dear.'

They started walking again. 'Maybe I've made a terrible decision. I mean, I'm living in my old housekeeper Maggie's spare room on a fold-out bed next to a half-built matchstick model of Tower Bridge, which her husband, Gordon, is no doubt livid about being unable to work on while I'm in the way.'

'I see.'

'I've gone from getting my food delivered by Selfridges to hunting around Lidl for bargains. A woman tried to fight me for the last box of frozen crispy pancakes last night. I didn't even want them – I was just looking at them in disbelief. I didn't know crispy pancakes were a thing!'

'I see.'

Hannah took a deep breath. 'I'm sorry. I'm rambling, aren't I?'

'It is fine. Ramble away.'

Hannah gave Grace a brittle smile. 'I'll tell you something else, though – I might've made a terrible decision, but at least I made a decision. You'd be amazed how long it's been since I made one of those for myself. At least one that wasn't "Where shall we have lunch?"'

'Well, now I feel bad,' said Grace, causing Hannah to turn and look at her. 'I should have let you pick whatever biscuits you liked.'

Hannah laughed harder than the joke warranted, but she was holding in a lot of pent-up tension that needed releasing somehow. 'Anyway, enough about my train wreck of a life. Let's talk about something else, like what's the deal with Stella?'

Grace shook her head. 'That girl will be the death of me, Lord as my witness.'

'Did Banecroft really catch her breaking in?'

'Yes, he did. I came in one morning a couple of months ago and he had taken the child prisoner with that evil crazy gun of his. He said either we handed her over to the police or she started working for us.'

'And her family are OK with that?'

'She is a runaway. She will not answer any questions about it. I tried to find out, but she said she'd run away again if I kept asking.'

'Oh, I see.'

'She can be difficult, but she is a good girl deep down. Very bright too. She needs to clean her room, though.'

'Wait, she stays with you?'

'Yes. She wanted to stay in the office but I put my foot down.

No way, no how. A young girl living there with two grown men, it is not decent. I am not having that.'

'Right. Hang on, two . . . ?'

As they turned the corner on to Mealy Street and the church came into view, all thoughts dropped out of Hannah's head. The building itself, even with the grimy windows and air of disrepair, still looked impressive. Its red-brick façade, faded as it was, gave it a certain presence amidst the humdrum houses and vacant lot that surrounded it – like an ageing Hollywood icon that nevertheless could still command a room.

The church was not what had drawn Hannah's eye, though – there was a queue of people outside it, stretching right around the block. Some had animals with them. Several were in fancy dress, although they might not have considered it so. One man was riding a donkey. The donkey was wearing a tutu.

'Oh my . . .'

'Yes,' said Grace, with a nod. 'Loon Day.'

CHAPTER 12

Simon passed the pad and pen back and forth between his hands, wiping the sweat from his palms on to his jeans. He'd never done this before. He was finally working on a proper story – it was so exciting.

Earlier, a reporter from the *Evening News* had arrived, taken a few details from one of the PCs and then slouched off to the pub. Not Simon. He'd got the tip-off from his 'network'. Well, from Keith who he'd been in chess club with. Keith's sister was in the police and she said they'd found the body of a homeless guy at the end of the night shift and there was something really weird about it. 'Really weird' was what Simon lived for. If he got a scoop, an exclusive of his very own, Mr Banecroft would have to let him join the staff of *The Stranger Times*, and that was all he'd ever wanted.

It was now 3 p.m. and he'd been on the case for six hours. When he'd got here, he'd taken as many pictures as he could from behind the cordon. When he'd been told to bugger off by a grumpy police-man, he had informed him that he was a reporter for *The Stranger Times* and that he was covering the story. This wasn't technically true, of course, but Simon considered it to be positive reinforce-ment rather than a lie. It wasn't as if it had helped, anyway. The officer had then told him to go away using a word rather stronger than 'bugger'.

Undeterred, Simon had gone looking for more information. He'd bought some Styrofoam cups and Hobnobs to supplement the contents of the massive flask of tea his mum insisted on giving him every morning. When he wrote his book of advice for the budding journalist – as he no doubt one day would – his first tip would be that nothing got you further with the Great British Public than a brew and a biscuit.

DI Sturgess stretched out his back; it ached from the amount of time he'd spent looking down at the crime scene, asking questions, grilling the SOCOs. The whole thing was a mess. An utter mess. After it had become clear that the victim must have somehow hit the wall from a distance, he'd sent a couple of PCs to the far side of the canal to look for signs of a struggle.

They'd found some spots of blood, but on a paving stone which, by that time, must've been walked over by a thousand pairs of feet on their way to work or elsewhere. He'd taken a sample and sent it to the lab for analysis, but he wasn't holding out much hope. If DI Clarke was remotely competent maybe they'd have had more to go on, but the lazy good-for-nothing had done bugger all except wait for Sturgess to take the investigation off his hands.

There'd been a few of these cases. Not quite like this one, but, well . . . strange. He'd had that murder down on Deansgate a few years ago. The victim, a young lad of only nineteen, had been found in the middle of a nightclub dance floor. He was as dry as a bone, but the cause of death was drowning. Sturgess had pushed and pushed on that, but it'd been weird. He had kicked over rocks and then, out of nowhere, the medical examiner's report was changed and the cause of death was given as a heart attack brought about by dehydration owing to a bad batch of ecstasy. It hadn't made any sense, and when he'd pushed it further he'd been warned off. Then he'd been reassigned and told to leave it well enough alone. As the DCI had said at the time, they had enough open murder cases without needing to reinvestigate the closed ones.

Since then, there had been a couple of other strange cases. Modern policing was all about statistics and nobody else wanted the unsolvables, so they tended to come to him – along with awkward questions and the potential to come out of them looking bad. In four years, Sturgess's previously meteoric ascent in the force had rather stalled. He was bad at knowing what was good for him.

Today, he'd asked for twenty officers to canvass the area over the course of a couple of days. He'd been given four, plus a couple for crowd control. It hadn't been said, but in the currency of death a homeless guy was spare change. If a student dies, the city looks bad. Things must be seen to be done or else Mummy and Daddy will send little Jeremy elsewhere to splurge their money on a useless education. A homeless junkie, though – dying is just what they do. Nobody wanted to hear about unusual circumstances.

He could feel one of his headaches coming on. He'd sent Wilkerson off to canvass the nearest two buildings, but he wasn't expecting much.

Sturgess glanced around. When he'd been working the case last year, there'd been a . . . He hated even thinking it, but there had been something odd. Everywhere he'd gone, he'd experienced a creeping sense that he was being watched. There had never been any evidence to back up the suspicion, but the feeling had stayed with him for weeks. It had got so bad that he'd considered taking his first holiday in six years. Gradually, after a few weeks, the feeling had started to fade. Or perhaps a certain level of paranoia had just become part of his daily life. Still, he glanced around again. Nothing to be seen.

The only person who seemed to be paying him any attention was a spotty kid in glasses on the other side of the crime-scene tape. Sturgess lifted it up and ducked under it, nodding to one of the PCs as he did so.

'DI Sturgess, Simon Brush from *The Stranger Times*,' the kid introduced himself as Sturgess breezed past.

'The who from the what?' Sturgess kept walking towards where his car was parked.

'Simon Brush from *The Stranger Times*,' he repeated.

Sturgess stopped. 'Wait, that joke weekly newspaper thing? Shouldn't you be off hunting Nessie or some such crap?'

The kid looked back at him with a face full of earnestness and acne. 'We report on all manner of unexplained phenomena across the globe, that is correct. Have you any statement to make regarding the nature of the occurrence last night?'

Sturgess started walking again. 'Give me a break.'

The kid scampered to keep up. 'I have witness testimony that says a creature might have been involved.'

Sturgess stopped again and noticed a woman staring at them, having caught the last sentence. He gave her a smile he wasn't feeling and waited for her to move out of earshot.

'All right, kid, who put you up to this? Was it that prick Clarke?'

'I don't – ehm – nobody put me up to anything. I'm a reporter from *The*—'

'Yeah, you said. Look, I know you like playing silly games, but a man is dead and I happen to take that seriously. Do not try to turn it into some bullshit sideshow or I will have your arse for obstruction of justice faster than you can say "abominable snowman", are we clear?'

The kid looked as if he might cry. 'As a member of the press, I am entitled to investigate goings-on as—'

'Fine.' Sturgess sighed and looked away. 'I'll tell you exactly what I told the real press earlier. A fifty-two-year-old man has been found dead in the Castlefield area. At this time we have not ruled out foul play. The Greater Manchester Police are pursuing several lines of enquiry and, as always, we welcome any assistance the general public can give us. Now off you pop, sonny, I'm a busy man.'

Sturgess strode towards his car and rubbed his hand over his eyes. He was definitely getting one of his headaches.

Ghost of Bowie Keen to Record New Material

Good news for fans of David Bowie: Jonathan Warwick, 38, from South Shields, claims that the ghost of the rock legend has possessed him and wants to go into the studio to record new work. According to Warwick, 'I woke up one morning feeling funny and I had no idea what it was until I picked up my lad Darren's guitar and started strumming away. I've never even played guitar before. Turns out I've only been possessed by David bloody Bowie and he wants to record an album.'

Mr Warwick, however, does not share the enthusiasm of hardcore Bowie fans. He claims that he himself has no time for the Thin White Duke's music: 'I'm a big fan of hardcore techno – y'know, something you can get off your face to and just bounce about. Mind you,

I like that "Jean Genie" song – I know that one.'

Mr Warwick's family say that his behaviour has been entirely out of character and that he had previously shown no interest in becoming a musical legend.

'I can't be doing with all of this nonsense,' says Mr Warwick. 'I've got plumbing jobs on. If I'm hanging around the studio, engaging in free association, boundary-pushing musical experimentation, who is going to get Mary Daniels' downstairs loo flushing properly? She can't get upstairs these days with her hips, and her downstairs is causing her no end of problems.'

The Bowie estate for their part have clarified that the star is still dead and is unlikely to have possessed a plumber from South Shields.

CHAPTER 13

Hannah had always liked to consider herself a people person. She was now realizing how badly she had misjudged herself.

She had spent the last two hours at the business end of a conveyor belt of humanity. It had been relentless. Grace had given each member of the queue a numbered raffle ticket – apparently there had been some altercations over queue-jumping in the past. As each person sat down in turn in front of Hannah, she took their ticket, and then their name and contact details – when they were willing to give them, at least – and then she listened to the tale they had to tell, the weird and wonderful thing they believed the rest of the world would be dying to know.

She was stationed in reception at a foldaway desk and chair, with a pad, pen and egg timer. Hannah had told Grace she wouldn't be using the timer, as it seemed very rude to limit people in that way. Grace had merely raised an eyebrow before going to hide behind her own desk. As she'd explained, she was admin staff and not a member of the 'journalism team' like Hannah, so it wasn't her job to gather stories. Hannah had felt a flush of pride – back in the day, she had always wanted to be a journalist.

How naive the two-hours-ago version of her had been. This

was to journalism what working in an abattoir was to fine dining. Hannah had no idea how long the queue was now; she could see only the next five people in the chairs at the other end of the room and the two on the sofa. Every time a seat was vacated, another person appeared from the top of the stairs to fill it. It was like trying to dig your way through water.

She had started using the egg timer after only the fourth person – a man who'd explained how everything from the weather to the price of a Pot Noodle was down to the Jews – and just before the woman who'd invented her own language, which she claimed everyone on the planet could understand instantly. It involved repeating the phrase 'oooohhhhh' in a series of subtle variations. It seemed to have been developed through the close watching of old Carry On films.

Hannah watched the egg-timer sand as it slowly – oh, so slowly – trickled from the top chamber to the bottom. The woman opposite was called Mrs Deveraux, and she had launched into a stream-of-consciousness rant about her husband as soon as she'd sat down. She was in her seventies and wore one of those hats that you never saw on anyone younger. It'd taken Hannah five minutes to get a word in edgeways – just to get her contact details. The most impressive thing about the woman was that she never seemed to draw breath. She spoke in one never-ending sentence.

'. . . and he never picks up after himself and he's always going down the pub and he never invites me, in fact he leaves if I turn up, and he expects me to darn his socks and he never cuts his bloody toenails, which is why he always needs me to fix his socks, and he doesn't maintain the car properly, which is why I had to fix the fan belt last month, and I had to take all that stuff up to the attic and I had to take it back down again when I changed my mind, and he never shuts up, he's always yack-yack-yacking – he just doesn't listen – and he never buys me flowers and—'

'Mrs Deveraux,' said Hannah, louder than she'd wanted to. 'Sorry, but what exactly is the story you think the readers of *The Stranger Times* would be interested in?'

Mrs Deveraux shot Hannah a look of outrage. 'Well, I was trying to tell you that next door's cat is a ghost, but screw you if you won't let a woman get a word in edgeways!'

And with that, she was gone, storming out of the office like a talkative tornado.

Hannah let out a sigh and looked over to the row of chairs – a man holding a chicken was standing up and looking at her excitedly. His face fell as Grace walked past and gave him the universally understood signal for 'one minute'. She leaned over Hannah's desk, blocking the rest of the room's view of her. Hannah took the opportunity to place her head on the nice cool surface of the table.

'How are you holding up?' asked Grace.

'Let me put it this way: you remember that scene in *The Shawshank Redemption* where Andy Dufresne escapes through a pipe filled with—'

'Yes,' interrupted Grace. 'Yes, I do.'

'Well, it's like that. Without the escape bit.'

'Hang in there. The worst of it is over.'

Hannah lifted her head slightly. 'You're lying to me, aren't you?'

'Not necessarily.'

'I'm on ticket' – Hannah raised her head just enough to look at her pad – 'forty-nine. How many more are there to go?'

'Actually,' said Grace, sounding chipper, 'hardly any.'

Hannah lifted her head again, her eyes full of hope. 'Really?'

'Yes,' said Grace. 'Wait, you're on the yellows now, right?'

'There are yellow tickets?!'

Grace winced. 'Not that many.'

'You really are lying to me now.'

'Look at it this way . . .' Grace stopped.

'What?'

She shook her head. 'Sorry. I cannot think of anything. I really thought something positive would come to me.'

Hannah put her forehead back down on the table. There was a jangle of bracelets as Grace placed her hands on either side of Hannah's head and gently raised it up. 'OK, come on now. You are tougher than this. You are a fighter. You got through a terrible marriage; you can get through this.'

'Really? That's your motivational gambit?'

'Sorry, all of my husbands died loyal and decent men. I have not got a frame of reference for infidelity.'

'Seriously, just stop.'

'Would you like a cup of tea?'

Hannah sighed. 'Yeah, OK.'

'That's the spirit. And pick your face up – the man with number fifty has a chicken! Who does not love a chicken?'

Certainly not the man with ticket number fifty. It turned out he really did love a chicken.

The next three hours passed in a tortuous blur of insanity and halitosis.

Fifty-seven pink – a short man with a wide grin and beady eyes: 'I seen a UFO – yours for ten grand.'

'I'm sorry, as a matter of policy *The Stranger Times* does not pay for stories.' Hannah was only guessing on that front, but seeing as they barely paid for biscuits, it seemed like a reasonably educated guess.

'Sure you don't. Wink.' He actually said 'wink'.

'We really don't.'

'Right. Wink.'

'Will you please stop saying "wink"? It's really annoying.'

The smile crumbled. 'I have to. I had a thing as a kid – means I can't wink.'

'Oh God, I'm so sorry.'

'Yeah. It's quite a story. Yours for five grand.'

'No. As I said, we don't—'

'Ten grand, I seen a ghost.'

'No.'

'I seen a tiger eating a ghost – fifteen grand.'

'How would a . . . Never mind, it's still a no.'

'Five grand – I had sex with a ghost.'

'A minute ago you wanted to charge me ten grand just because you'd seen one.'

'See, we're negotiating. You're an astute businesswoman and, may I say, a very attractive one at that. If you're free Thursday—'

'No.'

'To what bit?'

'All of it.'

'Is there anyone else I can speak to?'

'Sure. My boss.'

'Excellent. Well, can I—'

'It'll cost you ten grand, though.'

Seventy-three pink – a woman in her forties, long black hair, dangly earrings.

'And what is the story you'd like to share?'

'I have recently discovered that I was Cleopatra in a past life.'

'I see.'

'By which I mean Cleopatra the Seventh Philopator, the last active ruler of the Ptolemaic Kingdom of Egypt. Diplomat, naval commander, polyglot and medical author.'

'Yes, that's the one I thought you meant.'

'It's really quite extraordinary.'

'I can imagine. Can I ask, did you happen to find this out from a medium called Mrs Bryce who recently opened up in Stockport?'

'Yes, as it happens, I did.'

'I thought so. You're the third person I've spoken to today whom Mrs Bryce has assured they were Cleopatra in a past life.'

'Really? Fascinating. Well, she did have a very full life, didn't she?'

Hannah was distracted by a collective gasp from those waiting on the chairs, and looked across to see the cause of the disturbance.

The second most striking thing about the man who had just walked into the room was his long white dreadlocks, which were so long he wore them wrapped around his neck like a scarf. The most striking thing about him was that the dreadlocks were the only thing he was currently wearing.

Hannah turned to the reception desk for Grace, but she must have nipped off somewhere while the last gentlemen was explaining how he was haunted by the ghost of Macbeth, the fictional character.

'Ehm, sir,' said Hannah to the dreadlocked interloper, 'what are you doing?'

He lifted the mug in his hand and gave her a cheery smile. 'We just need milk for we cup of tea.'

'But, sir, you're not wearing any pants.'

He ambled into the kitchen just off reception, shouting back over his shoulder, 'S'alrite, chile. We don't need pants, we just need milk.'

'But . . .'

The double doors opened and Grace walked through, carrying a folder. She stopped when she sensed the tension in the room. 'Now what?'

'Ehm,' said Hannah.

'Is everything all right?'

'Ehm,' said Hannah again, because her brain had decided it had had enough of all this, put up the 'gone fishing' sign and left for the day.

'Everyting alrite,' said the man, re-emerging from the kitchen, presumably with milk in his tea, if no more clothing on his body.

'Manny!' cried Grace. 'What have we talked about?'

The man who was apparently called Manny stopped to ponder

this, as if he'd been asked a complex question. 'We talk 'bout many tings. We like to talk. You a good woman, Grace.' He favoured her with a warm smile.

'Manny, we agreed you'd wear pants during work hours.'

'We not . . .' Manny stopped and looked around at the people in the reception area as if seeing them for the first time. Some of them were averting their eyes, but one woman, who'd been half-way through a large bag of popcorn, was very focused on Manny, although Hannah doubted she'd be able to pick out his face in a line-up.

'Oh. We see. What time is it?'

'Three o'clock,' said Grace, before adding, 'in the afternoon.'

'Ah.' He nodded. 'What day?'

'Tuesday.'

He took a slurp of tea. 'Alrite. Sure nuff. We apologize. It's just the human body, man – natural thing. Nothing the peoples ain't seen before. Just what the good Lord gave us all.'

The popcorn woman spoke up. 'The good Lord was particularly generous to you.'

Manny gave her a smile and a wink. 'Thanking you. We appreciate your kindness.'

And with that, he sauntered back down the stairs.

Grace cleared her throat. 'Sorry about that, ladies and gentlemen – he is a bit of a free spirit.'

'Is he single?'

Grace ignored the question and walked back towards her desk. As she passed Hannah she shook her head. 'I will explain later.'

★

Forty-six yellow – a man who looked very tall until he sat down. Though his legs were very long, his body was tiny. Irish accent.

'Right, the government are suppressing this, but cats and dogs can have babies.'

'Ehm,' said Hannah. 'First off – hello.'

'Ah, right – yeah, sorry. Howerya. So, as I was saying, cats and dogs can have babies.'

'Yes,' said Hannah. 'Yes, they can. They're called kittens and puppies.'

'What? Ah, no – I mean, yeah – but they can have them together is what I'm talkin' about. Kippies. Cross between a kitten and a puppy.' He pointed a long finger at Hannah's notes. 'I came up with the name meself. I want credit for that. I've trademarked it.'

'Right. Smart thinking.'

'Oh yeah, I've given this some serious thought.'

'OK, thanks for—'

'Also, there's been a panda on the moon.'

'I see. And how did it get there?'

'I'm glad you asked.'

'At least one of us is.'

'I've narrowed it down to one of three possibilities. One: Chinese space programme experiment.'

'Makes sense.'

'Two: the moon is actually where pandas come from, and the question should be how did they get to Earth.'

'Ahhh, interesting.'

'Or three: stag do.'

'Really?'

The man nodded his head emphatically. 'Oh, yeah. Lotta weird stuff goes down on a stag do. On mine, me mate Paulie—'

'Sorry, I'm going to have to stop you there.'

'But there's still sand left in the timer.'

'I know, but I need to go into the other room and scream into a cushion before the next person.'

He paused to think about this for a moment. 'Ah, OK, fair enough. Thanks for your time.'

Ninety-eight yellow – a blonde woman, late thirties.

Hannah could sense it before the woman spoke. Maybe it was in the way she carried herself, or in the exhausted, beaten-down look in her eyes as she handed over her ticket, or maybe there was something less tangible that broadcast it to other people. Whatever was carrying the signal, the message was unmistakable: grief. This poor woman carried a weight of it on her shoulders. She sat down and gave Hannah a soft smile. She was no doubt attractive in other circumstances, ones in which she didn't look as if she hadn't slept in a month.

'Hi. I'm Hannah. Can I take your name?'

'Tina Merchant.'

Hannah noted it down. 'And how can I help you, Tina?'

Tina shifted nervously in her chair. 'It's . . . it's my husband. Look, I . . .' She waved her hand around at the office. 'I . . . No disrespect, but I don't understand any of this. I mean, normally . . .'

With alarm, Hannah noticed that the woman's eyes were welling up.

'It's OK. Take your time.' Hannah slipped a small packet of tissues out of her handbag and placed it on the table gently.

Tina took one with an embarrassed nod and dabbed at her eyes. 'Sorry. Been a long week.'

'No problem,' said Hannah. 'Take your time.'

The woman nodded and pulled out a photo from her coat pocket and handed it to Hannah. A tall, well-built man with tightly cropped hair was pushing a little blonde girl on a swing. The kid beamed a gap-toothed grin out to the world, full of the joys of life.

'That's . . . that's my daughter, Cathy, and my husband, Gary.'

'Right,' said Hannah.

'Cathy has cancer. We found out a few months ago.'

'Oh God, I'm so sorry.'

The woman waved it away. As if she'd been told how sorry people were so many times that the words had lost all meaning. 'It's a rare type. Bad. They tried some things but nothing is working.'

Hannah opened her mouth but no words came out. What could you say to that?

Tina carried on, her eyes fixed on the tabletop. She looked as if she just wanted to get it out.

'Somebody said they could do something in America. We tried one of those fundraising things, y'know – like you always see. We needed fifty thousand, didn't even make five. I guess we aren't that popular. Gary . . . he . . . since he came out of the service, he's had a few issues. Not been great at holding a job down.'

Hannah looked again at the man in the photo. On his right forearm was a tattoo of something that looked like some kind of dagger.

'We've been, y'know – taking turns sitting with Cathy. She gets scared in the hospital. Then, a couple of days ago, Gary says he's got a solution. Said a man is going to help us. At first I thought it was about money, that someone was going to give us it. You hear about stuff like that happening, don't you? Philanthropists and that. He said it wasn't that, though. Said it was even better. I told him he wasn't making sense. Told him not to do anything silly.'

Tina looked down at her fingers, as if only realizing at that point that they had been absent-mindedly shredding the tissue. 'He said it was . . . magic.' She said the last word in an embarrassed hush and then looked up, as if annoyed with herself. 'Gary said the man could help if he did some stuff for him. That was two days ago and I've not seen or heard from him since. Not answering calls. Cathy is asking for her daddy. I just thought maybe you people might, y'know . . . know who would be . . .' She looked at Hannah, suddenly angry. 'Who'd be filling a poor desperate man's head with stupid ideas.'

'Have you tried going to the police?' asked Hannah.

Tina nodded. 'They were useless. Said they'd keep a lookout but . . . whatever. There's a woman with a boy on the same ward as Cathy. Her husband killed himself a few weeks ago. They say men aren't good at dealing with stuff. I just . . .' Tina drew herself up. 'He's not perfect, but he's my husband and he loves his daughter. I just want to find him. Some bastard started filling his head with mad ideas.'

Hannah tried to think of something to say, but she never got the chance. Tina reached across the table and snatched back the photo.

'Sorry, this was a bad idea. I should get back to Cathy. Thanks for your time.'

'Hang on,' said Hannah. She didn't know how, but she wanted to help.

Tina threw a wave over her shoulder and disappeared down the stairs. Grace looked over at Hannah with a raised eyebrow. Hannah shrugged in response. She considered following Tina to make sure she was OK, but before she could move, a man had sat down in the chair opposite.

'OK,' said Hannah, 'I'm going to skip the contact details bit and go straight to the questions. First off, where did you get the fake moustache from?'

'I don't know what you're talking about, love. I seen a UFO fight a tiger. Eight grand.'

'Those are fake sideburns as well, aren't they? You're thorough, I'll give you that.'

'OK. I like you, love. I do. I think we've got a connection. I'll do you tiger fights UFO, I had sex with a ghost and – I cannot believe I'm giving you this deal – King Kong stole my wife, all for ten grand.'

'Do they come as part of a kit?'

'The stories?'

'The moustache and the—'

'Yeah. My mate Trustworthy Terence sells 'em down the market. And . . . ouch! This bloody woman just ripped off my moustache!' he cried. 'Wait until the papers hear about this!'

CHAPTER 14

Gary took a sip of his pint and looked around the Grand Central pub. He had located himself in the corner booth so he could enjoy a view of the whole room and no one could sneak up on him.

On the far side, two students were playing a game of pool while a third gave a tedious running commentary, thinking he was so bloody funny. A man sat at the bar, quietly drinking by himself, and a couple of women were having a natter in the corner. The barman looked bored and appeared to be spending most of the time reading his own tattoos. It wasn't as if the place couldn't do with a clean – there were dead glasses on half the tables.

Gary's phone buzzed in his pocket. He took it out, saw it was Tina and sent it to voicemail. He placed it on the table beside his pack of cigarettes and his lighter. It had been a mistake to try to explain this to her. He knew it sounded mad. Maybe he had been crazy to believe in it but he'd been desperate. Sometimes long shots really do pay off. He grinned as he took another sip of his pint.

He'd been trying to calm himself down all day. He'd seen action in the army but it had never been like this. After last night, once he'd . . . become himself again, he had tried to sleep, but it had been impossible, as it had been the day before. Moretti had explained it to him: at first, it would be easier for him to become the beast at night, but eventually he'd be able to transform whenever he liked. Even now, while he was 'himself', it still seemed to live inside of him. It was as if he'd been taken over – only he liked it. He really liked it.

His whole life, people had walked all over him, and now he was the one with the power. He could save Cathy and he didn't need to go begging and scraping, cap in hand, to do it. As he sat there, he could feel the beast prowling around inside him, just waiting for the night to come.

He jumped as Moretti sat down opposite him. Sneaky little sod. Every time they met, it was the weirdest thing – Gary never saw him coming, the fat little Yank just seemed to appear. Not with a pop or anything – one minute he wasn't there and the next he was. It was as if he'd been standing there the whole time and you'd somehow not noticed.

Moretti took off his baseball cap and ran his hand over his bald pate. 'You shouldn't be drinking.'

'Thanks, Mum.'

Moretti gave Gary a look.

'All right, relax, will ya?' Gary said. 'We're in a pub.'

Moretti shook his head. 'You Brits. Wouldn't even occur to you there was another option.'

'D'you want one?'

The Yank made a show of looking around. 'I'll pass. I make it a rule not to drink any place where I'll require a tetanus shot afterwards.'

Condescending little sod.

'So,' continued Moretti, leaning in, 'how do you think last night went?'

'Yeah,' said Gary, nodding. 'Fine. Mission accomplished and all that.'

Moretti's eyes widened. 'Really? All fine? You had one simple job. I gave you the scent, told you to locate one of what we needed, then come back and tell me the location.'

'Yeah, well, I saw the opportunity to take him, so I did. I improvised within the operational parameters.'

Moretti nodded. '"Improvised within the operational parameters"? Did they teach you that in the army? I suppose it's an interesting way to say "didn't follow orders".'

Gary bristled. 'I got him, didn't I? Put him where you told me to. Now we're ahead of schedule.'

'Yes, how perfect. Unfortunately, you killed somebody else in the process.'

Gary shrugged. 'Collateral damage.'

'Collateral damage,' muttered Moretti. 'Collateral damage. It's like the army trained you to be some kind of idiot parrot, with about three stock phrases at your disposal.'

Inside, the beast roared. 'Mind your manners.' Gary's hand tightened around his pint glass.

'Oh, please. I cannot believe I agreed to help a damn idiot with this. Thanks to you, the police and others are now looking into it. Worse than the fact that you left a body, you managed to leave a body with no explanation of how it could've happened. That is the kind of thing that gets attention.'

Gary shrugged. 'So what? Cops can't do nothing to us.'

Moretti rubbed his hand over his brow. 'Jesus, are you really this dumb?'

'I'm warning you.'

'*You* are warning *me*? Let me explain something to you: I don't care about the police. But they might cause enough noise to attract the interest of other parties, and believe me when I say we do not want that to happen.'

'You need to stop talking to me like I'm a fucking kid.' Gary jabbed his finger in Moretti's face. He'd had all of this he was prepared to take.

'You need to stop acting like one.'

'I'm gonna . . .'

Moretti clicked his fingers and Gary froze. Not deliberately. His body just stopped moving, leaving his finger in mid-air, inches from Moretti's smiling face.

'I think it's time for a little clarification of our arrangement, don't you?'

Gary could feel his heart pounding in his chest. He looked around the room in panic; his eyes seemed to be the only part of him that could move. He tried to breathe – just breathe – but he couldn't make whatever made that happen do anything. It was as if his entire body had just shut down.

Moretti picked up Gary's cigarettes and lighter calmly. 'You don't mind, do you?'

He drew a cigarette from the packet and lit it. Over his shoulder, Gary could see the barman, his eyes attracted to the flame.

'Hey, mate.' His voice was filled with outrage. 'You can't smoke in here.'

'Yes, I can,' said Moretti evenly.

The barman looked confused and embarrassed, as if he'd made some terrible faux pas. 'Yes, you can.'

Moretti looked at Gary as he puffed on the cigarette. 'I agreed to help you, remember? You begged me. You wanted to save your daughter, and I said if we did this, you had to do exactly as I said.'

Gary could feel the pressure building in his lungs – he couldn't tell if they were full or empty. Until this point in his life, breathing had just happened.

'So, let me be clear.' Moretti smiled as he spoke in a slow and deliberate voice. 'You will do exactly as I say.' He flicked the lighter into life again and casually held the flame under Gary's extended hand. Gary felt the surge of pain on his skin instantly. Every ounce of his being, every instinct, was telling him to pull away, but he couldn't move his hand – not even a fraction of an inch.

'This,' continued Moretti, 'is not a partnership. Your role in proceedings is to do what you are told. Clear?'

Gary did nothing. He couldn't even blink. He could feel tears rolling down his cheeks as his eyes remained frozen, staring across the table at Moretti's smiling face.

'I'll take that as a yes. Now, meet me tonight, same time, same place. Thanks to your screw-up, we have something else we have to deal with.' Moretti flicked off the lighter and stood up. He dropped the half-smoked cigarette into Gary's pint and picked up his baseball cap from the table. As an afterthought, he snatched up the pack of cigarettes. 'I'm keeping these. Damn things will kill you. See you tonight. Don't be late.'

He smiled again and calmly walked out the door.

Gary sat there, stock-still – his finger pointing at empty space. Since the flame was now gone, his body was focusing all of its energy on screeching at him to breathe. Every inch of him was willing his lungs to just *breathe*. He noticed that the three students had stopped playing pool and were looking over at him. Gary wanted to scream as they stood there, watching.

As quickly as it had been taken from him, his body was his own again.

He dragged in a gasping, blessed breath as he collapsed back into his seat, pulling his scorched hand to his chest, panting like a man who'd finally surfaced after being held underwater too long. The relief was exquisite.

Mingled with it all, the beast was roaring with impotent rage.

After about thirty seconds, he managed to calm his breathing to the point where he was able to focus on something else. He ran his sleeve over his face, wiping away the tears that had rolled down his cheeks.

As he looked up, he saw that the three students were still staring at him, mouths open.

His voice came out in a growl. 'What the fuck are you looking at?'

CHAPTER 15

Hannah sat at her desk, staring into the distance at absolutely nothing.

Stella looked down at her. 'I think we broke the new Tina.'

'Her name is Hannah!' shouted Grace from a distance.

'I dunno. All these white people look the same to me.'

'That is enough of your militant nonsense, young lady. Have you finished filing all those boxes?'

'Jeez, what did your last dogsbody die of?'

'Talking back!'

Stella disappeared from Hannah's field of vision and was replaced by Grace, concern etched across her face. She was holding a large mug of tea.

'I made you a cuppa, and look – custard creams. I keep some in reserve for, ehm . . . special occasions.'

'I don't think I'll ever be able to drink tea again.'

Grace looked horrified. Her world view was based on the core principle that a good cup of tea or the good Lord Jesus could fix all problems.

'Six hours,' said Hannah.

'There were a lot of people.'

'Six hours,' she repeated. 'It was like the opening scene of *Saving Private Ryan* only, y'know, longer. And the bullets were crazy people. And there was no Matt Damon at the end, just more crazy.'

'It is not normally that bad.'

'Six hours,' said Hannah. 'Who knew there was that much crazy in the world?'

'Anyone who was here last month,' called Stella from the far side of the room.

Grace's head swivelled round. 'File!' She turned back to Hannah. 'Normally Ox and Reginald would be here to help too. It was just bad luck that today was your first time.'

A thought struck Hannah. 'How come you two don't do it?'

'Ehm . . .' faltered Grace. 'Like I said, I am not part of the journalism staff . . .'

'Yeah,' said Stella, 'that's the reason, and not because a dude came in, said he was in league with Satan, and Grace tried to drown him in holy water.'

Grace shot daggers in Stella's direction. 'I wasn't trying to drown him,' she snapped. 'It was a misunderstanding.'

'That's not what the judge said.'

Grace forced a big smile at Hannah. 'Ox and Reginald will be here next month.'

Hannah pointed at Stella. 'So why doesn't she help?'

'Because I don't want to.'

Grace shot whatever was the next level up from daggers at Stella. 'We can't have her doing it. She is not. Good. With. People!'

'People ain't good with me. Ya get me?'

'I will something you in a minute, young lady!'

'I used to really like people,' said Hannah. 'I mean, most people –
not all people, obviously. I didn't like Osama bin Laden or Hitler . . .'

'Or the dude you married,' chipped in Stella.

'That's it,' said Grace. 'No dessert for you this evening.'

'Whatever.'

There was a slam of a door as Stella marched off to be in a huff
elsewhere in the building.

Grace pulled up a chair and sat down beside Hannah. 'You'll be
fine after a good night's sleep.'

'I'm not so sure. After listening to that woman who claimed the
CIA were using her dreams as a secret training base for an army of
space monkeys, I've got a horrible feeling they're going to start doing
that to me too. It's the kind of thought that sticks with you. She was
very graphic about the poo-throwing. God, I really hate people now.'

'You do not mean that,' said Grace in a cheerful tone of voice.
'You have just forgotten how nice most people are. As soon as you
meet somebody who does not think their tortoise is a vampire or
that Sigourney Weaver is trying to control them through the TV,
you will remember how much you like people.'

'Grace!'

The shout came from Banecroft's office.

Grace looked up and addressed the heavens. 'Seriously? Give
me a little help here!'

After a loud crash and some industrial-strength non-swearing –
Banecroft must have been giving it quite a lot of thought – the
door to his office flew open and he stomp-limped out.

'Where the hell are those two idiots?'

'That is a rude way to describe them.'

'Yes,' agreed Banecroft, 'but you knew who I meant, didn't you? Now, where are they?'

'Scotland,' said Grace. 'You do remember sending them to Scotland?'

'I do, but what I don't remember is hearing from them. I would like a report on their progress.'

'Well, then, why not just say that?'

'I just did!' Banecroft stopped and looked at Hannah. 'What's wrong with the new Tina?'

'She had to do the whole of Loon Day by herself.'

'Oh, big deal!'

Grace stood up. 'Do you remember the one time you tried to do it, in order to stop people whingeing about it?'

'That is beside the point.'

'That sweet old lady—'

'She was no lady. Ladies don't kick a man *there*. My point is . . .' Banecroft trailed off and looked at the floor. 'Wait, what was my point?'

'You came out to apologize for something.'

'No, that doesn't sound like me. Idiots – that's it. Get 'em on the phone.'

Grace sighed and picked up the extension on Hannah's desk. 'You have a phone in your office, you know.'

'Actually, Miss Smarty-Pants,' said Banecroft, 'I don't! It got shot yesterday.'

Grace finished dialling and held the receiver to her ear. 'Only you could say that like you think it proves some kind of point.'

★

Reggie looked up in alarm as an oncoming car honked at them. 'Keep your eyes on the road!'

Ox tugged the wheel to manoeuvre the car back into the left-hand lane. 'All right, all right. Chill out. You do your bit, map boy, and let me worry about the driving.'

'I think this map is erroneous.'

'Really? "Erroneous", is it? You only realized half an hour ago you had the thing upside down, now you're an expert in cartography?'

'If you would just let me use the GPS.'

Ox shook his head emphatically. 'No, no, no. GPS technology was developed by the US Air Force. I'm not having the military-industrial complex knowing my whereabouts, thank you very much.'

'Well, at the moment, you are particularly safe, seeing as *we* don't know our whereabouts. We should've arrived two hours ago.'

'Relax. It's a toilet. It's not going anywhere.' Ox pointed out the window. 'Does that cow look familiar to you?'

'Which cow?'

'The one we just passed.'

'It is a cow. I don't think they look familiar even to other cows.'

Beethoven's Ninth Symphony, arranged for the mobile phone, filled the car.

'You promised me you turned your phone off!'

'I made no such statement,' said Reggie, patting the various pockets of his jacket and waistcoat.

'Right. Well, I'm sticking me Primal Scream tape back on.'

'Oh, no.'

'It's a classic album!'

'Not that.' Reggie held up his phone. 'It's the office.'

'Ah, man. Don't answer it.'

'Yes, because he always responds so well to being kept waiting.' Reggie answered the call. 'Reginald Fairfax the Third.'

Ox couldn't make out anything other than the fact that it sounded like Grace on the end of the line. His car's engine was loud, but not that souped-up, obnoxious type of loud that some individuals embrace in an effort to make up for a massive short-coming in the personality stakes. No, it was the kind of loud that comes right before the very quiet – possibly permanently so.

The car was old. Not *classic* old, just *old* old. He'd tried to sell it last year but couldn't interest even the scrapyard in purchasing it. He called it 'the Zombie' because, despite bits falling off, the sickly engine and a near-constant groaning noise from the suspension, it inexplicably kept going.

'Yes,' said Reggie. 'We are still driving, due to some naviga-tional issues, but spirits are high and we remain confident of achieving our objective . . . What? Oh, Lord knows. Please don't put him on the—'

Reggie pulled the phone away from his ear as the unmistakable sound of Banecroft losing his rag filled the car's interior. Reggie held the phone in front of him, Banecroft's roar achieving the effect of a loudspeaker.

Reggie tried pleading with their boss as you would do an irate baby. 'No, we have . . . No, we are . . . Yes, we will . . . Honestly—'

Ox grabbed the phone out of Reggie's hand and sat on it.

'What on earth are you doing?'

'What?' replied Ox. 'It's not like he's gonna let you talk, is it?'

Reggie pursed his lips. 'Hmmm, that is true.'

'Jeez, I think I can feel his rage vibrating through my colon.' The car swerved alarmingly as Ox took both of his hands off the wheel to point. 'Seriously, man, there's that cow again!'

'. . . and if you don't, then I will have both of you chasing sewer monsters that don't exist for the next month. You see if I don't!'

Banecroft slammed down the phone. 'So help me . . .' He looked around the bullpen, surprised to find himself alone. 'Where the hell has everybody gone?'

Grace's voice carried from the reception area. 'I sent the new girl home.'

'What? When?'

'Twenty minutes ago.'

'But I was . . .'

Grace entered, carrying a stack of forms. 'You were doing one of your unnecessarily long and venom-filled rants. I have things you need to sign.'

Grace placed the forms in front of Banecroft and held out a pen.

'Since when do you have the right to send people home?'

'Since I decided I did. The poor girl does not need to stay late listening to you be horrible to someone. She can hear enough of that in ordinary hours.'

'But I . . .'

'But nothing. I like her, and more importantly, we need her. Much as you dislike the fact, this paper needs staff.'

Banecroft worked his way through the pile of papers, signing everything without reading it first. 'I'll have you know that people used to go to great lengths to learn the newspaper business from me.'

'Yes, but then you went crazy and now we need people who will put up with you.'

'Oh, really? So how come there's someone standing outside right now, literally begging for the chance to work here?'

'If you are referring to Simon, he did not show up this morning.'

Banecroft shook his head. 'Pah! Young people today. No patience!'

'This from a man who yesterday screamed at the kettle for not boiling fast enough.'

'Oh, speaking of which . . .'

'No, I am off home. Make your own cup of tea.' Banecroft winced as Grace shouted at the top of her lungs, 'Stella! Come on, we are leaving.'

'You don't need to shout.'

Grace gave Banecroft a long, hard look. 'If that is not the pot calling the pot a pot?'

'You're saying that wrong.'

'I am not blessed with your way with words.'

'Few are.'

'And for that, the rest of us are eternally grateful.'

Banecroft got to his feet and hobbled off. 'Right, you and I aren't friends any more.'

Grace couldn't keep the shock from her voice. 'We were friends?'

CHAPTER 16

Not much further. Only three floors.

Simon had never been particularly good at sneaking, despite considerable practice. Not in a 'thief in the night' way, but in the way that you develop from encountering some blowback from your more knuckle-dragging classmates when you take to school the rather fetching leather briefcase your uncle Alan has given you. Simon had been assigned the nickname 'His Lordship' and then treated in a way that made it clear none of the other children were royalists. School had not been fun, although it'd been nowhere near as bad as the hour directly after school when the knuckle-draggers went looking for him. Hence the sneaking.

He'd elected to take the stairs rather than the lift, as it was important he wasn't seen by the security guards – his source had made that very clear. Simon was worried that the lift might set off some kind of alarm. Well, that and the fact that he didn't like lifts at the best of times, especially not in a building that was still under construction. In any case, forty-two floors was a long way to climb. Luckily, he had strong legs from cycling everywhere. Unfortunately that also meant he had cycled here and so was already a bit tired before he'd even started.

Two floors to go. The inconvenience was nothing when it came to the chance to gain the scoop of a lifetime. After this, *The Stranger Times* would have to take him on. Mr Banecroft would be so impressed. Admittedly, this was a weird place and time to hold a meeting – on top of a not-quite-completed forty-two-storey building at midnight – but when he thought about it, it did make some sense. There was, after all, nowhere you'd be less likely to be overheard in the whole of Manchester. You'd probably have to shout just to hear yourself over the wind. Simon tried not to think about the wind. He wasn't a big fan of heights either.

One floor. The man had approached him earlier in the day, after he'd seen Simon talking to DI Sturgess. The detective inspector hadn't been very receptive to the information Simon had tried to give him, but that was the police for you. They had their set ways of thinking and they wouldn't keep an open mind. Simon's 'source' had said as much when they'd chatted. It had all been very rushed and hush-hush. He'd said he had information that would be of great interest to Simon, but it was very important that they discuss it in private. Nobody must know. Discretion was key. The man had advised Simon to keep the story to himself until he had all the facts. As he'd put it, Simon didn't want the police interfering or the mainstream press latching on until he was in a position to maximize its impact and fend off the inevitable naysayers and sceptics.

Simon had instantly liked the man. That was Americans for you. Despite what some people might claim, Simon had always found them to be considerably more polite than your typical British citizen. Though he might have been basing that opinion on the fact that no American had ever attempted to pull Simon's underpants over his head while he was still wearing them.

Zero floors. Breathing hard and with aching legs, Simon reached the door at the top. He took a moment, attempting to regain his breath. He hoped it would be a lot easier on the way down.

Bob-a-Job

James Rochester, from Orpington in Kent, was shocked to discover when he moved to a job in Reading that Bob, a colleague from his old office, was working there too.

James explained, 'Bob is a nice guy but a bit unusual. He makes very odd small talk, like asking people if they reckon Earth has developed light-speed travel capabilities, how would they feel if the government were replaced by nicer people from far far away, and how many kidneys the human body contains. To be honest, nobody minds as he does really good accounts and is happy to sign off a lot of things as expenses. Also, the watermelon outfit he wears for casual Fridays is fun.'

James was even more shocked when he rang one of his former co-workers, who confirmed that Bob was still definitely sitting at his desk in his old office. At that point, there was a loud popping noise and both Bobs vanished simultaneously.

'It was a nightmare first day,' confirmed James. 'The disappearance of the new office's Bob went down very badly as he was due to bring in cakes the next day.'

CHAPTER 17

As she walked through the park, Hannah was shocked to discover that she was whistling. From a distance, she must look like someone who was, at least temporarily, happy with her lot in life. Given how life had gone recently, this was really saying something.

Yes, yesterday had been long, exhausting and, frankly, full to the brim with crazy. She had been physically and emotionally drained, so much so that she'd fallen asleep on the bus home and had a very vivid dream in which a space monkey was trying to sell her stories about its sexual relations with a ghost. She'd awoken with a start to see other passengers looking at her – she had the horrible feeling that she had been talking in her sleep. Embarrassed, she'd got off the bus at the next stop, only to realize she'd already missed her stop – although luckily not by that much.

When she'd got home, she'd had a microwavable meal and, over a bottle of wine, chatted through her day with Maggie. Maggie had been fascinated – both with the onslaught of 'colourful characters' that made up Loon Day and with the boss from hell that was Banecroft. Hannah was not used to people being fascinated by what she had to say. Quite the opposite.

She had always had the fear, deep down, that she wasn't the

world's most interesting person. It came from a lack of self-worth, she realized. In fact, Dr Arno Van Zil, in chapter twelve of *Only One Direction* – 'Loving You, Loving Life' – had said as much. She had always felt nervous when chatting to others and, in hindsight, Karl hadn't helped. Her husband always gave off the vibe that he would be happier talking to someone else. On reflection, Hannah thought, she might have misjudged that – he was really just focused on having sex with other people as opposed to talking to them.

The other thing was that, back in her 'old life', she hadn't had much to talk about. She did now. Working at *The Stranger Times* was a lot of things, but it certainly wasn't boring.

Maggie had seemed genuinely disappointed to have to break up her conversation with Hannah to leave for the dinner reservation she had with her husband – Tuesdays were Maggie and Gordon's date night. The last thing she'd said was that she really wanted to hear more about Hannah's day when she got back. Hannah had been flattered. Then she'd gone up to her room and read a couple more editions of *The Stranger Times*.

Once you got past the silliness – and she hated to admit it to herself, but Banecroft's rant did come back to her – and once you read it as a chronicle of the weird and wonderful beliefs in the world, it was fascinating. Why were some people so convinced that their own government was out to get them? Why were others obsessed with proving that ghosts existed? Or UFOs? Or any of the other myriad peculiar beliefs and occurrences that filled the pages of *The Stranger Times*? Viewed in that light, it was, well, interesting – and it made her rather interesting by association.

As she neared the office, Hannah passed the spot where she had first met Reginald and Ox. When they got back from Scotland she was going to take some time to get to know them properly. She was, after all, the assistant editor. The more she understood their work, the better she'd be at her job.

She turned the corner to the front door of the church. Simon, for the second day in a row, was not at his station. The guilty thought that her hiring might have been the final straw for him popped into Hannah's head and deflated her good mood slightly. She had only met him briefly, once on her way in and then once while they'd been loading Banecroft into the ambulance after the self-inflicted shooting. He'd seemed like a nice lad, though, and he was keen. Maybe she should have a chat with him too? They did need more staff, after all, and taking care of that kind of thing sounded like the sort of task an assistant editor should be doing.

Hannah ran up the stairs, skipping neatly over the fourth-last step that needed fixing, and strode into the reception area.

'Grace, how are we this morning?'

Grace looked slightly taken aback. 'Oh, hello. You seem chipper.'

Hannah smiled. 'I do, don't I?'

She opened the box of doughnuts she'd picked up on the way in. 'Seeing as you're my favourite, you get first pick.'

Grace's face lit up. 'I should not really.' But she did.

'Where's everybody else?'

'Well,' said Grace, 'we have a bit of a problem there. When Reginald and Ox finally found the pub in Falkirk, they had had the toilet removed.'

'Oh.'

'Yes. The landlord had thrown it out. I cannot blame him – nobody wants the devil in their bathroom.'

'So what about Ox and Reggie?'

'I had to get them a hotel for the night. They reckon they can find the toilet this morning.' She nodded in the direction of the far end of the building. 'He is going to hit the roof.'

'Ah, relax,' said Hannah. 'He'll scream and shout but we can sort it.'

Grace gave Hannah a sceptical look. 'Are you on the happy pills or something?'

'Nope, I'm just high on life.' Hannah raised her voice. 'Stella?'

Her shout was met by tutting and a stomping of boots from down the corridor before the door flew open.

'What?'

Hannah held out the box of doughnuts. 'Would you like one?'

Stella moved her green hair out of her eyes and eyed the box suspiciously. 'What's the catch?'

'No catch, I promise.'

Stella reached out a hand towards the box, but at the last moment, Hannah pulled it back slightly. 'Actually . . .'

'I knew it.'

Hannah favoured her with a big smile. 'Just a teeny tiny thing, but to quote Beyoncé back in her Destiny's Child days: say my name?'

'Typical. This some kinda power trip, yeah?'

Hannah shook her head. 'No, no. Nothing like that. I just don't want to be the new Tina. I want to be me. We're all individuals after all, aren't we? Same as you want to be you – and by the way, I for one am loving this look you've got going on. It's sort of steampunk, isn't it?'

Stella looked wary. 'Yeah. Suppose.'

'Cool.' Hannah cringed internally, aware she was veering dangerously close to 'hey, I'm hip, I'm down with the youth' territory, but she held out the box and kept smiling.

Stella reached out slowly and took one of the pink-glazed doughnuts. 'Thanks, Hannah.'

'You are welcome, Stella.'

Hannah gave both Grace and Stella a big smile as she backed through the door and headed down the hall.

Hannah knocked loudly on the office door. Nothing.

She knocked more loudly on the office door. Still nothing.

Hannah pounded on the office door for a third time and was greeted by the sound of Vincent Banecroft groaning.

'I'm coming in.'

'What?' came the angry response.

Hannah threw open the door and walked in. 'I said I'm coming in.'

Banecroft was sitting at his desk, having presumably slept there. According to Grace, there was a bed somewhere in the back, but it must've been buried under the avalanche of crap that constituted the primary theme of the office's decor. Hannah ignored the half-empty bottle of whiskey on the desk and resisted the urge to check the bin to see if it had company.

Banecroft looked at her from beneath heavily lidded eyes

below his bird's nest of messy hair. 'What in the— I could've been naked!'

'That would've meant changing your clothes – something we'd all be excited to see happen. Here, have a doughnut.'

Hannah opened the box.

'We can't afford doughnuts!'

Hannah pulled them away. 'How much do you think dough-nuts cost?'

'I don't know. What am I, an accountant?'

'No, you're an editor, and I bought these out of my own pocket, so stop grumbling, shut up and have a damn doughnut.'

Banecroft snatched up a lemon one and took a large, messy bite.

'There you go! Now, there's a problem with the Falkirk toilet—'

'I knew it!' squealed Banecroft around a mouthful of fried dough.

'But,' continued Hannah, raising her voice to be heard, 'I'm going to deal with it. I'll have a report for you in twenty minutes at the morning briefing. You can get all shouty about it then if you like.'

He swallowed too quickly. 'I will shout whenever I bloody well like!'

Hannah left a gap but nothing happened.

Banecroft belched and then spoke. 'In nineteen forty, an Aus-tralian divorce court judge ruled that "bloody" was not a swear word. Precedent. Grace has agreed it therefore doesn't count.'

'That is correct,' came Grace's voice over the intercom.

'See?' said Banecroft. 'Now, where was I? Oh, yes – I will shout whenever I bloody well like!'

'OK,' said Hannah, 'but I'm leaving the office now, so you'll be shouting at yourself.' From her pocket she pulled a fresh tube of toothpaste, a toothbrush and a can of deodorant. 'Here are those toiletries you asked for.'

Banecroft looked at the items in confusion. 'When did I ask for them? I didn't ask for them!'

'OK,' said Hannah. 'I'll rephrase: here are those toiletries you desperately need.'

'Control freak. I can see why your husband—'

'STOP!' Hannah said it loudly enough that Banecroft actually complied. 'Now, you can continue to say something horrible or you can have another doughnut, but you can't have both. So, what's it to be?'

Hannah opened the box and held it out once more. There were still three doughnuts left.

Banecroft locked eyes with her. 'I'm not some dog you can train to do tricks for food, y'know?'

'No, you're a big scary dragon – but I'm the woman with dough-nuts. So, you can try for basic manners or you can just be you and go hungry. The choice is yours.'

He didn't take his eyes off her as he slowly reached forward and took one of the chocolate ones.

'There we go. See you at the meeting.'

'Yes, and we'd better have some bloody good answers on . . .'

The rest was lost as Hannah slammed the door behind her, humming loudly to herself.

'Manny!'

Hannah had tried knocking, but the sound of hammering from

the other side of the doors indicated he might not be able to hear her. Before she had gone home last night, Grace had explained Manny to Hannah. Apparently, he was in charge of the paper's printing department, which took up the entire ground floor of the building. He kept largely to himself, although from what Hannah had seen yesterday, he couldn't exactly be described as shy.

Carefully, Hannah pushed open one of the large wooden doors. The printing press took up what would have been the church proper back in the day. Indeed, some of the furniture looked as if it were made from repurposed church pews. An unmade bed sat in the left-hand corner. It appeared Manny lived here too.

Light flowed in through the dirty stained glass, filling the room with an ethereal glow. The room smelled of a not unpleasant mix of machine oil, smoke and a certain type of cigarette. Massive rolls of printing paper lay on either side of the door, along with a selection of random bits of metal, and plastic bottles full of what looked like ink.

At the centre of the room, dominating the space, stood the press. It was an intimidating piece of machinery, with metal arms and pistons, rolls, and all manner of appendages protruding at seemingly random angles. It was made of iron, and in a world of apps and laptops it had a weird feel to it. As if it were the most real thing she had ever been in the presence of. It had been here long before her and it would be here long after she was gone. It clunked away slowly, with a couple of pistons firing and steam sizzling out of one hole. Hannah was considering how the presence of steam must mean water was being used somewhere when Manny appeared from behind the machine.

Thankfully, he was wearing pants today – although that was all he was wearing. Well, underpants and some work boots. The long white dreadlocks wrapped around his neck made his age difficult to guess, as his physique seemed to belong to a younger man. He didn't seem to fit together logically. He was like one of those children's games where you could assemble different head, torso and leg combinations. The underpants might only have been there to give him something to which he could clip his Walkman. It was a proper Walkman too – one that played cassettes. It had been decades since Hannah had seen one of them. It was probably older than Stella, come to think of it.

Manny looked up at the press and ran his hands over it almost affectionately. Feeling oddly embarrassed to be intruding, Hannah paused for a moment before gingerly stepping into his eyeline and giving him a wave.

Manny's eyebrows shot up as he saw her, clearly shocked by her presence. He pulled off his headphones.

'We sorry, lady, we no hear you come in.'

'Sorry. I did knock but you mustn't have . . .' Hannah indicated the headphones. Now she was closer she could hear what sounded like classical music before Manny stopped the tape.

'Aye. We bad.' He had a warm, genial smile.

'No, no problem at all. I just wanted to introduce myself properly. I'm Hannah.' She extended her hand and Manny shook it enthusiastically. She ignored the oil.

'Pleasure to be making your acquaintance. We Manny and such.'

'Right. Yes. This is all . . .' Hannah looked up at the machine towering over them.

'Ya,' said Manny. 'We just giving the old girl a little tune. Keep her running right.'

'I see. Well, I won't disturb you. I just wanted to say hello and— Oh, sorry, I nearly forgot.' Hannah held out the box of doughnuts. 'Would you like one?'

Manny paused to consider this offer, as if he were listening for an answer. 'Yes and no. Me have one but she OK.'

'Right,' said Hannah, trying not to look confused.

Manny took one of the custards. 'We much obliged.' He smiled, put his headphones back on, and turned to stare up at the machine once again.

The morning meeting was proceeding reasonably well. Hannah had managed to get Reggie on the phone beforehand, and the news was better. They'd gone to the dump and found a toilet that matched the exact description the landlord had given them – it had a distinctive mark on it and was easy to verify. Ox had lost the coin toss and had had to go in and get it. Reggie had sent Hannah photos he'd taken of Ox being attacked by two seagulls as he did so. While entertaining in their own right, they did fit in with the story. The man in charge of the dump had told them that weird stuff had been happening all week, and he could well believe the toilet was to blame. He would never have taken it if he'd known it was the toilet from the Jolly Sailor – apparently it was quite the local celebrity.

Surprisingly, Banecroft had listened while Hannah explained all this, then he'd called them back and told them to drop by the local Catholic church and see if the priest might be up for a quick exorcism. 'If they say no, tell 'em you're going to the Protestants. That'll put it right up 'em.'

Then they ran through Hannah's notes from the day before, aka the Loon Day rundown. Throughout the meeting, Grace took notes and Stella wrote things up on the laptop, same as yesterday, while simultaneously reading a book. As Hannah went through her list, Banecroft stared at the ceiling, calling out 'plankton', 'icebox', 'throw-back', 'prawn', and so on. It gave her a thrill as she realized she was going to have articles published in the paper. Surprisingly, she'd not really considered this possibility, and here she was with her very own netful. She'd even got one shark! Banecroft said it was *The Stranger Times*'s duty to expose charlatans, and so later that afternoon Hannah would be trying to get Mrs Bryce of Stockport on the phone to see if she'd go on record to explain how so many people had been Cleopatra in a past life.

Hannah was nearly done when there was a knock on the door that led into reception.

'Go away,' shouted Banecroft. 'Loon Day was yesterday. Come back next month.'

Grace was standing up, about to say something, when the door opened and a short woman with a chestnut-coloured bob walked in.

She held up an ID. 'Excuse me. Sorry to barge in but there's nobody at your reception. I'm Detective Sergeant Wilkerson. I need to speak to the person in charge.'

'Ah,' said Banecroft, rising on to his crutch, 'excellent. Is this about you returning my gun? It's a family heirloom and—'

'No, sir. This is not about a gun.' She gave Banecroft a look. 'It's about one of your employees.'

Automatically, Grace and Banecroft looked at Stella.

'I didn't do nothing!'

DS Wilkerson cleared her throat. 'No, I'm afraid you're misunderstanding. This is about Simon Brush.'

'Oh, for God's sake,' said Banecroft. 'He's not our employee. He can't go around telling people that. This paper is not liable for anything he has done.'

'Would you shut up, Vincent?' snapped Grace, before turning back to Wilkerson. 'Is Simon OK?'

'No, I'm afraid not. He's dead.'

CHAPTER 18

'Dead?'

DS Wilkerson nodded. 'Yes, I'm afraid so.'

Hannah didn't know what to say. She looked around the room. Grace blessed herself, her eyes welling up. Stella looked numb, as if she didn't know how to process the information.

Banecroft sat back in his chair, his eyes fixed on DS Wilkerson. Eventually he cleared his throat. 'Where, exactly, did this happen?'

DS Wilkerson shifted nervously. 'He was found this morning – well, last night, really – at about three a.m. He'd . . . He was . . . He was found at the foot of the Dennard building – that one they're just finishing up on Cheetham Hill. The . . . big one. It appears that he may have . . . come off the roof.'

Grace gasped, her hand to her mouth. Hannah didn't know what to think. It wasn't as if she'd known him – she'd barely met him – but it was such a tragic waste. He could only have been a couple of years older than Stella; not much more than a kid.

Banecroft spoke in a quiet, measured tone. 'And you're sure it's him?'

Wilkerson nodded. 'He had his wallet on him. Also, he was wearing a T-shirt that said "I work for *The Stranger*—"'

Wilkerson broke off as Stella left the room, slamming the door behind her. Grace broke down into tears. Hannah moved over to comfort her, trying very hard not to look at Banecroft as she did so.

DS Wilkerson cleared her throat. 'I'm sorry for your loss – but you say he didn't work here?'

Hannah glanced at Banecroft, whose mouth opened and closed a couple of times, as if trying to decide how to answer. Nothing appeared to be coming. As Grace sobbed on her shoulder, Hannah decided to step in. 'No, I'm afraid he didn't. He wanted to work here. He used to turn up and stand outside.'

'I see,' said DS Wilkerson. 'Still, my boss, DI Sturgess, would like to request that someone from the paper come down to the station and answer a few questions.'

Hannah looked again at Banecroft, who was still staring at the detective.

'How exactly did this happen?' he asked.

'Well, Mr . . .'

'Banecroft.'

'Mr Banecroft, it isn't my place to speculate, but I think the circumstances do rather speak for themselves.'

'Do they?'

Wilkerson elected to ignore the question. 'So, sir, I believe you are the editor. Can you please come with me to answer a few questions? We'll drop you back afterwards, if you like.'

'Right,' said Banecroft. 'Hannah.' He nodded towards his office. 'I just need to take a moment to confer with my assistant editor.'

'Sure.'

Hannah patted Grace on the back. 'Are you . . . ?'

Grace nodded, brushing the tears from her face. 'Sure, I . . .' Her voice dropped to a near whisper. 'Such a young boy.'

Hannah dug a packet of tissues out of her handbag, which Grace took with a brittle smile. As Hannah followed Banecroft, limping in front of her, into his office, she caught the sound of Grace offering DS Wilkerson a cup of tea.

As soon as Hannah was through the office door, Banecroft slammed it behind her.

'Right, this is all a steaming pile of nonsense.'

'Excuse me?'

'This,' said Banecroft. 'This whole threw-himself-off-a-building thing – it's rubbish.'

Hannah looked at him as he hobbled around the office hurriedly, opening drawers and moving piles of books and papers around.

'I don't . . .' She didn't know where to start. 'What are you doing?'

'Doing? I'm looking for the keys to my car. I've not driven the thing in months.' Banecroft started pulling drawers out of his desk and emptying them on to the floor.

'The detective said they'll give you a lift to the station.'

'I'm not going to the station and neither are you.'

He was now kicking the contents of his drawers around the floor, mingling the mess with the other detritus.

'But they said we had to?'

'No, they didn't,' said Banecroft, moving over to his filing cabinet. 'They said they'd like us to. I'd like my staff to treat me with an awed reverence, that doesn't mean they do. The police aren't arresting us, because we haven't done anything wrong.'

'But shouldn't we cooperate with them?'

Banecroft started wresting open the overstuffed drawers of the filing cabinet as he spoke, first to himself and then to Hannah. 'Be under C for car, surely.' He raised his voice slightly. 'And good God, no. We're the free press – with the emphasis on "free". It's our job to make sure they're doing their job, and you heard her, they've clearly already made up their minds. They'll have this filed away by teatime, you see if they don't.'

'But,' said Hannah, 'I don't . . . Do you think it's possible that perhaps . . . y'know, like, the five stages of grief, you're in denial?'

'No. No, I don't. This smells all wrong.'

'Can't we tell them that?'

'Police don't care what we think. Not if we've no proof. Hmmm . . . Not under C for car. How about V for vehicle? . . . No? J for Jag? No.'

'Vincent!' Hannah spoke with such urgency that Banecroft looked up this time.

He fixed her with a glare. 'You can believe what you like, but I know what I know. The last article the lad submitted to us was not very good.'

'There's no need to speak ill of the dead.'

Banecroft shook his head. 'Yet again, you are missing the point entirely. Six months ago he was dreadful, three months ago he was bad – so "not very good" is a massive step up. He was trending upwards. The lad was mustard-keen and I was developing him . . .'

Hannah went to speak but Banecroft cut her off.

'Yes, he was outside. In which time, he'd learned shorthand, taken two online courses and worked on his writing style. Despite appearances to the contrary, I was paying some attention, and I'm telling you, he was not the jumping sort. Maybe I'm wrong, but that's why we need to investigate. One of two things has happened here. Either he's thrown himself off a building or someone has gone to great lengths to make it look like he has.'

Hannah ran her hands through her hair, trying to think this through. 'All right, then. Shall I tell DS Wilkerson we're not coming?'

'Absolutely not. H for hidden!' Banecroft held up a bunch of keys triumphantly.

'But why—'

Banecroft gave an exaggerated sigh. 'We're not telling them we're not coming because then they won't know where we are actually going. The thing about the police is they're very keen on looking into people, but they're not keen on people looking into them.' He tossed Hannah the keys, and she caught them clumsily. 'You're driving, because . . .' He pointed at his foot.

'But,' said Hannah, 'there's a policewoman waiting in reception right now. How are we going to get . . . ?'

In lieu of an answer, Banecroft opened the window to his office. 'First rule of journalism: know how to shimmy down a drainpipe!'

CHAPTER 19

Discounting a crappy marriage, Hannah had never escaped from anything before. Her impromptu departure from *The Stranger Times* building wouldn't be forming the basis of a beloved Christmas Day movie any time soon. She half clambered, half fell down a drainpipe and then served as a human crash mat for her boss, who landed unceremoniously on top of her. Luckily no bones were broken, but several things, not least her pride, took some serious bruising. Ever gallant, Banecroft opined that he regretted not having hired a larger girl.

His car was under a sheet in a sizeable shed behind the church, which was otherwise filled with half-used tins of paint and the kind of items nobody ever used but never threw out, convinced they might come in handy at some point.

As Hannah pulled off the sheet, she was surprised to reveal a large, dark-green Jaguar. It clearly had not been in service for quite some time, yet it was in considerably better nick than anything else Banecroft owned, or indeed Banecroft himself. After a couple of false starts, the engine coughed into life. Banecroft stretched himself out in the back seat, from where he proceeded to bark instructions and unhelpful criticisms as Hannah drove the getaway car.

The Dennard building was a massive, forty-two-storey sky-scraper that towered over the city from its position on Cheetham Hill. Glass stretched up to all but the top few floors, where the exposed girders of the building's skeleton could still be seen. Under Banecroft's snapped instructions, Hannah parked the Jag on the pavement behind a couple of police vehicles, her passenger explaining that nobody who wasn't meant to be there would dare park like that.

The site lay behind a massive chain-link fence. A couple of Por-takabins sat at the far end, surrounded by a lot of men in hard hats who were being paid to drink tea, and several tense-looking people who Hannah guessed would have to explain to the higher-ups exactly how they'd ended up paying quite so many people to do nothing but drink tea. About half a dozen uniformed officers stood guard around a hastily erected tent in the middle of the site, which figures in forensic overalls could be seen walking in and out of. With a jolt, Hannah realized that it must be conceal-ing Simon's body.

As she and Banecroft approached the gate, Hannah looked up at the building, keen to direct her attention elsewhere. She'd seen it before from the bus, but only now she was this close did she realize that its sides were slightly concave, bending inwards from the four corners. And only now she was this close did it hit home how incredibly tall the building was. The thought of how long Simon would have had to watch the ground hurtling towards him popped into her mind, and she really wished it hadn't.

Banecroft stopped in front of the uniformed policeman on duty at the gate – a young lad who Hannah guessed was fairly new on the job. He managed to give off a vibe of being both nervous and bored.

'I'm sorry, sir, the site is closed at the moment.'

'Yes, yes,' said Banecroft, 'it's a crime scene. We are very well aware. DI Sturgess has asked to see us.'

Hannah realized that this was technically true, but barely.

'Well, I . . .'

Banecroft kept moving. 'Is he up on the roof?'

'I, ehm—'

'It's fine,' said Banecroft, pushing through. 'I'll find him myself.'

Hannah gave the PC a smile as she followed her boss. She could see the thought bouncing around the constable's head that what had just happened was possibly going to get him into trouble, but he couldn't say for sure why.

Banecroft made his way across the site, criss-crossed with muddy tracks from heavy machinery. He stopped in the middle of the open area, looked up at the building and then around him.

'Are you sure we're allowed to be here?' asked Hannah. 'I mean . . .'

'The key to life,' said Banecroft, 'is looking and acting like you know exactly what you are doing at all times. Margaret Thatcher said that.'

'Did she really?'

He turned and raised an eyebrow. 'No, but thank you for having proved my point. Now, do you notice anything?'

'Ehm . . . Like what?'

Banecroft shook his head. 'Really? Nothing?'

'Well, I mean . . .' Hannah looked around. With the obvious

exception of the tented forensics area, it looked like a relatively ordinary building site, in Hannah's admittedly limited experience of such places.

'Come on,' said Banecroft. 'I don't have time to hold your hand right now.'

He limped off towards the building. Hannah followed while trying to look as if she was supposed to be there. He was heading straight for where the reception area would be when the construction was finished. Right now, it was nothing more than exposed concrete with plastic sheeting running across it. A female PC stood guard in front of the lifts. She eyed them suspiciously as they approached.

'DI Sturgess,' said Banecroft. 'He asked to see us.'

As he went to press the button to summon the lift, the policewoman moved in front of him. 'Sorry, sir, who are you?'

'Vincent Banecroft. DI Sturgess asked to see me and I'm a very busy man.'

Again, while everything in that sentence was true, the cumulative result was a lie.

The PC looked at the clipboard in her hands. 'I don't have you on the list.'

Banecroft shrugged. 'Then it's not a very good list, is it?'

'And he specifically asked you to meet him upstairs?'

'Of course not,' said Banecroft. 'I've just wandered in here because I'm curious and I've nothing else to be doing.'

'There's no need to take that tone, sir. I'm here to ensure that only people with the correct authorization gain access to this site. You can be as rude as you like, but it won't change that fact.'

Banecroft gave an exasperated sigh. 'Fine. Sorry, officer. Yes, DI Sturgess asked to see us on top of this building ASAP. Your colleague over there' – he waved a hand in the vague direction of the gate they'd come through – 'just rang up and got it confirmed. Feel free to check again if you like, but fair warning, he wasn't exactly thrilled when he got dragged away the last time. Now, would you like us to sign in or not?'

Almost every detail of those last couple of sentences had been an out-and-out lie. The part of Hannah's brain that had been keeping score was now poking the rest of it in an attempt to point out that the likelihood of this ending very badly had just increased. Hannah could see the PC weighing up what Banecroft had said, before begrudgingly presenting him with the clipboard. He scribbled a quick signature on it and handed it to Hannah, who did the same before returning it to the PC with a wan smile. The PC then pressed the button and the middle lift of three opened its doors.

'Take it to the top floor and then go around to the stairs on the left.'

Banecroft nodded as they moved inside.

When the doors had closed, Hannah turned to him. 'Did we just commit a crime?'

'Didn't you set a house on fire there a few weeks ago?'

'What's that got to do with anything?'

'I'm just saying – technically you're on a spree.'

The first thing Hannah noticed up on the roof was the wind. It hadn't felt that windy down below, but up here, with nothing to block its path, it cut right through her. She hadn't brought her coat, mainly because when she'd stepped into her boss's office an hour ago she'd not thought to dress for the possibility of finding herself on top of a skyscraper in the near future.

She and Banecroft nodded and smiled at a few uniformed police as they passed them hastily. They were met with some slightly confused expressions, suspicion clearly battling with 'well, if they weren't supposed to be here, they wouldn't be here'.

Banecroft limped towards the roof edge at the front of the building, with Hannah trailing in his wake. On the ground near the ledge she noticed a yellow numbered sign, presumably there to denote where something had been. Banecroft moved right up to the edge and looked over. Hannah stood a few steps back, and even there she was feeling nauseous.

'Hmmm,' said Banecroft. 'Interesting.'

'Can I help you?'

Hannah turned to face a man in his thirties with thick black hair, sporting a neatly trimmed beard and a cheerful smile.

'No, thank you,' said Banecroft. 'We're here to see DI Sturgess.'

'I see,' said the man. 'And he specifically asked you to come up here, did he?'

'Yes.'

'That seems unlikely' – the man pulled a wallet from his coat pocket and flipped it open – 'seeing as I am DI Sturgess, and you are under arrest for obstructing a constable in the execution of their duty.'

'Oh,' said Hannah.

'Yes,' continued Sturgess. 'Just for starters. You do not have to say anything, but it may harm your defence if you do not mention when questioned something which you later rely on in court. Anything you do say may be given in evidence.'

'Excellent,' said Banecroft, hobbling back towards Sturgess. 'Just one thing before we go.' He patted down the pockets of his coat, seemingly unable to find what he was looking for. Then he looked around them.

'Ah, just the ticket.'

He snatched DI Sturgess's wallet and tossed it off the roof.

Messy Nessie

Following a road accident last week in which six kegs of finest Scottish whisky fell into Loch Ness, watchers have become increasingly concerned about the reported behaviour of its most famous occupant. On Tuesday, a jogger reported seeing a dinosaur-like creature seemingly involved in an altercation with an electricity pylon while sporting a traffic cone on its head.

On Wednesday, Michael Barrymore (no relation), 24, from nearby Inverness, was taking his dog for a walk at 10 p.m. when he returned to the car park beside the loch to discover that Nessie was on top of his VW Beetle.

'He'd mounted me car and was pumping away on it, the dirty bastard. Ye could see the shame on his face while he was doing it too, the toe rag. It's not on, is it? And she's been pulling to the right something shocking since.'

Mr Barrymore's outrage has not prevented him listing the car on eBay where, at the time of writing, bids for 'the car Nessie shagged' have reached £22,500.

On a related note, Miss Irene Willis, who we reported as claiming to have married Nessie three months ago, has issued a statement that 'she is taking some time to consider their relationship after recent events' and is appealing for the press to respect her privacy at this difficult time.

CHAPTER 20

DI Sturgess entered the interview room at Stretford police station to find its occupant fast asleep on the table. He slammed down his folder as loudly as he could and enjoyed the pained expression on his interviewee's face as he reared back into consciousness.

'Ah, Mr Banecroft, I do hope I didn't wake you.'

'Sorry, sorry,' Banecroft said, rubbing his eyes. 'I was having this weird dream where I was suing the Greater Manchester Police for wrongful arrest. Any idea what Tahiti is like this time of year?'

'I wouldn't know,' said Sturgess, sitting down in the chair opposite. 'I'm just a lowly officer of the law, as opposed to you, Vincent Banecroft, former Fleet Street darling. Now, of course, you're the editor of . . .' He held up a copy of *The Stranger Times* from a few weeks previously, the one with 'Zombie Elvis Ate My Hamster' as a headline. 'That must've been quite the fall from grace. I imagine you do need a holiday.'

'Yes,' agreed Banecroft. 'I won't deny I've been through a difficult few years. At one particularly low point I considered joining the police. Can I ask, exactly what charges am I here on?'

'Before we get to that . . .' Sturgess turned on the recorder sitting beside them on the table. 'DI Sturgess interviewing Mr Vincent Banecroft, eleven thirty-eight a.m., March sixth.'

'Excellent,' said Banecroft. 'To repeat the question I just asked, what exactly am I charged with?'

'Let's kick off with obstructing a constable in the execution of their duty to start, but I'd imagine there's a case to be made for adding in wasting police time.'

'Really? Am I the one keeping you locked in this room?'

'Then we can move on to why, after I sent one of my officers to ask you to come in to assist us with our enquiries, I found you trespassing on my closed crime scene less than an hour later.'

Banecroft scratched at his hair energetically. 'Well, I'd imagine it comes down to poor communication skills. I'm sure it's not DS Wilkerson's fault. Maybe you could send her on a course?'

'Thank you – I'll take it under advisement. You're quite the expert in staff development. Speaking of which, could you explain your relationship with Simon Brush?'

'I don't have one.'

'Really?'

'No. He wanted a job working on *The Stranger Times*, I repeatedly and frequently told him he wasn't getting one.'

'And yet, according to his mother' – Sturgess looked down at notes on his pad – 'he turned up to your paper's premises every day. You tortured him – her words – by not letting him join.'

'No,' said Banecroft. 'With all due respect to a grieving mother, nobody tortured anyone. He was very determined to get a job with us.'

'And you delighted in not giving him one?'

'He wasn't good enough. I did monitor the articles he submitted, and if he'd improved, I'd have considered it. His work was getting better.'

'Do you think this constant rejection might have played a role in his death?'

'No.'

'Why not?'

'Call it a hunch.'

Sturgess raised an eyebrow. 'Is this the same finely honed instinct that led you from Fleet Street to' – Sturgess indicated the newspaper sitting on the desk in front of him again – ' "My Vagina Is Haunted"?'

Banecroft gave a tight, humourless smile. 'Speaking of instincts, did you get your wallet back OK?'

'Yes, thank you.'

'Where was it exactly?'

Sturgess casually flipped through his notes. 'About sixty feet due east of where you tossed it – as you'd expect, given a prevailing wind from the west, as there typically is in Manchester, and as there was last night.' He looked up. 'Really? Did you think you were the only person it occurred to that the late Mr Brush's remains were found to the west of the building? That none of us dumb coppers could've figured that out?'

'DS Wilkerson gave us the impression that foul play was not suspected.'

'If she did, that was not her place to do so. It was her job to ask you to come and assist us with our investigation. At this juncture, we have not ruled anything in or out.'

'I'd be inclined to rule out suicide,' said Banecroft.

'Why so? I've gone over it with our SOCOs and they assure me that with a running start and a variable wind . . .'

Banecroft scoffed. 'That is weak. Simon was a lot of things – a sprinter wasn't one of them. And that's at the best of times, not after he'd climbed forty-two floors of skyscraper.'

'How do you know he walked up?'

'None of the lifts in the building are being treated as part of your crime scene.'

'Well, aren't we clever?' said Sturgess.

'*We?* No.'

Sturgess gave a tight smile and leaned back in his chair. 'If you have a better explanation, Mr Banecroft, I'm all ears.'

'I don't, although just because I haven't doesn't mean I'd be inclined to reach for the most convenient and shoddily constructed version of events in order to close a case.'

'Yes,' said Sturgess, 'I know how enamoured you are with the implausible – I've read your paper. I, however, have CCTV footage that shows Mr Brush, alone, sneaking past security and making his way up the stairs to the roof. I've had two officers spend the whole morning going through the recordings from three different cameras covering the lifts and stairs, and the only people who appear on them are a couple of security guards, whose whereabouts we have verified, and the dearly departed Mr Brush. Have you got any theories to explain that away?'

Banecroft shrugged. 'Let's not rule out police incompetence at this early stage.'

Sturgess said nothing for a few moments. He simply looked across the desk at Banecroft, who returned his gaze and smiled.

'What was Simon working on?' asked Sturgess.

'I have no idea.'

'Really?'

'Really.'

'For the record, I'd like to remind you that this interview is being recorded and may be used in evidence.'

'Noted. I would also like it noted that I have not been offered a cup of tea since I've been here.'

Sturgess leaned forward. 'Here's the thing, Vincent – may I call you Vincent?'

'Absolutely not.'

'Here's the thing, Mr Banecroft. I met Simon Brush yesterday at the scene of an unexplained death down in Castlefield, and he identified himself as a reporter for *The Stranger Times*.'

'Is that so? Last week we had a woman come into the office and tell us she was the result of Boris Johnson breeding with the queen of the planet Mucktacki. My point is people can say they're anything – that doesn't make it so.'

'True,' said Sturgess. 'But while I can easily imagine people lying about whether they worked for your publication, it feels very unlikely that someone would do it this way round.'

'Is there a question here or are you just flirting with me?'

'Do you know a John Maguire, also known as Long John?'

'Not that I'm aware of. Who is he?'

'He . . . isn't, not any more. He was the victim in yesterday's unexplained death, although Simon did proffer an explanation.'

'Did he? And what was that?'

DI Sturgess leaned back. 'Seeing as you're being so very helpful,

Mr Banecroft, I think I'll keep that particular piece of information to myself.'

'Well, then, in the spirit of cooperation, how about I give you something and then you can return the favour.'

'That very much depends.'

'Of course,' said Banecroft. 'Have you checked the memory card in Simon's camera?'

'What camera?'

'Interesting,' said Banecroft. 'The camera he wore permanently around his neck. The one he took with him everywhere. It wasn't with the body, was it?'

'No, but then—'

They were interrupted by a knock on the door. DS Wilkerson popped her head around it sheepishly.

Sturgess checked his watch. 'DI Sturgess suspending the interview at eleven forty-one a.m. to speak to DS Wilkerson, who has just entered the room.' He paused the tape. 'Can't it wait, Andrea?'

'Sorry, boss. Mr Banecroft's brief has arrived.'

Sturgess turned back to Banecroft.

'I didn't call a lawyer. I don't have a lawyer, and I certainly don't want some court-appointed shirt-filler, thank you very much.'

'She says she works for the newspaper,' said Wilkerson. 'She's on a retainer or something like that.'

'She?' asked Sturgess. 'It's not . . . ?'

Wilkerson gave the slightest of nods and Sturgess swore quietly under his breath.

'Actually,' said Banecroft, beaming what was meant to be a smile, 'I think I'd quite like to meet this lady, whoever she is.'

Sturgess nodded at Wilkerson, who withdrew from the room.

'I bet you wish you'd given me that cup of tea now,' said Banecroft.

A minute later the door of the interview room opened again and Wilkerson stepped inside, ushering in a woman who was . . . Banecroft wasn't sure what he had been expecting, but this wasn't it.

Sturgess stood up. 'Hello, Ms Carter.'

The new addition to their number stood at maybe five feet tall, and that included a couple of inches of heels. Her blonde hair was cut into a short bob and her oval face was dominated by a smile that hardly left room for much else.

'Hello, Tom – you're looking well. Oh, I see they've still not redecorated in here.'

Her voice was high-pitched and could be considered grating – until you heard her machine-gun warble of a giggle that followed and quickly redefined the term.

She extended her hand to Banecroft while still across the room and then dropped her armful of folders as she approached. 'Oh, clumsy me! What am I like?' She giggled again.

With a roll of his eyes, DI Sturgess assisted Ms Carter in picking up her files.

'Now, Tommy, no reading anything, you naughty boy. There's defences for half the innocent men in Manchester in here – and a few of the guilty ones.'

Her files duly recovered and plonked on the desk, she offered her hand to Banecroft once more. 'Now, let's try that again. Veronica Carter at your service.'

Banecroft shook the woman's hand and attempted a polite smile as she giggled again for no earthly reason that he could fathom. She slipped into the empty chair beside him.

Sturgess turned the tape recorder back on. 'Let the record show that we have been joined by Ms Veronica Carter, who I am informed is counsel for *The Stranger Times* newspaper – is that correct?'

'Yes,' said Ms Carter, 'in large part, although, seeing as it is official, a teeny tiny correction, if you please. It is Dr Carter.'

'Yes, of course,' said Sturgess. 'Dr Carter.'

She gave Banecroft a pally nudge. 'I've got to get that in where I can.' This was followed by an extended remix of the grating giggle. Then she turned to Sturgess. 'Right, so let's kick off with me putting on record that I am appalled that the Greater Manchester Police have now taken to locking up journalists for nothing more than doing their job.'

'Their job does not include lying to the police.'

'Oh, phooey. Come on, now. A little bit of overenthusiasm – it's hardly Watergate.' The giggle made another unwelcome appearance.

'To be fair, Mr Banecroft and Ms Willis are not exactly Woodward and Bernstein. Have you read the publication you are defending?'

'Religiously,' said Carter, without skipping a beat. 'It is a fascinating exploration into the world of the unexplained, and the diverse and colourful beliefs that, as members of a free society, we are allowed to possess. Its very existence is a tribute to the society in which we live.'

'Yes,' said Sturgess, in a way that acknowledged a lot of words had just been spoken.

'And that is the point I will be making to the editor of every newspaper in this country if I do not leave this room in fifteen minutes, accompanied by my client and his associate, wherever she may be.'

'Are you threatening me, Ms Carter?'

'Doctor. And heavens, no, Tommy-Tom-Tom – I would never do that.'

There was another knock on the door.

'Ah,' said Dr Carter, 'perfect timing. That will very probably be DS Wilkerson to tell you your superintendent is on the phone. I rang him on my way here and threatened him.' This unleashed another fit of giggles.

The door opened, but before Wilkerson could say anything, Sturgess had pushed past her, slamming the door behind him.

'Well,' said Dr Carter, 'someone is a real grumpy goose today, isn't he?'

'So,' said Banecroft, 'not that I'm complaining, but you're the lawyer for *The Stranger Times*?'

'Yes.'

'Only . . . I'm the editor and I've never heard of you.'

'Have you needed a lawyer before now?'

'No, but—'

'Well, there you go, then. If it makes you feel better, I'll send you an invite to my firm's Christmas party this year.'

'I don't like parties.'

'Excellent, that'll save us some money on vol-au-vents and cheap plonk.'

The door opened and Sturgess re-entered, looking less than full of the joys of spring. 'Thank you for your time,' he said to the floor. 'You are free to go.'

'Super,' said Dr Carter, picking up her things. 'As always, Tom, lovely to see you. Are you taking care of yourself? You don't look well.'

'Now that you mention it, I do have a splitting headache coming on.'

Dr Carter tutted as she walked by. 'It's all that caffeine you drink – can't be good for you.'

'Thanks, but you're not that kind of doctor, Doctor.'

Banecroft walked past him. 'Inspector, I'm sure I'll be seeing you again.'

'You can count on it.'

Dr Carter stopped. 'Now, Thomas, you big silly billy. I know that wasn't a threat, as you're far too intelligent a man to say such a thing in front of little old me, but you should be careful. Other people don't have my understanding nature.'

'Yes, of course.'

Banecroft started to follow Dr Carter down the hall, but stopped and turned around.

'One more thing, Inspector.'

Sturgess sighed. 'Yes?'

'Simon's bike.'

'What about it?'

'It's locked to the chain-link fence outside of the building site.'

'Thank you for letting us know. I'll make sure it gets returned to his mother.'

'Good. It might be tricky, though. I noticed it earlier, and it's triple-locked. Do you think it's odd that a man intent on killing himself should put three locks on his bike?'

Neither man said anything, but they gave each other a long, hard look.

CHAPTER 21

The silence was weird.

Hannah had worked at *The Stranger Times* for only three days, but she'd never heard the place silent before. It was oppressive.

She'd spent most of the day sitting in a police interview room waiting to be questioned, but she'd been released before it could happen. It wasn't that she'd been looking forward to it – of course she hadn't. There was, however, a tiny part of her that'd been looking forward to getting grilled by DI Sturgess. Her soon-to-be ex-husband hadn't been big into conversations that weren't about him, so Hannah had been excited to spend some quality time with an attractive man who was interested in what she had to say. It was not lost on her how mortifyingly pathetic those thoughts were.

Instead, she had briefly met a short, rather odd woman who was apparently the paper's lawyer, before being instructed to pick up Banecroft's car and head back to the office. She'd managed to reach it just before it got towed but it had a few tickets nonetheless. She had them in her pocket, but it didn't feel like the right time to bring them up.

She'd returned to the office just after Reggie and Ox had got back from Scotland. Grace had rung them to break the news about Simon. Reggie sat at his desk, staring out the window, while Ox paced back and forth like a tiger in a too-small cage.

'Would anyone like another cup of tea?' asked Grace, not for the first time.

'No,' said Ox, 'I don't want a bloody cup of tea!'

Reggie turned in his chair and gave his colleague a pointed look. Their eyes met briefly and Ox looked down at the ground. 'Sorry, Grace, I didn't mean to . . .'

'It is all right, darling. We are all upset.'

Ox shook his head again and went back to pacing in silence.

Stella sat in the corner, staring at her phone, her green hair hanging over her face.

'Do we know when the funeral will be?' asked Reggie.

Grace shook her head. 'I suppose with all the police matters still outstanding . . .'

'Right. Yes. Of course.'

Ox picked up a small green toy alien from his desk and squeezed it, causing it to emit a high-pitched squeal. He looked at it for a minute and then tossed it in the bin.

More silence.

Hannah had never been good with silence. Back in primary school, her teacher had forced the whole class to sit in silence until the culprit confessed to stealing the Kit Kat from Timmy Walsh's lunch box, and she'd ended up doing so in under a minute. She wasn't even guilty – she just couldn't stand the tension. She even found it hard to sleep in silence, preferring to nod off with the TV or the radio burbling away in the background.

She considered the large item on Reggie's desk. 'So, is that the actual toilet?'

'Oh, yes,' said Reggie. 'The pub's landlord identified it. There's a mark on it from where one of his patrons broke a tooth.'

'Right,' said Hannah. 'How did it all go?'

'Well,' said Reggie, looking rather bashful, 'it wasn't the most dignified episode of paranormal investigation, but we did follow' – he nodded towards Banecroft's office – 'his suggestion. The local Catholic priest said no to the exorcism, then he found out the Protestant vicar said yes, and soon we had the two of them all but duelling over it in the pub's function room.'

'Really?'

Reggie nodded. 'Ox got pictures of the whole thing.'

Hannah looked in Ox's direction but he was just standing there, looking out the window, uninterested in the conversation.

'It ended up with the two men coming to blows, both sides claiming the other threw the first headbutt. It was terribly undignified. Then there was the throwing of some fried food. All in all, it was the most Scottish thing imaginable.'

'It sounds like it'll make a good article.'

'Yes,' said Reggie, without much enthusiasm. 'I'm sure he' – another nod in the direction of Banecroft's office – 'will be pleased. I mean, not that he's ever actually pleased about anything.'

'Where the hell *is* Banecroft?' This was from Ox, and the question was directed towards Hannah, despite her having no new information since the last time he had asked.

She shrugged. 'I don't know. Him and that lawyer woman left at the same time I did. One of the officers was nice enough to drive me to the car, but I . . . I assumed he'd be here when I got back.'

Reggie made a huffing noise. 'Odds-on the lush headed straight for the nearest public house.'

'Yeah,' said Ox. 'He's probably too ashamed to show his face.'

Hannah went to say something but thought better of it.

Where Banecroft was at that exact moment in time was about one hundred yards away, sitting uncomfortably in the passenger seat of a canary-yellow sports car. Dr Carter had offered to take him to lunch, which he had refused, then to the pub, which, somewhat to his own surprise, he had also refused. Then she had taken him to a drive-through coffee place, which he had also tried to refuse, but was given no option. He now had a coffee called something in Italian, which had cost more than a flight to Italy.

They were now parked on Mealy Street. Banecroft wanted to return to the office but his lawyer wanted to chat. He had tried to get out of the car, but it appeared she had engaged some form of child lock on the doors.

Banecroft didn't like lawyers – even those who'd got him released from assisting the police with their enquiries. Lawyers were very good at telling you what you couldn't do, and Banecroft was not very good at being told what he couldn't do. He was also a couple of proper drinks and several cigarettes away from the closest he came to normality, and he was irritable – or rather, more irritable than usual. If he had to put his irritability down to one thing, he'd have plumped for Dr Carter's giggle.

As if on cue, she did it again. Banecroft had no idea what she was laughing at. It didn't seem to matter.

'So,' she said, turning in her seat, 'we need to . . .' She paused and started looking around. 'Oh my God, do you think people think we're doing it?'

'What?'

'Every time I pass two people in a parked car, I wonder if they're doing it. I wonder if other people, passing us now, think that's what we're doing.' It turned out supposed embarrassment raised the giggle an octave. It was no improvement.

'No.'

'We could be.'

'No, we couldn't.'

'Oh, come on, now. You've got this whole gruff I-don't-care-what-I-look-like thing going on – some women go for that.'

Banecroft paused for a moment. 'Yes, actually I meant in this car. Seeing how incredibly uncomfortable it is to sit in, I can't imagine two individuals getting up to anything else. Given the available space, it would be a struggle for one individual to get up to anything else.'

Dr Carter gave Banecroft a playful slap on the shoulder. 'Hehe-hehehe. You! I've decided I like you.'

'I'm thrilled.' Banecroft tried the door again.

'So, we can't spend all day flirting. We need to discuss the case.'

'Oh, goody.'

Dr Carter pulled what she no doubt considered a serious face. 'Here's the thing: you can't go anywhere near this investigation. You must let the police go about their business.'

'We're the press. Everyone else's business is our business.'

Dr Carter ran a finger up and down the arm of Banecroft's over-coat. 'Oh, come now. You're not that kind of press.'

He gave the lawyer his best glower.

'Oh, look at Mr Grumpy Face.'

From the way Dr Carter pulled back, in what little room was available, perhaps even she realized that the cutesy pet name might have been a mistake.

'I am the editor of a newspaper, and as long as that remains the case, we will not ignore the news. And this – whatever it is – has the smell of news about it.'

Dr Carter nodded. 'I'm just saying that maybe there's a combin-ation of factors here – guilt, maybe wanting a little of your old life back – and you're trying too hard to see something that isn't there. A young man went up to the roof of a building alone and then . . . It's a tragedy, certainly, but what it isn't is a story.'

'I decide what is and isn't a story. To be clear, are you telling me to kill the story?'

'Well, I wouldn't put it in those exact terms, but—'

'In that case, let me put my response in crystal-clear terms. I do not kill stories.' Banecroft looked out the windscreen, watching the soft rain that had begun to fall. 'I am the editor of this news-paper until Mrs Harnforth says otherwise. Until that time, I will run it as I see fit. Now open this damn door.'

Dr Carter sighed. 'It's not locked – you just need to push it then pull it.'

Banecroft did as she suggested and the door popped open. He awkwardly grabbed his crutch from the back seat – narrowly avoiding catching Dr Carter as he did so and risking a lawsuit from his own brief – and then he was out.

Dr Carter watched him half stomp, half hobble through the steadily building rain. She pressed a button on the car's centre console to speed-dial a number. It was picked up on the second ring.

'We may have a problem,' she said. 'Another problem.'

'Thanks.'

Although she didn't want it, Hannah accepted another mug of tea from Grace. The mood in the room hadn't exactly improved, but the tension had at least eased somewhat. In the absence of anything else to do, Reggie had begun writing up his notes and Grace had given Stella some petty cash figures to put into a spreadsheet, a request that was met with only minimal grumbling.

Reggie sat down beside Hannah and spoke in a hushed voice. 'I feel weird pointing this out but . . . well, we keep an eye on unusual deaths and all because . . . well, we do.'

'Right,' said Hannah, wondering where this was heading.

'This – as in poor Simon – has happened before. That building – somebody . . .' Reggie looked uncomfortable saying it. 'Y'know . . .' He lowered his voice to a whisper. 'Someone jumped off it a couple of weeks ago.'

'Oh,' said Hannah, unsure what to make of that.

'Yes, I don't know if—'

Reggie was interrupted by a thumping noise coming from reception. The doors to the bullpen flew open and in clomped a soggy Banecroft.

'Bloody Manchester with its shitty weather.'

'One,' said Grace, as if on autopilot.

'God damn it, Grace – that was almost entirely a statement of fact.'

'Two.'

Banecroft mumbled something under his breath, safely out of even Grace's bat-like hearing range. Then he noticed the toilet on the spare desk. 'Ah, excellent. First things first, I take it this is the demon loo of Falkirk?'

It was only then that Ox wheeled around from looking out the window. 'Really?' His voice seemed to chill the room; the edge to it was unmistakable. 'That's the first thing, is it? That's the important thing we need to talk about? Some shitty toilet from shitty Falkirk we got for your shitty front page?'

'Ox,' said Grace, 'do not—'

'No, no,' said Banecroft. 'If he has something he feels he needs to say, let him say it.'

Ox took a few steps towards Banecroft. 'If I have something I need to say? Me? You hypocritical son of a . . . I'm not the one who tortured that kid—'

Reggie got to his feet but Ox waved him away. 'No, it needs saying. Leave off.' He pointed an accusing finger at Banecroft. 'You treat all of us like . . . Whatever. But that kid, he was a good lad.' Ox held out his hands. 'He was a good lad. He bloody loved this paper. It was his dream. This – this crappy, stupid paper – was his dream. And you took it away from him.'

Banecroft stopped, as if considering Ox's words for a moment, and then spoke in a confident voice. 'Crap.'

Reggie, Grace and Hannah all tried to stop him, but Ox charged at Banecroft, tackling him messily against the wall and sending them both tumbling to the ground.

Ox scrambled to his knees, his fist raised over the supine figure of Banecroft. Grace reached him first and grabbed his arm. Its momentum dragged her forward, causing her to trip over him and stumble clumsily to the floor.

Ox attempted to pull his hand free to get to Banecroft.

'Ox Chen, stop it this instant!' bellowed Reggie.

Hannah rushed over to check on Grace, who had banged her head on the way down.

Reggie stood between Ox and Banecroft. 'Our friend is dead and this is no way to honour his memory. Get back on your feet immediately.'

Ox, his breath coming in ragged pants, glowered at Banecroft, but he stood up begrudgingly. The anger fell from his face as he looked at Grace. 'Ah, jeez, Grace. I'm sorry, I—'

'It is all right,' she interrupted. 'No harm done. Reginald, take him home. Stella, come on – we are going as well.' Grace took Hannah's hand and got to her feet.

Banecroft lay sprawled on the floor. He spoke in what, for him, was a relatively quiet voice. 'We still have a paper to put out.'

'And we will catch up tomorrow,' said Grace, with more force than she perhaps intended. 'Nothing is getting done tonight.'

Banecroft made as if to speak but, unusually for him, heeded a warning glance from his office manager and didn't.

Hannah patted Grace's arm. 'Are you sure you're OK?'

'I am fine.'

'I really am——' started Ox.

'Forget about it. If you like, you two can drop me and Stella home. I know it is only around the corner, but I forgot to bring an umbrella with me.'

'Of course,' said Reggie.

They grabbed their coats from the hooks on the wall and walked to reception in silence, while Banecroft remained on the floor.

Hannah offered him her hand but he waved her away. Instead, he raised his voice loud enough to be heard by the four figures making their way down the stairs.

'Tomorrow, eight a.m. – editorial meeting!'

I Wax to Suck Your Blood

The proprietors of the Wacky World of Wax museum in Merthyr Tydfil have been left mystified by a series of bizarre attacks. Manager Glenys Davies, age undisclosed, said they first noticed something strange a few weeks ago.

'We kept getting called out with the alarm going off, thinking we'd had a break-in – only nothing was ever taken. After a while, we thought it was a fault, only the alarm company said it never was. Then our Gareth noticed some damage to one of the waxworks. Margaret Thatcher had peculiar indentations on her neck that looked like they might be teeth marks. To be honest, she's taken a lot of damage over the years – including an excrement-throwing incident that was very unpleasant. We laughed it off at first but then we found similar marks on the necks of Prince Harry, Tim Henman and Judi Dench. I mean, Judi Dench! Who doesn't like her?'

While police struggled to come up with an explanation, local 'paranormal investigator' Rhodri Halverson was far less reticent. 'Clearly what we're dealing with is someone who is having vampiristic urges and who is trying to assuage them by biting waxworks. Y'know, like people try and give up smoking by sucking on one of them fake ciggies.'

Ms Davies for one thinks Halverson might be on to something. 'It does seem like somebody is having a bite. They keep doing it too – we'd another break-in last week and this time it looks like they had a go on David Beckham. Whoever it was left Posh alone, which probably makes sense – there'd not be much eating in her.'

Staff have speculated that whoever the culprit is, they seem to be combining vampirism with Welsh nationalism as all of the waxworks attacked to date have been English.

CHAPTER 22

'Large white wine, please.'

The blond barman gave her a wide, customer-service smile. 'Sure. We've got Pinot Grigio—'

'Yeah, anything.'

The smile fell a bit. 'Right.'

DS Andrea Wilkerson had never drunk in here before; it wasn't her kind of place. She generally didn't go for Manchester's swanky wine-bar circuit, preferring the kind of proper pubs coppers typically frequented. The reason she wasn't in one of those establishments right now was because she really needed a drink and she was avoiding other coppers. It had been a properly crappy day and she did not want company. Still, this bar wasn't exactly in her comfort zone; she'd bet good money it was one of those places that gave you your change on a little tray, so you looked like a tightarse if you dared pick up the coins.

DI Sturgess had given her a proper bollocking. During her time on the murder squad, she'd worked mostly with DI Clarke and only occasionally with Sturgess. He wasn't a barrel of laughs at the best of times, but this was the first time she'd really seen him go nuclear, and it hadn't been pretty. To be fair, as much as she hated to admit it, he had not been wrong – she had made a pig's ear of the Simon Brush thing. As Sturgess had told her, at a volume loud enough for half the station to hear, when an investigation was ongoing it was not her job to speculate to witnesses as to what had happened.

Fair enough, but with anybody else in charge of the investigation – bloke goes to the top of a tall building alone and comes down the quickest way imaginable – it would've been an open-and-shut case. The conclusion she'd come to wasn't exactly a leap – no pun intended. DI Clarke would've rubber-stamped it and taken an early lunch. That was bad enough. For the witness she had been sent to collect to do a bunk out a window and then turn up in the middle of the crime scene – that had been a lot worse.

The blond and his grin came back with her large wine. 'Here we go.'

Wilkerson started to fish in her coat pocket for her purse.

'You can settle up now, or start a tab if you like?'

She looked at the wine and then back up at the pretty-boy grin. 'Tab, please.'

He turned the wattage of the smile up another notch. 'No problem. Wine o'clock, is it?'

God, she really hated people who said 'wine o'clock'.

She took a drink and looked down at her phone. When she raised her head again, the grin had taken the hint and gone back to the other end of the bar where it was busier and, presumably, there was a more receptive audience for his flirty little act. He wasn't her type. Not for a minute did she think she was his either. He was just flashing those baby blues at any woman who walked in, in the hope of scoring some tips.

Wilkerson tended to go for men who didn't take longer than her to get ready and who were also quite good at leaving quickly once they were. She preferred her own company most of the time, which was why she'd made the error of hooking up with married men in the past. That phase was over. Once you'd opened the door to your flat on a Sunday morning to a wronged woman and her two snotty-faced kids, whatever misplaced thrill there'd been soon turned sour.

She took another large sip of her wine. One of the main reasons she was avoiding the usual coppers' pubs was that news of Sturgess's latest meltdown would no doubt have got around, and there would be a queue of sympathetic souls eager to slag him off. He was not a popular man. Most everybody considered him to have serious tickets on himself, thinking he was too good to rub shoulders with the rank and file.

The thing was, he was right. Wilkerson was extremely unimpressed by a lot of what she'd witnessed since she'd joined the force. And when she'd made detective, she'd been further disappointed that the sloppiness and stupidity she had seen while in uniform were still evident further up the chain. It was by no means universal, but there were still a lot of people like DI Clarke who were happy to simply follow the path of least resistance. Sturgess was a perfectionist, and while that made him unpopular, it didn't make him wrong.

Coppers often dealt with people who were having the worst days of their lives. That deserved somebody's best, not just, 'Yeah, it's everywhere. These things almost never get solved. Please fill out this form saying we turned up.' On the rare occasions she'd been assigned to Sturgess, Wilkerson had pretended to be disappointed, but in reality she had been delighted. She wanted to be the best. And, besides, whether giving orders or a bollocking, at least Sturgess managed to do so while looking her in the eyes, as opposed to other senior officers, whose gazes tended to drift a bit further south.

'Hi there.'

Wilkerson looked up to see a Danny DeVito lookalike, complete with the Yank accent, hopping on to the stool beside her.

Oh great. She nodded and took another drink.

'So, what's good here?'

She shrugged. 'I dunno. Never been here before.'

'Me neither. I've only recently arrived in Manchester.'

'Great. Look, no offence, but I've had a hell of a day and I just fancy a quiet drink.'

He nodded and touched his index finger to his nose. 'Gotcha. Say no more.' He mimed locking his lips and throwing away the key.

'Thanks. Sorry.'

The grin turned up and the newcomer ordered a Jack Daniel's and Coke, which arrived promptly. He gave a big tip. Maybe he was hoping to bang the barman.

He took a sip of his drink. 'So, what do you do?'

Wilkerson gave an exasperated sigh. 'Really? You thought you'd try again?'

'Hey' – he gave her a wide smile – 'I'm very engaging company when you get to know me.'

'Let me save you some time, fella. I'm never ever, ever going to sleep with you. I know you probably figured coming over to merry old England with your Yankee Doodle accent would make you somehow exotic or exciting and you'd suddenly be catnip for the ladies, well, I'm afraid not. We've got annoying little short-arsed slapheads over here already – we don't need to import them.'

Not that she'd been thinking this far ahead, but she would have expected him to be either embarrassed or angry. Instead, he just kept on smiling at her.

'Relax, I'm not trying to sleep with you.'

'Good to know.'

'I mean, I could if I wanted to.'

Wilkerson gave a mirthless laugh. 'I really doubt that.'

He took a sip of his drink while casually glancing around the bar. 'If I wanted to, you'd have no choice.'

Wilkerson's eyes widened and her voice came out as an irate hiss. 'What did you just say?'

'You heard me.'

She shoved her hand into her pocket, pulled out her wallet and flipped it open to her police ID card. 'Say it again.'

He reached his hand inside his own pocket and pulled out a gold coin. As he spoke, he twirled it between his index finger and thumb, showing a bird on one side and an upside-down pyramid on the other. 'I know you're a police officer. In fact, I followed you here from the station.' He dropped the coin and let it dangle from a silver chain. 'You see, we need to talk.'

Wilkerson was possessed by the strong urge to punch this arse-hole in the face. 'Stalking a police officer? Are you out of your tiny mind?'

With a twist of his wrist he started the coin spinning. 'Almost certainly, but not in the way you imagine. But first, this works better when you're emotional. So you need to focus all that anger here . . .'

Moretti watched Wilkerson's eyes as they focused on the coin. Then he saw the tell-tale sag in the eyelids and he knew he was in. He stopped the coin spinning and quickly slipped it back inside his pocket. He surreptitiously glanced around the bar again and noticed the concerned expression on the barman's face as he watched from the far end.

'OK,' he said to Wilkerson, 'now you need to give me a big, warm smile.'

She did.

'Throw in a hearty laugh . . .'

She did.

From the corner of his eye, Moretti saw the barman relax and rejoin the conversation he'd been having.

'That's right. I'm a funny, funny guy.'

'You're a funny, funny guy,' Wilkerson repeated.

'And for the record, I could have you do anything I wanted you to, but I have neither the time nor the energy. In fifteen minutes, you will walk out of here and all you will remember is having a quiet drink all on your own. But before that, you're going to tell me everything about your investigation into the body in Castlefield and the guy who jumped off the building.' Moretti took another sip of his drink. 'Because, sweetheart, you ain't never met a short-arsed slaphead quite like me.'

CHAPTER 23

Gary Merchant didn't mind the feeling of the rain pelting down on his skin. It felt good. It felt like he was somehow still himself. His clothes were soaked through – not that it mattered. On the street below, traffic whooshed by – people rushing to get home where it was dry. Up here in the darkness, the lights from all the windows made him all but invisible. Besides, nobody ever really looks up.

He'd managed to walk through the security simply by acting like he was meant to be there. The guard had clocked him and then looked away. It was the beast. Even when Gary was still himself, the beast still was there. Others could sense it. No minimum-wage hospital security guard was going to get in his face. From there, he'd found the door to the roof and made his way up the stairwell. If the last few days had taught him any-thing, it was that true power meant the normal conventions of society didn't apply to you. The rules were there only for those willing to obey them.

Only, if he was truthful, he wasn't himself any more. He could feel it taking him over. He couldn't control the beast. He'd done things now, things he couldn't come back from. It had always been part of the deal. He would have to do some bad things, but he didn't care about any of it – only Cathy. As long as he could save her then his whole sorry life would mean something.

When he'd woken up this morning, back in his human form, he had remembered the night before – when, as the beast, he had hunted rats in the warehouse – and he'd thrown up, repulsed by the memory. Inside, the beast had roared. It did not like to be judged. It had no conscience. It was just the beast and it was getting stronger. Strangely, that had bothered him more than the killing. Maybe it was his training coming through.

The blinds of the room on the fifth floor of the building opposite were open because Cathy liked to look at the view, even when there wasn't much to see bar other buildings and rain – lots and lots of rain. Gary watched as Tina came into the room carrying one of those magazines full of pop stars and make-up tips that Cathy liked to read. His wife showed it to their little girl, trying to get her interested in it, but she just glanced at it briefly and closed her eyes again. He saw that look on Tina's face, as another little piece of her heart broke. He had seen that too often. He had sat there opposite, unable to do anything about it.

Not now.

Now he could do something. He had made his deal with the devil. He would do all that Moretti asked and Moretti would save Cathy. Gary knew now, with a cold certainty, that soon he would no longer exist. Soon the beast would take over and Gary's life, to all intents and purposes, would be gone. He didn't mind. It was a sacrifice any parent would make in a heartbeat. His little girl would be all right and maybe Tina would know that she hadn't made a mistake in marrying him after all.

A surge of pain ran through Gary's body, causing him to crumple to his knees. It was time. The beast had work to do.

CHAPTER 24

Logically, Hannah knew, rain was rain.

She'd been caught in countless storms on several different continents, and the essentials were cast in stone. Laws of nature. It was drops of water falling from the sky at a certain rate. They would be angled in a certain direction due to prevailing winds. They'd be a certain temperature due to . . . something. There was probably a formula involving atmospheric temperature, humidity, windspeed and other stuff. The point was, rain worked in a certain way. It was definable and measurable.

Not Manchester rain. For a start, predicting it was beyond the capacity of meteorological science. She had been naive enough to believe the weather forecast this morning, which was why she had left the house without an umbrella. The rain also seemed to be falling in every direction at the same time, seeing as no matter which way she turned, it beat against her face.

It also appeared sentient in its malevolence. At least she was wearing a coat. It was still England in March and she hadn't been that much of a fool. And yet, despite having it fully buttoned up, water had inexplicably found its way inside. It crawled down her neck, up her sleeve, reaching parts of her that raindrops falling from the sky should simply not be able to. This was how Hannah found herself standing at a bus stop, utterly drenched and utterly miserable, staring balefully into the distance, looking for a bus that was seemingly never coming.

And to think, the day had started so well. She had got out of bed that morning full of beans, determined to grab life by the throat. Now she just wanted to crawl back between the sheets and never leave. Simon's death had been shocking. She had only met the poor guy twice, but he'd been brimming with energy and enthusiasm. It was hard to process the idea that while she'd been tucked up in bed last night, he had been throwing himself off a forty-two-storey building. It didn't make sense.

She had found a soaking-wet copy of the *Evening News* on the ground at the bus stop: an improvised temporary shelter that had been cast aside by some lucky sod whose bus had shown up. She tried to read it even as the sodden paper fell apart in her hands.

Simon's death, added to the suicide that had happened there a couple of weeks before, had led to dark mutters that the Dennard building was cursed. Its owners had issued a statement expressing shock and giving assurances that their security would be stepped up yet again. There was a barely disguised subtext of 'everybody is getting fired'.

If Simon's actions were incomprehensible, then arguably Banecroft's didn't make a great deal more sense. His automatic assumption that the police were the enemy had been odd. Hannah had been brought up always to respect the police. The ones who had dealt with her after her entirely accidental act of arson against her own house had been very nice about it. Though trying to explain what had happened there had been mortifying. She wondered if Banecroft's insistence that things were not as they seemed was born out of a sense of guilt. Had he pushed a fragile young man too far? It was impossible to say. After all, nobody can ever really know what is going on in someone else's mind.

And yet, if you looked at it in a certain way, maybe Banecroft did have a point: the triple-locked bike, the peculiar location in which the body was found, and the absence of Simon's camera, which Grace had said she hadn't seen him without for months. Perhaps it was all wishful thinking, but it at least gave the impression of it not being quite as open-and-shut as it first appeared. None of that changed the biggest fact of all, though: Hannah had been informed by DS Wilkerson that they had CCTV footage that showed conclusively Simon entering the building and walking up all of those flights of stairs entirely alone. That was hard to argue with.

A Ford Granada pulled in to the bus stop and its passenger-side window began to lower. Oh God, not again. A man had done the same thing earlier. Trying to be helpful, Hannah had leaned in to explain that she didn't know the area and would be of no help with directions. The man had avoided eye contact as he'd spoken to his own steering wheel.

'Are you working?' he'd asked.

Odd question, she'd thought.

'Yes, thank you.'

'What do you do?'

'Ehm . . . I'm a journalist.'

He had slammed the car into gear and driven off so quickly

that Hannah had barely managed to pull back her foot to stop it from getting run over. It was only as she watched the car's brake lights flare in the distance that she realized what the conversation had been about. She wouldn't have thought it possible to feel even more miserable, but there it was. Grim.

This time Hannah looked off into the distance and ignored the window as it whirred down. She'd have to find another bus stop, one that was less – well, whatever you could call this.

'Would you like a lift?'

Hannah took a step further back and kept her gaze firmly fixed on the horizon, which was remaining stubbornly bus-less.

'Ms Willis?'

Hannah ignored that too, for a couple of seconds. Truth be told, she had been Mrs Drinkwater for so long that Willis didn't instantly register as being her name. When it did, she lowered her head tentatively to see DI Sturgess leaning over and looking at her from the driver's seat.

'Oh God,' said Hannah. 'Sorry. I thought you were . . .'

'What?'

'Never mind.'

'Would you like a lift?'

Hannah felt drops of rain fall off her head as she shook it. 'No, thank you.'

'Look, it's chucking it down cats and dogs. C'mon, I'll drop you home.'

'I see,' said Hannah, stepping forward to look in the window. 'And you just happened to be passing, did you?'

'No. No, I wasn't. I've just come back from seeing Simon Brush's mother and I was about to swing by your office on the off-chance you might still be there. I was hoping you'd be more reasonable than your boss.'

'Well, at least you're honest.' Hannah had to shout over the rain, which, against all probability, appeared to be getting heavier. 'How was she? Simon's mother?'

Sturgess shrugged. 'Bad. I mean, when are they not in this situation? Her husband died several years ago, so it was just the two of them.'

Hannah shut her eyes. 'Oh God.'

'Yes. She's not a massive fan of your paper, I'm afraid.'

Hannah wasn't sure what to say to that. Luckily she was saved from trying by the sight of the 46 bus rounding the corner in the distance. She pointed at it. 'Thanks for the offer, but I'm fine. You're blocking the bus stop, Inspector.'

He glanced in his mirror and nodded. 'OK, if you're sure.'

He pulled away and Hannah stuck out her thumb. Two minutes later, she was still there with her thumb out as the number 46 bus, packed with commuters, went by. It didn't even bother to slow down. Instead, it hit a rather large puddle as it sped past, sending up a thick spray of water to drench any bit of her that by some miracle was still dry.

Everyone has a breaking point – Hannah had just reached hers. She screamed after the bus, a formless expulsion of rage, pain and frustration that could probably keep a Master's course in psychology busy for a whole semester. When she finally ran out of air, she kicked the bus stop, which only had the effect of sending pain shooting through her foot. She put her hands around the metal post and summoned all her strength in an effort to pull it out of the ground. The thing was infuriatingly sturdy.

She looked up when a car horn honked loudly. Only then did she notice DI Sturgess's car, pulled up exactly where it had been before. Hannah's whole body sagged, her humiliation complete.

He wound down the window again. 'It would appear your bus did not stop.'

'No kidding.'

'Would you like a lift?'

She closed her eyes again. It felt somehow disloyal, in ways she couldn't express coherently.

'If it helps,' said Sturgess, 'we could say I'm arresting you for attempting to vandalize a bus stop?'

'Super,' said Hannah, moving across and opening the passenger door. 'Just what I need: something else to add to my ever-growing rap sheet.'

He hurriedly tossed the folders that were occupying the passenger seat into the back as she got in. Her feet crunched on the collection of empty Diet Coke cans that occupied the footwell.

'Oh, sorry.'

'It's fine. Just drive.' Hannah caught herself. 'I mean . . . Sorry. Hell of a day. Thank you for, y'know . . .'

'Not a problem. You should probably tell me where you live?'

She did. Sturgess turned the car's heater to high and pulled out into traffic.

Hannah caught a quick look at herself in the visor mirror and winced. The phrase 'drowned rat' came to mind.

'So . . .' said Sturgess, after a couple of minutes during which

Hannah had tried to do what she could to look less like she'd been hauled ashore in a net. 'How are you enjoying Manchester?'

'Well,' said Hannah, suddenly aware of the Mancunian twang to his accent. 'It's very . . . different.'

'I see. Where did you live before?'

'London, on and off, and Dubai.'

'Oh right,' said Sturgess. 'Yeah, that'd be a big change all right. What made you decide to move up here after—'

Sturgess stopped abruptly, aware he'd put his foot in it.

'After I accidentally burned down my own house while trying to get my melodramatic revenge on my cheating bastard of a husband?'

'Sorry.'

'It's not your fault. You're one of the few people on the planet he didn't sleep with.' She glanced across at him. 'I mean, I'm making a big assumption there.'

'No,' said Sturgess. 'He's definitely not my type.'

'OK.'

Hannah looked out the window, watching a few brave souls trying to hurry through the downpour.

'Oh God, sorry,' said Sturgess. 'I didn't mean to sound homophobic. I meant your husband wasn't my type because he was a City boy, not . . .'

'It's all right,' Hannah said with a smirk. 'I knew what you meant.'

Sturgess's steely countenance slipped and he looked embarrassed. It was a good look on him.

'I'm tenth generation Manc,' he said. 'I've got a hereditary chip on both shoulders.'

'So is that why you joined the police? Hoping for a shot at locking up some fat cats?'

'If it was, I'd be sorely disappointed. Our system is set up to only really catch the—'

Hannah's coughing fit interrupted him. Great, now she might be getting sick too.

'That doesn't sound too good. Do you need a drink?'

Without looking, Sturgess reached into the back seat and held out a can of Diet Coke to her.

'No, thanks. I'm OK.' She looked down at the empty cans that crunched beneath her feet. 'Bit of a fan of Diet Coke, I see?'

He placed the can in the drink holder in the central column. 'Yeah, you could say that. I've got some painkillers too, if they're any good to you?'

He flipped open the compartment in the middle of the console and Hannah was greeted with a mini pharmacy's worth of tablets.

'Bloody hell.'

'I get some killer migraines.'

'You've got half the drugs in Manchester in there.'

'Yeah. Luckily I know a couple of guys on the drug squad. They sort me out.'

Her eyes widened.

He pulled up at a set of traffic lights and glanced across at her. 'That was a joke.'

'Right.'

Their eyes met and she smiled awkwardly. Oh God, were they flirting now? The man had arrested her a few hours previously.

She looked out the window again: a woman was dragging a wheeled shopping bag with one hand and a kid in a parka with the other. The child was jumping in puddles happily, the only person in a several-mile radius who seemed to be enjoying their life.

'So,' said Sturgess, 'your boss seems to be quite the character.'

'Seamless segue,' said Hannah.

'I'm not known for my subtlety.'

'Good, because if that was considered a real strength of yours, then you'd be in big trouble.'

Sturgess pulled a left turn into the estate where Maggie's house was situated.

'Why do you think he's so convinced that Simon Brush didn't commit suicide?'

'I don't know that he is. I think he was more annoyed that the police immediately assumed that he had.'

Sturgess sounded offended. 'For the record, that is not the approach I am taking, and this is my investigation.'

'Right. Good to know.'

'What does your boss think happened?'

'I'm afraid you'll have to ask him that.'

'I tried. It didn't go terribly well.'

He pulled up outside Maggie's house and turned off the engine.

'Well, you could always try again. Maybe give him his gun back – that might win him over.'

Sturgess pulled a face.

'Thanks for the lift – I appreciate it. Sorry about soaking your car.'

'It's fine.'

She gave him a tight smile and went to open her door.

'I met him, you know.'

Hannah turned. 'Who? Banecroft?'

'No. Simon. Yesterday, at the scene of an unexplained death down in Castlefield. I probably could've been nicer to him.'

Hannah lowered her voice. 'You weren't to know.'

Sturgess gave a brief nod. 'He was . . . He said he worked for you – the paper, I mean. He had a fairly wild theory about the death. He claimed he'd got a witness. Someone who had seen a . . .'

Sturgess looked away again.

'A what?'

'Stupid as it sounds, he said they'd seen a "creature".'

'Right. What sort of creature?'

'I mean, it's nonsense, obviously.'

Hannah nodded. 'OK.'

'Only, well, whoever that witness is, maybe they know something – about the other death, or Simon's. I need to know what he was working on.'

Hannah sighed. 'Look, honestly – he really didn't work for the paper and I don't think anyone had any idea what he was up to.'

'Fair enough.' Sturgess pulled a card from the inside pocket of his suit and scribbled something on the back of it. 'Here's my card. My personal mobile number is on the back. You think of anything, day or night, you ring me.'

Hannah took it and looked at it. 'Right.'

She tucked it into her coat pocket and turned to go again.

She was half out of the car when Sturgess spoke again. 'Do you believe in it?'

'Excuse me?'

'All the, y'know, the stuff in your paper. The supernatural stuff.' He said the word 'supernatural' like he expected it to be met with derision.

'Well,' said Hannah, 'I don't know. I mean, bits of it, maybe. To be honest, I've worked there three days. I've never really thought about this stuff.'

'Right. Yeah.'

'Do you?'

He left a pause long enough that Hannah was wondering if he was going to answer at all. She nodded and finished getting out of the car, finding that the rain had eased off to a downpour.

'I don't . . .'

She bent her head slightly and looked down into the car, the rain pitter-pattering on the vehicle's roof.

Sturgess turned to her. 'I've seen a lot of weird stuff in this job. I could tell you some stories.'

'I'd like to hear them.' Hannah blushed at the way that sounded.

Sturgess opened his glove compartment and took out a bottle of pills. 'Yeah, maybe. You'll have to excuse me – I think I've got one of my headaches coming on.'

CHAPTER 25

Vera Woodward awoke with a start.

The room was dark, and although it wasn't silent, it was filled with a sound she had come to expect after thirty-two years of mostly happy marriage. She turned and looked at Declan, who was snoring away contentedly, wrapped in the cloak of deep sleep. She had friends who had been driven to distraction by their partners' snoring. They'd tried all manner of earplugs on themselves, and chin straps, mouth guards and vibrating pillows on their partners in the vain hope of getting a decent night's sleep.

Vera had just got used to it. In fact, she sort of liked it. It meant she knew where he was. Vera was one of life's great worriers. If she had her way, their two girls would sleep in the same room too, then she'd know where they were as well. She and Declan had been told they could never have children – and then their two miracles had arrived. People who thought happiness and worry didn't go hand in hand had never been parents.

One of the rare serious rows she and Declan had had in those thirty-two years was when he'd forced her to take the baby monitor out of the girls' room when they were six. They were fourteen now, and last year Declan had caught her looking on the internet at those teddy bears you could hide cameras in. He laughed that laugh he had and told her for the hundred thousandth time that she worried too much. She'd forced a smile and kept her thoughts to herself. Their family had a lot more to worry about than he could ever understand.

She heard the slightest of noises. So slight it might have been entirely in her imagination. She glanced at the clock on the dresser – 3.34 a.m. She had to be up in less than four hours to do the school run and drop Jupiter to the vet to get his booster shots before she went to work. She should turn over and close her eyes, but she knew it would eat away at her. Her accursed mind would leap to wild speculations, it'd itch and poke away at her subconscious, and tired as she was, sleep would not come.

With a shake of the head at her own neuroses, she lifted herself carefully to a sitting position on the edge of the bed and wiggled her feet into her fluffy pink pussycat slippers. Secretly, she loathed them, but they had been a Christmas present from the girls. She had even left them down in the kitchen a couple of times in the hope that Jupiter might regress to his shoe-chewing phase, but it appeared she had been too successful in training him out of it.

As she stood, Declan stirred beside her and spoke in his sleep.

'Mwaff meh, fabricated half-inch pipe.'

Vera smiled. She was married to a man who dreamed of plumbing supplies.

She made her way past the girls' room and then, cracking under the weight of her own anxieties, doubled back and peeked in to see them both sound asleep: Keira, as ever, a tangle of limbs with the bedding kicked off; Siobhan so neat and tidy it looked as if she were faking sleep.

Vera headed downstairs. Any noise would almost certainly have come from Jupiter, otherwise he would be barking at it. Perhaps he'd got into the bin again. She reached the bottom of the stairs and quickened her pace when she heard a whine from the kitchen. She hoped the big softie hadn't been eating inedible objects again.

She opened the door and froze. The first thing to catch her eye was Jupiter's terrified expression as he tried to squeeze himself into the corner by the sink. Then she followed his gaze. Standing in her kitchen was something that could not be. Nine feet tall, stooped, the sight of its blood-red eyes and slobbering jaws sent a jolt of terror through her. It was standing unnaturally still and quiet, yet its eyes were screaming for blood.

Its foul stench hit her nostrils as she started instinctively to circle her left hand in the air and form the words. Then her hand stopped moving, held in the air against her will. She and the beast now stood in a frozen tableau. All she could move were her eyes, which only now scanned the rest of the room.

Distracted by the beast, she had sensed him too late. The man – short, round and bald – sat at the far end of her kitchen table. He smiled at her.

'We both know I can't hold you long,' he said in a calm voice, his accent American. 'At least, not while I'm holding him too.' He nodded at the beast. 'I do suggest you listen, or else' – he glanced at the Were – 'I will have to let him go.'

The beast's red eyes turned towards the man. Vera could feel the hatred.

Her mind was racing. She was outmatched, no question, but above all else, she must . . .

'You need to protect your family. I want to give you that opportunity. To do that, though, we must talk.' He spoke in the reasonable tone of a man advising her on mortgage options. 'If we fight, I'll win, and it will be . . . unfortunate. I wish to prevent that. Do we understand each other?'

She couldn't move, but perhaps he saw compliance in her eyes. He released his hold and her body sagged.

'Thank you for your cooperation.'

'What the hell?' she started. 'You can't— There are rules!'

He rubbed his fingers casually across his cheek. 'Not for me.'

She looked up at the beast again. 'This abomination should not exist. Under the Accord—'

'Yes, yes. We do not have time. We must move quickly if we are to avoid a messy outcome.' The man pointed across the table at her. 'I need you, or I need one of the two upstairs—'

'They're adopted!'

He gave her a wan smile. 'No, they aren't.' He nodded at the Were. 'You know what he is, and therefore we know what you – all of you – are.'

She ran her tongue over her dry lips. If she could buy some time or . . .

The man leaned back. 'This is a lovely home.' He held up a framed picture. It was the one from the mantelpiece in the front room. 'And you have a lovely family. Give yourself up to us, without a fight, and they shall be spared.'

'Why would I trust you?'

'Because,' he said, 'as you mentioned, I am, let's say, breaking with tradition. That means I don't want attention brought to what I'm doing. It will complicate things for me.'

'You're . . .' Realization hit her and Vera's eyes widened. 'You're making, aren't you?'

'I am trying to save a child's life.'

'Oh please!'

A momentary annoyance flashed in the man's eyes. 'If you come quietly, then it won't look suspicious. But if you fight, you will lose, and it will be loud. At that point, I might as well take the two fledglings, and he' – he nodded to the Were – 'can have his fun with the nothing you married.'

Vera could taste the bile at the back of her throat. 'That word . . .'

'I don't care for your opinions. Do we have a deal?'

Vera tried to think. Tried to find an angle where she knew none existed.

The man calmly slid a pair of shackles across the table. She had never seen them before, but she knew what they were. The markings on their sides showed they were more than just metal. They had featured in the stories her grandmother had told, the ones that had first made her such a bad sleeper.

With tears on her cheeks, Vera stepped forward and picked up the restraints. As she clicked first one and then the other around her wrists, a terrible emptiness enveloped her. A part of her that had always been there was suddenly gone, as if one of her senses had been shut off.

'Good,' he said. 'And now you will write a note, explaining why you are running away. Let's make it an affair.'

He moved his finger, and a pad and pen slid themselves across the table.

Vera rubbed her cheek with the sleeve of her nightdress. This man did not deserve her tears. She took a deep breath and started writing.

'I strongly suggest you resist the urge to attempt to be clever.'

Her lip curled with disgust as she looked at him. She nodded in the direction of the beast, still watching her with those burning-red eyes. 'Does he know what he is?'

'He knows why he is. That is more than enough.'

'Someone will stop you. There are systems in place to stop men like you.'

He yawned. 'Enough with the amateur dramatics, please. You have never met a man like me.'

She finished the note and scrawled her name beneath it, then she tossed the pen down on the table and attempted to straighten her back. 'There are always men like you.'

CHAPTER 26

It was only as Hannah turned the corner and the Church of Old Souls – aka the offices of *The Stranger Times* – came into view that she realized she didn't have any way of getting into the building. Grace had mentioned something about giving her a key, but between one thing and another they'd never got round to it.

She'd managed a couple of hours of sleep last night before waking up in a cold sweat. In the nightmare, she had been falling off the top of the Dennard building again and again and again, each time more horrible than the last. After failing to find a way back to sleep, she had eventually got up and headed to the office. Technically, they were supposed to be sending this week's edition to press tomorrow, and although she didn't know much about the process, she knew it required actual articles. Whatever else happened, she was going to see to it that they were spelled correctly.

As it happened, she didn't need a key. She was the last one to arrive. Hannah was surprised to see Reggie and Ox already sitting at their respective desks, typing away: Ox's fingers were flying over the keyboard; Reggie was hen-pecking away with one finger from each hand. Stella was seated in the corner at the computer with the big screen, using a graphic design package to move blocks of text around some pictures. Grace was circulating with a tray, wordlessly delivering cups of tea to all and sundry. When she turned and saw Hannah standing at the door, she gave her a broad smile.

'What's everyone doing in so early?' asked Hannah.

Grace moved towards her, keeping her voice low. 'We have still got a paper to put out.'

'Right,' said Hannah, feeling like a shirker, even though she hadn't really understood she was one. She lowered her voice. 'Is everything all right with . . . ?' A nod of the head in Ox's direction. 'And . . . ?' A nod in the direction of Banecroft's office.

Grace's bracelets tinkled as she dismissed Hannah's concerns with a wave of her hand. 'Do not worry about it. If you will insist on being Vincent Banecroft, you cannot expect to go through life without people attempting to rip your head off. The man is permanently asking for it.'

'He does have that way about him. Simon's mother is apparently blaming him too.'

Grace furrowed her brow. 'You went to see her?'

'Oh God, no. That, ehm . . . DI Sturgess gave me a lift home last night.'

'Did he?' Grace waggled her eyebrows to an extent Hannah would not have thought possible on the human face. To be fair, in Hannah's old crowd of Botoxed 'friends', facial expressions were something you picked from a catalogue and stuck with for the rest of your life.

'Oh stop,' said Hannah. 'He was just being nice. And pumping me for information.'

Grace's eyebrows did the fandango.

Hannah blushed. 'Not like that.'

'Fifteen per cent of people meet their future partners at work. I read that in a magazine.'

'He arrested me.'

'Nineteen per cent of people have used handcuffs at some point in their relationship. I read that in a slightly less God-fearing magazine.'

'I'm going to go do some work now.'

'Of course you are,' said Grace with a smile. 'Oh, not to tell you your job, my dear, but have you gone through the messages yet?'

'Messages?'

Grace raised her fingers to make bunny ears. 'The "Loon Line".'

'The what?'

'Oh,' said Grace. 'With all of the toing and froing, we might have forgotten to tell you about that.'

Hannah closed her eyes. 'Let me guess: we have a phone number that the loons can ring to give us stories?'

Hannah opened one eye to see Grace giving her a comforting smile and nodding.

Hannah sagged. 'Of course we do.'

'You had better get to it. The meeting is in an hour and he will ask. The man has a spectacular talent for asking questions people do not want him to.'

Hannah sat at her desk at the far end of the office, notepad and pen at the ready, and dialled the number on the Post-it note. She typed in her PIN when requested. An electronic voice spoke to her: 'You have . . . eighty . . . seven . . . messages.' She let out a groan. On the upside, at least she didn't have to maintain a professional facial expression when the other person couldn't see her. 'Press one to listen to message, two to delete message, three to save message.'

Hannah pressed '1'.

Beep.

'Message one,' came the electronic voice.

'Hello, yes. This is . . . It doesn't matter who I am. I want to keep my identity secret. My next-door neighbour, he's an alien. His address is . . . Oh, wait a sec . . . I'll call you back.'

Beep.

'Message six.'

'Hello, yes, I wish to complain about last week's edition. The ghost of Elvis Presley cannot be haunting some madwoman's vagina and I am appalled that you would report such utter tripe! I know it's utter nonsense as Elvis has been living happily with me for six years now, ever since he was reincarnated as a parrot. I asked him and he assures me he has not been anywhere near that harlot's—'

Beep.

'Message nineteen.'

'Right, this is your lucky day. I'm willing to do you "I had sex with the ghost of an alien" for only six grand and—'

Beep.

'Message twenty-three.'

229

'Have you been involved in an accident that wasn't your fault?'

Beep.

'Message twenty-eight.'

'I had sex with a unicorn – only five gr—'

Beep.

'Message thirty-six.'

No talking – just panting.

Beep.

'Message forty-two.'

'Hello, yes, I'd like to report that I met a UFO in Stalybridge last night. I was coming home from the pub, right, minding me own business, and then there's this bright light and I wake up four hours later and I've been interfered with.'

There was a clicking noise and another voice, angry and female, came on the line. 'Don't mind any of that bollocks. You're talking rubbish, Darren.'

'Doreen, shut up! I'm on the phone to the nutter people.'

'It's all bollocks,' she repeated. 'He got pissed and went over to see that Sophie slag.'

'Doreen!'

'No, he did. He bloody did. Either she was there or he went and interfered with himself and fell asleep, the drunken—'

Beep.

Messages forty-three through to forty-eight were the same

couple ringing back to continue the argument, each message being a maximum of only three minutes long. At the end of forty-seven, Darren proposed.

'Message forty-nine.'

It took Hannah a few seconds to realize what she was listening to. She held her hand to her mouth, shocked. The message was twenty-three seconds long in total. At the beep to signal the end of the recording, she fumbled with the buttons.

'Message saved.'

She listened to it again, twice, and then stood up.

'Ehm, everyone – everyone, could you all come here, please?'

She looked down the office to see Reggie and Stella looking at her. Ox, locked into his headphones, carried on typing, oblivious.

Grace came running in. 'What now?'

'Seriously, everybody, come over here right now.' She pointed at Ox. 'Reggie, get him.'

She ran over to Banecroft's office door and pounded on it. 'Wake up, you drunken Irish git, this is important!'

A selection of unintelligible syllables were barked from behind the door, accompanied by the sound of glass breaking.

The others gathered around Hannah's desk in a rough semicircle.

'What is it?' asked Ox.

Hannah took a deep breath. 'OK, I was going through the Loon Line messages—'

'Oh, is that all?'

'Shut up, Ox, I'm not finished.'

Ox looked taken aback. 'Right, Hannah. Sorry, Hannah.'

She gave him a smile to show there was no harm done. 'So, I was going through the messages. A lot of, well, loon stuff, but then . . .' She looked around. 'Where the hell is Banecroft? Grace?'

Grace nodded and stepped over to bang on Banecroft's door hard enough that it shook. 'Get out here right this instant, you—'

The door opened so quickly that Grace almost fell through it.

'I'm coming! Good God, can a man not take a moment to put on his trousers in the name of common decency?'

'Actually,' said Reggie in a tremulous voice, 'your trousers are on the wrong way round.'

Everyone bar the owner of said trousers looked down to verify this was the case.

'Yes,' said Banecroft, 'but we're all in agreement that they are in fact on, which is clearly the main thing.'

'Whatever,' said Hannah, pressing buttons on the unfamiliar and not terribly modern phone on her desk. 'I'm going to put it on speaker. Everybody stay quiet.' She shook her head while pressing a couple more buttons. 'Right, I think this will . . .'

She trailed off when the beep that introduced the message came over the phone's tinny speakers.

'Hello, Mr Banecroft, Simon here . . .'

Reggie's hand flew to his mouth. Grace gasped and blessed herself.

'I just wanted to let you know that I'm out working on a story and it's going to be an absolute whopper! You'll have to hire me after this! I'm just off to meet my source and then I'll drop in tomorrow morning to tell you all about it. I've always wanted to

say this . . . Hold the front page!' He giggled. 'OK, see you tomorrow. Bye.'

Beep.

The room was completely silent for a long moment.

Hannah nodded. 'I need to check that the timestamp on
this message is right, but if it is, that message was left at eleven
thirty-four on Tuesday night. Which is, what – twelve minutes
before he started climbing the stairs at the Dennard building and
about forty-five before he . . . y'know. He doesn't sound suicidal,
does he?'

He didn't. He sounded excited. Happy. Full of life. He sounded
like someone who was doing exactly what he said he was doing.

'We need to tell the police,' said Grace.

'No,' said Banecroft. 'We don't. They've already made up their
minds. We need to investigate this ourselves.'

'To be fair,' said Hannah, 'DI Sturgess said he wasn't ruling
anything in or out.'

'When did he say this?' Banecroft gave Hannah a suspicious
look.

'I bumped into him on my way home last night.'

'Did you? Well, I know Sturgess. I've known a hundred Stur-
gesses. They'll say anything to try and trip you up, or to achieve
whatever he was trying to achieve last night. What we need,' continued Banecroft, 'is a plan of attack. You!' He pointed his crutch
at Reggie. 'What Simon was working on had something to do with
an unexplained death in Castlefield on Monday night. Go down
there and find out what happened.'

Reggie nodded nervously. 'Of course, but I . . . It's not really my field of expertise.'

'It involves dead people, doesn't it? That's right up your street.'

'Yes,' said Reggie, wincing and nodding, 'but not normally that recent. Could Ox come with me and—'

'No, he can't. You'll have to figure it out without having your hand held. Ox has another assignment.' Banecroft locked eyes with Ox. 'You were friendly with Simon?'

The tension in the room grew. The two men hadn't spoken since the fight. Ox gave a terse nod.

'Excellent. Then go and find out what happened to that bloody camera of his. Meanwhile, the new Tina—'

'Hannah,' interrupted Hannah.

'—is going to drive me somewhere.'

'No, I'm not.'

'Excuse me?'

'If Reggie is going to be sniffing around a crime scene then he needs somebody with him. Seeing as we've already pissed off the authorities' – she tried not to look in Banecroft's direction when she said it – 'it makes sense to have two of us down there, and for one of us to be the only person who has a relationship with someone from the police force.'

Banecroft considered this. 'All right, fine. Where are my car keys?'

With everything that had happened, Hannah had forgotten to give them back. She took them out of her handbag and tossed them to him. He, in turn, tossed them at Stella, who wasn't expecting them – they hit her right in the chest.

'What the hell?'

'Yes,' said Banecroft, 'it's those lightning-fast reflexes that make you the perfect choice for the job of my chauffeur.'

Stella's face looked as close to happy as Hannah had ever seen it. 'For real?'

'Absolutely not,' said Grace.

'She needs to learn. She's been bugging you about it for weeks.'

'How did you know that?' said Grace.

'Because,' said Banecroft, 'I know everything that happens in this office.'

'Really?' said Grace. 'What's my surname?'

Banecroft hobbled off in the direction of the toilet. 'I don't need to know that – we're on first-name terms. Everybody get going – we're going to press tonight, come hell or high water. And why the hell do these trousers have no fly?'

Battered Sausage

Sharon Marmont, 23, from Essex has been arrested for assaulting her former partner with a battered sausage. Ex-boyfriend Liam Willis, 25, is a committed vegan, and calls have been made for the case to be dealt with as a hate crime.

CHAPTER 27

In what was turning out to be a week full of revelations, Hannah found herself having yet another.

Throughout her life, for reasons she had never understood, strangers would talk to her. Not just sleazy men – although, yes, that – but people in general. Her old college roommate Samantha had wanted to make a study of it. They could both be sitting on a train, wearing headphones while reading a book, and people of all manner and description would start talking to Hannah. Samantha said it was because she had 'resting friendly face' – the implication being that she permanently looked like somebody who was happy to chat. Samantha, on the other hand, had self-diagnosed 'resting bitch face', which meant she got to read her book undisturbed.

So it was that Hannah spent long-haul flights being shown pictures of strangers' cats or grandchildren, or sometimes – to much hilarity – cats with grandchildren. She spent one long train journey discussing what it was like to be a widower with a man called Derek, aged eighty-two, who casually dropped in halfway through that he liked his women 'large and in charge'. She would get stopped on the streets of London about every thirty minutes to give tourists directions, and once, memorably, she'd turned down an offer of marriage from a nice Indian man and then directed him to Piccadilly Circus. It had been a burden, until today.

Castlefield was a brisk fifteen-minute walk from the office. It was a collection of apartment buildings that wound along a slow-moving canal, which in turn was criss-crossed by railway bridges, the lines converging at nearby Oxford Road station. A mix of modern apartment buildings and converted mills offered balconies with views of the canal, which had tree-lined paths running alongside it and barges chugging happily along its waters. It was all rather lovely – a relatively calm oasis of waterside living that was only a few minutes' walk from the city centre.

In a corner of her mind, Hannah made a note to check rental prices. She would need to find somewhere permanent to live. Come to that, she would also need to find out how much she was being paid. With everything that had happened, there hadn't been a right time to bring it up. Plus, given the general state of disrepair of the office, a part of her didn't want to know. She was still feeling good about having a job and she didn't want to ruin that little boost by discovering it was a very badly paid one.

On the walk over with Reggie, Hannah had made the decision not to talk about what had happened with the Fenton brothers outside the Admiral's Arms on Monday, which now seemed like a lifetime ago. She was, after all, someone who was trying to re-invent herself. If Reggie had decided to do the same, then who was she to judge? Besides, as she walked into the unknown, there was a little part of her that was reassured to know that, while he might not look it, her companion was able to handle a tricky situation. So instead, she had listened as Reggie happily ran down a list of restaurants he had visited and the reasons why they were terrible.

Hannah's previous experience of investigative work stretched only to failing to notice her husband's industrial-scale infidelity, and Reggie's seemed to extend only to a thorough criticism of a second-rate wine list. This was how they had come to find themselves standing in the middle of Castlefield, looking about, not knowing where to start. It had, frankly, been rather embarrassing.

They'd started googling 'Castlefield murder' on their phones. The press reports had been scant. On the first day, little more had been said than the body of a fifty-two-year-old man had been found in the area and police were investigating. The following day, the reports had been only a rehash of the previous day's, with the addition of one new piece of information: the man had been formally identified as John Maguire, a Manchester native of no fixed abode.

Hannah still had DI Sturgess's card in her pocket, but the idea of ringing him was a non-starter. He didn't strike her as the kind of man who'd cheerfully answer her questions – not without having rather a lot of his own. Also, while she would rather die than admit it, she had caught herself thinking about him every now and again since yesterday. It was probably some variation on Stockholm syndrome – after so many years in a dreadful marriage, she was wildly over-reacting to her first contact with an eligible male since her emancipation. All of which left her and Reggie standing around with no clue where to start.

Which is when Hannah's lifelong 'curse' had revealed itself to be a blessing. Absent of any other ideas, she had been wandering around looking for police tape when a woman standing in the smoking area of a nearby office block, hugging herself to fend off the chill, took notice. 'Y'all right there, love?'

Fifteen minutes later, Hannah found Reggie eating a breakfast roll by the canal while a trio of ducks gave him the evil eye. When Hannah appeared beside him, he pointed at a sign that showed a cartoon quacker thanking you for not feeding it bread. It went on to point out that bread made its tummy hurt, contained the wrong nutrients and caused algae in the water, which killed his/her fish friends and gave the ducks diseases.

'All of that may well be true,' said Reggie, 'but I can't help thinking that the massive flaw in this system is that nobody has explained it to the ruddy ducks. And it says we're supposed to feed them half-cut seedless grapes. Who on earth has half-cut seedless grapes about their person?'

Hannah patted him on the arm and they both took a step back as one of the ducks quacked angrily in their direction.

'Right,' she said. 'The body they discovered on Tuesday morning was found over there – some poor homeless guy. It was found first thing in the morning and they reckon that it happened Monday night, which tallies with what the papers said.'

'Oh, I see.'

'Yes. See those workmen?' Hannah pointed at two men up on scaffolding, fixing damage to a red-brick wall. 'That's the spot. The police had it closed off for all of Tuesday.'

They started to walk towards the wall. 'How did you find all this out?' asked Reggie.

Hannah gave a shrug and a sheepish smile. 'Oh, y'know, I just asked about.'

They stood on the far side of the canal and watched the men work.

'That damage can't be related to the body, can it?'

Hannah looked around them. 'I don't know. I mean, the woman I spoke to said that the body was found right underneath where those guys are.'

'Oh,' said Reggie.

They both stared up at it for a couple of minutes.

'OK,' said Hannah. 'Let's think this through. Something about this death was suspicious, and somehow Simon got involved. That must mean it was the kind of suspicious he would've been interested in.'

'Well,' said Reggie, pointing across the canal, 'that damage to the brickwork, fifteen feet in the air – that'd be rather odd, wouldn't it?'

'I guess.' Hannah clicked her fingers. 'He also said on the message that he had a source. What kind of a source could Simon have?'

'That's . . . I don't know. I mean, the poor lad spent most of his time sitting outside our offices. Maybe there's something in his notes?'

'If there is, the police have it, and Banecroft was very clear about not involving them.'

They turned to scan the overlooking flats, the railway arches, the cranes in the distance. The brief period when it had felt as if they might know what they were doing was fast running out.

Just then, a figure shuffled up to them, carrying a sleeping bag.

'Sorry to bother you, folks, but could you spare some change?'

Hannah had the suspicion it was nothing more than blind luck. When engaged in an investigation, she assumed it was unlikely that the most obvious line of enquiry, which you'd somehow missed, sidled up to you and asked for spare change. Not that that guy had been of much help, telling them only that John Maguire had been known as Long John and he'd been an all-right bloke who never did nothing to nobody. After some prodding, he'd also revealed a few different locations where they could find other members of the homeless community.

It was shocking at first, and soon it just became depressing. Even here, in a fairly well-to-do area, the issue was rife if you knew where to look. People who had fallen through the cracks of life, surviving by living in whatever crevices they could find. Hannah and Reggie passed two rough sleepers who had laid out actual mattresses in a pedestrian walkway under one of the several railway bridges in the area. Gaps between buildings, areas up on the far side of the canal across from the busy walkway, under railway arches – anywhere there was a little space and a little shelter, homeless people could be found.

As the pair walked further along the towpath, away from the apartment buildings with their prized canal-side views, they came upon a mini encampment of tents.

'How is it so bad?' asked Hannah.

'Well,' said Reggie, 'people are allowed to be homeless here. In London, the richer areas do everything they can to make it all but impossible – installing spikes, moving them along, et cetera, et cetera.'

Hannah nodded, feeling dreadful. He was right, of course. In London, she'd lived in Knightsbridge with her husband, and the reason they'd not seen any rough sleepers was because money had been spent to hide, if not fix, the problem.

'And,' continued Reggie, 'Manchester is a nice city. At a guess, if you have to be homeless somewhere, I'd imagine the thought is that it might as well be here.'

That did make sense. They'd spoken to a lot of people, and while there'd been plenty of Manc accents, there had been no shortage of people from elsewhere.

Reggie had had the presence of mind to bring a picture of Simon with him on his phone. They showed it around, receiving automatic shakes of the head from people suspicious about why they were asking. Reggie had explained to those who would listen that they weren't the police, that Simon had been his friend, and that they just wanted to find out who had talked to him. Several people begrudgingly admitted having met him. He'd asked questions about Long John and whether they'd seen anything on Monday night.

Hannah wondered how long it had taken Simon to come up with the idea of asking the homeless what they'd seen, given the embarrassingly long time it had taken her and Reggie. Maybe he really would have made a good reporter.

They came to an abandoned barge moored in a run-off of the canal, which some homeless people had occupied. Two men sat on the deck, drinking cans of something Hannah didn't recognize. One had a lot of tattoos and sported a cast on his right wrist; the other had a long, scraggly beard and wore an anorak over a 'Frankie Say Relax' T-shirt that had seen better days.

'Hi there,' said Hannah. 'I was wondering if you'd mind having a quick chat? We're asking about for people who might have met a friend of ours.'

The man with the cast spoke in a Yorkshire accent. 'You the fuzz?'

'No,' said Reggie.

'Then bugger off.'

Reggie held up the picture of Simon on his phone. 'Honestly, it'll be no trouble. We just want to find out who he might've been talking to. He worked with us.'

'Don't know him. Don't want to know him.'

Reggie put away his phone. 'I'm afraid you won't get the chance now. He's dead.'

'Boo hoo,' added the beard, in an accent with a strong dash of cockney. 'Go on, get out of it.'

Hannah felt Reggie tense and she put her hand on his arm.

'OK,' she said in a cheery voice, 'thanks very much for your time. We'll be back up that way if you change your minds.' She pointed in the direction they had come from. 'We're going to find a bench and have ourselves some lunch.'

'Oh, la-di-da,' said the displaced cockney.

They turned to go. Reggie spoke out the side of his mouth. '"Thanks for your time"? I'm all in favour of good manners, but they were dreadful.'

'I know,' said Hannah, 'but it wasn't them I was talking to. It was the girl who was looking out at us from the window below deck. Her expression when she saw the picture – she definitely knew Simon.'

'Oh.'

'So let's walk slowly, find a bench, and then do as much hanging around as it takes for her to come find us.'

CHAPTER 28

As Ox entered the vestibule of the Church of Old Souls, there was an unmistakable scent of herb coming from the printer downstairs. On the rare occasions when Banecroft wasn't on the prowl, Ox sometimes nipped in and joined Manny for a toke, but he wasn't in the mood today. Instead, he headed up the stairs, automatically hopping over the fourth step from the top. As he climbed, his record bag banging against his hip, he could hear Grace's booming voice on the phone.

'Well, I am sorry, sir, but *The Stranger Times* cannot be held responsible for the products advertised in our publication. You should contact the manufacturer directly.'

Ox turned the corner. With her headset on, Grace was on her feet, giving the reception desk a vigorous polish. It was notable for being the only part of the office that ever looked clean. A couple of months ago, he'd made the mistake of leaving a bag from an Indian takeaway on it. For a fortnight he'd been pointedly left out of the lunch order as a result. Unusually, there was a big bunch of flowers displayed in a vase on it today. Ox didn't know much about flowers, but they were a variety of colours and smelled nice.

Grace looked up and smiled at him, then her brow furrowed as she addressed the caller on the other end of the line. 'You have done what? Well, I mean, that is not designed to go up there, is it?'

Ox stopped in front of the desk. He knew better than to lean on it in its just-polished condition.

'It does not have to specifically say do not do that. I mean, sweet Jesus and all the saints in heaven, some things you just know you should not do.'

Grace opened her mouth wide, anger filling her eyes. 'Now, you listen to me . . .' She looked up at Ox. 'He hung up on me! Rude man! Whoever manufactured him needs a serious talking-to.' Grace pulled off her headset and sat down.

Ox pointed at the flowers. 'Where'd these come from?'

Grace's face lit up. 'I do not know, but the card says "from a secret admirer"! I think Hannah must have caught the eye of that policeman.'

'The one investigating Simon's . . . ?' Ox left the sentence hanging.

The smile dropped from Grace's face as she leaned forward and looked up at him. 'Oh, sweetheart, I am sorry. You are just back from visiting poor Simon's mother, aren't you?'

Ox nodded.

'How was she?'

Ox let out a long sigh. 'Bad. I mean . . . I'd expected her not to be, y'know . . . but . . .'

Grace patted him on the arm. 'I know it is tough. I'm sure she appreciated you dropping by.'

Ox shrugged. 'Honestly, I'm not sure she realized I was there.

There were a few women with her. She just sat on the sofa, staring blankly at the floor. Poor woman.'

'Well,' said Grace, 'that boy was all she had. I cannot even begin to imagine.' She clasped her hands together as if in prayer.

'Yeah,' said Ox. 'You know how you're religious and that, Grace?'

'Yes, Ox.'

'Well . . .' He paused, looking for the right words. 'I mean, I've never been. No disrespect and that, just not my thing.'

'You know I do not judge, Ox.'

Ox nodded. He liked Grace, but one of the things he definitely knew about her was that she loved to judge people. He'd seen her go through an entire magazine, issuing judgements on every person mentioned as she did so. He'd worried she might be weird when she found out he was gay, but, to be fair to her, she hadn't been. The only thing that had changed was how instead of giving him pamphlets to come to services at her church and find himself 'a nice decent woman', she'd just swapped it to 'a nice decent man'. Clearly the Manchester New Reformed was on the more liberal end of the spectrum.

'I was just . . .' said Ox. 'I mean, do you really believe in heaven and hell and all that?'

Grace nodded. 'I do. I try to keep myself right with the Lord. I know my dear departed husbands are up in heaven right now, waiting patiently for me.'

'Right,' said Ox, who did not want to ask further questions relating to how Grace saw that working exactly. 'Yeah. Thing is, if you do something really bad . . . Is that, like, you're out for definite? Or can you, like, make it right?'

'Well,' said Grace, with a dangerously enthusiastic light in her eyes that told him he was going to start getting pamphlets again, 'the blessed Lord washes all souls who truly want it in the sweet waters of his forgiveness.'

'Right,' said Ox, with an unsure nod. 'Yeah.'

'Why?' asked Grace, her tone shifting from evangelical to suspicious. 'What did you do?'

'Well,' said Ox, rubbing the back of his neck with his hand. 'Y'know how Banecroft told me to go and, y'know, find out what happened to Simon's camera?'

'Yes.'

'Well, his mum, poor woman . . . She's, y'know, out of it. No point asking her nothing.'

Grace's eyes narrowed. 'What did you do, Ox?'

He held up a hand. 'Just give me a sec. So, I . . . And remember, we're trying to find out what happened to the poor lad. I mean, he was my mate. I was the one who went down the pub with him and I gave him advice on his camera gear. Like, back-ups and all that. He was able to set it up so it backed up over wi-fi. I helped him do that. We were proper mates, like . . . I mean, he lent me a hundred quid!'

Ox looked at Grace's darkening expression and realized that sharing the last bit might not have been one of his best ideas. 'And I'm absolutely going to give it back to his ma, with interest. Once I, y'know, have it.' Ox ran a hand across his beard. He was beginning to seriously regret trying to explain this. 'So, all right, I go upstairs – to use the loo, like – and I nip into Simon's room, just to see if I can spot the camera.'

'Right.'

'And it isn't there. But, like I said, I helped him with his gear, and I remembered that the camera is set to back up over wi-fi. Any photos and that.'

'What is the point you are trying to make, Ox?'

'I'm trying to tell you. His photos backed up to the cloud, and then, because you can't trust nothing on the net, man – the big corporations are in the pocket of—'

'Ox,' said Grace, trying to stop him going off on one.

'All right, I'm just . . . I did a bad thing . . . Maybe not that bad?'

'Ox!'

'But I did it for a good reason. Trying to, y'know, find out what happened to the poor lad.'

'So help me God, if you don't get to the point this instant!'

Ox reached into his record bag and pulled out a black box about the size of a paperback. 'I . . . I sorta temporarily borrowed his hard drive back-up. I'm gonna give it back.'

Grace folded her arms. 'That was a very stupid thing to do, Ox.'

'I know! I sorta panicked.'

'You have to give it back.'

Ox nodded emphatically. 'Yeah, absolutely. No doubt. No doubt. Thing is – I've done it now.' He gave a shrug. 'Might as well see what pictures he took.'

CHAPTER 29

It took about forty-five minutes in the end.

Hannah and Reggie had found a bench near a pub and watched a couple of narrowboats pass by slowly. They sat huddled together, their coats pulled tight around them. While it was at least dry, this was brisk-walk weather, not sitting-around weather. A couple of Canada geese hissed as they waddled past.

'Geese,' said Reggie, 'not unlike swans, seem to get by in life exclusively on their looks.'

'Do you think?' said Hannah absent-mindedly. She was keeping watch on the bend in the canal around which the abandoned barge was moored.

'Absolutely. The grace, the poise, the elegant long necks and beautiful feathers – it all rather distracts from the fact that they are utter, utter bastards.'

'Yeah. Aren't swans owned by the Queen?'

'Oh yes,' said Reggie. 'Just like most of her grandchildren.'

'Yes, well . . .' This diverted Hannah's attention. 'Wait, what?'

Reggie nodded. 'Yes, under some weird royal charter or other, she is the legal custodian of the quote-unquote "minor grandchildren". Apparently it dates back to King George the First thinking his son, the eventual King George the Second, was an utter buffoon.'

'Right,' said Hannah. 'Wow. Are you a big royal-watcher, then?'

'Good God, no. It was in an old copy of *Marie Claire*. Only magazine in my GP's office last week.'

'Oh, right. I . . .' Hannah trailed off. She had finally spotted whom she had been waiting for.

The girl came around the corner, her shoulders hunched and her hands shoved into her coat pockets, moving at a choppy near-run and glancing around her nervously. When she saw Hannah and Reggie she stopped, and for a second Hannah thought she might run the other way. Instead, she turned to her right and, with a subtle nod, headed across the lawn and out of view behind the pub.

'She seems very nervous,' said Hannah.

'Yes,' agreed Reggie, 'she rather does.'

Hannah stood up. 'You stay here – I'm going to go talk to her alone.'

Reggie's brow furrowed. 'Are you sure that's a good idea?'

'She's our only lead – I don't want to scare her off.'

Reggie didn't look at all happy about this.

'Relax, she's tiny.'

'Yes, but her two mates aren't. What if they're waiting around the corner?'

Hannah had to admit she hadn't thought of this. 'I'll be careful. I promise, no dark alleyways.'

'Dear girl, spoken like someone who has never been robbed in broad daylight.'

★

Hannah found the girl lurking nervously in the pub's car park. She tried to give her a reassuring smile as she approached. It was only as she got closer that she realized the 'girl' was probably in her late twenties. Her emaciated appearance had made her look younger from a distance, but not in a good way. She was hunched and jittery, and her chewed fingernails tugged nervously at the zip of her anorak.

'Hello,' said Hannah, trying to sound cheery.

The young woman shushed her and flapped her hand nervously. 'Keep it down. I don't want people seeing me talking to you.'

'OK,' said Hannah. 'No problem. Would you like to go inside for a drink?'

She shook her head. 'They don't let us in there. Was that true, what you said? About your friend – the guy with the glasses?'

'Yes,' said Hannah. 'He's dead.'

The girl's eyes became wide saucers of fear. 'Fuck.' She started to walk away.

Hannah held out her hand. 'Please – wait. I just want to talk to you.'

'No, no, no.' She shook her head again.

'Look, I need to find out what you talked about. That's all. I promise I won't tell anyone. Just two minutes.'

The girl looked around again, her left leg jiggling as she did so, scanning her surroundings like a trapped animal. 'Fuck,' she repeated. She nodded towards one of the pub's fire exits and they stood inside the doorway. 'What happened to him?'

'Simon? He . . .' Hannah flinched at having to describe it. This woman had already nearly bolted once. 'That's what I'm trying to find out. That's why I need your help.' She extended her hand. 'I'm Hannah.'

The girl looked at her hand but didn't take it. Then, after a pause that Hannah reckoned was spent making up something, said, 'Karen. I'm Karen.'

'Right. Thanks. So when did you meet him? Simon?'

Karen sniffed and spoke while looking everywhere but at Hannah. 'Few days ago. I didn't know his name. He was nice, though. Gave me a cup of tea from his flask thing.'

Hannah nodded. 'Yes, he was a good guy.'

'He came around asking about Long John. It was the day they found him.'

'Tuesday?' said Hannah.

Karen shrugged. 'I dunno. He said he'd be back the next day. Said he was going to bring his boss with him.' She looked into Hannah's eyes directly for the first time. 'He said there'd be cash in it.'

'Right,' said Hannah, unsure what to say next. 'Well, there might be. What did you tell him exactly?'

She shifted nervously. 'Did he not tell you?'

Hannah shook her head.

'It's gonna sound mental.'

'Try me,' said Hannah, trying to look encouraging. 'You'd be surprised what I'd believe. It's been a hell of a week.'

Reggie slumped with relief when he saw Hannah re-emerge from behind the pub. He'd been on the verge of going to look for her, his desire not to spook the girl and blow their morning's investigative endeavours outweighed by his concern to make sure that Hannah wasn't bleeding in an alley somewhere.

Hannah gave him a nervous smile as she approached with the girl walking behind her fretfully. 'Ehm, Reggie, could you lend me some money, please?'

Reggie looked from Hannah to the girl and back again. 'Is everything OK?'

'Yes,' said Hannah, her smile tightening. 'I mean . . . I'll explain in a minute, but could you . . .'

'Oh. Right. Yes.'

He pulled out his wallet and opened it. He had two twenty-pound notes. 'Is twenty enough?'

The girl spoke for the first time. 'The fella said it'd be a couple of ton.'

'OK,' said Hannah. 'Well, for the minute, we'll give you forty. When we meet again, we can talk about proper payment.'

The girl scratched at her arm and then bit her lip before nodding.

Hannah looked at Reggie, who reluctantly handed her both notes. The girl reached out for them but Hannah pulled away gently. 'Ah, first things first, Karen. Remember, you said you'd show us the spot.'

'Right, yeah. C'mon, then.'

The girl turned and scurried back down the path at such speed that Reggie had to practically run to catch up with her and Hannah. Then she came to an abrupt halt. 'I was standing here.'

'OK, and where was . . . ?'

Karen nodded across the water to the far side of the canal, at the wide-open space where Reggie and Hannah had stood earlier, watching the workmen fixing the brickwork. 'See where that woman with the blue bag is? There. Few feet further back maybe – hard to tell.' She looked away again quickly.

'Sure.'

Karen turned and put out her hand. Reggie noticed it was shaking.

'OK,' said Hannah. 'Remember: ring me later on. And you promised me you'd spend this money on food.'

Karen nodded again. Hannah held out the notes, which she snatched before hurrying off without another word.

'Are you sure that was a good idea?' said Reggie.

'I honestly don't know,' said Hannah. 'I mean . . . I'm not an idiot. I know that she's . . . But I'll tell you this, she's also terrified.'

'Of what?'

Hannah nodded in the direction of the bridge. Then she took a deep breath. 'You know how our paper is full of some pretty incredible stuff?'

'Well, yes.'

Hannah pointed. 'See that building over there, the tall one?'

'Yes,' said Reggie, feeling increasingly confused.

'Now, this will sound odd, but how far would you say it was – roughly – from the spot she pointed out to the top of that building?'

Reggie looked back and forth between the two. 'I mean, I'm never great at this kind of thing, but I would imagine three or four hundred feet?'

'Yeah,' agreed Hannah, 'that's about what I thought.'

Reggie folded his arms. 'You realize you're being infuriatingly vague, don't you?'

Hannah nodded. 'OK. Just . . . I know how this is going to sound, but keep an open mind. OK?'

Reggie gave a firm nod.

'Right. Karen – although I'm pretty sure that's not her name, but anyway – was walking past at about three o'clock on Monday night. Well, Tuesday morning, technically. She was standing about here when she saw something go flying through the air and hit that wall – the one with the damaged brickwork.'

'Are we saying it was this Long John fellow?'

'Yes.'

'But that's . . . I mean, what could do that?'

'Well, she said it looked like a big hairy ape or something – only bigger – but she couldn't be sure how big. It was dark. But she saw it. She watched as it put what she reckons was a second person over its shoulder and then—'

'What?'

Part of Hannah felt ridiculous saying it out loud. 'Then,' she repeated, 'it took a couple of steps and leaped from that point on the ground to the roof of that building.'

'I see.' He couldn't keep the scepticism from his voice.

'I know,' said Hannah.

'I mean, not to be rude, but are we sure she's the most reliable of witnesses?'

'No, we're not. Thing is though, if she's making it up she's got a hell of an imagination. I mean, it would explain that damage to the brickwork at least, right?'

Reggie nodded. 'That's true.'

'And,' said Hannah, 'here's the other thing. We're here because Simon's message said he was meeting someone that night, but there's no CCTV evidence of anybody else on that roof. Or rather, there's no CCTV evidence of anybody going up to the roof via the lift or stairs.'

Reggie put his hands to his mouth. 'Oh my . . .'

'Yes,' said Hannah. 'Exactly.'

CHAPTER 30

DI Sturgess would never forget the first dead body he ever saw. Nobody does – it is one of those life experiences that never leaves you, regardless of the circumstances. The circumstances of his had been quite peculiar.

His first week in uniform on the streets of Manchester had coincided with university Rag Week, which meant students trying to outdo each other in the stupid stakes – be it drunken dares, drunken pranks or just drunken drinking. Mostly, it had meant dealing with disorderly behaviour, occasional property damage and the odd fight. In all honesty, it was more of a pain in the arse for the ambulance crews than for the police, seeing as they had to stomach-pump the little nuisances.

The dead body in question had not been a student. He had been a man in his late forties. Sturgess didn't know his name but he had been Cadaver 427X – whatever that meant. The medical students to which Cadaver 427X had been assigned for the term had nicknamed him Ralph. For Rag Week, they'd decided to dress up Ralph and take him out on the town – on a pub crawl, to be exact. Incredibly, they had proceeded to lose him.

In a panic, one of the students had made the regrettable

decision of ringing the Greater Manchester Police to report Ralph as having been kidnapped. Sturgess and his training officer had escorted the three rapidly sobering-up students, who had realized belatedly that they were in all sorts of trouble, as they retraced their steps. Eventually Ralph was located in the corner of a nightclub, looking dishevelled and holding half a pint of mild. Most disturbingly, his face was smeared with lipstick.

What brought Ralph to mind was the fact that DI Sturgess was standing in the morgue at Royal Oldham Hospital. And it wasn't the presence of the bodies that reminded him of the rogue cadaver, but rather the appearance of Dr Charlie Mason. In addition to the medical qualifications required to be a pathologist, one of the bare minimum standards you might be expected to uphold was looking healthier than your clientele. Mason looked as if he'd slept in a dumpster, only his bloodshot eyes indicated he probably hadn't slept at all. He smelled of booze and regret.

'Are you all right, Doctor?'

'No, not really. It was Colin from the lab upstairs' stag do last night. I'd have called in sick but I've used up all my sick days recently and, y'know . . .' He waved a hand around. 'Death waits for no man. Who are you here for?'

'Two, actually. Simon Brush, who you got in yesterday, and John Maguire from the day before.'

'Oh, handy.'

'Handy?' asked Sturgess, but Mason ignored the question and turned around.

'C'mon, then.'

Sturgess followed the doctor down the hall, walking a step behind to avoid the man's breath – it put him in mind of the time they'd found a body in a sewer. Mason himself seemed oblivious to his own halitoxicity as he used the walk as an opportunity to launch into a monologue.

'I say it was the stag do, turns out it wasn't *the* stag do, or even the alternative one. No – only found out last night when one of the lads let slip there'd been a weekend in Budapest last month and then a night in Blackpool last weekend. Apparently, I'm on the C team. Can you believe that?'

Sturgess didn't answer, because he didn't care, and even if he did, he guessed Mason wouldn't have wanted to hear it.

'Six years I've been playing five-a-side with Colin. Six! I invited him to the game when he'd just moved here from Glasgow, and now he's heading off to bloody Budapest with lads I introduced him to. Without me. Come to that, I introduced him to his bloody wife-to-be as well.'

He pushed his way through a swing door into the mortuary proper, the normally overpowering smell of disinfectant battling with the funk around the good doctor.

'I'll tell you what it is,' he continued. 'It's the divorce. They're choosing Yvonne's side, same as everybody else. I'm getting stereotyped as some mid-life crisis loser who ran off with a younger woman, only to find the younger woman doesn't want him, and all right, technically – *technically* – all that is correct, but it is never that simple.' Mason stopped between two bodies covered with white sheets. 'Things are never that simple, are they? I mean, you're a detective, I don't have to tell you that. And now it looks like I might not even get an invite to the wedding. I mean, does that seem fair?'

Sturgess was taken aback when Mason looked at him as if he were actually expecting an answer. He'd been tuning him out. What had he meant by 'handy'? He could also feel the dull throb behind his left eyebrow that meant one of his damned headaches was coming on.

He looked blankly at the doctor, having no idea what the ques-- tion had been. 'So, where are these two bodies?'

Mason shook his head and pointed at the gurneys either side of him. 'Here and here – Messrs Brush and Maguire respectively.'

Sturgess looked around at the banks of lockers that were presumably mostly full of bodies, and then back again at the only two that were sitting out for inspections. 'Really?'

'Yeah,' said Mason.

'This place deals with, what – about six thousand deaths a year?'

Mason nodded. 'Nearer eight now, since they closed the—'

'Right,' interrupted Sturgess. 'The Maguire autopsy – I was told that was done two days ago. And the Brush one yesterday?'

Dr Mason nodded as if he were wondering exactly what point the detective was trying to make.

'So,' continued Sturgess, 'seeing as the autopsies have been completed and you don't leave corpses sitting out for days on end, it strikes me as incredibly unusual that both these bodies just happen to be on display and sitting side by side when I come to see them.'

Mason's face would've gone pale if it hadn't been a deathly

shade already. He tried to laugh off the question. 'What can I tell you? We're surprisingly efficient.'

'Not to mention psychic, seeing as I didn't tell anyone I was coming, and these two cases are not officially linked in any way.'

Mason said nothing but stood more upright. Sturgess could visibly see him sobering up, as he realized this casual chat was no longer casual. He got an odd flashback to those three drunk students, when they realized that losing a body was probably a very bad idea.

'Now, Doctor,' said Sturgess. 'I want you to consider the next question carefully as it is an official one. As the lead officer on both of these investigations, can you tell me if anyone else has been in to see these bodies?'

The two men stood for a long moment, staring at each other. Eventually, Mason cleared his throat. 'If you have any questions regarding access to this facility, I feel you should direct them towards my superiors.'

'I will.'

'And,' the doctor added under his foul breath, 'the very best of luck with that.'

The steadily building throb in Sturgess's head was exacerbating his rising temper. 'The only people who are supposed to be in here are medical professionals and police officers.'

'I'm well aware of the rules. I'm not sure you are, though.'

'Look, just give me the names and nobody needs to know where I got them from.'

Mason gave a humourless laugh. 'Cop yourself on, Sturgess. Now, if you've no questions regarding the post-mortems that have been carried out on these subjects then I've got plenty of other work to get to. We rushed these to the top of the queue at *your* request.'

Sturgess bit his lip and ran the back of his hand across his brow. He was starting to sweat now. 'Fine. Please give me your report.'

Mason nodded. 'John Maguire, male, fifty-two years old. Shows signs of sustained alcohol and drug abuse. There were some lacerations, but the cause of death was massive blunt force trauma to the back of the head.' He turned to the other body. 'Simon Brush, nineteen. Appears to have been in good health prior to his death. Body shows signs of massive trauma, consistent with a fall from a great height. Death would have been instantaneous.'

'And did you find anything unusual?' asked Sturgess.

'Define unusual.'

'Really, Charlie? Do I really need to define unusual?'

Mason shrugged. 'It's just you seem to have some very specific questions, DI Sturgess, so I'm trying to assist you as much as possible.'

'Right,' said Sturgess. 'How about this, then: is there anything, other than being dead and both deaths involving blunt force trauma, that links these two bodies?'

Mason looked at him for another long moment and then seemed to decide something. He pulled back the sheets from both bodies to reveal the heads of the two men. Sturgess looked away for a second and gathered himself. It was not a pretty sight.

Mason pointed at the neck of John Maguire. 'See here, on the neck? There are marks.'

'What kind of marks?'

'I'm not sure. The bruising looks as if it might have been caused by someone grabbing the subject around the throat, but both the placement of the bruises and the lacerations are inconsistent with those made by a human hand.'

'What does that mean?'

'I don't know,' said Mason. 'The pattern isn't something I've seen before. It looks almost like it might have been caused by an animal, although obviously that's very unlikely given the circumstances. There's also evidence of it on the neck of Simon Brush, although not as clear due to the body's overall condition. I've sent pictures to colleagues down in London who specialize more in this area, to see if they can come up with anything.'

'Right,' said Sturgess. 'Anything else unusual?'

'No,' said Mason. 'Just that.'

'OK.' Sturgess took a breath and closed his eyes for a second.

'Are you all right?'

'Fine. Just a headache.' Sturgess rolled his head in circles. 'I should let you know, as soon as I leave here I shall be putting in a request to review this facility's CCTV recordings for the last twenty-four hours. Are you sure there's nothing else you'd like to tell me about who might have shown an interest in these bodies?'

Mason shook his head. 'Are you really this stupid?'

'Excuse me?'

'A word of advice, DI Sturgess, from a man in his forties who is now sleeping alone on a futon in a flat where the heating doesn't work and the bathroom from the place upstairs leaks every bloody morning: learn when you should leave something well enough alone.'

'If you don't want to play ball, Dr Mason, then I have no choice but to get more senior officers involved to get answers to my questions.'

At this, Mason actually smirked. 'Yeah, and as a medical professional, I'd strongly advise against holding your breath waiting for answers.'

'Aren't you sick of it?' asked Sturgess. 'You must get it too. That feeling that when certain things happen around here, there are people working in the background, interfering, covering things up. Doesn't that bother you?'

Mason looked away. 'I've no idea what you're talking about.'

'Right.'

On his way out the door, Sturgess pulled the blister pack from his jacket pocket and popped four tablets, swallowing them dry. This headache felt like it was going to be a doozy.

CHAPTER 31

Stanley Roker belched, winced and then rubbed his chest with his hand, ignoring the disapproving look from a woman walking by, pushing a pram. He patted his pockets, looking for his indigestion tablets. Maybe this was it? The heart attack he'd always known was coming. Or a stroke? It could be a stroke. He could smell toasted bread, but then he was outside a sandwich shop, so it was hard to know for sure.

Part of him liked the idea of having a heart attack. Even Crystal couldn't have a go at him for not making enough money if he was in hospital, could she? He tried to play it out in his mind: his wife standing over his sickbed, her eyes filled with tearful concern, telling him to take it easy and that everything would be all right. Then he remembered the night they'd been sitting on the sofa in their habitual frosty silence, watching *Come Dine With Me*, and she'd turned to him, apropos of nothing, and asked him if he knew that if he died the insurance would automatically pay off the mortgage in full. From that night, he had started to lock the door of the spare room he now permanently slept in because apparently his breathing had become 'revolting' and earplugs hurt her ears.

Stanley popped two tablets in his mouth. He took them so often these days that everything had an aftertaste of chalky peppermint. He looked at his watch: 10.45 a.m. He didn't have time for this today. He had a lead on a footballer who was banging his hairstylist, and the kid had knocked in a hat-trick at the weekend. If Stanley was really lucky, the lad might have a call-up to the national team coming. 'England International in Secret Love Tryst' would pay a good five grand more than 'Premiership Footballer', and Stanley needed the money badly. Crystal wanted a holiday. All of that meant that even though Stanley had no time for this today, he had also been left with no option – the phone call he had received had been very clear on that point. And so he waited.

He looked up at the building on the other side of the street. He had pitched an article about the Dennard and its spate of associated suicides – he felt comfortable calling two a spate; he'd stretched language considerably more than that over the years – but the editors who were still taking his calls in London either already had the story or had no interest in it. One of the celebrity reality shows had kicked off on TV that week, so they had plenty of 'getting to know you' scandals to use already. Stanley hated those programmes – they allowed editors to dust off old stories about celebs who'd fallen out of the public eye rather than pay for dirt on the new lot. It was devaluing the noble tradition of tabloid journalism.

He turned to see what all the honking was about. A green Jaguar was coming around the corner, but only just. Its movement was slow and jerkily sporadic. Other cars were pulling around it, their drivers making their feelings known through universal gestures that probably weren't officially recognized in British Sign Language.

Stanley took a few quick steps back as the Jag surged forward, mounted the kerb and made a beeline for him. He'd long suspected that one of the many people he'd knifed in the metaphorical back over the years would try to have him killed, but he had always hoped he'd warrant a more professional attempt than this.

The car juddered to a halt, skewed across the pavement. The driver's door flew open and a young black woman with green hair got out and stomped off, ranting to herself as she went. 'Absolute 'mare. Absolute. What was I thinking?'

One of the rear doors swung open and Vincent Banecroft – or, to give him his full title, Vincent 'Bastard' Banecroft – clambered out, crutch in tow.

'Excellent,' Banecroft roared. 'Well done. Lesson one completed.'

The girl twirled around. 'Lesson? Lesson! You spent the whole drive shouting "faster, faster, faster" at me.'

'Well' – Banecroft held out his hands – 'we got here, didn't we? I mean, the parking needs work, but—'

She pointed a finger at him. 'You're mental, mate. You're absolutely . . . completely . . .' At a loss for words, she threw her hands up in the air and marched off around the corner.

'Don't go far. We've to head back soon.'

Only then did Banecroft notice Stanley.

'Ah, Stanley. Kid's a natural. Prodigy, no less.'

'I see your interpersonal skills are as strong as always, Vincent.'

Banecroft slammed the door shut and hobbled towards him. 'Why thank you, Stanley. That means a lot, coming from you.

Thank you so much for coming. I'd shake your hand only, well, let's be honest, you're a festering landfill of a human being and I'd rather not touch you for fear of where you've been.'

'Thanks,' said Stanley. 'I'm glad I made the time to see you.'

'Yes,' said Banecroft, pulling a pack of cigarettes from his pocket and shoving one into his mouth. 'Let's pretend you had a choice.'

Stanley glared at Banecroft as he cupped his hands and lit the cigarette. He hated the man. Really, the word 'hate' was woefully inadequate to express the depth of his feelings. Stanley had liked his job at the *Herald*. Ten years ago, Banecroft had come in as editor, to huge fanfare, and cleared out Stanley and those he termed 'the rest of the pond scum'. He'd taken the paper in a more . . . well, upmarket was one way of describing the direction. Banecroft wasn't immune to celeb gossip, but he had much preferred holding the feet of politicians, judges and businessmen to the fire. He'd pissed off a lot of people, and that wasn't just limited to the hacks who had suddenly found themselves out of a job.

The fallen had gathered in the Regency pub on the day they were canned, and hatched devious schemes and plans to destroy the high and mighty Banecroft. Everyone had got paralytic, slept it off and then forgotten the whole thing by the morning after in the rush to find another job in a tricky economy. Everyone, that is, but Stanley. He was apparently the only one who had really meant it.

In hindsight, Stanley had to admit, he had become ever so slightly obsessed. He'd done surveillance on Banecroft for three weeks, but it had emerged that the man was the wrong kind of weirdo. He had no extracurricular activities and no interest in screwing around on his wife. Admittedly, she was fit as. Banecroft had seemed content to spend his days being the Rottweiler snapping at the establishment's heels, and then he'd go home, snuggle on the sofa and read a book. Stanley had needed to get creative. It had seemed like a fantastic idea at the time. Besides, in his second week as editor of the *Herald*, Banecroft had done a big exposé on the expense accounts of some top coppers, and they'd wanted to take him down almost as badly as Stanley.

Stanley had been very careful. He knew a guy who knew a guy, and he had spent more than he needed to – not just to get the stuff, but to have everyone involved forget that he had. Then he had stashed the gear in Banecroft's shed and put in the anonymous tip. Stanley had parked down the street and watched gleefully as the drugs squad raided Banecroft's house. Then, confused, he'd watched as the cops had apologized and run out of there with their tails between their legs. The bloody idiots. It hadn't been that hard to find.

Stanley had been about to log an irate anonymous call when the passenger door of his car had opened and Banecroft had got in. 'Hello, Stanley.'

'What do you want?'

Banecroft had just smiled and handed him the envelope. It had been thick.

'Something to remember me by. Footage of you planting a kilo of cocaine in my shed – tut-tut. The envelope also contains some detailed evidence of you doing very naughty things over the years to get stories. I'm sure the Metropolitan Police would be interested in your . . . let's call them "unconventional" methods. You've got until morning to get out of London, and if I ever even smell that you might have come back here, I'll hang you out to dry.'

Then he'd calmly climbed back out again. 'Oh, and do drive carefully, Stanley. There's a kilo of cocaine in your fuel tank, and I've honestly no idea what effect it'll have. It might make you go really fast, or it might just force you to pull over and then bore you to tears talking about a screenplay it's going to write.'

That had been ten years ago, and since that fateful night, Stanley hadn't laid eyes on Banecroft. Until now. He'd heard about the breakdown and taken heartfelt delight in it. The mighty Vincent Banecroft, laid low. It had been glorious. He'd had no idea Banecroft was in Manchester, though – not until that morning.

'So,' said Stanley, 'what do you want?'

'Want?' said Banecroft. 'Do I have to want something? Can't I just be excited to catch up with an old friend?'

Then Banecroft smiled that smug little smile. He looked like shit, a real mess of a man, but still, that smile was the same one Stanley remembered. His chest burned again.

'Can we just . . . ?'

'Oh, very well,' said Banecroft. 'You used to be more fun, Stanley.' He nodded towards the Dennard building. 'Tell me about this?'

'What about it?'

Banecroft blew out a large plume of smoke. 'A little bird tells me you've been pitching it, so what's the story?'

'Do you mean other than the suicides?'

'Well, yes. The two "supposed" suicides are facts. You've never been one for just reporting facts, Stanley. What's the angle?'

'What's it to you?'

Banecroft leaned against the bonnet of his car. 'Oh, Stanley, for someone with your experience, you've forgotten how this works. I've got the dirt on you, so I'll ask the questions.'

'Fine. Whatever. I was pitching human interest.'

'Really? Not your usual area of expertise, Stanley.'

Stanley shrugged. 'It's a small town – got to work harder for it up here. The first guy – the one a couple of weeks ago – was a fireman and his kid is sick in hospital. Like, terminal. I wanted to do one on the widow – husband killed himself, can't cope, kid on the way out. Real tear-jerker.'

Banecroft pulled a face. 'Christ. You really are something, Stanley.'

'Thanks. Means a lot, coming from you.'

'Is that it?'

Stanley held out his hands. 'Look, I told you on the phone it wasn't much. This meeting is a waste of everyone's time.'

'You say that, Stanley, but I wanted to see you again. Remind myself that things could be worse.'

'I'd give up going for high and mighty, Banecroft – you can't carry it off any more.'

'Oh, Stanley, Stanley, Stanley. Dung beetles still look down on you. Now, before I let you get back to whatever truly dreadful thing you've got planned for the rest of the day, I need you to do me a little favour.'

Moretti stood outside the pub and watched Banecroft talking to the fat man. He was too far away to guess at the tone of the conversation, but suddenly the big guy started flapping his arms around, as if the pair were arguing. The two men then pointed over at the Dennard building. They were really shouting now. The fat man stomped across the street, earning honks from oncoming traffic, while Banecroft, with a final wave of his hand, disappeared into the sandwich shop. Moretti leaned against the wall and watched as the fat man approached the security guards at the gate of the building site and proceeded to get into an argument with them.

Moretti had passed the site earlier. There was a lot of extra security, which wasn't a surprise. Circumstances had forced him to improvise a lot more than he would have liked this week. His original reasons for using the Dennard building in his attempt to create a Were had been straightforward. While it wasn't the tallest building in Manchester, the fact that it wasn't completed and was relatively isolated in its location meant that it would provide them with much-needed privacy. Yes, the height was important too – for the mixture to work, the subject's adrenalin levels had to spike dramatically, and a long fall was the best way to make that happen.

In the olden days, subjects had hurled themselves off cliffs to achieve the effect, but sadly cliffs were in short supply in Manchester. When the first subject failed, it had at least looked like a simple suicide, no questions asked. And so he'd used it again with Merchant, and thankfully that time it had done the job. When Moretti had discovered the kid snooping around following the 'collateral damage' death of the homeless guy, he'd been forced to think on his feet. The Dennard building had been the first place that had popped into his head.

He'd expected, as with the first failed attempt to make a Were, that the resultant crater would be chalked up to another tragic suicide, waste of life, blah blah blah. Sure, two suicides at the same location so close together would attract attention, but nobody was going to suspect foul play, not when both jumpers appeared on CCTV entering the building alone. At least that should have been the case, but this Banecroft character seemed determined to make a nuisance of himself. Moretti was just keeping an eye on him, making sure he didn't create enough noise for it to be an issue.

The fat man was continuing his argument with the security guards, and two more now entered the fray. It had just dawned on Moretti that Banecroft had been in the sandwich shop for a considerable amount of time when . . .

'Hello.'

Moretti turned to find the man in question standing right behind him, holding his hand out and grinning.

'Vincent Banecroft, but seeing as you followed us here from the office, I'm guessing you already knew that.'

'I'm sorry,' said Moretti. 'I've no idea what you're talking about.'

Banecroft smiled. 'Sure you do. You were driving an Audi TT, and we were a nightmare to follow because my protégée hasn't quite got the hang of the whole driving thing yet.'

Moretti shrugged. 'I'm sorry, you've got me confused with someone else. I'm just a tourist visiting for a few days.'

'Yes, because Manchester in March is a big deal with our American brethren. You must really love rain. Now, who are you and what is your interest in Simon Brush's death?'

Moretti's smile twitched slightly. 'I . . .'

People walking by were noticing them now. Moretti tried to change his body language, make it look as if they were two friends chatting rather than two men squaring up to each other.

'It's fine,' he said. 'There's been a big misunderstanding. Let me show you something that will clear this right up.'

He took the gold coin on a silver chain out from the inside pocket of his jacket and, with a practised twist of the wrist, set it spinning. 'It's a funny story actually. If you take a look at this, everything will become clear.'

Banecroft stared long and hard at the coin – then his clear eyes darted back up to Moretti's. 'Seriously, if you're going to start using close-up magic . . . I'm not a violent man, but I'm willing to make an exception.'

Moretti pulled back in shock, causing the coin to swing erratic-ally. 'That's not possible. How did . . . Who . . . Who are you?'

'We've covered that,' said Banecroft. 'But I would rather like to know who you are and what the hell you have to do with all this.'

Moretti slipped the coin back in his pocket and looked around nervously. 'How are you . . . ?' Without another word, he stepped away from Banecroft quickly.

'Hey, come back here.'

Moretti walked briskly to the corner and then turned left.

'Hey!'

When Banecroft came around the corner, he found himself shout-ing after a man who was nowhere to be seen. There was no doorway – nothing but solid concrete wall. Either the man was an Olympic sprinter or he had vanished into thin air.

CHAPTER 32

Ox sat looking at the screen with Grace standing behind him. Neither of them said anything for a very long time.

Eventually, Grace cleared her throat. 'Are you sure that is . . . ?'

'I don't know,' replied Ox. 'I don't know what I'm looking at. I mean . . . it's . . . I can see that it's . . .'

'Could it be fake?'

'Absolutely. Only . . .'

'What?' asked Grace.

'Only I don't know how somebody – why somebody – I mean, it don't make no sense.'

'No.'

'It doesn't feel fake, does it?'

Grace said nothing in response, just blessed herself.

They both looked up at the sound of rapid footsteps across the wooden floor in reception. A moment later, Hannah and Reggie walked in, looking flushed.

'Oh my God,' said Hannah, 'you are not going to believe this.'

'She's right,' said Reggie. 'I'm not sure I believe it. I mean, I do, but I can't believe I believe it.'

The two of them looked positively giddy.

'Right,' said Ox. 'Well, we've found something pretty incredible as—'

Hannah looked at Reggie. 'Do you want to tell them or should I?'

'You do it. You found it.'

'I couldn't have without your help.'

'Oh, stop it. You were positively Sherlockian and you know it.' Reggie pointed at Hannah and addressed the rest of the room. 'The kid is a natural.'

'Yeah,' said Ox, 'but listen. I—'

Hannah spread her hands. 'OK, I know this will sound crazy, but hear me out.'

They all turned as a door slammed loudly and in stomped Stella. She pointed back in the direction from which she had come. 'That dude is unbelievable. He is stone-cold insane! I can't believe I got back in the car with him. He just sat in the back, necking a bottle of whiskey, shouting, "Go faster! Don't hit stuff!" over and over again. He is—'

The door crashed open and Banecroft too stomped in, as much as was possible for a man on a crutch to stomp. 'Ah, excellent, you're all here. Something very peculiar happened.'

'I guarantee it's not weirder than what happened to us,' said Hannah.

'Yes,' agreed Reggie. 'This story is incredible, but it does make sense. Sort of.'

'Ehm, guys?' said Ox.

'Forget all that,' said Stella. 'I want to talk about this lunatic and the mental torture he put me through.'

Banecroft scoffed. 'Torture? Nonsense. It was character-building.'

'Character-building?!'

'So, we're down at the scene of the first murder—' Hannah began.

'Hannah is an absolute natural at this investigating thing, by the way,' interrupted Reggie.

'I met with my source,' announced Banecroft. 'But more importantly, we were followed.'

'Yeah. It was dead character-building. Why—'

'SHUT UP!'

The entire room turned as one and looked at Grace.

She took a deep breath. 'Right. I appreciate you all have things you wish to talk about, but with the sweet Lord Jesus as my witness, you all need to shut up and listen to Ox.'

This was met with a selection of nods.

Grace turned to Ox. 'Go ahead.'

'Right,' said Ox, looking slightly shell-shocked. 'So, short version: I went over to Simon's house and, well, I sort of temporarily took his back-up hard drive.'

'Oh, Ox,' said Hannah.

'I'm only . . . I'm gonna give it back. It's just . . . I remembered he had it and I couldn't find his camera nowhere.'

'Ox . . .' said Reggie, shaking his head disapprovingly.

'It was a spur-of-the-moment thing. I remembered, y'see, that his camera backs up to the cloud. I helped him set it up.'

'I have little interest in your petty thievery,' said Banecroft, 'but I assume there is another shoe that is about to drop?'

'Well, yeah,' said Ox. 'So it backed up like it was supposed to, all on to this hard drive. It's set up to use that cloud wi-fi that's in lots of different spots in the city. Whoever had or has it – the camera, I mean – I'm guessing they didn't know. They must've passed a wi-fi hotspot, because it backed up. We've got all of Simon's pictures.'

'And?' said Banecroft.

'And,' said Ox, 'there's a . . . Well, there's pictures that . . .' He looked up at Grace.

'Just show them,' she said.

'Right,' said Ox, turning his screen around. He pressed a key and a picture of the Dennard building at night filled the screen. They all watched as he pressed another key and a couple more pictures of the building skipped by. Next was a dimly lit stairwell.

'Can we—?' started Banecroft.

'Shut up, Vincent,' snapped Grace.

Ox continued to scroll through the pictures: a few more of the stairwell and then images of Manchester at night, taken from a great height. The rooftop.

'Well, this is all lovely, but . . .'

Banecroft didn't need to be told to shut up this time.

The picture on the screen changed again – to a blurred shot of what looked like fur.

Then the angle flipped. The next photo looked as if it had been taken from below. Like the person taking it had been lying on the ground. Above the camera towered a terrifying beast with massive teeth, a protruding snout and wild, red pupils in bloodshot eyes. The pictures moved on.

Hannah gasped as the point of view altered dramatically once more. The camera was now slightly above the beast, which had its arm extended as if holding the photographer high off the ground, possibly by the throat.

The final image was of the blurry Manchester skyline, the lights of the city jerky smears on the screen. Then the screen went black.

Reggie spoke in a whisper. 'Did we just see Simon's final moments?'

Ox nodded. 'I . . . I think so.'

'What was . . . What was that thing?' asked Stella.

'Whatever it was,' said Hannah, 'it matches the description we had of whatever was responsible for the murder in Castlefield.'

'Excuse me?' said Banecroft.

Hannah just nodded.

'I can't believe I'm saying this,' said Reggie, 'but didn't it look a bit like . . . I mean, if you saw it on a TV programme, you'd call it a werewolf.'

'Could it be somebody in a suit or something like that?' asked Grace. 'I mean, Lord knows there are a lot of weirdos out there.'

'If that was a suit,' said Stella, 'then it was a seriously expensive one. I mean – it don't look like no special effects to me.'

'Plus,' said Hannah, 'from what we've heard about that . . . thing, it can jump impossible distances, which explains how it got on top of a forty-two-storey building without being seen, but . . .'

Banecroft stepped forward. 'Show me the second-to-last picture again.'

Ox nodded and pressed a couple of keys, and the image of the beast holding Simon above him reappeared on the screen. It sent a shiver down Hannah's spine as she looked at it again. Part of her was still trying not to believe it, but somewhere deep down it felt real. Those eyes . . . She thought of how terrified Simon must have been, coming face to face with that monstrosity. The sheer terror. And despite it all, he had still had the presence of mind to keep snapping pictures. Hannah looked down at the floor and pushed a knuckle into the corner of her eye.

'I thought so,' said Banecroft. 'I recognize him.'

Reggie didn't attempt to keep the incredulity from his voice. 'You recognize that? How could you possibly recognize . . . ?'

'I met him an hour ago.'

'That's bullshit, man,' said Stella. 'I was watching you. You met a couple of old dudes. You didn't meet no werewolf.'

Banecroft slowly looked at each of them in turn. 'Really? Well, this is disappointing. A room full of supposed journalists . . .'

'Vincent,' said Grace, 'for once, just stop being so . . . you.'

Banecroft stepped towards the screen and pointed at the beast. 'I didn't meet that. I think meeting that in the middle of the day would attract some attention, even in Manchester. No, I'm referring to him.'

To be fair, thought Hannah, what with the monster in the foreground being quite so monumentally distracting, it was easy to miss. The flash of the camera caught mostly the beast – its brown fur, the massive, fang-like canines with ribbons of saliva hanging from them, and those eyes . . . Those eyes would distract anyone. It was only when you attempted to look past it that you noticed what Banecroft was referring to.

There, in the background, just over the beast's right shoulder, was a figure – or at least a partial one. The man was wearing black, which had hardly been picked out at all by the flash, giving the illusion that his head was floating in the air with no body attached. All you could see was half of a face. It was that of a bald man, and he appeared to be grinning.

Everyone's a Critic

Researchers studying the Wantaki tribe, one of the few uncontacted peoples left in the world, have made a shocking discovery. In the last two years, the Wantaki have developed their own form of social media. According to Dr Serena Daniels, 38, from Boston University, 'some members of the tribe have taken to drawing pictures on a large rock at the edge of the village. Every night, other tribespeople then come and look at the pictures and either applaud or throw faeces. Sadly, this has not led to a greater appreciation of art and artists in their culture, but we have noticed that the natives capable of producing the most faeces have started to become dominant.'

CHAPTER 33

The bullpen was a hive of activity: Ox alternating furious typing with speed-pumping his stress ball while he read, reread and then, more often than not, deleted; Reggie hen-pecking away at his keyboard at a relentlessly slow but steady pace.

'Where in the hell is . . . ?' started Banecroft.

'It's coming to you right now,' finished Ox.

The previous four hours had been an intensive crash course in how a newspaper was assembled. Hannah felt as if she was being carried along by a flood. She'd helped Reggie write up what they had learned, in between Banecroft hollering stuff at her, reading and rereading everything being sent to her, correcting the grammar and, in Ox's case, rationing his excessive use of exclamation marks. Not that the subject matter wasn't exclamation-worthy.

Hannah was standing beside Banecroft, who was standing over Stella as she worked at her computer.

'Stop crowding me,' said Stella.

'I need to see the screen.'

'Well, then, either get some glasses or take a bath. You smell like manky bacon, man.'

'There's no need to get personal,' said Banecroft.

Stella glanced up. 'Have you met you?'

On her computer, Stella was running a software package that could format the text into columns around the artwork, slot in adverts and basically do everything that makes a newspaper a newspaper. Occasionally, Banecroft would say something that made no sense to Hannah, and Stella's screen would become a whirr of activity. Before she knew it the pages would be formatted entirely differently. Pictures and text danced about in a way that would have been almost hypnotic had Banecroft not been shouting in her ear every other minute. When the chaos was over, Hannah would need to sit down with Stella and figure out how on earth she did it all.

'Right,' said Banecroft. 'Front page, we go full picture of that – whatever the hell it is. We need the headline.'

He looked around the room.

Ox didn't look up from his furious typing, but he managed to continue one-handed as he waved the other in the air. 'Big letters – "What the f—"'

'Ox!' scolded Grace, who was circulating with yet another tray of teas – this time accompanied by Viennese whirls. She couldn't write an article but she, too, wanted to bring her A game.

'Sorry, Grace.'

'"Werewolves in Manchester"?' offered Hannah.

'No,' said Banecroft. 'We will not use that word. We use that word and it's easy to dismiss it as some kind of hoax.'

'Won't people do that anyway?' asked Reggie.

'Most will,' said Banecroft. 'But we're not writing for them. We're writing for the truth. I'll come back to it.' He turned back to Stella. 'Page two – Woodward and Bernstein's article on the Castlefield murder.'

Hannah glanced over at Reggie and he gave her a nod.

'Page three,' continued Banecroft. 'Blown-up shot of our mystery man in the background – and push the ads. Then – yes – put this: "*The Stranger Times* is offering a ten-thousand-pound reward for any information on this individual that leads to a conviction."'

'Can we do that?' asked Hannah.

'Yes.'

'I mean, can we afford that?'

Banecroft shrugged. 'If this paper finds the man standing behind whatever that' – he pointed at the picture again – 'is, then I'd imagine we'll be able to afford it by the time any conviction happens. Stick Ox's article under it.'

'Don't you mean "the Chinese one"?' asked Stella.

'Don't be so racist,' said Banecroft.

'OK,' said Hannah. 'Can I suggest again—?'

'No,' said Banecroft. 'For the last time, we are not handing over our evidence to your boyfriend in the police.'

'He's not my boyfriend.' Hannah winced at her own voice as it climbed a full octave. She was aware of the whole room stopping to look at her. She reddened. 'Oh, shut up. All of you. The man gave me a lift home in the rain.'

'Indeed,' said Banecroft. 'Is that what they're calling it now?'

'Can we talk about something else?' chimed Stella.

'Yes. Thank you, Stella.'

'Because the idea of old people having sex is frankly making me want to hurl, innit.'

'Super,' said Hannah. 'Thanks for that. To go back to my original point . . .'

'No,' said Banecroft. 'If they want to see our evidence, they can read it in the paper like everybody else. I'm not having this brushed under the carpet.'

'We don't know . . .'

'We do,' said Banecroft with an air of finality. 'Trust me, I've been in this game a while. Don't forget, I used to put out real papers overflowing with actual news, and I'm telling you, the way to get the boys and girls in blue to do anything is to point out that they aren't doing anything. If we want Simon's killers brought to justice, then this is what will get it done. Speaking of which . . .' He turned his attention back to Stella. 'Pages four and five – pictures of the Dennard building and the full explanation of what we think happened.' He looked pointedly at Ox. 'Of course, that's assuming we ever have that explanation . . .'

'Sent!' shouted Ox, pulling his fingers away from the keyboard and shaking his hands at the wrist as if they were in danger of bursting into flames.

'Right,' said Hannah, rushing back to her desk. 'You'll have it in five minutes.'

'I'll have it in three,' said Banecroft.

'You can have it now, but if you want it edited, it'll be in five.'

'I preferred you when you were the clueless new girl.'

'I'm still clueless. I've just realized the rest of you are too.'

'Right,' said Ox. 'I need a smoke.'

'Request denied,' said Banecroft.

'I wasn't asking—'

'Page six,' continued Banecroft.

'Actually . . .' said Reggie. Ox looked at him and the two of them had a brief, wordless conversation before Reggie continued. 'Ox wrote an obit for Simon yesterday. It's really good.'

Banecroft locked eyes with Ox for a long moment.

'Fine. Obit. Picture. Push the ads back.'

'Right,' said Hannah. 'Send me that too, Ox.'

'OK,' piped up Stella, 'I've got a page of adverts that should have been placed by now. Are we bringing out a supplement just full of ads?'

'Find space near the back,' said Banecroft.

'There'll be complaints,' warned Grace.

'Let them complain,' said Banecroft. 'This edition will sell more than any other in the sad history of this rag or I'm a monkey's uncle.'

'It would explain the smell,' muttered Stella.

Heads turned as they heard boots on the stairs.

'Grace,' said Banecroft, 'we are not accepting visitors.'

Grace slammed down her tray and headed towards reception. 'I'm on it.'

Banecroft turned to address the room. 'Right, I know you're all tired. We've been working solidly now for hours. Here's the thing – I don't care. In the history of this printed loo roll we call a paper, this is that rarest of things: an important issue. So please, limit your incompetence as much as possible.'

'Inspiring as always,' said Reggie.

Banecroft looked over at Hannah. 'Oh, for God's sake, what the hell is wrong with you now?'

'Shut up,' said Hannah, looking up from her PC and dabbing her eyes with a tissue. 'Ox' – she pointed at her screen – 'this is . . . this is really good.'

'Right,' said Banecroft. 'Well, if we're all finished—'

'You are.'

They all turned to see an ashen-faced Grace standing in the doorway, flanked by DS Wilkerson and DI Sturgess. Several uniformed police stood behind them.

Sturgess held up a folded piece of paper. 'You being finished is pretty much what this document says. Please step away from your computers.'

'What in the hell is the meaning of this?' bellowed Banecroft. 'You can't just come tramping in here.'

'Yes,' said Sturgess. 'Yes, we can. This is a court order. This publication is being shut down and all your devices seized.'

This news was met with a clamour of voices as everyone in the room tried to talk at the same time.

'The hell it is,' said Banecroft. 'I don't know what you've heard . . .' He glared at Hannah, who looked horrified by the implication.

'Actually,' said Sturgess, 'I haven't heard anything. What I have seen, though, is that a hard drive belonging to Simon Brush was taken from his home by someone who I am reliably informed is a member of staff at this – for want of a better word – newspaper. My tech officers have confirmed its removal and Mrs Brush assures us that only one individual could have had access to it. Mrs Brush knows him as Ox?' Sturgess surveyed the room. 'And seeing as you all just made a great effort not to look at this gentleman,' he said, pointing at Ox, 'I'm assuming that he is the individual in question.'

'We absolutely deny that accusation,' said Banecroft. 'We did not take any hard drive.'

DS Wilkerson pointed to Ox's desk. 'I can see it. It's right there.'

'That is a hard drive,' said Banecroft. 'We never said we didn't have *a* hard drive. And I assume you are not arresting everyone in possession of a hard drive. Although, frankly, it wouldn't surprise me.'

'You're welcome to appeal the decision,' said Sturgess.

'Rest assured we will.'

'In the meantime, we are confiscating your computers and the hard drive we have reason to believe belongs to Simon Brush.' Sturgess nodded and the uniformed PCs moved into the room. 'It turns out that stealing from the dead is still considered a bit of a no-no.'

'We're doing nothing of the sort,' said Banecroft, hobbling towards Sturgess. 'We are finishing the story that Simon started.'

Sturgess stepped towards him. 'Would this be the same guy you left standing outside?'

'Yes. The one you are going to conclude committed suicide, despite evidence to the contrary.'

Sturgess bristled. 'I will follow the facts. Nothing is getting covered up.'

'Really?' said Banecroft. 'Tell me, how many inexplicable deaths have you chased to a satisfying conclusion?'

'What would you know about it?'

The two men were getting dangerously close to each other. 'I used to be the editor of a national newspaper. Do you think

I've not seen the stories getting killed? The cases being quietly dropped?'

Sturgess ran his hand across his forehead and rubbed a finger into his temple. 'That doesn't happen on my investigations.'

'Yet,' said Banecroft. 'You should have added "yet".'

Sturgess pointed at Ox. 'DS Wilkerson, arrest that man. The rest of you, assuming you don't want to be joining him down the station, take your hands off your keyboards now and do nothing to prevent my officers from carrying out their duties.' Sturgess held out the court order, and when Banecroft didn't take it, he tossed it on the desk beside him. 'Consider yourself formally notified. Pending review, *The Stranger Times* is out of business.'

CHAPTER 34

Reggie, Hannah and Grace leaned against Hannah's desk and surveyed the office. Hannah realized it was now dark outside. She'd been too busy to notice the day slip into night. There was no point in any of them being there, not since the police had shut them down, but nobody had gone home.

'Do you think,' said Grace, 'that we could use this as an opportunity to give the place a proper clean?'

The others just looked at her.

'What? I am simply saying, with all the computers gone, we could, you know, tidy up the place.'

Reggie sighed. 'Dearest Grace, while, as always, your enthusiasm is appreciated, I'm not entirely sure you've grasped the magnitude of the situation.'

'As in?'

'As in,' continued Reggie, 'seeing as the photocopier broke down over two years ago and we haven't been able to get it fixed, I wouldn't hold out a great deal of hope that we can afford a lengthy legal fight with Greater Manchester Police. It'll be weeks, if not months, before we get our stuff back, and that's assuming they'll allow us to publish at all, given . . . well, everything.'

'Oh,' said Grace.

'Shit!' said Hannah, loud enough to be on the receiving end of an admonishing look from Grace. 'Sorry, but I've just realized I'm going to have to do job interviews again.'

'Well,' said Grace, 'they cannot be worse than the one you had for here.'

'You'd be surprised.'

'Oh, hellfire,' sighed Reggie. 'I'll have to go back to giving ghost tours. Walking around with a yellow umbrella while German tourists ask questions and hen dos from Bolton keep trying to form conga lines behind me. Somebody kill me now!'

'What about you, Grace?' asked Hannah. 'What'll you do?'

Grace shrugged. 'I can type and answer phones – people always need that. I will go back to temping and getting let go every month or so. I do not do well with so-and-sos called Clive telling me to "tone it down".'

All three of them went back to staring glumly at their surroundings.

'By the way,' said Grace, 'he may have sent you flowers, but I do not like your new man.'

'What are you talking about?'

'That Detective Inspector Sturgess.'

'He sent me flowers?'

'Well,' said Grace, 'flowers turned up and the card said "from a secret admirer". How many men in Manchester do you know?'

Hannah did not appreciate Grace's tone. 'None. And I don't know Sturgess either – he gave me a lift home once. I've seen the bus driver more regularly.'

'Well, he is clearly smitten.'

'Was my name even on the card?'

Grace looked unsure – which was something of a new look for her. 'Well, no, but who else would they be for?'

'They could be for you! Or Stella.'

Grace's tone went up a notch in the haughtiness stakes. 'They are most definitely not for me – and they had better not be for Stella! She is too young to be courting.'

'They could be for me,' interjected Reggie. Both women looked at him in surprise.

'I mean, I highly doubt they are, but you never know. It is the twenty-first century, ladies. They could be for anyone who works here.'

Banecroft's office door flew open and he hobbled out.

'Almost anyone,' added Reggie quickly.

Hannah ignored him and addressed Banecroft. 'Well?'

'I've rung our lawyer, Ms Carter, but I keep getting her voice-mail. I have left several detailed yet pointed messages. I assume she'll get back to us before long.'

'Shouldn't we go down to the station?' asked Grace.

'There's no point,' said Reggie. 'Ox will be being processed and then interviewed, and at this time of night, they'll keep him in. Trust me, I've . . .' Reggie left it hanging and looked away, clearly changing his mind about sharing whatever he'd been about to say next.

'Besides,' said Banecroft, 'he's a paranoid who's convinced that "the man" is out to get him. I'd imagine there's a part of him that's enjoying finally being proved right. Here.' Banecroft supplied

Hannah with four plastic cups. 'Hand those out. Seeing as it's a special occasion, I thought I'd break out the good china.'

'Are these clean?'

'You can be picky or you can be drunk,' he said, pulling a nearly full bottle of whiskey from his pocket.

'I do not really drink,' said Grace.

'You're in luck,' replied Banecroft. 'Few get the chance to learn from a master.'

He filled the cups, giving himself a large enough measure that it was in danger of spilling over. He put down the bottle and raised his drink in the air. 'What shall we drink to? I know – to *The Stranger Times*. The dilapidated old boat went down while trying to report the news. Not enough of it about.'

Hannah felt the whiskey burn her throat as she downed it.

'Lord, that tastes horrible,' exclaimed Grace.

'Ah,' said Banecroft, 'classic rookie mistake. Don't try to taste it. Knock it back as fast as humanly possible and then you don't have to. Same again . . .'

They held out their cups and Banecroft refilled them.

'Whose turn is it?'

Reggie raised his cup. 'To Ox. The daft sod spent a life doing wrong and now he will go to prison for trying to do right.'

They all drank again.

Banecroft topped up everyone without asking. 'Well?'

Hannah held her cup aloft. 'To Simon, for . . .' She hesitated, unsure what to say next.

'To Simon,' said Grace, lifting her drink. 'May he spend less time outside St Peter's gate than he did outside ours.'

They all joined in the toast and drank again.

'Lord, how is it tasting worse now? How can that be?'

They were interrupted by a pointed cough and looked up to see Stella, hands on hips, glowering at them.

'Christ,' said Banecroft, 'we've been busted by the fun police.'

'One,' said Grace, before belching softly.

''Scuse me,' said Stella. 'Sorry if I'm interrupting, but I thought we had a newspaper to put out?'

Banecroft shook his head. 'Dear oh dear. Her generation is so used to having technology, she literally cannot understand when it is taken away.' He raised his voice and spoke slowly, waving his cup around to emphasize his point. 'Remember – the nasty police-men came, took all the computers. We've got no computers.'

Stella responded by raising her voice and talking even slower. 'I know. That's why when you were arguing with the po-po, I sent the pictures to Manny.'

'Yes,' said Banecroft, even more slowly and loudly, 'but they took his PC too.'

'I . . . know . . .' Stella now shouted, delivering a word every three seconds or so. 'But . . . not . . . before . . . he . . . printed . . . them!'

'Oh, for God's sake,' said Hannah, standing up. 'Stop behaving like children.'

'She started it.'

Hannah walked over to Stella. 'Are you saying Manny still has his PC?'

'No. I'm saying Manny says he doesn't need his PC. He says we can print some kind of newspaper without it.'

'Why the hell didn't you say so?' Banecroft stood up and snatched the cups out of Reggie and Grace's hands. 'Don't stand around here getting drunk – we've got a paper to put out.'

Meanwhile, a couple of hundred yards away, a lady called Caroline Redford yelped in alarm. She was out walking her dog, Toto, and had been pretending to pick up Toto's doings with a poo bag – she didn't like the feel of it, but in her eyes, doing the mime at least showed willing, should anyone be watching – when a short, bald man wearing headphones, sitting in a nearby parked car, repeatedly punched the steering wheel in a fit of anger. Toto barked ferociously at the disturbance; he had always been a sensitive dog.

Caroline looked in the car's window. 'Are you all right?'

The man waved her away dismissively.

'Well, no need to be so rude about it. You need to work on your anger management skills.'

The man looked at her for a long moment in a way that made Caroline feel very uncomfortable. A shiver ran down her spine, as if someone had just walked over her grave, then she turned and hurried off, tugging the still-barking Toto in her wake.

Twenty minutes later, Caroline Redford and Toto reached their front door. She dipped her hand into her coat pocket and screamed. For years afterwards she would still think back on it and struggle to find any kind of logical explanation. Had she been having some kind of breakdown? Had she been the victim of some elaborate and cruel practical joke?

How had she ended up with a pocket full of dog shit?

CHAPTER 35

'You go.'

They were standing in Banecroft's office, or rather Hannah was. Banecroft was sitting with his injured foot on his desk, scratching around the bandages with a riding crop he had obtained from somewhere.

'Excuse me?'

'Damn, these bandages are itchy. Do you think I can take them off yet?'

'No,' said Hannah. 'And sorry, can we loop back to the part where I said we need to talk to our printer, who can apparently still produce a newspaper?'

'You go. I said that already.'

Hannah leaned on the desk. 'Are you . . . ?' She stopped as a whiff of Banecroft's feet assailed her nostrils. As diplomatically as possible, she took a step back. 'Are you scared of Manny?'

'Don't be ridiculous. I am not scared of Manny.'

'You are. You're scared of Manny.'

'It's almost hard to believe a man is divorcing you.'

'I'm divorcing him, and you are scared of Manny. Why are you scared of Manny?'

'Shut up.'

'Is it the hair?'

'Don't be—'

'Is it the nakedness?' Hannah worked her eyebrows. 'Do you find his propensity for nakedness intimidating?'

'No.'

'Arousing?'

'I can fire you, y'know.'

'From what?' asked Hannah. 'We've already been shut down.'

'No, we haven't. Not while we can still put out a paper. Even if it is only locally, at least that is something.'

'I agree,' said Hannah.

'So?'

'So I'll go down and see how we're going to print a newspaper.'

'Good.'

'Because you're too scared of Manny.'

Banecroft snapped. He pitched the riding crop, which whizzed past Hannah's ear. 'I'm not scared of Manny!'

'Did you just throw a riding crop at me?'

'No. Or you'd have been hit by a riding crop. I have superb aim.'

'Says the man who shot himself in the foot.'

Banecroft dragged his foot back off the desk, sending a pile of papers flying in the process. 'Don't you have somewhere to be? Urgently?'

Hannah raised her hands. 'All right, all right. I'll go, because you're—'

'It's the press!' cried Banecroft.

Hannah, who had just turned towards the door, spun on her heels. 'Excuse me?'

'The printing press. I don't . . .' Banecroft's expression was pained. 'I don't . . . I always feel like it's watching me.'

'The machine?'

'I am fully aware it makes little sense. That doesn't mean I don't feel it. It makes me uneasy. It's like the damn thing is always hungry.'

'Thank you for sharing this with me.'

'Get the hell out of my office.'

Loath as she was to admit it, Hannah got it. She had been standing in the press's vicinity for about fifteen minutes now, and it did rather loom. It felt as if it were gradually getting closer to her, which logic told her was, of course, impossible. Still, she took another step back. While pointedly not looking at the machine, Hannah noticed something odd about the rest of the room – namely that no one else was looking at it either. It sat there, quietly hissing, the occasional metal limb clanking or piston firing, like a great beast waiting to spring into action.

From her limited exposure to him, and on one occasion *of* him, Hannah knew that Manny was not the easiest individual to communicate with at the best of times. This was not the best of times. This was a time when Manny had heard the police raiding the paper's offices, and had seemingly swallowed any and all recreational/medicinal substances he may have had lying about the place. At this moment, if relaxation was an Olympic sport,

Manny would miss his flight to the Games – that's how relaxed he was.

Grace had spent the last fifteen minutes pouring tea into him, which, if nothing else, meant that he would need to go to the toilet at some point. Hannah strongly hoped that he'd make it to the bathroom, although it was by no means guaranteed. He really was very relaxed.

'Manny,' said Grace, sounding exasperated. 'You need to focus, dear, all right? Focus!'

'We is focused. We is laser-focused,' he said, simultaneously standing up and falling down. Reggie made a move towards him and grabbed him under the arms, hauling him upright.

'Who be moving de floor?'

Hannah stepped forward and looked into Manny's eyes. She could see his pupils dancing around as he tried to focus on her.

'OK, Manny. Stella said you said we can still print the paper without all the stuff the police took. Is that right?'

Manny nodded emphatically several times. 'Yeah, yeah, mon, we tell you. We tell you true. We got the pictures from da chile on the machine already.' He pointed at the press. 'She got them. We just need the words.'

'Oh, right,' said Hannah. 'We don't have them.'

'Yeah,' said Stella, holding up her phone, 'we do. I sent all the articles to my personal account while you lot were gawping at the fuzz.'

'Then we golden!' said Manny, giving a cheerful wave.

'Really?'

Manny regained the use of his feet and Reggie carefully let him go. After a slight wobble and a few steps in the wrong direction, he executed a turn – all of his limbs somehow involved at different times – and led them to the corner of the room. 'Come, come, come, come.'

With a flourish, Manny pulled a paint-splattered sheet from what looked like a big metal picture frame on a worn, rusted stand.

Everyone who wasn't Manny looked at everyone else who wasn't Manny and shared a collective shrug. Manny chuckled to himself and heaved a large chest off the floor, placing it on a crate beside the frame. As he opened it, trays and trays of lead letters of various sizes concertinaed out before him. 'What we headline?'

Hannah watched in amazement as Stella read out the front-page article and Manny's hands became a near blur, grabbing letters from shelves and slotting them in place, seemingly without needing to look. He wasn't just arranging what Stella said; he was doing it right to left and back to front. As he worked, the press made an occasional whirring or hissing noise behind him.

Over the next two hours, Manny assembled an eight-page newspaper out of lead and sweat. Hannah had questions. Lots of questions. But after the first couple, which Manny attempted to answer with the kind of Manny-isms that are short on detail, Reggie pulled her aside.

'Aeroplanes,' he said.

'Excuse me?'

'Hannah, sweetheart – aeroplanes. Do you know how aeroplanes work?'

'Well . . .' Hannah gave him a confused look. 'There's something about thrust and, I guess, aerodynamics.'

'Exactly. You don't know. I don't know. I assume the only people who do know are the people who build them and possibly the people who fly them. Still, it's a big metal tube shooting through the sky, isn't it?'

'I suppose.'

'Now you, I'm sure, are fine with that concept, but I'm a nervous flyer. Do you know what I don't do when I get on an aeroplane, though? I don't go and find the pilot and start asking questions. Because on a base level, to which none of us admits, we all secretly think it's pretty much done by magic – and on an even deeper level, we all know that you don't question magic with logic, or else the magic might get the hump and stop working.'

Hannah nodded. 'I think I see your point. You think me asking questions might distract Manny?'

'Well, no. I mean, yes, that too – but no. While you were asking questions, I made the mistake of walking around . . . that . . .' He nodded at the press that stood behind him. Hannah was trying not to use the word looming in her head. 'Here's the thing: I've lapped it three times and I can't figure out where the power goes in or why there is steam coming out.'

Hannah furrowed her brow. 'OK.'

'Don't make that face. I'm not saying . . . Look, need I remind you of the picture that will be on the front of this paper? "There are more things in heaven and earth, Horatio, than are dreamt of in your philosophy." In short, don't question the magic.'

Hannah nodded again, then raised her voice. 'Reggie and I are going to leave you to it.'

'Good,' said Stella, without looking up from her phone.

It made no rational sense, but Hannah still felt as if the press was watching them as they turned and hurried out the door.

CHAPTER 36

'How much longer?' asked Banecroft.

The entire room – Hannah, Reggie and Grace – groaned as one. They were gathered in the bullpen like expectant fathers. There was nothing more for them to do, their role in proceedings having been completed. Right now, Stella was downstairs, continuing to dictate the contents of this week's edition to Manny, who, while still rather more 'relaxed' than usual, was transforming her words into something that could be printed. Hannah was trying very hard not to think about the many ways it could go wrong.

'We need to get the damn paper out,' barked Banecroft. 'Hannah, go down and—'

'No,' said Hannah.

'What do you mean, "no"?'

'I mean no, the same way I meant no the last seven times you asked. They're doing what they're doing and it'll take as long as it takes. I appreciate you think everything in life should be fixed by you shouting at it, but sadly that is not the case.'

Banecroft mumbled unintelligibly to himself, unwilling to accept that this was the case.

'Would anyone like a—' started Grace.

'No,' finished the rest of the room.

She looked more than a little put out by this response and Hannah felt immediately guilty. She reached across and patted the bit of Grace's forearm that wasn't covered in bracelets. 'Sorry, Grace, didn't mean to snap. I think we're all fine for tea, thanks.'

Grace gave a curt upward nod, at least mildly assuaged. 'Oh,' she said, 'I forgot to mention: Mrs Harnforth rang earlier, when everybody was out. She will be popping in.'

Banecroft threw his hands in the air. 'Oh, for – swear word, swear word, swear word. The owner is going to "pop in" and you're only mentioning it now?'

'It slipped my mind,' said Grace, 'what with the picture and the police raid and Ox getting arrested and all of that. Don't you snap at me, Vincent Banecroft, I am not paid to take your nonsense.'

'Perhaps we need to find someone who is?' countered Banecroft.

'Relax,' said Hannah. 'In case you forgot, I think we'll all be looking for gainful employment in the morning. So let's just take a breath, wait for Manny to get done doing what he's doing and then we can deal with the next thing when it's time for the next thing.'

Banecroft walloped his crutch against the side of the desk. 'I want the next thing to happen now!'

Grace gasped.

The words Hannah was about to utter died in her throat when she saw the expression on Grace's face: her mouth was hanging open and she was physically shaking, abject terror writ large across her face. Hannah followed her gaze.

There had been no noise, no warning. One second there had

been nothing but empty, mundane space and the next it was filled with the beast.

It stood there, ten feet tall, streaks of slobber trailing from its jaws, its eyes glowing red like portals to hell. Its long arms almost touched the floor, the tips of its black claws dangling inches above the floorboards. Drops of water dripped on to the floor beneath it.

A part of Hannah's brain that was refusing to engage with her surroundings fully noted that it must be raining again.

'I wish to withdraw my previous remark,' said Banecroft.

The beast moved towards them slowly. As it did so, Hannah watched its taut muscles straining beneath its matted brown fur. Nothing she had seen in her whole life compared to it.

The group of four started to move backwards simultaneously. Hannah felt the cold, damp plaster of the rear wall against her palms as she pressed her back against it.

'Oh, Christ,' said Reggie, in not much above a whisper.

Grace had her eyes closed, an unintelligible babble of prayer spilling forth from her.

Banecroft hurled his crutch at the beast, and it swatted it away casually as if it were a fly.

'Oh, bollocks,' said Banecroft.

'Two,' said Grace, working on autopilot.

It was all of eight or nine feet from them now, Hannah's desk the only thing between them and it. With a flick of its wrist, the beast sent the desk hurtling into the wall that divided the bullpen from Banecroft's office. It shattered on impact, taking a chunk out of the plaster. The beast continued its slow, steady

progress towards them, its unhurried movements entirely deliberate. Hannah got the sickening feeling it was enjoying itself.

'I'm going to rush it,' said Reggie quietly. 'Get ready to run.'

'No,' said Hannah. 'It'd be—'

The sound of a voice from the other end of the room cut her
short.

'Manny says that . . .'

Stella had appeared in the doorway, her mobile in one hand and
a book in the other. She looked at the beast and froze in place, as
her book fell to the floor.

The beast half turned and stared at her, its snout tilting upwards
slightly, sniffing the air. Then it reversed course and moved towards
her instead.

'Stella,' said Hannah, 'get out of here, now.'

She and the others followed the beast as it moved towards the
girl.

'Stella!' said Grace. 'You get out of here this instant, young
lady.'

Hannah scanned the surrounding desks. Paperwork. Nothing
that could be used as a weapon. She was dimly aware of the sound
of the door to Banecroft's office opening.

Stella's feet stayed glued in place. Her only movement was her
phoneless hand rising into a shaky point at the beast that was now
advancing towards her.

Reggie rushed towards the creature's back. Hannah saw a flash
as the blade in his hand caught the light. He was moving fast and
yet, apparently without seeing him, the beast's claw shot backwards and caught him in the chest with a blow that sent him

hurtling through the air, then on to and over one of the unused desks.

'STELLA!' screamed Hannah. 'RUN! JUST RUN!'

Stella's lips moved, mouthing unheard words.

And then Banecroft was in front of the girl, barging her out of the way. In his hands, he held, of all things, a notepad and pen.

'We are about to publish a story implicating you in the deaths of Simon Brush and John Maguire, aka Long John. Have you any comment you wish to make?'

The entire room shook as the beast roared, its long arm shooting out and sending Banecroft spinning away. The editor landed in a crumpled heap in the corner.

Stella stood once again, with nothing between her and the beast. She tossed her phone at it, but it bounced uselessly off its snout.

Hannah took a deep breath and began her run towards its back, only to find Grace matching her stride for stride.

And then Manny stepped calmly in front of Stella. There was a peculiar look in his eyes that caused the beast, Hannah and Grace to all stop in their tracks. It was as if the world had paused. Manny slumped forward as his feet rose off the ground, leaving his body suspended in the air, like a puppet dangling from invisible strings. The beast made a low, guttural sound in its throat, confused by this development in proceedings.

Hannah and Grace stood rooted to the spot as a cloud of white smoke began to flow from Manny. It wasn't coming out of anywhere; it seemed to rise off him like steam. The beast took a step back as the smoke thickened and expanded. Hannah and Grace grabbed on to each other reflexively and they too stepped backwards. The smoke kept coming thick and fast. It reached the ceiling and, amidst the swirls, a shape emerged – it was forming into a definite shape. Wings. Broad wings stretching outwards, becoming something if not solid, then certainly more solid-looking. At its centre, the air was roiling and shifting faster and faster.

Then it stopped.

A face. A face and then a body grew distinct in the writhing mass of smoke. A woman. The figure filled all available space, right up to the high ceiling, becoming more and more opaque. The face was beautiful. For a moment it hung there in the air above them, serene and regal, a munificent goddess staring down upon her loyal worshippers.

It surged forward without warning and warped into the thing of nightmares, a screeching face of terror. A voice issued forth from it – only it wasn't one voice. It was a legion, all screaming as one. 'Be gone, foul beast, this place is protected.'

The beast staggered backwards before leaping towards the smoky figure that hung above it. There was a blinding flash of light, then an animalistic squeal of pain as the beast hurtled between Hannah and Grace, sending them sprawling to the ground on its way to slamming into the back wall.

Hannah looked up in time to see the creature picking itself up and hurling itself through one of the three large stained-glass windows and out into the night.

As if it had never been there, the angelic figure was already smoke once again, retreating into the unresponsive form of Manny, who collapsed on to the ground.

CHAPTER 37

As she waited outside, it occurred to Hannah that this was the second time in a week that an ambulance had been called to the offices of *The Stranger Times*. She was expecting a lot of awkward questions. Her luck being what it was, as it pulled up she noticed that it was the same crew that had attended the first incident – the one where the boss had literally shot himself in the foot. A short woman in a high-vis jacket and a bad mood hopped out of the passenger seat.

'Was it you that made the call?'

'Yes,' said Hannah. 'He's upstairs. Broken arm and some cuts. Possible concussion.'

'Right. If it's the same guy as last time then we're not taking him.'

'It isn't.'

'Paramedics do not have to put up with that kind of abuse.'

'Honestly, it's not—'

'Emotional abuse is still abuse. The things he said to poor Keith . . .'

'I promise it isn't the same guy.'

Keith, a ludicrously tall younger man with a rake-thin body

and the wariest of wary expressions appeared from the far side of the vehicle. 'Debbie, it's not him again, is it?'

'No,' said Hannah quickly. 'This man is absolutely lovely. Honestly.'

'How did he get injured?' asked Debbie.

'That is a fantastic question,' said Hannah, with a very big smile and not the first idea how to answer. 'Fantastic.'

Reggie was sitting on the worn leather sofa, gingerly holding his broken arm against his chest while he took deep breaths. Meanwhile, at the far end of the room, Grace had plonked Manny into her chair behind the reception desk and was plying him with tea and a selection box of biscuits that Hannah guessed she kept in reserve for really big emergencies.

Debbie and Keith bent down to Reggie and examined him. They soon concurred that his arm was indeed broken – the protruding bone was a bit of a giveaway.

Reggie looked up at Hannah. 'I'll be all right, sweet girl – honestly. It's just a scratch.' He smiled at the ridiculousness of his own statement.

'Do you want me to come with you to the hospital?' asked Hannah.

'No need. No need at all. Besides, I think you might be required here.'

As if to emphasize his point, a crashing noise came from the direction of Banecroft's office, followed by a bellow of 'Unbelievable!'

As soon as they had seen to Manny, Hannah and Grace had

checked on Banecroft's wellbeing. Despite having being hurled across the room, he seemed to be nothing more than bruised – clearly the relaxing effects of whiskey had played their part.

'He's not coming out, is he?' asked Keith.

'Relax, he's just . . .' Hannah couldn't think of what to say next. *He's just a man-sized baby*, while entirely truthful, felt somewhat disloyal.

'OK,' Debbie said to Reggie. 'We'll put your arm in a sling to stabilize it, then you get to have a ride in the whoo-whoo bus.'

'Marvellous,' said Reggie. 'Will there be drugs? While I'm being frightfully brave and stoic, I'm in bloody agony here.'

'We can't give you much, but I happen to know one of the doctors on tonight and the man gives out more drugs than Glastonbury.'

'Wonderful.'

'OK,' said Debbie, nodding to Keith, 'we need to get you up. One . . . two . . . three.'

With an expulsion of air through gritted teeth, Reggie was on his feet again.

'Good, good,' said Debbie. 'That's the worst of it.'

'You have no idea,' replied Reggie. 'Can I have a quick moment with my colleague, please?'

Hannah moved closer as, with a grumble, Debbie took a step back. Reggie leaned forward to whisper, 'You need to have a word with Stella.'

'I do?' Hannah looked across to the corner of the room where the girl sat, staring at her phone, her green hair covering her face.

'You do,' said Reggie with a nod. 'I don't know anything about her past, and frankly I – more than anyone – can respect some-body's wish to reinvent themselves.' He gave a brief, pained smile in acknowledgement of the incident with the Fenton brothers. 'But I have noticed how keen the poor girl is to avoid any and all attention and how, beneath the street-ruffian act, she is terrified most of the time.'

'Oh,' said Hannah, looking in Stella's direction. 'Really?'

'Trust me,' said Reggie. 'I have a sense for such things. The average teenager's first move when entering a room isn't always to check where the nearest exit is. The poor kid always has one foot out the metaphorical door – and that was before a mythical beast was moments from ripping her head off.'

Hannah nodded, feeling rather stupid. 'Yes, I take your point.'

'Also, when you find out what on earth just happened with Manny, ring me.'

'I don't . . .' started Hannah, 'I don't know where to start with that.'

'Well,' said Reggie, 'I guess we now know why he always refers to himself as "we".'

'Right,' said Hannah, nodding her head while lost in thought.

Reggie placed his good hand on her arm. 'Honestly, for some-one in their first week, you're doing great.' Then he raised his voice. 'Right, folks, I'm off for a lie down. Keep the chins up. And now, Deborah dear, show me to the drugs!'

'Hi,' said Hannah.

Her greeting was met with an unintelligible grunt.

Stella was sitting in the corner on one of the fold-out chairs.

'Unbe-bloody-lievable!' came the roar from Banecroft, which carried down the hall.

'Golly, he is something, isn't he?' Hannah tutted, then winced.

Golly. Had she really just said 'golly'? She hadn't used the word since she was maybe ten – and even then . . . She didn't know what it was about trying to talk to Stella, but every time she tried, Hannah felt as if she transformed into someone called Trinny who came out with inane nonsense like 'Such fun!' and 'Golly gosh!'

Her comment was greeted with another grunt.

She grabbed a chair, folded it out and sat down opposite Stella. 'So, bit of a mental day, wasn't it?'

'S'pose.'

A word. Progress.

'How're you feeling?'

''Bout what?' As Stella spoke, Hannah caught the slightest flicker under the curtain of green hair that indicated Stella might've looked up from the game she was playing on her phone.

'Well, that . . . thing did sort of go for you, didn't it? That was scary.'

'I guess.'

'Are you feeling OK?'

Stella ran her fingers through her hair for the briefest of moments, and her face was revealed. It struck Hannah how young she was – and then the curtain descended again. 'It's my fault.'

Hannah was genuinely taken aback. 'What is?'

'The thing coming in. It's my fault.'

Hannah touched Stella's phone. 'Stella, look at me.'

Reluctantly, the girl looked up.

'It is not your fault. That thing was big and scary and . . . So you left the door to the roof open? If you hadn't, it would've got in some other way. It's not your fault. And if Banecroft says otherwise, I'll put him right. OK?'

Stella looked at Hannah for a long moment and then nodded. 'Yeah.'

'OK. Good. You're an important part of the team here. We'd be lost without you.'

Stella shrugged, too embarrassed to say anything.

'It's been a crazy day. Maybe you and Grace should head home soon and get some sleep?'

'Yeah.'

Hannah gave Stella a pat on the shoulder and then got to her feet and walked away. Two down, one to go. She was absolutely nailing this.

Manny was sipping his tea while Grace fussed over him.

'Hey, Manny. Are you OK?' asked Hannah.

'We fine. We fine.'

'I think he should go to hospital too,' said Grace, sounding far from happy.

Manny patted her hand. 'Hush y'self now, Grace, we fine. Just dog-tired's all. Just need a nice long sleep.'

Hannah looked at Grace. 'Maybe you could check in with Stella? It's probably a good idea if everyone starts to head home. It's been a long night.'

Grace looked in Stella's direction and nodded. 'I will go and get our coats.'

Hannah smiled and sat down opposite Manny as Grace headed off into the bullpen.

'Thank you, chile. She a fine woman, but she worry.'

'Yes,' said Hannah. 'Although, well, not without reason. Are you OK? I mean, really?'

Manny gave a weak smile. 'She frighten you, huh?'

'Your friend? Well, I guess you could say that. I mean, she saved us.'

'Don't be fear of her now. Ya not seen her at her best.'

Hannah nodded as she tried to think of the right words to say next. 'What exactly . . . is . . . she?'

Manny chuckled. 'Well, not like we have big chats about it, but, best I can tell, she dis place.'

'She's . . . ?'

'This place,' Manny repeated. 'Every place got a spirit of a kind. This a very different kinda place – need a different kinda spirit. We job protecting this place. There be all kinds out there, chile. All kinds.'

'Are you telling me that you're possessed by the spirit of the paper?'

Manny waved his hand. 'Don't be saying that word. She not be liking it.'

'Paper?'

Manny looked at Hannah.

'Right, sorry – you meant . . .'

'The other P-word.' He nodded.

'OK. But how did . . . ?' Hannah left the sentence hanging, mainly because she had no clue where it could go.

'I been here long time now,' he said, giving her a smile full of large, crooked teeth. 'Long time. Back in the day, I stumbled in here. I was . . . I was bad version of meself. Done bad tings, was in a bad place. Not an evil man, but I had evil in me body. Hurtin' me. The needle was me mistress and she cruel.'

Hannah nodded again, at least getting the gist.

'Friends, money, hope – all gone. Nothing but a shell of a man. Hungry. Empty. Hurtin'. She took me in, made me well. Look at me now.' Manny held out his hands. 'I'm living good, feeling good. Me and her, we together.' He drew his hands palm to palm and intertwined his fingers. 'I in her. She in me. We happy. We protect this place. This place us now. You understand me?'

Hannah sat back. 'I guess so. Makes as much sense as anything else that happened tonight. So, did you know that things like that horrible creature existed?'

Manny shrugged. 'Not my ting. I know she there, so I guess anything possible, but I'm just the printer man.'

Hannah patted him on the knee. 'You're a lot more than that.'

He chuckled. 'Me happy with that. Don't want for nothin'.' He leaned forward. 'I think ya no need worry about that ting comin' back.'

'I wish I was as sure as you seem to be.'

'No, ya not understanding . . . She don't speak to me, but I feel her. That thing – first time was a warning. It come again, she gonna kill it.'

Hannah leaned back. 'Right. I see.'

Manny shrugged. 'She nice, but she no like people coming in, wrecking up the place.'

'OK, then. Well, I guess we can get back to . . .' Then the thought struck. 'Oh God, in all the commotion – is the paper ready to go?'

Manny pointed at her and then pulled a small, neatly folded stack of sheets out of his pocket. 'Yes, chile. Here it is.'

Hannah unfolded it and felt a thrill rush through her body. It was eight pages of tabloid-sized newspaper. You couldn't even really describe it as a paper, it was that thin – but still, she had helped produce it and now it was a real thing. She held it in her hands. She looked at the front page.

Behind her, she could sense Stella and Grace standing there, peering over her shoulder. It was surreal, seeing the picture of the beast that had attacked them not much more than an hour ago there, on the front page.

'I like the headline,' said Hannah, looking at Manny. He pointed behind her. Hannah turned to see Stella looking bashful.

'We needed one,' she said. 'And I wasn't asking Grumpy.'

'It's great,' said Hannah. 'Well done. "What Stalks the Night?" Really good.'

Grace beamed a big smile at Stella. 'Simon would've liked it.'

Stella shrugged. 'Maybe. I bet someone won't, though . . .'

They all turned at the sound of Banecroft's office door slamming open.

Hannah laughed. 'Speak of the devil.'

'Right!' came the holler, punctuated by the *stomp-thump, stomp-thump* of Banecroft hurtling down the hallway as fast as a crutch and his outrage could carry him.

Hannah looked at her watch. 'Three a.m.' She looked at Manny.

'Do you think you'd be OK to start printing it soon? What time do the trucks get here?' This question she directed at Grace.

'Six.'

Manny nodded and closed his eyes.

Banecroft came crashing through the door. 'Where the hell is everybody?'

Hannah waved. 'We're over here. Calm down.'

'Where are the other two?'

'The other two?' repeated Hannah. 'Do you mean the member of staff who got arrested and the one who broke his arm?'

'Broke his arm? It was just a scratch. The paper doesn't stop for minor inconveniences. The presses should be . . .'

Banecroft stopped as the rumbling noise of the printer firing up reverberated through the building.

'How did . . . ?' started Banecroft.

Hannah looked down at Manny, who was wearing the benign smile she was beginning to realize was his default expression. She turned back to Banecroft. 'It doesn't matter. What matters is that it's getting printed – so just relax, would you?'

Banecroft's voice took on a mocking lilt. 'Relax? Relax!' He flapped his arms. 'Yes, let's all relax and take the rest of the night off. What a super job we've all done. Never mind that we got attacked by a supernatural beast, and nobody, not one member of staff at this so-called newspaper, had the presence of mind to take a picture of the bloody thing! Seriously, is there anyone in this building with an ounce of journalistic instinct in them?'

Something snapped inside Hannah. 'Oh, would you shut up? You irritating windbag of a man! These people have gone through hell for this paper. We lost poor Simon, Ox is under arrest, Reggie is in the hospital, and the rest of us just got attacked by a bloody werewolf! An actual bloody werewolf! Something that isn't -supposed to exist very nearly killed us all – only for Manny and his . . .' She pressed her fingers to her eyes. 'Whatever. So, for the sake of everyone's sanity, for five bloody minutes can you just stop being you?'

'That's it. You're all fired.'

Banecroft ducked as the vase of flowers Hannah had picked up from the desk flew past his head.

It smashed against the wall beside the stairs and shattered – causing the woman standing there to step back smartly to avoid getting water on her coat. Then she calmly stepped forward and began to remove her leather gloves, a sardonic smile playing across her lips. 'I'm sorry, is this a bad time?'

The room stood still.

'Hannah,' said Grace, 'this is Mrs Harnforth.'

Satan Don't Play That

Dougie Reed, 28, from Glasgow, and the self-proclaimed emissary of Satan on this plane of existence, has issued a press release clarifying that while numerous heavy metal bands have expressed their love of Satan over the years, Satan himself is actually a big fan of the musical stylings of the Irish songstress Enya. Dougie says, 'The biggest misunderstanding about the Dark Lord – all hail Satan! – is people think he's into metal. He's really a pretty chilled guy who, after a hard day torturing souls, just likes to kick back and relax with a nice Merlot and the *Watermark* album on repeat.'

CHAPTER 38

Mrs Harnforth sat quietly beside Hannah, carefully reading the edition of *The Stranger Times* that was literally hot off the press. Hannah had been surprised that it had been hot. She'd always assumed that was just an expression. Mind you, after all the other events of this long night of revelations, it wasn't unreasonable to wonder if their press worked in quite the same way as everyone else's.

Now that Hannah had time to take a good look at her, Mrs Harnforth was an impressive woman. She had swept in, apologized for the late hour and asked to speak to Banecroft and Hannah privately.

How did she know they would be here? How did she even know Hannah's name?

Hannah guessed the owner of *The Stranger Times* was in her late sixties but remarkably well preserved. She was of slim build and wore an elegant but understated coat. Her hair was dyed a light shade of pink, which really shouldn't have worked but somehow did. On her, it looked elegant, with more than a touch of rebellious charm. The woman had a certain poise, and a relaxed yet commanding presence that Hannah guessed was something you were probably born with.

Grace had insisted on bringing in her chair from reception for Mrs Harnforth to sit on, so that the newspaper owner would not have to make physical contact with anything in Banecroft's office. (Grace had previously mentioned to Hannah that they'd hired a cleaner once, who had taken one look at the room and then ran out of the building screaming.)

'Can I just . . .' started Banecroft, but he was silenced by Mrs Harnforth's raised finger as she turned a page and continued reading. She'd been doing this for nearly fifteen minutes. Commanding presence indeed.

She turned to the last page, the one where Stella had found room to throw in a couple of adverts.

'Ah,' said Mrs Harnforth, 'I see Mrs Wilkes and her "implements of romance" are still advertising with us. My, my.'

'If you will just let me explain,' said Banecroft.

'What?' replied Mrs Harnforth, finally looking up. 'Mrs Wilkes's implements? That is unnecessary – I am a woman of the world. Speaking of which . . .' She turned towards Hannah and extended her hand. 'Where are my manners! Alicia Harnforth, pleased to meet you.'

'Oh,' said Hannah, shaking her hand. 'Hannah Drink— sorry, Willis.'

'Yes, indeed,' she said with a smile. 'Lovely to meet you. I've heard so much about you.'

'You have?' said Banecroft.

She turned back to face him. 'Yes, Vincent. Of course I have. Grace keeps me fully informed.'

Banecroft's eyebrows ascended so quickly that for a millisecond they looked in danger of breaking free from his face entirely. 'Our receptionist is your spy?'

'Oh, do calm down, Vincent. Such a drama queen. Grace informs me of all the goings-on in the office in a daily email. She is not spying on anyone. If you'd asked her, I'm sure she would have told you exactly what she was doing. Did you ever take the time to ask her? Or, indeed, have a civilized conversation with her of any kind?'

'No, he hasn't,' came Grace's voice over the intercom.

'Grace, dear, you're slightly undercutting my point,' said Mrs Harnforth.

'Oh. Sorry.'

'I told you to go home!' barked Banecroft.

'No, you didn't.'

'Well, I'm telling you now.'

There was a loud beeping noise.

'When this is done, she and I will be having words.'

'No,' said Mrs Harnforth, 'you will not.' She turned to Hannah again. 'I don't blame you at all for hurling that vase at him. Vincent has a penchant for being beastly.'

Banecroft drew a cigarette from the packet on his desk. He stopped with the lighter in his hand as Mrs Harnforth gave him a certain look. Hannah did her best to appear not to notice as the pair locked eyes wordlessly. Banecroft removed the cigarette from his mouth and tossed it on the table. He glared at Hannah, daring her to mention it.

'So,' continued Mrs Harnforth, placing her finger on the newspaper that now sat on the table in front of her.

'Right,' said Banecroft. 'I know it seems unbelievable, but—'

'Oh no,' she replied. 'I believe every word of it.'

'But if you'll just let me— Wait. What?' Banecroft's eyebrows were getting more exercise than possibly his entire body had experienced in quite some time.

'Yes. The creature in this picture is what is known as a Were. The "werewolf" thing is a complete nonsense. Nothing to do with wolves. For a start, Weres always hunt alone, while wolves are, of course, pack animals.'

'What?' said Banecroft.

'What?' said Hannah.

Mrs Harnforth looked at them each in turn. 'I appreciate that the last few days will have been a big culture shock for both of you. The world is not what you thought it to be.'

There was a long moment of silence, followed by everyone who wasn't Mrs Harnforth saying 'What?' again.

In lieu of an answer, Mrs Harnforth turned to Hannah and touched her on the knee. 'Can I ask, did you really burn down your cheating husband's house?'

'Well, I . . .'

'Hang on,' said Banecroft. 'Don't change the subject. You knew about this?' He slammed his hand down on the paper to emphasize his point.

'No,' said Mrs Harnforth. 'I mean, I knew such creatures had once existed, but they are not supposed to any more. In fact, to be precise, they are not *allowed* to exist any more.'

'At some point, are you going to stop talking in riddles? It's really getting annoying now.'

Hannah nodded in agreement.

Mrs Harnforth uncrossed and recrossed her legs. 'Sorry. I shall endeavour to be clearer. There's a lot I can't explain to you – at least not now – but I shall tell you what I can.' She glanced at her watch. 'I'm afraid I have little time.'

'Well,' said Banecroft, 'thank you for squeezing us in to your busy schedule.'

Mrs Harnforth spoke as if addressing the room rather than any one individual. 'Who was it that said sarcasm is the lowest form of wit?'

'I don't know,' replied Banecroft, 'but I guarantee they'd not seen the internet before they said it.'

Mrs Harnforth smoothed the line of her skirt as she spoke. 'Before we begin, trust me on this: things will be easier if you can embrace the idea that what you have known as myths, fairy tales, legends – much of it is, well, not true per se, but it does contain echoes of the truth.' She gave them a weak smile.

A voice in Hannah's brain wanted to dismiss this all as nonsense, but then the image of the creature she had seen with her own eyes just a couple of hours previously came back to her.

Mrs Harnforth continued. 'The world has always contained what can be thought of as, for want of a better word, "magic". In centuries past, it was an everyday thing. Humanity, as we now know it, lived side by side with many creatures who, to a greater or lesser extent, were "other". Notice I don't say lived peacefully. Sadly, such is human nature that peace is a rarely achieved ideal. The others have many names and come in many shapes and sizes, but can loosely be referred to as "the Folk".'

'Hippy claptrap!' blurted Banecroft, who was not used to staying quiet while others spoke.

'Really?' said Mrs Harnforth calmly. 'So, do you have an explanation for the creature you encountered tonight?'

'Well, I mean, I . . . but . . . what I . . .' Banecroft gradually ran out of steam.

Mrs Harnforth nodded and continued. 'So, humanity and the Folk lived side by side, if not entirely in peace then at least in what could be termed balance. Then mankind, ever the striver, slowly evolved. Villages became towns, stone became metals, and slowly the world bent to man's will. It is important to note that humanity and the Folk were not entirely separate. Far from it. I'd imagine both of you have some Folk blood in your ancestry – almost everyone does. Why it all started to change is attributed by most people to the tale of Alexander and Isabella.'

'Oh good,' said Banecroft. 'Story time!'

Mrs Harnforth sighed. 'Vincent, Vincent, Vincent. This will go so much more easily if you try just a little not to be so, well, you. Now, where was I?'

'Alexander and Isabella,' prompted Hannah.

'Ah, yes. Thank you, dear. As the story goes, Alexander was a great and wise king, beloved by his people. The lands he ruled were known for their peace and prosperity, places where the pauper and the prince were equal in the eyes of justice. The king, however, was a lonely man. It was rumoured that he had been cursed at birth to be unable to feel love. Princesses from far and wide came to call, but none could capture his heart, and he vowed he would not – could not – marry without love.'

Banecroft pulled a face, which everyone else ignored.

'And then one day, while out riding, he came upon a poacher on his land hunting a stag. He chased down this hooded figure and they fought to a standstill. The king's private guard wanted to kill the interloper, who had the temerity not only to defy the king but also to stand up to him in single combat. The king, however, was impressed. He offered the figure clemency in exchange for learning the identity of such a fine warrior. The figure removed their mask to reveal they were . . .'

'Isabella,' said Hannah.

'Isabella,' confirmed Mrs Harnforth with a sad smile. 'So the story goes, she was the most beautiful woman the king had ever seen. So beautiful that he fell off his horse. In a matter of weeks, they were wed. They made a wonderful couple and the kingdom rejoiced. Then, almost immediately, she fell ill. The king called forth the greatest doctors and healers, but nobody could save her as she faded away before his eyes. He was inconsolable. The cruellest love is that which is granted late and taken early.

'He had all but given up hope when, as he kept vigil by his love's deathbed, a sorceress came to him. She told him that there was a way. By stealing the life from three of the Folk, his queen would live. Blinded by his own grief, the king gave the order and three members of the Folk were duly taken. The sorceress performed the ritual which took their lives, and it did indeed save Alexander's queen. But at the final moment, the sorceress laughed a cruel laugh, for she knew what she had truly done. She had granted Isabella eternal life.

'But in that moment Isabella had seen what would happen if it were ever taken away: a vision of hell – a very real hell – to which her soul would be committed if she ever did pass. The king, while meaning well, had stolen his bride's soul from her and she could not forgive him for it. You see,' continued Mrs Harnforth, 'the sorceress had not explained it all. What she had done would keep Isabella alive, but only for ten years. After that, the blood of more of the Folk would be required, or else she would be doomed to suffer the eternal torment she had seen in her vision. And so, good King Alexander became something else. The Folk became his enemies, because only through their deaths could Isabella continue to live. The Folk tried to kill her—'

'Hang on,' interrupted Banecroft. 'I thought you said she was immortal?'

Mrs Harnforth shook her head. 'No, she could die, just not by natural means. Her body was impervious to illness, but the well-placed blow of a sword could still end her. She became terrified, haunted by the fate that awaited her. Alexander swore to protect her for all eternity and so, in an act of misplaced love, he too underwent the ritual and embraced eternal life. He and Isabella became the first two of what have been known by many names over the ages but these days are most commonly referred to as "the Founders".'

'These days?' repeated Banecroft disbelievingly. 'These days? Are you telling me that this fairy story is supposed to be real?'

Mrs Harnforth shrugged. 'There are many versions of the tale, of course, but yes, the Folk and the Founders are very real. The Founders grew in number over time. It is the most human of human emotions to fear death. If given the opportunity, who wouldn't want to live for ever? Over time, they gathered people of power to their side, and with this power they hunted the Folk, because they needed them to ensure their survival. The Folk were much greater in number, but they had none of the power the Founders enjoyed. The only option open to the Folk was to run, to hide, but the Founders had ways of finding them.'

'The Were!' exclaimed Hannah.

Mrs Harnforth turned to look at her. 'That's right: the Were. It is not size nor strength that makes the Weres so useful – it is their sense of smell. They can use it to detect members of the Folk. You see, not all Folk are the same – far from it. There are many different "species", to use a scientific term, and only certain ones can be used to make a Founder.'

'So, that Were thing,' said Banecroft, jabbing at the picture on the front of the paper, 'is immortal too?'

'No,' said Mrs Harnforth, shaking her head. 'Quite the contrary. Think of it as a weapon, and a temporary one at that. It will have been an ordinary man or woman that a Founder has transformed into that beast. They cannot be controlled for long, though. Soon, the human's mind is subsumed and they become a wild, rabid, thoughtless beast, of use to no one.'

'So why would they do it?' asked Hannah. 'Why become one of them?'

'Well,' said Mrs Harnforth, 'they were generally men who had been condemned to death – back in ancient times, at least. When the choice is certain death or anything else, many people will take the other option regardless. As for this poor soul you met tonight – who knows? Now that the knowledge of such things has faded from human memory, this poor man almost certainly will not have known what he was signing up for.'

'Wait,' said Banecroft. 'Say I do, for a second, believe all of this. You said earlier that this Were thing should not exist?'

Mrs Harnforth nodded. 'There is an accord: an uneasy truce of sorts between the Founders and the Folk, which has been in place for over a hundred years now. As part of that, Weres should be a thing of the past.'

'They've been decommissioned?' asked Banecroft.

'In a manner of speaking. For centuries, the Folk ran and the Founders hunted. That was the way it was. The Founders were always selective, of course, as to who they'd let in. Any new member meant yet more of the Folk were needed to keep them all alive.'

'Wait,' said Hannah. 'Sorry, but . . . you said that all the myths and stuff were true?'

'Well, many of them,' replied Mrs Harnforth. 'I'm not saying there's a Loch Ness monster.'

'Right, but, does that mean . . . One of the names the Founders are known by, is it . . . vampire?'

Mrs Harnforth nodded. 'That name isn't used much by the Folk, and it is detested by the Founders, but yes, the vampire myth can be seen as an allegory for the Founders.'

Banecroft blew a loud raspberry.

Mrs Harnforth sighed. 'Vincent, do you have a point you wish to make?'

'Yes, I do. If these Founders, as you call them, were running about sucking the blood out of people, I'm pretty sure we'd know about it.'

'Now, Vincent, I know you know what an allegory is. They do not do that, at least not directly. Don't think of fanged figures in cloaks. Think of what you know from your Fleet Street days. You've seen it. Certain stories quietly killed? The hidden hands of power? Some of that is just how the world works, but some of it is the Founders. Think about it: the Folk don't want themselves known to the quote-unquote "ordinary world". Would you, if the fountain of youth ran through your veins? And the Founders want their existence kept quiet for the same reason. They'd rather live in this world and guide it from the darkness than stand in the light.'

'All right,' said Banecroft. 'If all of that is true, then how on earth is this "accord" in place now? Who achieves total victory and then negotiates a truce?'

'Ah,' said Mrs Harnforth, 'now you are asking the right questions.'

'Whoop-dee-do.'

There was a moment's pause and the briefest of looks exchanged between the two — just enough for Mrs Harnforth to allow Banecroft to remember the nature of their relationship.

'What changed things was, shall we say, an unintended consequence of man's inhumanity to man. Or, to put it in simpler terms, when the twentieth century rolled around it became a lot easier to kill. Guns, bombs, artillery. Suddenly the Founders, despite all their power, were vulnerable. Castle walls couldn't protect them any more. The Folk — or rather, a small but dedicated band of them — were able to find ways to kill Founders, and that is their one great, collective weakness: their absolute terror of death and the tortured eternity that awaits them afterwards. Remember, as part of the "making", every Founder experiences a vision of the certain terrifying hell that awaits them should they ever die. Once modern warfare was conceived, even they did not have the power to put that genie back in the bottle.'

'Ah,' said Banecroft, 'speaking of which.' He pulled a bottle of whiskey and a glass from his desk drawer. 'The two of you can keep going, but I've no intention of listening to this stuff sober.'

'I don't understand,' said Hannah.

Banecroft barked a laugh that caused the amber liquid to spill from his glass on to the table.

Mrs Harnforth turned to face her. 'Sorry, dear. Which part?'

'This . . . accord?' Mrs Harnforth nodded to indicate Hannah had got it right. 'You said the Founders could stay alive only through these Folk people dying?'

'Ah,' she replied, 'yes, I did, didn't I? My apologies – I left out a crucial point there. You see, that was the case, but then certain Founders – the more progressive of them, if you will – began doing some research. They discovered that it was possible to extract what they call "life force" – but, for simplicity, think of it as the "magic" for the moment – from the Folk without killing them.'

'Right,' said Hannah. 'Doesn't that mean it's all sort of fine, then?'

Mrs Harnforth wrinkled her nose. 'Not exactly. It comes at a terrible price. The procedure is brutal and it greatly shortens the life of any member of the Folk who goes through it. The Folk themselves refer to it as "the cost". Effectively, Folk lives are still taken so that the Founders may live, but it is done in a less immediate way. It is merely the best bad solution. There's a lot more to it than that – but for the moment, think of it in those broad terms.'

'So,' said Hannah, 'this Were thing – does that mean that the Founders have broken the Accord?'

'Yes and no. Unless I'm very much mistaken, I'd imagine it means that one of the Founders is breaking the Accord. A rogue element.'

Banecroft snatched the paper and held it up, showing Mrs Harnforth the front-page image. 'By any chance are you referring to this little slaphead thunder-anus in the background?'

'Well, I wouldn't have put it quite so colourfully, but yes, that gentleman. I may be wrong, but I believe the most logical explanation is that he is breaking one of the three guiding principles of the Accord. Rule number one was that the Folk agreed to cease all attempts to kill any of the Founders. Rule number two was that the Folk would pay "the cost" in exchange for the Founders no longer hunting them. And rule three?' She looked at Hannah and Banecroft expectantly.

'No new Founders?' said Hannah.

Mrs Harnforth gave a smiling nod, like a proud parent. 'No more "makings", as they are known. This gentleman is breaking that rule. Your report identified him as an American. I would imagine he has come here hoping to do whatever he is doing in secret. The mainstream press and the general public will, of course, dismiss your headline as hokum.'

'Oh, terrific,' bristled Banecroft.

'But when this evidence is made public, those who need to know will see it for what it is and deal with it accordingly. That is exactly the purpose that this paper was intended to fulfil.'

'Well,' said Banecroft, 'we won't be doing it again. The police are shutting us down, unless your lawyer can pull something pretty damn spectacular out of the bag.'

Mrs Harnforth looked taken aback for the first time in the conversation. 'Lawyer? What lawyer?'

Banecroft stared at her for a long moment and then tilted back his chair to a precarious angle and shouted up at the ceiling, 'Oh, you are kidding me!'

'Sorry,' said Mrs Harnforth. 'I think you have had the wool rather pulled over your eyes.'

'But she . . .'

'By any chance did this lawyer encourage you to kill the story?'

Banecroft slammed down the front legs of his chair and reached for the bottle of whiskey again. 'I think you know the answer to that. Just so I'm clear, is there anyone actually on our side?'

'We don't have a side. That is very much the point. Besides, you didn't take this lawyer's advice.'

'Well, no,' said Banecroft, pouring himself another indecent measure. 'I've never been one for following orders.'

'That is why you are here,' said Mrs Harnforth.

Banecroft's glass stopped halfway to his lips and he gave Mrs Harnforth a long, hard look. 'Which brings me to my next question—' Annoyance flashed across his face as he was interrupted by a knock on the door. 'What the hell is it now?'

Manny's voice wafted through. 'You said we tell you when the trucks is here.' There was an odd pause, and then, 'The trucks is here.'

CHAPTER 39

Moretti took a bite of the doughnut and then spat it back into the bag. Another food these Limey a-holes couldn't get right. The sooner this was over and he could get back to the States the better. Of course, after yet another screw-up from the dog, the likelihood of that ever happening was in serious jeopardy. He tossed the bag on the ground as he turned the corner and headed towards the warehouse. This time he was going to have to hurt the dog – really hurt him. Their previous talk about the price of failure had clearly not penetrated his thick skull.

Moretti had to admit that the initial error had been his own. Getting rid of the nosy reporter had made sense, and having him throw himself off the same building – well, he'd figured that would have the authorities barking up all the wrong trees. In his own defence, what the hell was a wi-fi-enabled camera? He still didn't understand it completely, and seeing as he'd smashed the camera to pieces as soon as he'd picked up the chatter on the bug he'd placed inside *The Stranger Times*, he would not be undertaking further investigation.

Somehow, while the camera had been in the back of his car as he'd driven through Manchester, it had picked up a wi-fi signal and sent its content to the little dweeb's hard drive.

Desperate times called for desperate measures, and he had instructed the dog to slaughter the remaining staff of that silly rag and burn the place to the ground. Moretti didn't know why his powers hadn't worked on the Irish guy, but claws still ripped and fire still burned. If you couldn't avoid leaving a mess, then leave the biggest mess possible. If the dog had any awareness of the beast taking over, he was too dumb to realize. Or maybe the guy would always have been fine with the order to liquidate civilians. Regardless, it should have been simple. Then he'd seen the dog crashing through the window and hightailing it out of the church like a whimpering cur.

Moretti stopped in front of the metal shutters to the warehouse and, after glancing around briefly to make sure nobody was watching, performed a quick series of movements with his left hand. The shutters juddered upwards with a complaint of grinding metal, and the gloomy interior was flooded with the dawn's early light. Moretti stepped inside, his eyes taking a moment to adjust.

The dog lay in one of the raggedy armchairs – back in human form and naked. He cowered pathetically as the lights came on.

'Ah, did I wake you up, puppy?' Moretti casually took a handkerchief out of his pocket and cleaned the sugar from his hands – far too much of it. They really didn't know how to do a simple frickin' doughnut. 'So, how did it go?'

Gary Merchant didn't look up. 'You know how it went.'

'No,' said Moretti. 'I know how it was supposed to go. What I don't understand is what the hell went wrong?'

The dog finally raised his eyes to look at him. 'There was a – I don't know – this bloody great demon or summat. The black fella – it came out of him. Had wings. You didn't tell me about nothing like that, did ya?'

'Oh,' said Moretti. 'I see. So your failure is my fault, then, is it? Is that what we're saying?'

Merchant looked down at the ground again and hugged his legs to him. 'No, I just . . .'

'You just what?'

'I just . . .'

'Speak up. I want to know. I bet they want to know too.'

Moretti turned to the two figures chained high on the wall, their mouths muzzled. The homeless Type 2 looked at him with the terror he'd come to expect; the Type 6 looked at him with the pure hatred he'd known would be there. They both hung there, entirely helpless, their wrought-iron bindings holding them in place. Normally Moretti would've hosed down the homeless guy to get rid of the stench, but the whole place smelled so bad it seemed pointless. The witch looked amusingly incongruous, up there in her dressing gown and nightie, but Moretti wasn't in a laughing mood.

'C'mon.' Moretti skipped towards them, his arms outstretched. 'These brave souls have volunteered to give their lives so that your poor daughter might live. So tell me – tell us – why you couldn't do the simple task that needed to be done in order to save poor, cancerous Cathy.'

'Don't you say her name!' His voice came out in a snarl and he switched from whipped cur to snarling beast in a second. His eyes flashed red as he hurtled forward. With a casual wave of his hand, Moretti grabbed the dog and spun him around and around in the air, like a marionette, up towards the ceiling and back down again, finally bringing his face to rest mere inches from his own.

'I really think, of the two of us, I should be the one getting upset.' He spoke calmly again. 'Thanks to you, the third and final piece of our puzzle will now be virtually impossible to catch. We'll need a Type Eight. Type Eights are hard to find at the best of times, but now they'll be cloaking their scent and we'll never find them. All of this will be for naught. I'll have to go somewhere else and start again. My time has been wasted. Do you know how unhappy that makes me?'

The dog tried to speak. After a moment's contemplation, Moretti loosened his grip enough to allow his jaw to move. 'Does doggy want to say something?'

'There was something else, at the paper place.'

'Yes, the big bad demon. You said. That is of no use to us, believe you me. It sounds like a . . . Well, never mind, it seems pointless to attempt to educate you now.'

'No, no, no. Something else. Not that. It smelled, y'know, powerful.'

Moretti moved a little closer, trying to determine if this was truth or lies born from desperation.

'Are you saying it was a Type Eight?'

'Stronger than that. It felt . . . I mean, I don't know what it was, but—'

Moretti waved his hand in the air and the Book of Scent appeared. 'You'd better not be wasting more of my time.'

'I'm not, I bloody swear it. It was . . . incredible.'

'Well, then . . .' Moretti opened the book and began flicking through. 'Say when.'

'No. No. No. No.' Moretti kept skimming through the pages. He moved on, past the normal, past the rare, on to . . . 'That one!'

Moretti looked down at the page and then up again. 'Really?'

'It was like that, but combined with the one from two pages back.'

'That is not possible.'

'It definitely was, I'm telling ya. I've got a crazy sense of smell now.'

'But that's not . . . That would be the most extraordinary of things.' Moretti turned, talking more to himself now than to anyone else. 'I mean, theoretically maybe, but . . .' He clapped his hands together excitedly.

'So will it work for what we need?'

'What?' said Moretti, turning. 'Oh, yes. I mean, it's a shocking waste in some ways, but it'll definitely do for that.'

'Right, then.'

Moretti stopped. 'If you're lying to me . . .'

'I'm not. Why would I make that up?'

Moretti looked into the dog's eyes again. There was no deception there. It didn't know enough to come up with a lie this good. Moretti danced a little jig of genuine delight. 'Oh me, oh me, oh me, oh my – these are the days to be alive.'

'So, is it good, then?'

Moretti turned back around and slapped the dog on the cheek affectionately. 'Oh, my dear little moron, this is news of such unexpected, inexplicable good fortune that I could be drawn to the highly unlikely conclusion that someone up there likes me!'

He turned and held his hands out to their guests. 'Good news, my friends – you shall be dying in the very best of company. Free at last. Great God almighty, I'm free at last!'

'Can you . . . ?' asked the dog.

'Oh, yes, of course.' Moretti clicked his fingers and the dog fell to the ground. 'C'mon, c'mon, up you get,' he said, turning on his heel and heading towards the door. 'You need to change into something a little more hairy. We're going hunting!'

CHAPTER 40

Banecroft sat up on the roof and watched as, in the wan light of early morning, the delivery trucks below him were loaded.

'Is it safe for a man with your blood-alcohol level to be sitting up here?'

He didn't turn around. 'Perfectly. I've worked it out, and sadly I'd almost certainly survive the fall.'

'Yes, but I do worry about the poor sod you'd inevitably land on. This paper can't afford a lawsuit.'

Mrs Harnforth stepped forward and perched on one of the short, stone bollards. Banecroft was reclining in the rusted and weather-worn sun lounger he'd found up here.

He picked up his bottle of whiskey again.

'Don't you think you've had enough of that?'

'No, no, I don't.'

He poured himself another unhealthy measure.

'You're angry.'

'I'm always angry.'

Mrs Harnforth sighed, not unkindly. 'That's not anger, Vincent – that's pain. A great well of pain. Instead of dealing with it, you've just tried to drink yourself to oblivion. How has that worked out for you?'

Banecroft held up his glass in a toast. 'Too early to tell. Cheers.'

Mrs Harnforth looked out at the city waking up. Even now, the Mancunian Way elevated motorway held a steady flow of traffic, and lights could be seen in apartment windows in the distance. 'Ask your questions, Vincent. I know you have them.'

'Oh, how terribly kind of you. I do appreciate how you like to give the impression I have some kind of control. You lied to me.'

'I did no such thing.'

'A lie of omission is no less of a lie and you know it. I had no idea what you were getting me into.'

Mrs Harnforth turned to look at him. 'Would you have believed me?'

'That is irrelevant.'

'No, Vincent. Quite the contrary. If I had told you the truth, you would have scoffed at it. You always had to see it to believe it. A mind like yours has to be allowed to get most of the way to the truth by itself, or else it just will not take.'

He jabbed a finger in her direction. 'You brought me here under false pretences.'

Mrs Harnforth considered this and then gave a nod. 'That's fair – I did. I would apologize for it, but I think we both know that would be hollow. I did what had to be done. I would do it again in a heartbeat.'

Banecroft glowered at her and then threw back a large gulp of whiskey.

'Whilst you're so enjoying being angry, please do not forget where you were when I found you, Vincent. You'd hit rock bottom and were attempting to dig your way through it. You'd be dead by now if it weren't for me.'

'There are worse things.'

Mrs Harnforth gave him a long, hard look – one of the few in his entire existence that Banecroft was unable to match. 'One day we will have to have a serious chat about that statement, but not today. In the meantime, yes, I lied to you, but I did it for both your own good and the greater good.'

This was met by a mirthless bark of laughter.

'Mock all you want, Vincent, but I knew if I placed you here – somewhere amidst the crackpots and the wild conspiracies and the monsters of the imagination – at some point the truth would come knocking and that mind of yours, still sharp despite the extraordinary lengths you have gone to in order to deaden it, would recognize it when it presented itself to you.'

'A boy is dead! Just a kid, chasing a story. And because I didn't know the truth, he's dead. That is on you.'

Mrs Harnforth shook her head. 'I don't believe so, but, to be honest, you may be right. I don't know. My position . . .' She looked at the skyline again. 'I've seen so much, been responsible for so much, I've . . . Undoubtedly, there is blood on my hands. I can't deny it. Maybe poor Simon should be added to that. That is for others to judge. Still, I believe in the truce I have made it my life's work to preserve. I left rather a lot out down there. It is not going well – the Accord, I mean. There is pressure from all sides, and it wasn't the best of deals to begin with. At times it feels like an impossible task, but someone has to do it.'

Banecroft gave a sarcastic trio of claps and Mrs Harnforth's calm demeanour slipped for just a moment, anger flashing in her eyes. He spoke in a mocking falsetto. 'Blessed are the peacemakers.'

'As I said, Vincent – I am very busy. There are an awful lot of places I need to be, so I would appreciate it if you could dispense with the histrionics and ask your damned questions.'

He reached down to find the near-empty bottle of whiskey. Mrs Harnforth moved two of her fingers in a precise motion and the bottle rose into the air and moved silently across the rooftop away from him. He watched it go.

'Well, that answers one of them.'

The bottle came to rest beneath the ledge of the window that led out to the rooftop.

'Ah,' said Mrs Harnforth, 'this reminds me of something I should have mentioned. The man behind the Were – you said that when you met him, he dangled something in front of you?'

'Yes,' said Banecroft. 'Like he thought the shiny object would somehow distract me.'

She nodded. 'He was trying to perform what is commonly referred to as a glamour. It allows a practitioner to gain control of another's mind.'

'I see,' said Banecroft. 'And was I saved by my aforementioned razor-sharp mind?'

'No. You were saved by the key that is currently resting in your trouser pocket.'

Banecroft shoved his hand in and extracted the tarnished bronze key to the front door of the church. 'This?'

Mrs Harnforth nodded. 'Exactly that. It is what is known as a totem – quite a powerful one. As are all the keys to this place. Anyone carrying one of them is shielded from magical interference. Mostly.'

'If I'm "protected" from hocus-pocus, then how come . . . ?' He nodded in the direction of his dearly departed whiskey bottle.

'It protects you, not objects. It also does not prevent that bottle from being walloped against the side of your thick skull, I'm afraid. Invincible you are not.'

'So the opposition has magical powers and all we have is a key-ring's worth of protection?'

'That and, as you met this evening, Manny's associate.'

'Do I want to know what in hell that was?'

She shrugged. 'Probably not, but rest assured, when you're in this building you are protected. She is old magic, and all but the most foolhardy or the most powerful would avoid facing off against her.'

'I knew all that hippy peace-and-love stuff from the Rastafarian was nonsense.'

'She is not him. She is . . . I suppose "with him" would be the best way to put it. Which does rather bring us to . . . ' Mrs Harnforth hugged her coat around her. 'It is cold up here, Vincent, and as I said, time is ticking on. Shall we get to the question you really want to ask?'

Banecroft leaned forward and spoke mostly to his own feet. 'My wife.'

Mrs Harnforth walked towards him and placed a cold hand against his cheek. 'Your wife,' she said softly.

It took a few moments for Banecroft's voice to emerge, and when it did, it was stripped of all its bravado. 'I . . . I knew, when they found her, that it wasn't her. Even when the tests – when everything said it was her – I knew it wasn't. I knew.'

He looked up at her, his eyes filled with tears.

She spoke softly. 'And then you spent every penny you had, let your life crumble around your ears, trying to find the woman you loved in a world where everyone said she was dead.'

'That body' – his voice was a hoarse croak now – 'was not her.'

Mrs Harnforth took a step back and turned away. 'I know you believe that. I wish I had answers for you. I'm afraid I don't.'

Banecroft ran a sleeve across his face and reached down reflexively for a bottle that wasn't there.

'I've looked into it,' she continued, 'and I'm trying to get an old friend of mine to take a look at it.' She turned back to him. 'Maybe there is a truth to be uncovered. If there is, she will find it. Although it might not be one you want.'

Beneath them, the doors of a truck slammed shut and an engine started up.

'What am I supposed to do?' asked Banecroft.

'About that?' said Mrs Harnforth. 'Nothing. Not right now. You have to give it time. I promise you, my friend will do what she can when she can. In the meantime, you have a paper to run.' She pointed at the truck as it pulled out on to the road. 'In a few hours, every member of the Folk within forty miles will know that a Were is on the hunt, and they will be ready. Similarly, the

347

"powers that be" will be forced to act. You have done good work this week.'

'It came at a cost.'

He looked up at Mrs Harnforth. In the half-light of morning, she looked considerably older than she had previously.

'It always does. This, I fear, has been only the first shot. A cold wind is coming.' She took a seat back on the bollard and they sat in silence for a few moments, watching the city start to rise.

Banecroft pulled a cigarette from behind his ear and lit it.

'By the way, can you pull a rabbit out of a hat? I've always enjoyed that one.'

'Oh, do shut up, Vincent – there's a good chap.'

Psychics' Convention Cancelled Due to 'Foreseen Circumstances'

The 15th annual convention of Portuguese Psychics has been cancelled due to what organizers are calling 'foreseen circumstances'.

In a press release, they revealed that next week's event will not take place because 'if it did, something very bad would happen. We cannot give any further details, as unfortunately that would cause something even worse to happen.'

The organizers go on to explain that the cancellation has absolutely nothing to do with poor ticket sales.

CHAPTER 41

Hannah leaned back in her chair and cradled the phone to her ear. A part of her had been excited to have her own desk. It was now a pile of kindling lying beside the wall, having been a momentary inconvenience to a rampaging beast. She looked at it, feeling that the incident from a few hours ago was already starting to seem like a particularly vivid dream. Surprisingly, her phone still worked, although Hannah hadn't yet decided if she was happy about that or not.

After the long night, now that the newspaper was published and everyone else had gone home, the adrenalin was finally leaving her. Still, the buses wouldn't start running for another hour, and seeing as she would soon be unemployed again, she couldn't afford a taxi. She realized that going through the phone messages again was not only unnecessary but also entirely futile, given the edition of *The Stranger Times* that had just been printed would be the last. However, it was that or try to process everything that had gone on, followed by everything she had been told, and this side of the morning, that felt like far too big a task to undertake. Instead . . .

The electronic voice spoke to her. 'You have . . . thirty . . . nine . . . messages.'

Hannah groaned to herself and slammed the phone back on its cradle. 'Oh, screw this.'

'Well, that's a fine attitude!'

She looked up to see Banecroft standing in the doorway, leaning on his crutch and holding the remnants of the flowers that had sat on Grace's desk prior to Hannah hurling them at his head.

She immediately sat forward in her chair. 'Oh, sorry, I was just going through the voicemails. Killing time before the buses start running and I can go home.'

'Home?' said Banecroft, sounding outraged. 'Home? We've got a features meeting for next week's edition at nine, and attendance is mandatory.'

'For who? I don't know if you've noticed, but one half of the features department is in hospital and the other has been arrested.'

Banecroft sniffed. 'Bloody excuses. I've been shot in the foot and I'm still here.'

'You did that to yourself.'

'And I got tossed around by that big hairy lummox too, and you don't hear me whining about having a broken arm.'

'Well, with the amount of alcohol in your system, I'd imagine we could hit you with a building and you wouldn't feel it.'

Banecroft shook his head disdainfully. 'Fine. Be back here for eleven – no, wait, ten thirty. We need to get cracking on next week.'

Hannah closed her eyes and ran her fingers through her hair. She couldn't remember the last time she had felt this tired. 'Oh, why don't you go and . . .' Her eyes shot open. 'Wait a sec, I thought we wouldn't be publishing next week? Or ever again?'

'Nonsense,' said Banecroft. 'I have used my considerable powers of persuasion and negotiation and—'

'Mrs Harnforth,' interrupted Hannah. 'She's fixed it, hasn't
she?'

Banecroft gave her a look as he lit a cigarette. 'It was a team
effort.'

'Who did she ring at this time of the morning?'

Banecroft took a long drag and pushed out a cloud of smoke. 'I
would imagine quite a few of the people she has to deal with are
not exactly big sleepers.'

Hannah was surprised by the elation she felt. Maybe it was the
exhaustion, or maybe it was the relief that she would not have to
go through another job interview.

'Well, that's good news, I suppose,' she said, trying to sound
non-committal. 'And if you're looking for an apology from me for
throwing those flowers at you, you'll be waiting a while. You thoroughly deserved it.'

'Oh no,' said Banecroft, 'I'm just glad you didn't try to burn
down the building.'

Hannah, for the first time in God knew how long, stuck out her
tongue in a childish gesture of defiance. It was amazing how good
it felt.

'I'm testing a theory,' continued Banecroft.

'If it's whether or not holding flowers makes you more charming, the initial results aren't encouraging.'

Banecroft limped across the office. 'Don't forget you are still on
probation. It's a slow economy – people would kill for your job.'

'Really?' said Hannah, standing up. 'Well, they're in luck,

because I'm way too tired to put up much of a fight. So, what's your theory?'

'Why did that . . . thing attack us?'

Hannah shrugged. 'I don't know. I mean, it's a monster. It . . .'

'Don't think of it in those terms. You heard Mrs Harnforth: it is a weapon. So the question is, why did its owner aim it at us?'

'I don't know.'

'Oh come on, woman, think!'

Hannah glowered at him. 'I don't . . . We had the photo. They knew that if it was published it would be big trouble for them.'

'Right. And how did they know that?'

'I . . .' Hannah stopped.

'Think about it,' said Banecroft. 'The only people who knew about it were in this office, and incompetent though they may be, I doubt even they would have found a way to somehow leak that information to the enemy.'

'Then . . .'

Banecroft tossed the bunch of flowers to Hannah. 'Say it with flowers.'

She found the device, about the size of a two-pence piece, stuck just above where the stems were tied together.

'Someone bugged us?'

'Yes,' said Banecroft. 'And I think we know who that certain someone is. The good news, at least, is that we found out who your secret admirer is.'

Hannah dropped the device on the floor and stamped on it repeatedly with her heel, not stopping even when it had most certainly been rendered inoperable.

'Men,' said Banecroft. 'You can't trust any of the bastards.'

'Oh, shut up.'

'So you know, I had a whole little speech planned, in which I'd tell our American friend how we'd beat him, but you literally stepped on it.'

'That's a shame. I know how much you enjoy the sound of your own voice.'

Just then, the office phone rang. The phone system, antiquated though it was, was set up to ring in the main office if Grace was not behind her desk.

'Grace!' shouted Banecroft. 'Get the phone!'

'She's not here.'

'Why not?'

'Because it's five thirty in the morning and nobody should be here.' Hannah looked at the phone. She had had her fill of crazy for the night, but it might be about the trucks that had just left, full of newspapers. Reluctantly, she picked up the handset.

'Hello, *The Stranger T*—' Hannah sat forward. 'OK, calm down, Grace. Calm . . . Are you sure? Where are you?'

'What in the—?'

Hannah raised her hand to silence Banecroft.

'OK. We'll be right there. Which hospital?'

Hannah stood up as she listened. 'OK. We're on our way.'

She slammed down the phone and grabbed her coat. 'Come on. Grace is in hospital. They've taken Stella.'

CHAPTER 42

Hannah heard Grace before she saw her.

'Get your hands off of me!'

They'd taken Banecroft's car. Hannah had torn through the early morning traffic at a reckless speed, ignoring a couple of inconveniently coloured lights on the way. Banecroft had hopped out of the car as soon as they'd arrived at the hospital, and rushed into the accident and emergency department as fast as his crutch could carry him.

Hannah had thrown the car into the first thing that looked like a parking space and raced after him, catching him up as he stomped down the hall. They passed a rotund nurse whose beaming smile crashed to the ground when she clocked Banecroft. 'Oh no, not you again.'

'Lovely to be back,' said Banecroft, not stopping. It had been five days since his visit, but he had clearly left an impression.

There was no need to talk to the woman behind the reception desk. As soon as Hannah entered A & E, Grace's presence was unmistakable. Her voice carried from the ward and down the halls: 'You do not understand. Let me go. I need to help her.'

A harassed-looking police constable stood outside the curtain.

As Banecroft and Hannah moved towards him, he held out his arms to block their passage.

'Whoa, whoa, whoa. This is a closed-off area.'

'The woman in there is my employee,' said Banecroft, 'and I wish to speak with her.'

'You can't do that, sir. It isn't safe.'

'Safe?' asked Hannah, doing nothing to hide her disbelief. 'Grace is a lovely, sweet woman who wouldn't hurt a fly.'

Grace's voice grew louder. 'You let me go this instant or so help me God, I shall rip off your arms and use them to beat you to death.'

'Her bark is worse than her bite,' finished Hannah.

'There was an explosion at her house,' continued the PC, 'and we think she might have concussion – she's raving like a lunatic. The medical staff are restraining her for her own safety.'

Grace's voice lifted over the quieter voices from behind the curtain, the ones using that specially trained, calming tone of reassurance. 'You'd best let me out of here, or with the good Lord as my witness, I will not be responsible for what happens. None of you are listening to me! You have got to listen to me!'

'What kind of explosion?' asked Hannah.

'We're not sure, madam. Probably gas. Lot of it about.'

'I'm going to talk to her,' said Banecroft, and went to move past. The PC placed a hand firmly on his chest. Banecroft glanced down at it for a moment and then looked the PC dead in the eye. 'I'm the editor of a newspaper and the lady in there is my employee. If I were you, I'd think hard – this is about to be a career-defining moment for you.'

Hannah could see the panic in the man's eyes.

'Look,' the PC said. 'The poor woman is ranting and raving. She keeps talking about a monster. She needs medical assistance.'

Banecroft looked down at the hand again. 'She won't be the only one in a minute.'

Hannah stepped forward. 'Is she under arrest?'

'What? No. Course not.'

'Right, then.' Hannah raised her voice. 'Grace. Grace!'

'Hannah? Hannah, is that you? They will not listen to me.'

'It's OK, it's OK. Grace, I want you to take a deep breath, stop struggling and calmly say that you want to speak to me.'

There was a moment's silence and then, 'I wish to please speak to her.'

Banecroft nodded. 'She sounds calm and in control of her faculties to me.'

Hannah nodded. 'I agree.'

'I bet the paper's lawyers will too. What do you reckon' – Banecroft glanced at the name badge on the PC's jacket – 'Constable Sinclair?'

PC Sinclair hesitated, then turned and stuck his head around the curtain. After a brief whispered conversation, he drew back the flimsy material. Hannah stepped beyond it to see two flustered nurses standing either side of a bed occupied by an irate and sweat-covered Grace. She had leather straps around her arms and cuts on her face.

'Oh my God, Grace. Are you OK?'

'Silly question,' said Banecroft, before raising his voice and addressing the nurses. 'Thank you, ladies. We'd like to speak to our associate privately for a couple of minutes, please.'

The nurses looked at PC Sinclair and then back at Grace, who was now a little calmer than she had been. They moved out of the cubicle, pulling the curtain closed behind them. As soon as they did, Hannah undid the restraint on one side of the bed and Banecroft did the same on the other.

Grace's voice came out in a torrent. 'You have got to save her. Oh, good Lord, that poor child. You have got to. They have got her. They have got her. They have got her.'

Hannah tried to keep the panic from her own voice as she spoke. 'Grace, it's OK.'

'It's not, it's not! Oh Lord, oh Lord!'

'Grace,' said Banecroft sharply. 'Calm down and stop ranting like a lunatic. Christ on a bike.'

'One,' said Grace automatically, as she somehow seemed to regain a semblance of self-control. 'Listen to me. They have got Stella!'

'All right,' said Hannah. 'Grace, I know you're upset, but you've got to focus. What happened exactly?'

Grace closed her eyes, and for a second Hannah thought she was going to burst into tears, but then they reopened, looking more focused. 'We had not been home long. Stella had gone upstairs to bed. I was making myself a cocoa – I can't sleep without my cocoa – and then there was a knock on the . . .' Her brow furrowed. 'No, there was . . . I don't know. But suddenly, they were there. That . . . thing.'

'The one from last night?' said Hannah.

Grace's head pistoned up and down furiously. 'Yes, that abomination was in my kitchen. My kitchen! And a man was with it. And then . . .' Tears welled in her eyes. 'And then it went for me, and Stella was there suddenly, and she screamed. Then there were chains in the air. Full metal chains, flying through the air. I know that does not make any sense, but I swear to God, chains. The little bald man, he threw them at her, only . . . not. And then she screamed so loud, and there was this blue light. So bright. And the explosion . . .'

'What exactly exploded?' asked Banecroft.

Grace looked at him, her eyes filled with confusion as tears rolled down her face. 'Stella did – or, I mean, it sort of came out of her. She . . . Bless her. She cannot control it when she gets upset. Blew out the whole back wall of the house. And then she was standing over me, telling me to get up, and then . . . It went dark, things fell, and when I came around they were all gone and part of the roof had fallen on me.'

Banecroft and Hannah looked at each other.

'I tried to explain it to the police,' Grace continued, 'but they looked at me like I was crazy.' She grabbed Hannah's hand. 'You know, though – you saw it. They have got our Stella.'

Banecroft spoke to Hannah. 'When that thing was in the church earlier, remember? It was going for us and then . . .'

'When Stella came up the stairs,' said Hannah, 'it turned and went for her. Like it was, I don't know, drawn to her.'

Banecroft looked back down at Grace. 'Did you see where they went?'

'I didn't. I was . . . They were there, then it all fell down, and when I opened my eyes again they were gone. Oh Lord, oh Lord. I have not got my phone.'

Hannah put her hand over Grace's, partly to comfort her and partly to try to ease her grip, as her fingernails were digging into the skin of Hannah's forearm. 'I tried ringing Stella on the way over but there was no answer.'

'No, you don't understand.' Grace looked up at Banecroft. 'A few months ago, when we had that fight – me and Stella – and she disappeared for a couple of days?'

Banecroft nodded.

'I asked Ox,' Grace continued, 'and he . . . he did it as a favour.'

'Grace,' said Hannah, as calmly as possible, 'what are you try-ing to tell us?'

'My phone!' said Grace. 'I made Ox put a thing on it so I could see where she was. I made him . . . I just wanted to know she was safe, and she always has it with her.'

Hannah placed her hand on Grace's cheek so that she would meet her gaze. 'Are you saying you've got a tracker on Stella's phone?'

'Yes,' said Grace. 'I told Ox I wanted something she would not see, and he did it for me, eventually. There is a thing on my phone, only it was on the kitchen counter and the wall blew up. I've not got my phone.'

'It's OK,' said Hannah. 'Ox will be able to find her.'

'Yes,' said Grace. 'Yes. Ox will be able to. She's a good girl. You've got to find her.'

'We will,' said Hannah. 'We will.'

Banecroft turned and headed out of the cubicle. 'C'mon, then – clock's ticking.'

Hannah looked down at Grace. 'It'll be OK. I promise. We'll find her.'

She rushed to catch up with Banecroft as he brushed past PC Sinclair and the two nurses, who were huddled in conversation.

'Would you just . . .' Hannah shouted after him. 'Hang on! What are we going to do?'

Banecroft didn't look back as he spoke. 'We're going to find Stella.'

'We need to tell the police.'

'Really?' said Banecroft. 'Our employee has been snatched by a werewolf and his demented Yankee master. Do you want to end up strapped into a bed beside Grace?'

'Well, what are we going to do, then?'

Banecroft pushed through the swing doors and stomped on. 'We're getting in the car and then you are ringing your boyfriend.'

CHAPTER 43

Tom Sturgess stared at the notices on the information board. Apparently, cats could carry some kind of killer flea now.

He was sitting in the large waiting area of the Ancoats Urban Village Medical Practice. About twenty people sat around in uncomfortable moulded plastic chairs, waiting for their names to scroll across the LED display, followed by a room number. At some point, visiting your GP had gone from waiting in a hallway to see a man in what was essentially the converted front room of his house to sitting around in what looked like a rather shoddy airport gate, waiting for your flight on Air NHS – maximum flight time: ten minutes. There were some subtle differences, of course. On the few occasions he had flown somewhere, nowhere near as many of his fellow passengers had been showing the effects of serious smack addiction.

He'd only dragged himself out of bed and come here today as the headaches were getting even worse, and besides, he suddenly had the time, having been suspended from work.

Following yesterday's raid on *The Stranger Times*, he'd gone straight back to the station and had Patel from the tech squad go through the hard disk for him. They'd found the picture pretty quickly. He and Patel had sat there for quite a long time, just looking at it.

'Is it possible,' Sturgess had asked, 'to fake something like that?'

'Well, I mean, you know,' said Patel, for whom a typical sentence had about five redundant sections before it got to the good bit, 'it's theoretically possible to fake anything these days.'

'Right.'

'I can, like, if you want, I can, y'know, tell you the timestamp on the file. When it was taken and that.'

The picture had been taken just minutes before Simon Brush's fatal dive off the top of the Dennard building. As Patel had confirmed, checked and rechecked the timings, Sturgess's headache had reached truly excruciating proportions, throbbing so hard that his perception of colours seemed to change, as if someone were turning the contrast on a TV up and down in time to a thumping bassline. He'd closed his eyes while, for the fourth time, Patel rechecked everything.

'Detective Inspector, are you – I mean, none of my business – but are you OK and that?'

Sturgess had opened his eyes again to find Patel leaning over him. 'You sort of, slumped over a bit there.'

'I'm fine. Just tired. Well?'

The recheck of the recheck had come back with the exact same results. Patel had also run a series of tests on the photo and he couldn't find any evidence of manipulation.

'OK,' said Sturgess. 'Don't mention this to anyone.'

'Right. Yeah. No problem. Whoever faked that, they must be, y'know, like, seriously, really good.'

'I thought you said it wasn't faked?'

Patel had looked at Sturgess and then at the screen again. 'Well, I mean, like, y'know, it must be fake, mustn't it?'

Sturgess had studied Patel's monitor one last time, and the demented eyes of a massive beast that seemed to be effortlessly holding the photographer off the ground with one long, powerful arm. 'Yeah,' said Sturgess, 'obviously.'

He'd gone back to his office and, behind the closed door, had taken four painkillers and even attempted those breathing exercises that he always felt foolish doing. Then, when the pain had at least receded to a dull, steady roar, he'd headed straight for the interview room where Mr Ox Chen was stashed. He'd started talking before he even reached the table. He was angry.

'Are you proud of yourself?'

Ox had held up his hand. 'All right, I shouldn't have taken the hard drive.' Then a look of panic crossed his face. 'Not that I'm saying I did, or I didn't. I'm saying "no comment" is what I'm saying.'

Sturgess had rested his fists on the table. 'Not that, you piece of shit.'

'Hey!'

'How else would you refer to somebody who uses a kid's death as an opportunity to fake a photo?'

Ox had looked outraged. 'No way, man. I would never do that. That picture is real.'

'It can't be real!' Sturgess had all but shouted it.

'It is. Simon was my friend. I would never—'

'Bullshit!'

'What the hell would you know about it?' Ox had shouted, raising his tone to meet Sturgess's. 'Working for "the man". You people oppress everything.'

'I'm trying to get to the truth.' Sturgess had thumped his fists into the desk, his head throbbing again.

'You've seen the truth. That thing killed Simon, and it killed that homeless bloke too. We've got witnesses.'

'It can't be . . .' Before he'd known what he was doing, Sturgess had grabbed Ox by the shirt and pushed him up against the wall. 'Tell. Me. The. Truth!'

Then there had been hands on him, pulling him away. DSs Wilkerson and Murphy. He'd held up his hands and they'd let him go. He'd seen the looks of shock on their faces.

In all his time on the force, that was the first time Sturgess had ever put his hands on a suspect. He held them out in front of him now, as if they had somehow betrayed him.

Wilkerson had spoken in a soft tone. 'The boss wants to see you.'

'I'm busy.'

'She wasn't asking.'

As he'd left the room, flanked by Wilkerson and Murphy, he'd stopped and turned. He'd winced with embarrassment as he felt his colleagues tense, ready to hold him back again. Ox was standing in the corner, looking at him like a man looks at a vicious guard dog that has been temporarily restrained.

'Mr Chen, I wish to apologize for what just happened. I shall report myself to the Independent Office for Police Conduct and submit a full written statement and an unreserved apology. I would encourage you to contact them – these officers will give you the details of how you can do so. Once again, I apologize unreservedly for placing my hands on you. There is no room in the modern police force for such behaviour.'

Ox had said nothing, just looked at him in confusion.

Then he'd been taken into Clayborne's office, where she and the chief inspector had informed him that it had been noted he was showing signs of stress and was overdue a break.

'No, thank you, boss,' said Sturgess. 'I'd like to continue with my investigation. I'd also like to know if my request to see the CCTV at the morgue has been granted?'

Clayborne had spoken to him with faux concern. 'Tom, be sensible. Take the long view here. You're a good detective – you still have a fine career ahead of you.'

'Then let me do my job.' He turned to look directly at the chief inspector. 'Let me complete the case I'm working on. What on earth are you trying to hide?'

'Tom!' Clayborne's voice had been full of warning, the fake friendliness gone.

Sturgess's eyes had remained locked on the chief inspector's. 'Who's applying pressure to get this case dropped?'

'There is no case here, DI Sturgess,' the chief inspector said in a casual manner. 'A homeless man died due to drunken misadventure and a confused young man tragically took his own life. All I see is an officer showing signs of a breakdown and exhibiting very poor judgement.'

'With all due respect, sir, that's crap.'

Clayborne had made to speak but the chief inspector had

silenced her with a raised hand. 'Think very carefully, DI Sturgess, as the next words out of your mouth are going to have a massive impact on the rest of your life. There is no case here, and we would like you to take a couple of weeks' holiday to relax and regain some of your lost perspective. Are you willing to do so?'

'No.'

'Fine.' The chief had shaken his head and then suspended him pending a disciplinary review.

Wilkerson had met him outside Clayborne's office, looking awkward. She had tried to pretend she was just being friendly, not under instructions to escort him back to his office and stay with him until he left the building. While he'd been taking a few things from his desk, Wilkerson had made every effort not to notice the bottles of pills he removed from his drawer. Instead, she had closed the door carefully and spoken in a hushed voice. 'I don't think Chen will go to the IOPC, boss, and Murphy and I won't—'

'He should,' said Sturgess. 'And you should encourage him to do so. I also expect both of you to report the incident.'

DS Wilkerson had stood there, unable to think of anything to say.

'Though I doubt it'll make any difference,' continued Sturgess. 'In case you haven't noticed, I've been suspended already – for doing my job. I don't know what they'll trump up but we both know my career is finished.'

He had gone home, taken a long hot bath and tried to sleep. His head had been full of that photo and the pain from the headaches, so this morning he had finally decided to go back to the GP and organize the tests they'd suggested the last time he had been in.

As he sat in the waiting room his phone vibrated in his pocket. He fished it out and took a long look at the screen. It was an unknown number and he was tempted to let it go to voicemail. Given his lack of a social life, it was undoubtedly work-related. Still, a nagging voice wouldn't let him ignore it. He pressed the green button.

'Hello.'

'Hi, DI Sturgess.'

'Hello, Ms Willis.'

'Hi. I, umm, had your number from when you gave me your card.' She sounded nervous.

'Yes, of course.'

'How are you?'

'Just ask him,' a male Irish voice barked in the background, followed by a muffled exchange he couldn't make out.

'How can I help you, Ms Willis?'

'All right, look. I know this will sound mad, but our friend has been taken by . . . It's hard to explain . . .'

'The thing in that photo?' Sturgess could feel his headache starting up again.

'Oh. Yes. That.'

'I see.'

'And the only way we can get her back is . . . We need to talk to Ox. The guy you arrested yesterday. He knows how to find her and . . .'

A message scrolled across the LED display above the door instructing T. Sturgess to go to examination room four, but he didn't see it, being halfway out the door by that point.

'I'll meet you outside Stretford police station in ten minutes.'

Still No Martians in Masham

The town of Masham in North Yorkshire is one of the very few in the UK never to have documented a UFO sighting, much to the chagrin of local ufologist and undertaker Jacob Ransdale.

To redress this, Mr Ransdale has opened an intergalactic tourist information centre in the hope of attracting them.

'Masham is a blooming great town and I think if visitors from other galaxies would just give it a chance, they'd find themselves pleasantly surprised. We've got two working breweries, and we have the sheep festival in September, which is always very popular. I mean, bloody Thirsk had one last year – a proper triangle being chased across the sky by the RAF. Why won't they come here? We're miles better than sodding Thirsk. All they've got is that the bloke who wrote *All Creatures Great and Small* comes from there, and they're always banging on about it.'

If any intergalactic visitors are intending to add Masham to their itinerary, Mr Ransdale respectfully asks that they avoid the first two weeks in June as he has a holiday in Torremolinos booked.

CHAPTER 44

Speed and confidence, thought Sturgess. *That was the key. Speed and confidence.* Throughout his life, he had never broken the rules. In fact, if his life had a driving motivation, it was an obsession with bringing to justice those who flagrantly disregarded rules. And yet here he was.

When he had pulled up across from Stretford police station, Hannah Willis had been standing beside a green Jaguar, looking around nervously. He had been happy to see her. He had been less happy when the back window rolled down and her boss's voice had chimed forth. 'Ah, excellent, here's the jackbooted thug of oppression we've been waiting for.'

'Shut up,' Hannah had hissed.

'Both of you are against freedom of expression. I can see why you get on so well.'

Sturgess had sat in the front seat while Hannah quickly made her pitch: that thing was real; it was being controlled by some American; and it had taken Stella, the young girl from their office, of whom Sturgess had only the dimmest recollection.

'Look,' said Hannah, 'we can try to go the police route with this, but we need to do something fast. We don't know what this guy is planning . . .'

'We do,' Banecroft chipped in, 'but it isn't good and it will take far too long to explain.'

Sturgess had looked out the window and taken a deep breath. Some things you don't come back from. But there wasn't a decision to be made. He had thought about it on the drive over and had already made his choice. He had nothing to lose and, more than anything, something deep down inside him wanted to know the truth – to hell with the consequences.

He nodded to himself. 'The police won't do anything. They've suspended me for chasing this. Somebody with a lot of power wants it to go away.'

'Terrific,' said Banecroft. 'The standard of policing in this—'

'Shut up,' Hannah told him again. She had given Sturgess a pleading look. 'If the police won't do anything, then we have to. If Stella has her phone, Ox knows how to track it, but we need to get him out.'

Sturgess shook his head. 'I can't do that.'

Hannah had looked crestfallen.

'But I can get you in.'

Speed and confidence. Sturgess strode into the station and past Brigstocke on the reception desk. There was no point going in the normal way: Sturgess would bet that his pass no longer worked. 'Hello, Jim – can you buzz me in?'

The sergeant looked up at him, eyes filled with suspicion, and then at Hannah standing behind him, trying to look relaxed and charming. 'Sturgess, I thought you were . . .'

'I'm on holiday. Just dropping in to pick up a couple of things.'

He rested his hand on the door and looked at Brigstocke expectantly. He could see his colleague's training battling with the natural human instinct not to make things awkward. Brigstocke hit the button and buzzed them through.

Sturgess walked down the corridor as quickly as he could. 'We'll have to be fast. Sooner or later, someone's going to notice I shouldn't be here.'

He took a left and a right before hurrying down the stairs to the basement. A couple of people he passed did double takes. He was aware he was not a popular man, and he guessed the news of his suspension had been a gleeful topic of conversation since yesterday.

As Sturgess opened the door that led down to the holding cells, PC Duncan Deering looked up from his paper with a start. Deering was utterly terrible at his job and had managed to get himself sick-noted into doing indoor work only. He was the deadest of dead weight, which meant that doing a sloppy job – as Sturgess needed him to – would come as second nature.

'This woman needs to see the guy in cell four,' Sturgess announced. 'Family emergency.'

'Right,' said Deering, who had somehow got chocolate on his cheek. 'Should we not bring him up to an interview room?'

'There's no time,' Sturgess said, not having to fake his impatience. 'I'm approving it. His sister needs to speak to him.'

Deering looked at Hannah and gave a nervous smile. 'Sister?'

Sturgess took a step forward. 'Yes, sister. What? Do you think a man of Chinese heritage cannot have a Caucasian sister? Have you never heard of adoption? Are you opening the cell or am I writing you up for racial insensitivity?'

This was the great advantage of having a reputation for being a bastard: people believed you were perfectly happy to be one at the drop of a hat.

As the holding cell opened, Sturgess was ashamed to see Ox flinch at the sight of him. Sturgess took a step to the side, and when Ox saw Hannah, his expression changed to a mixture of confusion and relief. She quickly sat down beside Ox on the bench-cum-bed.

'Thank you, PC Deering,' said Sturgess. 'You can leave the door open and I'll call you when they're done.'

Deering nodded and scurried away.

Sturgess waited until the officer's footsteps had faded, then turned to Ox and Hannah, and lowered his voice. 'Be quick!'

'What's going on?' said Ox.

'No time,' said Hannah. 'We need to find Stella and Grace says you'd know how.'

Ox looked up at Sturgess nervously. 'I don't know what you're talking about.'

'Ox,' said Hannah, 'that thing has got Stella.'

'The . . . ?'

'Yes. The bloody great monster. Now tell us how to find her – fast.'

Ox glanced around again furtively and then scratched at his stubble.

'Ox?'

'My phone. There's an app called Bloodhound. I downloaded it when I installed it on Grace's so—'

'PC Deering,' shouted Sturgess, walking out into the corridor, 'I need this detainee's personal effects immediately.'

CHAPTER 45

Stella had tried alcohol only once in her entire life. It had been back in the old place, in what she now thought of as her old life. She'd been far too young but, as always, she'd been attempting to fit in. One of the older girls had got hold of a bottle of vodka and they'd gone out to a clearing in the woods. The girls had given her some mixed with Coke and it had tasted, well, mostly of Coke. Like slightly off Coke.

Huddled around a fire, they'd all been chatting and she'd felt, for the first time in her life, as if she had friends. Then she'd started to feel unwell, like the world was tumbling off its axis. She'd stood up and tried to excuse herself before stumbling away from the fire to be sick, a very different kind of laughter now ringing in her ears. When she'd come back, she'd found the clearing empty. It had taught her two valuable lessons: one, you couldn't trust people; and two, alcohol was only the answer if the question was 'How can I make everything worse?'

She had made her way home eventually and been met by Jacob as she attempted to sneak in the back door. He had looked even more disappointed than usual. For a moment, she'd thought he was going to say something, but instead he just sent her to her room. When she woke up the next morning, her head had been throbbing and she would have welcomed death.

As she opened her eyes this time, if anything she felt worse. But on this occasion she didn't wish for death, mainly because it was so clearly imminent.

She was sitting on a plastic chair in some foul-smelling warehouse. In the background, the outlines of piles of furniture could be made out in the patchy light coming through the grimy windows near the ceiling. There was a smell of rotting wood, decay and rust, and somewhere behind her she could hear the constant drip, drip of water. One electric bulb hung from the ceiling in front of her, offering a pool of light, in the centre of which sat something that looked like a marble font. It was made of a shiny white stone that seemed to give off its own softly throbbing light.

Spread on the floor surrounding it was a collection of weird-looking objects: a knife with a serrated edge, a ball of twine, some apples, a cup, something furry that Stella couldn't see clearly and, most inexplicable of all, a bottle of tomato ketchup. Looking down at them with an appraising eye was the short bald guy who had been in the photo, and whom Stella had seen in the flesh for a brief moment back at Grace's house.

Grace! Stella immediately tried to scream – she desperately needed to know what had happened to Grace – but her lips would not move. No part of her body would move. All she could do was breathe through her nose. She was restrained somehow. Something metal was wrapped around her wrists; it felt cold and yet it burned at the same time. It didn't explain why the rest of her was immobilized, though. She willed her legs to come to life so she could stand up and run, but nothing happened. Her skull felt as if it were vibrating as she attempted to speak, but despite it all, her lips would not part.

A shadow passed over her, and then, as if ripped from a nightmare, the face of the beast was in front of her, its wild, demented eyes looking into hers, its rancid breath washing over her. Stella felt her body attempt to retch as the creature's coarse tongue slobbered up the side of her face.

'Bad dog!'

The beast yelped and jolted backwards as if it had been shocked. The short man walked towards her, a wide grin on his thin lips. 'Oh, excellent – you're awake. Do forgive the doggy, I'm afraid he's yet to be house-trained.'

This elicited a low growl that would have stopped another man dead in his tracks, but the short man seemed unfazed. Instead, he gave an ostentatious bow, waving his hand as he did so.

'Charlie Moretti at your service, madame.' He straightened up and moved closer. 'It is honestly a real treat to meet you. Frankly, I thought your kind were a myth. If time allowed, I would study you – but alas, a certain matter is pressing.' He gave her an appraising look. 'I wonder, do you even know what you are?' After a long moment, he shook his head quickly, as if snapping out of a reverie. 'Oh, such fun.' He took a handkerchief from his pocket and wiped the slobber from Stella's face. 'Sorry about that. And where are my manners? I've not introduced you to the rest of the team.'

Moretti twirled his finger in the air and Stella felt herself being lifted by unseen forces and spun around. She was suspended in the air, about five feet off the ground, so she was more or less level with the other two prisoners. They looked to be welded to the corrugated metal wall. Thick metal restraints bound their hands, feet, waists and necks, leaving them pinioned in the crucifix pose. Some form of leather muzzle was also wrapped around their mouths, preventing them from speaking.

Moretti moved first to stand beneath the man, who was wearing worn jeans, a stained hoodie and a thick anorak. His eyes, looking at Stella from above an unkempt beard, were filled with terror.

Moretti waved his hands like a host on a quiz show introducing contestants to the prizes. 'This is . . . Well, to be honest, I never did bother to learn his name. Let's call him the unluckiest hobo. He's a boring old Type Two.' Moretti moved across to the woman in the torn nightdress and dressing gown. She looked about fifty and had curly brown hair. 'This is Vera Woodward. Good old Vera is a Type Six, and a feisty one at that. She enjoys long walks along the beach, needlework and sacrificing herself so that her family might live. She's also a little bit ticklish.' He ran his fingers across the bare soles of the woman's feet. Panicked as she was, Stella noticed that the woman's eyes didn't seem to carry the same fear as the homeless man's. More than anything, she looked angry.

Moretti twirled his finger again and, with a sickening jolt, Stella spun around and was plonked roughly back into the chair, from where she could still not move.

'I want you all to know that the sacrifice you will make today is for the most noble of causes. You will die so that a sick child may live.' Moretti clutched his hands to his chest melodramatically.

'Ain't that just the most beautiful thing. You should feel proud – you'll be part of something truly special. It'll be the highlight and the finale of your sad little lives.'

Moretti made his way over to Stella and placed his finger on her nose. 'It does seem a waste of your unique qualities, but sadly I made an agreement and I am very much a man of my word. And now . . .' Moretti turned on his heel and clapped his hands in the air twice, like a flamenco dancer. 'On with the show!'

Stella heard what sounded like a fist being banged against the metal door. The beast snarled.

'Aha,' said Moretti. 'Perfect timing. The last piece of the puzzle, arriving right on schedule.' He turned to the beast. 'Be a good doggy and pick up that pile of metal rods over there.'

The beast stared at Moretti for a moment too long, and the smile fell from the short man's face.

'Don't make me ask twice,' Moretti warned. 'You know I don't like to do that.'

The beast turned and effortlessly snatched up the pile of six-foot-long rods.

'Good boy!' Moretti turned to his audience of three again. 'You know, when I first met Mr Merchant here – or "doggy", as he likes to be called – I was not impressed. He seemed boorish and dim. Still, I needed a doggy and my first attempt at making one had resulted in a nasty crater in the ground.' He grinned at the beast. 'Oh yes. You weren't my first attempt. Heavens, no. I'd imagine in your whole crappy life you've never been anyone's first choice.'

The beast's mouth opened in a snarl, which Moretti ignored. 'His one redeeming quality was the sincere love he had for his poor sickly daughter, Cathy. He would do anything to save her. Anything, that is, except follow simple orders.' Moretti took a step closer to him. 'Still, despite the endless screw-ups, the carnage you left in your wake, and the unwanted and downright inconvenient attention it attracted, I managed to make lemonade out of the shitty little lemons you brought me. So I just want to say this . . .'

A more insistent fist thumped on metal this time.

'Coming!' hollered Moretti cheerfully, before lowering his voice again. 'I've been looking forward to this moment so much.'

Moretti's hands became a blur of movement. The metal rods spun out of the beast's grip and started to wrap themselves around its body. It let out a roar of frustration as it fought in vain against the constricting metal before losing its footing and tumbling messily to the ground, its arms pinned tightly to its sides, its legs bound. Stella could see its muscles straining against the restraints, but there was no way it could free itself. Another rod wrapped itself around the beast's snout, forcing its mouth closed and leaving it only able to whimper pathetically.

'Moretti,' came a raised voice from somewhere outside.

'Just. A. Second!' Moretti snapped, irritated at having his fun interrupted. He leaned over the beast and looked into its glowing eyes. 'I'd say it's nothing personal, but it really is. You remind me of every mouth-breathing knuckle-dragger who made my life hell as a child, not to mention the ones in prison. People like you made me what I am. So, you see, all of this is kind of your fault.'

Moretti straightened up and motioned in the air. Stella could hear what sounded like a large metal door opening with a screech of ill-maintained metal.

'What the hell are you doing, leaving us out there?' said the accentless voice of someone who was making no effort to hide their irritation.

Moretti looked directly at Stella and waggled his eyebrows. 'Ohhh, I'm in trouble now.'

The owner of the voice appeared beside Moretti: a bald man with a hawkish demeanour, who was dressed in a black suit. He was freakishly tall – almost seven feet when drawn to his full height. He walked with a stoop, however, as he pushed a wheelchair in front of him. In it sat a teenage boy, entirely hairless, whose skin was a pallor that Stella had never seen on the living. An oxygen mask was strapped to his face, attached to a cylinder that sat beneath the chair.

'Everyone,' said Moretti, 'this is Xander and his young friend Daniel. Daniel and Xander, this is everyone.' Xander, the tall man, avoided looking at Stella and the other prisoners. The boy's eyes looked so dim it seemed he was unaware of where he was. Moretti looked pointedly at the beast as he spoke again. 'Daniel is the poor sick child we shall be curing on this fine day.'

On the ground the beast rocked and gave forth a pitiable whine.

The tall man did not divert his eyes from Moretti. 'Could you please minimize the histrionics? My employer engaged your services to do this quickly and quietly, something I hear you have singularly failed to manage thus far.'

Moretti stood over the font and moved his hands in a series of complicated gestures. 'Sorry, it's so hard to get good help these days.'

'You've turned this simple task into a freak show.'

The joviality dropped from Moretti's voice entirely. 'Simple? Simple? Nobody could have done this but me.'

'Nobody else was willing,' said Xander, shifting the blanket draped over Daniel's legs, 'which is not the same thing. My employer granted you your freedom for a very specific purpose. He can take it away again just as quickly.'

Moretti dropped his hands to his sides. 'Oh, I'm sorry – should I leave you to do this simple task yourself, then?'

'Do not attempt to bluff, Moretti. You do not have the cards. We both know you would do anything not to go back there.'

Moretti spun around, his eyes bulging. 'And you think it is a great idea to threaten somebody who has nothing to lose?'

Xander looked momentarily taken aback by the ferocity of Moretti's tone. 'Calm down, Mr Moretti. Despite the setbacks, it appears this is about to work out well for all parties.'

'Yes, it will, if I'm allowed to go about my business uninterrupted.'

Xander ran his long bony fingers down the front of his suit and gave the slightest of nods.

'Very well, then.' Moretti turned his attention back to the font and resumed the sequence of hand gestures. 'And I trust you have remembered the rest of our agreement?'

Xander took out a handkerchief and patted it against his cheeks. 'Get this done and you will get exactly what was agreed.'

'Excellent.' Moretti stared into the font for a good twenty seconds before raising his head and favoured the room with a broad smile. 'Well, then . . .' He spread his arms out wide. 'It's showtime!'

CHAPTER 46

'Take a right here,' said Sturgess.

Hannah looked at the road sign. 'It says no right turn.'

'Take a right!' hollered Banecroft from the back seat.

'Christ,' said Hannah, executing the turn and heading down the thankfully empty one-way street. 'I can see why Stella so enjoyed the "driving lesson" she had with you.'

'Unless you two stop making goo-goo eyes at each other and get a move on, she won't get a chance at another.'

'Left here,' said Sturgess. 'Is he always this charming?'

'You're actually catching him on a good day.'

'Pull up here.' Sturgess checked the screen of the phone in his hand and then studied their surroundings. They were in a warren of backstreets that seemed to comprise mainly storage units covered in rather dull graffiti, an MOT garage that had gone out of business, and a large abandoned warehouse. It was now 10 a.m. on a bright March day. 'If this thing is right,' he continued, 'then Stella's phone, and hopefully Stella, are in that warehouse over there.'

'OK,' said Banecroft, opening the back door. 'Let's go get her. She's already late for the Friday morning meeting.'

'Wait,' said Sturgess. 'We should call in back-up.'

'Right,' replied Banecroft, 'from the police. Remind me again: what did they do when there was the first hint of hairy-monster involvement in proceedings?'

Sturgess opened his mouth, but no words came out.

'Exactly as I thought. They shut you down. The police turn up, what're the odds they arrest us, seeing as you are in possession of stolen evidence?'

Sturgess looked down at Ox's phone.

Banecroft slammed the car door behind him and hobbled up the pavement. Hannah and Sturgess exited the car wordlessly and followed him. Hannah ran a few steps to catch up with her boss and lowered her voice. 'Do you have to go out of your way to offend people?'

'No, I find I don't need to. They keep putting themselves in my path.'

The trio stopped before the warehouse behind its wire-mesh fence.

'How are we going to get in?' asked Hannah.

'There's a gap in the fence over there that we could crawl through,' suggested Sturgess, pointing, 'but I don't know how we can get inside.'

'Aha!' said Banecroft, snatching a small leather case from the pocket of his overcoat and holding it up. 'Allow me to introduce you to the freedom of the press.'

CHAPTER 47

It turned out that the 'freedom of the press' was what Banecroft called his lock-picking kit. They found a padlocked entrance to the side of the building, at the end opposite the huge loading-bay doors. They stood outside and listened, but they could hear absolutely nothing, which was odd. Hannah put her ear against the corrugated metal wall and heard muffled voices and an animalistic whine. It was as if any noise from inside was being dampened somehow.

Banecroft seemed to take a perverse delight in picking the lock while being observed by a detective inspector. As he worked, Hannah had a chance to study Sturgess's face. He seemed incredibly uncomfortable and kept opening and closing his eyes.

'Are you OK?' she whispered.

Sturgess nodded. 'Yes, just a migraine.'

Banecroft opened the padlock in roughly a minute and then admonished himself for being out of practice. They opened the door painfully slowly, for fear of attracting unwanted attention. In the end, they needn't have worried, as piles of old furniture stacked high were blocking the far end of the room from view. Precarious-looking columns of chairs, sofas on top of sofas, old-fashioned wooden wardrobes and chests of drawers were piled side by side in a haphazard fashion. The place stank of decay and rot. Behind it all, they could hear what sounded a lot like a voice chanting.

Banecroft set off through the jungle of remaindered furniture at an awkward, crouched hobble. He held out his crutch, useless as a support, like a makeshift weapon. Hannah and Sturgess followed, and the trio worked their way through, making their way to a vantage point behind an old cabinet upon which some prehistoric tins of paint rested.

As she looked over the top of the cabinet, Hannah had to place her hand over her mouth out of fear that she would make an involuntary noise. Two figures hung from the wall, arms splayed out as if being crucified. In the middle of the room, Stella sat awkwardly in a chair, her body rigid, her hands cuffed. A freakishly tall man stood beside a young man in a wheelchair, and at the centre of it all, she could see the short, bald man. He had his back to them, and was waving his arms over something that was emitting a glowing light. He was chanting words in a language Hannah didn't recognize, and the light was growing steadily brighter.

The three of them hunched back down behind the cabinet.

'Right,' said Hannah softly. 'Now we're here, what are we going to do?'

'Personally,' said Banecroft, 'I'd be in favour of Johnny Law here popping a cap in the little slaphead's ass. I'm happy to testify that he was armed.'

'I would not shoot a defenceless suspect,' said Sturgess quietly.

'He's unarmed – I very much doubt that's the same thing.'

'And besides, I don't have a gun.'

'What?' replied Banecroft. 'Is it in your other suit or something?'

'We don't normally carry guns, and they certainly don't let you take one home with you after you've been suspended.'

'Well, we could use my gun, but, oh yeah, the bloody police took it away.'

'Shut up. Both of you,' hissed Hannah. 'Or at the very least, keep your voices down. We're not shooting anyone, and besides, in case you didn't notice, right behind him are innocent hostages. I'm pretty sure bullets pass through people.'

'Well, we'd better do something,' said Banecroft, 'and fast. Laughing boy is building up to something and I don't think it'll involve pulling a rabbit from anywhere.'

Behind them, the chanting grew louder, as if voices from unseen people were now joining in. Banecroft stood up and looked over the cabinet again.

'I've got an idea. A really terrible idea.'

Stella watched as Moretti waved his hands above the font, his eyes closed, vocalizing words she couldn't understand. Xander watched on, while the boy seemed only vaguely aware of his surroundings. If he was looking at anything, it was at the beast who now lay on the ground, trussed up helplessly. It was only because Stella tried to look away and shift her eyes, the one part of her body she could control, that she saw something move. The old furniture was piled seemingly at random around the warehouse, and it was hard to make out because of the now almost painfully bright light coming from the font, but there had definitely been some kind of movement to her right.

The chanting stopped abruptly. In front of Moretti, who now beamed the grin of a demented Cheshire cat, a column of water rose up from the font, standing steady. Not because it was frozen; it was liquid that had decided the laws of gravity did not apply to it.

'And there we go,' declared Moretti, gleefully clapping his hands. 'We are ready! Ladies and gentlemen, please make sure your tray tables and seats are in the upright position – we are coming in for landing.' His hand wafted through the air and the dagger with the serrated blade leaped from the ground and rotated slowly in the air beside the column of liquid. 'All we need now are the blood donations from our three plucky volunteers. But in which order? Oldest first? Bit ageist. Ladies first? A tad sexist. We could go by type? Most common to rarest.' He gave Stella a gleeful smile. 'Or we could . . .'

'Just get on with it, Moretti,' said Xander. 'This is not good for the boy.'

'I don't tell you how to lackey. Don't tell me how to—'

'Greater Manchester Police, you're all under arrest.'

Moretti and Xander spun around to see the man Stella recognized as DI Sturgess. He was standing to Stella's left, barely in her field of vision, and he was holding his ID open above his head.

'Stop what you are doing immediately. We have the building surrounded. Hands in the air.' He hesitated and pointed at Moretti. 'Not you. Hands by your sides.'

Xander glared at Moretti. 'I thought you said this place was secure?'

'I said hands in the—' The words died on Sturgess's lips as the knife zipped through the air and came to a stop inches from his forehead. Stella saw him try to dodge it, but with another wave of Moretti's hand, he seemed to go as stiff as a board, his mouth frozen open mid-word.

'Relax,' said Moretti. 'He wouldn't be coming in here alone if he really had back-up.'

As Moretti spoke, Stella felt unseen hands touching hers. Hannah's face appeared in her field of vision and her colleague briefly touched her finger to her lips. Stella glanced at the backs of Xander and Moretti, who remained facing away from her, distracted by Sturgess – his hand still raised in the air, holding his ID aloft. The only eyes on her were those of the boy, who looked on without saying or doing anything. Hannah's hands tugged at Stella's cuffs and she felt a tiny vibration of metal scratching on metal.

Stella watched the blade fly back to land in Moretti's hand, and the figure of Sturgess began to lift off the ground and drift slowly towards Moretti, Xander and the boy.

A waft of BO and whiskey reached Stella's nose. Banecroft.

'We need to make sure we're not compromised,' she heard Xander say.

'Calm down,' said Moretti, taking something from his pocket and dangling it in front of Sturgess's face. 'Watch the birdie and—'

Xander and Moretti took a step back in surprise as Sturgess's head suddenly started to spasm on his neck, as if he were having a seizure that affected only one part of his body.

'Well, now,' said Moretti. 'That really is interesting.'

Xander went to speak and Stella noticed his head twitch, as if he'd spotted something out of the corner of his eye. He turned in their direction.

'MORETTI!' Xander's scream was surprisingly high-pitched.

Stella felt something being slipped into the pocket of her jeans and had just enough time to register the terror on Hannah's face as both she and Banecroft rose into the air, frozen in their crouched positions. Stella felt her own body sag as hope was replaced with despair.

'You people,' snapped Moretti, 'are getting really annoying.'

Xander moved towards the boy in the wheelchair. 'That's it. This has been compromised.'

'SILENCE!' screamed Moretti, his face now bright red from exertion and agitation. 'Do you really want to go back and tell your boss you walked away when the boy was about to be made immortal?'

Xander said nothing.

'Exactly. So shut up and let me handle this.'

He waved his hands in the air, like a conductor managing an orchestra, the knife his baton. In response, the figures of Hannah, Sturgess and Banecroft all straightened out and stood to rigid attention before him, like soldiers on parade, albeit ones standing three feet in the air.

'You people,' Moretti repeated. 'You need to stop interfering in things that don't concern you. As far as rescue plans go, this one is essentially the classic "Look, your sneaker is untied". Pathetic.' He pointed at Sturgess. 'And you, who are you working for?'

Moretti waited for a moment. 'Oh,' he said, realizing why a reply wasn't forthcoming. He clicked his fingers and all three of their heads moved, freed from whatever force had rendered them immobile.

'Lovely to see you again,' said Banecroft.

'You will speak when spoken to or else I'll put this knife straight through the woman's throat.'

Moretti gave Banecroft the opportunity to open his mouth and close it again. 'Wise choice,' he said, before pointing at Sturgess. 'Now, you – who are you working for?'

Sturgess looked confused. 'What?'

Moretti spat out the words slowly, as if speaking to a confused child. 'Who. Do. You. Work. For?'

'The Greater Manchester police force.'

Moretti raised the knife and pointed it at Hannah. 'Don't play games with me.'

Sturgess looked baffled.

'He doesn't know,' said Xander.

Moretti turned his head to look back at Xander. 'Is that even possible?'

'Clearly.'

Moretti shrugged. 'Hmm. Interesting.'

He dropped the coin on its chain and dangled it in front of Sturgess. Once again, the detective's head started to spasm violently.

'Please. Stop!' begged Hannah.

And just like that, it did. Sturgess slumped forward, unconscious, as if someone had flicked a switch and turned him off.

Moretti stepped forward and tapped the top of Sturgess's head with the edge of the knife. 'C'mon. Out you come.'

Hannah gasped as the hair on the top of Sturgess's scalp started to move. The skin began to part and up popped an eyeball on a stalk. It spun around, looking in all directions.

'What in the—' said Hannah.

'Yeah,' said Banecroft, 'I don't know if that's an STD, but you probably want to get yourself tested.'

Hannah said nothing. She was too busy concentrating on not throwing up.

Moretti held the blade directly in front of the eye. 'And who do you work for?'

Sturgess's mouth moved and a voice came from him, though it was clearly not his own. 'That is none of your concern.'

'I beg to differ.'

'Mr Xander's employer already has enough questions to answer without adding damage to the property of another member of the Council.'

Xander threw up his hands in irritation. 'Wonderful!'

Moretti lunged the knife at the eyeball, which dodged backwards.

'Leave it,' shouted Xander. 'What's done is done. Finish the procedure. My employer's instructions were very clear. Save the boy.'

'What about these two?' said Moretti, waving the knife in the direction of Hannah and Banecroft.

'We,' said Banecroft, 'are employees of *The Stranger Times*, which is protected under the terms of the Accord.'

Xander rolled his eyes. 'Of course you are.'

Hannah looked at Banecroft in confusion before adding, 'So is Stella. She works with us.'

'Yes,' said Banecroft.

'Is this true?' asked Xander.

'Ahhh,' said Moretti, 'that explains what happened when we met before. When my powers didn't . . .' He trailed off and looked up at Banecroft. 'Wait. Why were you protected before and yet—'

'Yes,' said Banecroft ruefully, 'looks like I picked a very bad day to leave my totem at home. Anyway, as we said – protected. So just let us go and we'll be off.'

Moretti tossed the blade into the air. It came to rest hovering at Banecroft's throat. 'I'm going to enjoy killing you slowly.'

'Not now,' said Xander, his patience running thin. 'Complete the making and do what you like with these two after.'

Stella felt tears begin to run down her cheeks. Without thinking, she raised her hand and brushed them away.

She could move.

How could she move?

In all the confusion, she had somehow not noticed. Her hands were still chained, but she could move. The thing she had felt being slipped into the pocket of her jeans. Something metal. She brought down her hand. A key – like one of the big brass ones Grace had for the door of *The Stranger Times*.

On unsteady legs, she got to her feet.

'We need to . . .' Xander's words died away as he caught sight of Stella.

She took a step forward and, after coughing to clear her throat, said, 'Let them go.'

Moretti turned to look at her. For the first time, she saw fear in his eyes.

'How did . . . ?'

'That's right,' said Banecroft. 'Silly me. I didn't leave my totem at home – I slipped it into Stella's pocket. Doesn't that mean your jiggery-pokery no longer works on her?'

Stella shifted her hands and looked down at the manacles binding them. 'Just let everybody go.'

Xander backed away.

'It's all right,' said Moretti dismissively, 'she can't control her power. She's useless.'

Stella looked around her. 'Just . . . Please. I want to go home.'

Moretti laughed. 'Oh dear, how pathetic.' He waved his hand and the plastic chair pushed into the back of her legs. 'Sit down. There's a good girl. Don't make this harder than it needs to be.'

Stella felt panic rising in her. She didn't know what to do. There was nothing she could do. She looked from Hannah to Banecroft to the two figures chained to the wall. It was all too much.

She looked down at the chair behind her.

'He's right,' Banecroft chimed in. 'Sit back down like the silly little girl you are. Bloody useless.'

Stella's head snapped up as if she'd been slapped. She glared at Banecroft, and she could see Hannah doing the same.

'We went to all this trouble and you can't even save yourself,' Banecroft continued.

'Vincent!' exclaimed Hannah.

Moretti laughed. 'Someone doesn't like losing.'

'Stupid, pointless child,' Banecroft carried on. 'Letting everyone down, again.'

Hannah's head whipped back and forth between the two of them.

'Shut up,' whispered Stella.

'No,' said Banecroft. 'I won't. Thanks to you, I'm going to die. Hannah's going to die. Simon died.'

Moretti clapped his hands gleefully. 'Tough love!'

Stella could feel the rage building in her chest. She took a step forward. 'That was not my fault.'

'It's all your fault,' said Banecroft. 'You are worthless.'

Hannah looked at Stella, her mouth suddenly dry. 'Yes, you are.'

Stella flashed a hurt look at Hannah, bewildered by her betrayal.

'Moretti . . .' Xander's voice sounded a warning.

Moretti stopped clapping and the smile fell from his face.

'Thanks to you,' continued Hannah, 'this man killed Grace!'

'No!' screamed Stella.

The feeling began to surge through her. Uncontrollable. The cuffs on her wrists fell away and she strode towards Moretti.

'You killed her!'

Moretti's hands were a blur in the air. Random hulks of furniture began to rise and fly towards Stella. She let out a scream, and all of it – wood, fabric, metal – disintegrated and fell to the ground as dust.

Hannah, Banecroft and the unconscious form of Sturgess dropped to the floor as Moretti backed away from the advancing Stella.

'No, don't. I . . .'

Stella spoke, more to herself than anyone else. 'She was a nice lady. She was good to me. She took me in. YOU. KILLED. GRACE!'

She was dimly aware of Xander standing to her right, waving his hands in her direction. She shot out her own hand and a shaft of blue light sprang from her fingers and sent him pinwheeling across the room. Moretti's hands flapped about in the air above him, no longer casting, now just the actions of a desperate man looking for help that would not come. In the background, Stella could hear Hannah trying to talk to her, but her words were rendered unintelligible by the roaring sound in her ears. Stella raised her arms and felt the thing – the thing that scared her more than anything – rising within her once again.

And then . . .

A sudden feeling of emptiness washed over her. What had been rising didn't calm so much as disappear entirely. There was no sound. It was as if the universe had frozen itself into one moment.

And then the large metal doors behind her blew in.

CHAPTER 48

As the smoke around the door cleared, a dozen armed men in balaclavas rushed in, a clamour of voices screaming for everyone to get
on the floor. Hannah, already on the ground, stayed where she
was. She looked up to see Stella standing above them, looking
down at her own hands as if in a daze, before being slammed to the
floor by two of the storm troopers in balaclavas.

'Leave her alone!' shouted Hannah, but then hands were on her
too, roughly turning her over, pinning her arms behind her back
and cuffing her. Her face bashed against the wet concrete floor.
'Ouch. Go easy!'

Hannah's experience with handcuffs was limited to the two
occasions when she had been arrested recently, and one other incident when she had tried to do something a bit different on her
soon-to-be ex-husband's birthday, which had been excruciatingly
embarrassing for everyone involved. While those experiences
hardly qualified her as an expert, these cuffs felt different.

Thicker, heavier and somehow colder. The word 'manacles'
popped into her head but she wasn't sure if that was right either.
They felt like more than just metal.

She looked around to see Banecroft, Moretti, and even the

unconscious form of Sturgess being similarly hog-tied. In the confusion, Hannah turned and saw Stella looking at her. She felt horrible about what they had done to her, but belatedly she had caught on to Banecroft's idea. Grace had told them that Stella's outbursts were related to her losing her temper.

Grace.

'Stella! Stella!' Her young colleague seemed to focus and looked at Hannah in surprise, as if only just realizing she was there. 'Grace is fine. I'm sorry. Grace is fine.'

Stella closed her eyes.

Before Hannah could say anything else, the lanky figure of the man called Xander was pushed down on to the ground between them.

'This is a mistake,' he was saying. 'I am one of the . . .'

He stopped speaking as the circle of gun-wielding men parted and a diminutive figure walked in. It took Hannah a moment to process. The last time she'd seen Dr Carter was at her brief appearance in the police station to inform her she was free to go. She had struck her as an odd but weirdly cheery woman. The juxtaposition of that memory with the sight of the woman now surrounded by storm troopers was jarring to Hannah's sleep-deprived brain.

Adding to the surreal nature of proceedings was the pair of red-haired boys who flanked her, holding out their hands with strained expressions on their faces. The children looked about twelve and appeared to be identical twins.

Dr Carter turned to the nearest storm trooper. 'Well?'

'Containment confirmed, ma'am.'

'Excellent. You can relax, boys.'

The two children dropped their hands to their sides. One of them wobbled unsteadily on his feet.

'Very well done, my darlings. Mummy is very proud of you. You can go wait in the car. Maranda?'

A matronly woman appeared, took each of the boys by the hand and led them away.

Dr Carter raised her voice without turning around. 'And don't let them play with the radio!'

She looked down at the figures on the ground. 'Honestly, a dampening field that big, they're going to be overtired and grouchy all week. I'll have to crack and take them to Nando's.'

'Can I just—' started Moretti.

'No,' said Dr Carter, and gave a small wave of her hand. Moretti's voice was instantly silenced.

'If I may . . .' began Xander.

This interruption, Hannah noticed, was not met with the same hand gesture. 'No, Mr Xander, you may not. We shall discuss the actions of you and your employer later. Right now, we have guests.'

Hannah looked at Xander's face. He looked like a man who could see a great deal of awkward conversations in his future.

'Yes,' said Banecroft, 'and while I hate to pile on, Dr Carter here is our lawyer. I don't know about anyone else, but I intend to sue for emotional distress.'

Dr Carter giggled — at least that's what Hannah assumed the noise that came out of her mouth was. It sounded more like someone strangling a chipmunk.

'Ah, dear Vinny. Charming as always.' Dr Carter pointed at

Banecroft, Sturgess and Hannah. 'That one, that one, that one, we're throwing back.'

Two sets of hands grabbed Hannah under the arms and plonked her firmly on her feet. A second later, the cuffs were released. She stood beside Banecroft, rubbing her wrists. Two of the storm troopers hauled up Sturgess and then had to catch him as he began to slump to the ground.

'Oh, for . . .' said Carter. 'He's unconscious, you ninnies! Take him outside and give him a cup of tea.' The storm troopers did as instructed and began to carry the senseless form of Sturgess back outside.

'He needs to go to the hospital,' said Hannah.

Dr Carter looked at her for the first time. 'Oh, dearie, believe me when I say that's the last place he needs to go. That thingy in his head, with the . . . y'know.' She crooked her arm up at the elbow and mimicked the roving eyeball with her hand. 'It will kill its host – by which I mean him – if it thinks it is in danger.'

Hannah tried to process this new piece of information, but found herself lacking the capacity. She would think back later and cringe at the fact that she nodded and said, 'OK. Thank you very much.'

Dr Carter gave her a condescending little smile. 'You're welcome.' Then she turned her attention to Banecroft. 'Vinny, if you wanted to see me again, there were easier ways to manage it. You've got my digits.'

'Yes, I think I've definitely got your number now.'

'Oh dear. I really didn't think you'd be the type to be intimidated by a powerful woman.'

'Not at all,' said Banecroft. 'I just don't think it would work out. I'm the editor of a newspaper while you appear to work for a shadowy organization whose express purpose is to run the world for its own evil ends.'

Dr Carter shrugged. 'Oh, come now, can't I do that and still be your lawyer? I mean, a little pro bono work is good for the soul.'

'Yes, but I'm not entirely sure you've got one. Besides' – Banecroft pulled a cigarette from somewhere and patted down his coat, looking for a lighter – 'I think we've got an excellent case for false imprisonment here. It might be a real conflict of interest for you, though – what with you being the head honcho of this little fascist cub scout outing.'

Dr Carter gave a mocking pout. 'Oh Vinny, sweetie, are you upset about me telling you a few teeny-tiny fibs?'

'Of course not,' said Banecroft. 'I work on the assumption that anything coming out of a lawyer's mouth is invariably a lie. Although I'm sure you had my best interests at heart.'

'You might not see it, but I really did.'

Banecroft looked around, having been unsuccessful in his attempts to find a light. 'I don't suppose any of you have a . . . ?'

Dr Carter clicked her fingers and the end of Banecroft's cigarette lit itself. He took a puff and looked at it appreciatively. 'D'ye know, I've been inundated with this hocus-pocus nonsense for the last couple of days, and that's the first bit that's actually been useful.'

'As a doctor, I should point out that those things will kill you.'

Banecroft took the cigarette out of his mouth and looked at it. 'Really? From the woman who's putting boggle-eyed parasites into people, that is really saying something.'

Dr Carter gave a soft little clap. 'Well deduced.'

'Not really. You're here, and you must've followed us somehow, so it stands to reason you must be the person who is responsible for whatever the hell that was in PC Plod's head. I bet it's been there a while too.'

'DI Sturgess is a conscientious and relentless detective. It has been advantageous for us to keep tabs on his work.'

'Clearly,' said Banecroft. 'Lucky you did too, seeing as you apparently couldn't find this wingbat Yankee window-licker yourselves.'

Hannah noticed a flash of irritation in Dr Carter's eyes. 'I'm sure we would have, eventually.'

'Really?' said Banecroft. 'You seemed keener to hush things up than to catch any perps. Not to fault your sense of timing, but it looked like we interrupted proceedings at a crucial juncture.'

'Enjoy the victory while you can, Vinny dear – you won't remember it in the morning.'

'Guess again,' said Banecroft. 'I and my two colleagues here are employees of *The Stranger Times* and therefore protected under the terms of the Accord.'

'Ah,' said Dr Carter. 'I see that Mrs H has popped in for a visit.'

'Yes. Very enlightening. She clarified quite a few things.'

'Did she now?' said Dr Carter. 'Well, you and I will have to have a clarification session of our own one day.' She turned to the nearest man in a balaclava. 'These two can go.'

'Three!' said Banecroft, pointing down at Stella.

Carter shook her head. 'She is a person of interest.'

'What she is, is my employee. Protected. Given what happened here today, I would have thought your lot would be keen to be seen to be sticking to the Accord in all its glory.'

'She is undocumented.'

'Don't you worry,' said Banecroft. 'I'm more than happy to document her and everything else that happened here in great detail.'

'That will not be necessary,' said Carter stiffly.

'Well,' said Banecroft, 'that very much depends, now, doesn't it?'

Dr Carter looked down at Stella and then back at Banecroft. 'Fine. Her too.'

Two of the storm troopers stepped forward and freed Stella.

'And,' said Hannah, 'the police must return all of our stuff and DI Sturgess must be reinstated.'

'I don't control the police,' said Dr Carter with a shrug.

Banecroft barked a mocking laugh. 'Yes, you do.'

Dr Carter rolled her eyes. 'All right. Fine.'

'And I want my gun back!' added Banecroft.

'Sure, why not?'

'Oh,' said Hannah, feeling embarrassed. 'And, of course, those two poor people.'

'What?' Dr Carter glanced up at the two figures pinned to the wall. 'Yeah, whatever.'

With a wave of her hand the two prisoners tumbled to the ground. Hannah ran over to them with Stella by her side. The two freed hostages were busy pulling the leather muzzles off their faces, gasping for air as if they'd been rescued from an angry sea.

The man rubbed at his jaw. 'Bloody Founder bastards,' he said, his voice a gummy lisp.

'I heard that!' Dr Carter's voice carried across the warehouse.

'Are you OK?' asked Hannah.

The woman looked up from rubbing her legs. 'We're alive. Let's leave it at that.'

'Right.' Hannah felt herself blush – not her smartest of questions.

Two of the storm troopers moved forward to try to pick them up.

'Do not place your hands on me,' said the woman. 'I need nothing from your sort.'

The men stepped back and the woman looked up at Stella. 'You, on the other hand, love, I could really use a hand from. I'm Vera, by the way.'

Stella nodded and helped Vera up from the floor. Her legs wobbled and Stella placed herself under her arm to prop her up. Hannah did the same for the man.

Dr Carter waved cheerfully. 'Sorry for the inconvenience.'

Banecroft met them as they walked slowly towards the doors, having reclaimed his crutch. 'Let's get out of here.'

'Is that it?' said Hannah. 'What about Moretti, Xander and the boy?'

As she spoke, she looked across at young Daniel, a storm trooper standing awkwardly beside his wheelchair. He still looked only vaguely aware of his surroundings. Still, there he sat with cuffs on.

Vera spoke, her voice exhausted and yet laced with anger. 'There will be no justice for them,' she said grimly. 'That Moretti monster is a Founder – and they do not kill their own. It is their core belief. Nothing is more sacred than the life of a Founder. He'll be locked away somewhere until they decide they need him again, and the rest they shall sort out amongst themselves. There will be a testy meeting and that will be it.'

'That's awful,' said Hannah. 'After all they've done, they get off scot-free?'

As they approached the threshold to the outside world, the spring sunlight dazzling after the gloom of the warehouse, Vera patted Stella on the arm and then stood on her own two feet. 'That is the way of their world. However, there is one thing they did not account for.'

She spun her body around with a dexterity Hannah found almost impossible to believe, forming shapes with her hands as she did so. The two storm troopers who had been walking a few steps behind them rushed forward but they were too slow. A screech of metal cut through the air.

Hannah heard the roar of the beast and then saw a flash of movement as it leaped across the room. Banecroft threw himself on top of her, dragging her to the ground as the air filled with the deafening crackle of automatic gunfire and a terrifying scream from the dying beast.

In the maelstrom, something thumped against the corrugated wall beside Hannah.

She looked up to see the Were dancing in place as bullet after bullet thumped into its body, before finally it crumpled to the ground.

Dr Carter's words echoed around the warehouse at a volume not achievable by human voice alone. 'Cease fire. Cease fire. It's dead.'

As the echo of gunfire faded away, Hannah looked across at where the circle of storm troopers had been. A body lay on the ground.

Dr Carter looked in their direction, her face filled with rage. 'Get them out of here. Now.'

The storm troopers grabbed them roughly under the arms and started frogmarching them towards the exit.

'What happened?' asked Hannah.

An object lay on the ground in front of them, as if the universe were providing an answer. As they walked past, Hannah realized what it was. The severed head of Charlie Moretti.

Banecroft barked a manic laugh. 'He'll feel that in the morning.'

CHAPTER 49

Hannah turned off the ignition and listened to the engine as it made soft clicking and whirring noises. She didn't know enough about cars to say if it was supposed to do that or not. She also couldn't care less either way. She was back outside the hospital again. Had it really only been a few hours since her last visit?

She had offered a lift home to the two survivors from the warehouse. The woman named Vera had eagerly accepted, but the man called Jimmy had shaken his head and said no, thank you. Hannah thought he was Scottish, but it was hard to be sure given his lack of front teeth. She'd also offered to drop him at the hospital – or anywhere else – but he'd turned down flat that offer too. Banecroft had looked at the tremble in Jimmy's hands and, without a word, had handed him the half-empty bottle of whiskey he unsurprisingly had about his person.

Stella had carefully guided Vera into the back seat of the Jag. Banecroft had climbed in beside her and promptly fallen fast asleep. Vera gave Hannah an address in Chorlton and Stella, sitting in the front passenger seat, had directed her there.

On the way, Hannah had received a text from DI Sturgess in which he told her that he'd woken up on his sofa and was confused as to how he'd got there. Hannah had just texted back that all was well and she'd explain more later. At that moment, she had no idea what she could tell him, seeing as the truth about the thing living in his skull could literally kill him. That, she decided, was a problem for another day.

Feeling moved to make conversation, Hannah had commented on how Vera's family would no doubt be delighted to see her safe and sound. She hadn't responded, simply sat in the back seat and stared out the window, lost in thought. When they'd arrived at a nice semi-detached house in suburbia, Vera had thanked them and exited the car. They'd watched as she rang the doorbell, looking incongruous, standing there in her dressing gown in the middle of the day. The door had been opened by a middle-aged man with salt-and-pepper hair. Vera had clearly been trying to say something, but the words wouldn't come, not before she was swept up in a bear hug. Two teenage girls rushed out of the door after their father, and Hannah and Stella watched from the front seat of the Jag as the family hugged and cried.

And now here they were, sitting in the hospital car park. Neither Hannah nor Stella made to move, and Banecroft was still unconscious in the back seat. Hannah knew they needed to talk, but she was struggling to know where to start. After an awkward stretch of silence, it finally came to her.

'I'm sorry about saying Grace was dead. That was awful.'

'Forget it,' said Stella.

'No, I . . .' She nodded in Banecroft's direction. 'Grace told us that when you got angry your, y'know, thing happened, and . . .'

'It's all right,' said Stella. 'I get it. I know what you were doing and why.'

Hannah noticed that Stella's accent was different now. Instead of the cod London 'y'get me', it now had a hint of a West Country burr about it.

'So, how long have you . . . ?' Hannah laughed nervously. 'Sorry. I'm doing a rubbish job here. I don't even know what to call it.'

Stella shrugged. 'Neither do I. I've just . . . It's always been there, I guess, but as I got older it happened more. I can't control it or anything.'

'That must be scary?'

Stella nodded.

'Am I right in assuming that you didn't end up at *The Stranger Times* by accident?'

'I . . . I ran away from . . . Well, I don't think you could call the place "home", exactly. I was being kept in a place and I decided to escape. Got on a train to Manchester because it was the first one that turned up. Then I was looking for somewhere safe and . . . It's hard to explain, but the church – it had a feeling.'

'So when Banecroft found you breaking in, you weren't trying to rob the place . . .'

Stella shook her head. 'No. I was trying to just get inside.' She glanced back at his dozing form and lowered her voice. 'Him taking me in – that was better than I'd hoped for. I was just trying to find somewhere safe for the night until I had to run again in the morning.'

'Well, that worked out well.'

And then, because life sometimes likes to take the easier punch-line, Banecroft farted loudly.

Hannah could feel some of the tension release from her body as laughter overtook her. She looked across to see Stella similarly trying to hold herself together as her frame shook and tears rolled down her face.

Hannah put her hand over her mouth and gradually regained a semblance of self-control. 'God, I needed that.'

Stella nodded.

They both watched as a man walked by the car wearing just a surgical gown, glancing over his shoulder furtively as he did so. Without comment, they watched his bare-arsed escape from wherever he was supposed to be.

Hannah nodded towards him. 'Do you think he's changed his mind about having an operation?'

'I dunno,' replied Stella. 'He looks like a man who's expecting to be chased. Maybe he's escaping from custody?'

'Is it wrong that I really don't care? I just don't have the energy.'

Stella shrugged again. 'Was Grace mad?'

Hannah turned to look at her young colleague, taken aback by the question. 'Why would she be mad?'

'It was because of me that those . . . whatever . . . came to her house.'

Hannah reached across and moved Stella's hair away from her eyes. 'Right, you listen to me. I can't pretend to understand what you're going through, but there's one thing I definitely know. None of this was your fault. Are we clear on that?'

Stella nodded, but avoided Hannah's gaze.

'Stella?' Hannah pressed. 'I need you to say it. None of this is your fault.'

Stella finally looked up, tears in her eyes. She smiled. 'Are you trying to do that scene from *Good Will Hunting*?'

'I . . . Well, I might be drawing on it as inspiration, yes.'

Stella smiled and nodded. 'It's a good film.'

'And,' said Hannah, 'to use a phrase I heard on the bus yesterday – I'd drink Matt Damon's bathwater.'

'What does that mean?'

'I think it means he's hot. I should probably check I'm using it right, though.'

'Yeah, you probably should.'

'And the other thing might be from *Good Will Hunting*, but it doesn't mean I'm wrong.'

Stella smiled again, then drew in a deep breath that caught in her throat. 'I was going to kill him, you know. That Moretti guy.'

'But you didn't,' said Hannah.

'But I—'

'But you didn't. What you did was save me and those two poor people Moretti had taken. You saved us all. Even . . .' Hannah jerked her head towards the back seat.

'Yeah,' said Stella. 'Well, there's a downside to everything.'

'Seriously, though – thank you. While it's been touch and go lately, I think I might still prefer being alive.'

'Don't mention it. You bought doughnuts, so let's call it even.'

Stella and Hannah watched as two harassed-looking police officers came rushing out of the doors to A & E and looked around.

Hannah pointed at them. 'I think you might have been right about our friend. Should we say something?'

Stella shook her head. 'Nah. Speaking as someone who has to run again, I say give him a head start.'

Hannah was shocked. 'What are you talking about?'

'Those people, that Dr Carter woman – they know about me now. Trust me, it isn't safe. I've got to go.'

'No, Stella – you can't.'

'I have to. It won't be safe for the rest of you.'

'I don't know if you've noticed, but it looks like it might be pretty unsafe either way. Maybe we need somebody with your . . . thing on our side.'

'No,' said Stella firmly. 'I don't want to put anyone in danger. I need to—'

'You're not going anywhere.' Hannah jumped with shock as Banecroft's voice boomed from the back seat. 'You're my employee and I do all of the hiring and firing. You don't get to leave *The Stranger Times* until I say so. Have you forgotten our agreement?'

'But—'

'But nothing, young lady. Like you said, the church is a safe place.'

'You were listening?' asked Hannah.

'Of course I was listening. If you ever want to find out useful information, pretend to be unconscious.'

'The farting was a nice touch,' said Hannah, pleased to see Stella's smirk.

Banecroft ignored her. 'You are an employee of *The Stranger Times*, ergo you are protected by the highest power imaginable.'

'The Accord,' clarified Hannah.

'Sod the Accord,' said Banecroft, 'I was talking about me. I will not be . . .'

Banecroft left his thought unfinished as the man in the surgical gown sprinted past the front of the car, the two police officers in hot pursuit.

'What in the . . . ?'

In a rather nifty manoeuvre, the patient managed to evade his pursuers and dashed back the other way, leaving one of them holding the article of clothing that hadn't been covering much anyway.

All three of them watched in silence as the naked man trotted out on to Oxford Road, scurrying along the pavement with his thumb out.

'Now that,' said Hannah, 'is optimistic.'

'Is it me,' said Banecroft, 'or does this city get weirder by the day?'

CHAPTER 50

Hannah opened the box of doughnuts and watched as the one-eyed homeless man's face lit up.

'Really?' he asked.

'Absolutely. And you get first pick too.'

He gave her a suspicious look. 'What's wrong with them?'

'There's nothing wrong with them,' said Hannah. 'I promise. In fact . . .' She balanced the box of a dozen doughnuts in one hand so she could free the other. 'Cross my heart and hope to die.'

'Oh no,' said the man, 'never say that. There are enough things around here that can kill you.'

A week ago, Hannah would have dismissed his comment, but it had been a very long week. Nothing looked the same now.

'I . . . No offence, love, but I probably shouldn't accept sweets from strangers.'

'OK,' said Hannah. 'Well, my name is Hannah and I work just over there, in that building that used to be a church.' They were beside the same bench and bin that Hannah had first stood next to a week ago. It felt like another life now.

'You work at the loony paper?'

'Yep!' she said with a grin. 'I do.'

He shook his head. 'Well, you seem trustworthy. Nobody would lie about that, for a start.'

'What's your name?'

'They call me Two Eyes,' he said.

'Oh,' said Hannah. 'That doesn't seem like a very nice name.'

'Ah no,' he said, 'it's fine. It's because I wear glasses to read, you see.'

'Oh, right. What's your actual name?'

'Paul, but nobody calls me that.'

'Well, they do now. Hello, Paul – pleased to meet you properly.'

He nodded. 'You're all right, Hannah. I've decided I like ya.'

'Likewise, Paul. Now take a doughnut.'

'I'm going to take the pink one, if that's OK?' He still looked unsure.

'Excellent choice.'

Just then, Hannah's mobile rang. She flapped her free hand around, trying to find it.

'D'you need some help?'

'Thanks.' Hannah gave Two Eyes the box and dipped her hand into her coat pocket, finally locating the phone.

An unknown Manchester number.

'Hello, Hannah speaking.'

The voice on the other end was female and posh. 'Hi, Hannah, my name is Chelsea Downs, I'm calling from the Storn boutique here in Manchester.'

'Oh right, yes. Thanks for calling but I already know I didn't get the job.'

'Oh no. I'm ringing to apologize. I was out last week and my second-in-command took the interview without checking her emails. Joyce Carlson recommended you highly, and frankly, you're exactly what we need – as this bloody screw-up shows. If you'd consider it, the job here at Storn is yours. I should add that the package is very competitive.'

Hannah looked at the box of doughnuts and Two Eyes's face as he bit reverently into the pink-glazed doughnut. Then she looked across at the church.

'Hello? Hannah . . . Are you there? Hannah?'

'I've got doughnuts!' This revelation was met with great approval from the occupants of the bullpen. 'But I'm going to hold off handing them out until the meeting starts.' This was met with less approval. 'Think about it – it might actually cheer up Old Grumpy Pants.'

Hannah took a seat beside Grace. The office manager had plasters covering some cuts on her face and a bandage on her wrist, but other than that she looked well. 'And how are you doing?'

'I am super, thank you, darling. A nice man came around to the house yesterday, said the insurance company would cover all the costs of the repair, no questions asked.'

'That's brilliant news,' said Hannah.

'Yes,' said Grace, 'especially as I did not have any insurance.'

'Oh,' said Hannah.

Grace raised her hands towards the sky. 'The good Lord moves in mysterious ways.'

Hannah lowered her voice. 'And how is . . . ?' She glanced over to the corner, where Stella was sitting behind her computer, phone in one hand, book in the other.

'She is doing OK. There is a way to go.'

Hannah nodded. She imagined there was. While their chat outside the hospital had at least cleared the air, there was still a lot to figure out.

'Ox!' That came from Reggie, on the far side of the room.

'What?' came Ox's response.

'Don't you "what" me, you base ruffian. I said you could only sign my cast if you didn't monkey about.'

'I'm drawing your favourite meal – cooked breakfast. That's a sausage and two—'

'It's a penis.'

'Reginald!' said Grace, outraged. 'Please. There are children present.'

Stella spoke without looking up. 'If Ox's thing looks like that, he wants to get it seen to.'

Hannah laughed, as much at Grace's outraged face as at Stella's response.

The door to Banecroft's office slammed open and Hannah glanced at the clock on the wall: 9 a.m. precisely. He limped out, minus his crutch, but with his blunderbuss perched jauntily on his shoulder.

'Laughing?' said Banecroft. 'Why on earth are people laughing?'

'They're enjoying the company of their co-workers,' said Hannah.

'Oh, how lovely. I'm amazed you all think we have the time. In case you've forgotten, you all missed Friday's meeting.'

Ox raised his hand. 'I was in a cell.'

'I was in hospital.'

'So was I.'

'I'd been kidnapped by a maniac.'

'Yes, yes, yes,' said Banecroft, 'you've all got your excuses. None of which change the fact that this bastion of inability still has to produce a newspaper on Friday. Right, we're going around the room.'

Groans.

EPILOGUE

Banecroft awoke with a start.

Had it been the nightmare again? He was having it with increasing frequency. Throughout the day, it had become, well, not exactly easy, but at least possible to keep Charlotte out of his mind. In the night, though, his memory of her had free rein.

The dream was always along the same lines. It would be a replay of some happy moment from their life together – their wedding day, the holiday in Rome, the weekend in Cornwall. Or just mundane moments. They would be sitting together on the sofa, or at the kitchen table eating breakfast, or in any other number of everyday locations. He would be happy – that was the worst part. He would feel an echo of what his life had been and then it would stop and Charlotte would turn to him and say the same line every time.

Why didn't you save me?

He would plead. Beg. Explain how he'd tried and tried and tried. She would sit there, watching him without any reaction save for repeating those words again and again. He would reach for her but he was never able to touch her. And then he would wake up with that horrible empty feeling. The nightmares had never gone away, but now, after recent events, they seemed more vivid than ever.

He automatically reached for the bottle on his desk – and then he heard it. The noise. Someone was in the main office.

He looked at the clock on the wall: 4.23 a.m. Nobody who worked here was that keen, and though Manny slept downstairs, he kept himself to there, the kitchen and the bathroom. He would have no reason to be wandering around the bullpen.

Banecroft was about to dismiss it as the work of his imagination when he heard it again.

He got to his feet and picked up the blunderbuss. In light of recent developments, he was aware that the word 'intruder' covered a lot more ground than he had previously imagined. Still, someone or something was in the offices of his newspaper, where they shouldn't be, and that was not something he could let stand. Slowly, trying to avoid putting too much pressure on his still-bandaged left foot, he limped towards the door.

He took a deep breath, and in one fluid motion opened the door and walked through it.

'Freeze, motherf—'

He stopped. Someone was sitting at the desk in the far corner – one of the empty desks that had never been occupied in Banecroft's time as editor. The person was quietly reading through something, not even looking up at Banecroft's shout.

Banecroft walked slowly towards where the figure sat. A part of his brain was shouting in recognition, but the rest was studiously ignoring it. It couldn't be. It literally could not be.

He noticed as he moved forward that the first rays of morning light were seeping in through the large stained-glass windows, and that they appeared to pass through the figure. Banecroft realized he was still pointing the gun, and slowly he took it down and placed it on the table.

Only then did the figure look up and seemingly notice him for the first time. And when he did, Banecroft saw a face filled with irrepressible excitement, like that of a child on Christmas morning. 'Oh, hello, Mr Banecroft.'

Banecroft sighed and leaned on another of the empty desks.

'Hello, Simon.'

FREE STUFF!

Hello, C. K. (or Caimh) here. Thanks very much for reading *The Stranger Times* – I hope you enjoyed it. If you'd like to download an exclusive, not-available-in-the-shops ebook of my short story collection *In Other News*, full of tales from *The Stranger Times* world, then hot-foot it over to thestrangertimes.com right now and sign up to the newsletter. You can also find *The Stranger Times* podcast wherever you get your podcasts – each episode features stories narrated by many of the finest comedians available in my price range.

If you're reading this in 2021, you can look forward to another book in *The Stranger Times* series coming out next year. If you're reading this in 2061, then let's be honest, the planet lasted way longer than any of us expected. If you're reading this while standing in a bookshop because you're one of those people who likes to read the end of a book before starting it, then, on behalf of authors everywhere, stop it!

It is both traditional and entirely proper that I now thank all those people without whom this book would not have been possible. I thought I'd give that process an update nobody asked for by assigning the task to *The Stranger Times*'s resident pre-emptive obituarist. The results are on the following pages and I'd like to apologize for them now.

Cheers muchly,

Caimh (C. K.) McDonnell

ACKNOWLEDGEMENTS

(Written by Minty Van Der Flirt – psychic
obituarist for *The Stranger Times*)

The author has asked me to thank the following people:

Simon Taylor, editor extraordinaire, who dies in a boating accident while on holiday in 2076. The accident is especially tragic as the UK is still in lockdown at the time, and he will be sitting in his front room reading a book when it happens. Authorities will initially be baffled as to how a speedboat hit his landlocked apartment.

Rebecca Wright, a different but equally important type of editor, who dies while trying to scale the Forth Bridge, in an effort to correct a particularly egregious misspelling of the word 'transcendental' in some graffiti.

Judith Welsh, all-seeing, all-knowing managing editor, who dies while riding an enraged bull through the streets of Leamington Spa, dressed as all of Henry VIII's wives and being chased by a pack of irate, one-eyed Boy Scouts on mopeds. There's a fascinating story behind how that comes to happen, but sadly, space in this publication is limited.

Marianne Issa El-Khoury, genius cover designer, who dies a tantalizing six feet from the summit of Mount Everest – a particularly galling way to go as she'd initially only nipped out to the corner shop for tea bags, and things sort of escalated.

Sophie Bruce and Ruth Richardson, for their marketing expertise. Sophie will die tragically when the skywriting plane she is piloting runs out of fuel in the middle of a promotional stunt for a book she is launching. The inquest will agree that *The Sequel to the Previous Book Where What's-His-Face and Thingy-Me-Bob Look Like They're About to Finally Get It On But Somehow Don't But At Least They Manage to Solve a Crime Amidst All the Sexual Tension and There's a Good Bit with a Dog* – is really too long a title for a book. Ruth dies when the aforementioned skywriting plane lands on her house, which really is spectacularly bad luck.

Tom Hill, for his PR brilliance. He will die when crushed by a stampede of delirious readers, desperate to get hold of a copy of a book he is promoting. He shall be remembered as having died from a job well done, although the autopsy will go with the rather less prosaic 'massive internal injuries'.

The author would also like to thank all of the other wonderful staff at Transworld, who live long and happy lives before dying in weird and interesting ways, all inexplicably involving cauliflower.

Gushings of thanks to super-agent Ed Wilson, who is initially feared dead when swept up in an avalanche of unsolicited manuscripts from would-be writers. However, it is later discovered that he merely used that as an opportunity to start a new life with his family. He renames himself Eddie 'Big Ideas' Monchengladbach and embarks on a new career as an inventor. He eventually dies by execution, being the first person in over a century to do so, when it is discovered he was behind a tragically ill-conceived 'speed-boats delivered to your door' scheme. His wondrous partner in crime and foreign rights, Helene Butler, goes on to enjoy great success writing, directing and producing the hit film *Speed Kills – The Ed Wilson Story*. She dies from a particularly bad glass of champagne at the Oscars.

Thanks to Scott Pack, who shuffles off this mortal coil while disrupting and reinventing the publishing world in general, but in particular from not looking up from his phone while simultaneously tweeting and walking.

Thanks to Kahn Johnson, Sam Gore, Graham Goring and Gary Delaney – who join the long line of people who unsuccessfully reinvent the submarine. And to all of those who would go on to contribute to *The Stranger Times* podcast and website – before being tragically hunted down and killed by some guy who was, ironically, a big fan, because people in general, and men in particular, are weird.

Thank you to Mammy and Daddy McDonnell, who die as they lived, spelling out the name McDonnell to people over the phone who will still inexplicably write it down wrong anyway.

Finally, thank you to Elaine Ofori aka Wonderwife for a list of things far too long to be contained in print. She lives for ever but never remarries.

ABOUT THE AUTHOR

Born in Limerick and raised in Dublin, C. K. (Caimh) McDonnell is a former stand-up comedian and TV writer. He performed all around the world, had several well-received Edinburgh shows and supported acts such as Sarah Millican on tour before hanging up his clowning shoes to concentrate on writing. He has also written for numerous TV shows and been nominated for a Kid's TV BAFTA.

His debut novel, *A Man With One of Those Faces* – a comic crime novel – was published in 2016 and spawned *The Dublin Trilogy* books and the spin-off *McGarry Stateside* series. They have been Amazon bestsellers on both sides of the Atlantic.

C. K. McDonnell lives in Manchester. To find out more, visit whitehairedirishman.com